THE LIGHTS OF TENTH STREET

"*The Lights of Tenth Street* will give both faithful and struggling Christians strength to meet the challenges of our sexualized society. Men and women who feel trapped by sin or whose marriages are struggling will find hope and insight in these pages, as the author reminds us that none of us are exempt from the seduction that is permeating our culture. Feldhahn has given us a riveting, thoughtful, and yet highly enjoyable read."

DR. JERRY KIRK, FOUNDER
NATIONAL COALITION FOR THE PROTECTION OF CHILDREN AND FAMILIES

"Who knew Christian fiction could be so exciting—and so relevant to the times? A fascinating tale of people caught up in immorality, spiritual mediocrity, and high-tech terrorism, *The Lights of Tenth Street* is an edge-of-your-seat spiritual thriller."

BILL MCCARTNEY, FOUNDER AND PRESIDENT
PROMISEKEEPERS

"This book made me long to be part of a huge response of Christians who say no to sin and yes to following God without reservation. It's a novelist's way of calling the church to repentance and watching God's power be released to impact the world through His children."

DR. BOB RECCORD, PRESIDENT
NORTH AMERICAN MISSION BOARD, SOUTHERN BAPTIST CONVENTION

THE VERITAS CONFLICT

"In *The Veritas Conflict*, Shaunti Feldhahn paints a disturbingly accurate picture of the liberal climate surrounding our most hallowed academic institutions, and of the intense spiritual warfare that exists there. Not only is this thrilling novel a pleasure to read—it gives powerful, Christ-centered perspectives on many difficult situations Christian students face in today's classroom. Highly recommended for every student and parent!"

DR. BILL BRIGHT, FOUNDER AND PRESIDENT
CAMPUS CRUSADE FOR CHRIST INTERNATIONAL

"*The Veritas Conflict* is a fictional story that is packed with truth. This novel gives a compelling glimpse into the spiritual warfare behind the scenes of one of our nation's great universities and sounds a trumpet call for Christians to be *salt* and *light* in our often-challenging, secular culture. This story will draw you into a deeper walk with Christ, and inspire you to stand for His truth."

DR. CINDY JACOBS, BESTSELLING AUTHOR
WOMEN OF DESTINY AND *THE VOICE OF GOD*

"A carefully woven plotline that, through the medium of story, delves deeply into intellectual and emotional issues and the invincible power of prayer. Shaunti has written an engaging novel that provides answers to some of life's most difficult questions about God and truth."

RAVI ZACHARIAS, CHRISTIAN APOLOGIST AND AUTHOR
THE LOTUS AND THE CROSS

"Having trained Christian students for over twenty years how to apply their faith in a secular educational setting, I know the hazards they face in attempting to be salt and light within an increasingly tasteless and dark campus environment. *The Veritas Conflict* challenges Christian students to think about the invisible battle they face on campus—with forces of spiritual darkness, as well as deceitful philosophies, vying for their hearts and minds. Shaunti Feldhahn has woven together practical ideas for waging war on these two simultaneous battlefronts in a compelling and imaginative way."

CHUCK EDWARDS, DIRECTOR
BIBLE STUDY CURRICULUM SUMMIT MINISTRIES

"Ms. Feldhahn has an enormous writing talent. I cared about her main characters—rooting for them and hoping they'd come through in the end. Her intricate plot left me breathless in awe at how she tied up everything without dropping a thread! Overall, a message of love was given—love that is patient and love that gives to people unselfishly, right where they are. *The Veritas Conflict* takes a few little facts and becomes a full-blown work of contemporary fiction that will certainly cause readers to think."

KAREN LARSEN
SCRIBES WORLD REVIEW

THE LIGHTS OF
TENTHSTREET

A NOVEL

SHAUNTI FELDHAHN

Multnomah®Publishers

THE LIGHTS OF TENTH STREET
published by Multnomah Publishers
A division of Random House, Inc.

© 2003 by Veritas Enterprises, Inc.

International Standard Book Number: 1-59052-080-7

Cover image of angel by Kamil Vojnar/Photonica
Background cover image © Owaki-Kulla/Corbis

Unless otherwise indicated, Scripture quotations are from:
The Holy Bible, New International Version © 1973, 1984 by International Bible Society,
used by permission of Zondervan Publishing House

Multnomah is a trademark of Multnomah Publishers
and is registered in the U.S. Patent and Trademark Office.
The colophon is a trademark of Multnomah Publishers.

Printed in the United States of America

For information:
MULTNOMAH PUBLISHERS
12265 ORACLE BOULEVARD, SUITE 200
COLORADO SPRINGS, CO 80921

Library of Congress Cataloging-in-Publication Data

Feldhahn, Shaunti Christine.
  The lights of Tenth Street / by Shaunti Feldhahn.
    p. cm.
  ISBN 1-59052-080-7 (pbk.)
  I. Title: Lights of 10th Street. II. Title.
  PS3556.E4574L54 2003
  813'.54--dc21   2002156081

06 07 08 09—10 9 8 7 6 5 4 3 2

Dear Reader,

When Shaunti first told me she wanted to write a story that would expose the destructive forces in our world's expanding sex industry, I must admit I was surprised. It's not the usual subject I expect for Christian fiction! But as she explained the story and the mission of the book, I realized there was no better venue than the Christian fiction market for the message the Lord was placing on her heart.

This book is about choices, about temptation, about the consequences of sin, and about unconditional, nonjudgmental Christian love—the love Jesus displayed when He walked the earth. After all, Jesus befriended prostitutes. Today, He would condemn the sin but love the sinner. He would befriend exotic dancers, those ensnared by pornography, and even those for whom innocent lives are cheap. God's love is the most powerful force in the universe, and it is most mightily shown in its ability to transform depraved and hurting lives. Where better than the Christian market to show and celebrate that transformation?

Shaunti has handled some difficult subjects with great sensitivity and skill. She has written a powerful story that draws the reader into the world of her characters, yet without being titillating. Early on in her writing, she told me her goal was to not write anything that would cause my then-fourteen-year-old son to stumble. I believe she has succeeded in that goal, but I still think it's important for me to let you know that the subject matter is for a mature audience.

As I read *The Lights of Tenth Street,* I found myself praying and being renewed and challenged in my relationship with the Lord and with his lost and hurting children. My prayer is that you would experience the same delight in this story.

Donald C. Jacobson
President and publisher

PROLOGUE

Y
ou be good, pumpkin."

Ronnie leaned into the broad chest as the owner of the deep voice knelt for a hug by the driveway. She squeezed her arms tight around his waist, breathing in the scent of sawdust and engine oil. She stood quiet in his embrace until she felt him kiss the top of her head. Her fingers gripped tighter.

"Do you have to go? Can't I go with you just this once?"

"Nope." The callused hands gently pried her fingers loose. "I told your mom I'd have you back by five o'clock. It's already past that. I hope you had fun with the other kids at that church, at least."

"I did!" The little face beamed. "That teacher lady this morning told us a story about how this man got beat up by some bad guys, and how another good man helped him. She said I was kind, like the good man!"

She prattled on about her morning. He finally stood up, silencing her. Then he took one of her hands in each of his and gave her a small smile. He chucked her under the chin, his voice quiet.

"Go on in now, Raggle-bear. I love you."

Out of the corner of her eye, Ronnie saw movement at the front curtains. She took a step backward.

"I love you too, Daddy."

He climbed into the familiar sedan, and she waved good-bye as the only father she'd ever known backed down the driveway.

Bye, Daddy...

She heard the screen door squeak open behind her, heard the familiar female voice.

"Come on in, sweetheart."

She turned and shouldered her small bag, then clambered up the uneven porch steps. She accepted another hug, a kiss on the cheek.

"Oh, I *missed* you. Go on now, put your stuff away. Then set the plates for dinner."

Ronnie started to walk around the corner just as another figure appeared in the kitchen doorway.

"Hello, Veronica."

She looked up at the tall man in the doorway, squinting against the ceiling light. "Hi, Seth."

His expression darkened. He glanced at her mom, still standing by the front door, and then back at her. His voice was calm. "I have told you repeatedly to call me Dad."

Ronnie looked back down. "I have to go put my stuff away."

Seth stared at her a moment longer, then waved a hand. Ronnie hastened down the hallway toward her room. She put away her pajamas, a few toys, and the white teddy bear that went with her everywhere, and then headed back toward the kitchen.

The swinging door was slightly ajar, and Ronnie could hear voices lowered in intense conversation. She padded softly down the hallway.

"But, Seth, she—"

"No. That's it. He's dangerous to this family, and I won't stand for it."

"But it'll *kill* her not to—"

"So you want to risk it, is that what you're saying?" Seth's voice rose just slightly. "I saw the bruises he left on you. You want that to happen to Veronica?"

Ronnie stopped a few feet from the kitchen door, eyes wide, straining to listen.

"He wouldn't do that to Ronnie."

"And that's another thing. You need to get over this juvenile nickname. Her name is Veronica. She's almost eight, for crying out loud. The sooner we stop mollycoddling her, the quicker she'll grow up and accept her new life."

"But to cut off all visitation—"

"Tomorrow morning," the voice lowered again, "you call the court. It shouldn't take long to convince the judge, once you show your police pictures. Especially since he's not even her biological father."

There was a long silence, and Ronnie stood still, trembling, afraid to move. *Daddy!*

"I can't—I can't do that. She needs her father."

"If you won't, I will. *I'm* her father now, and it'll be better for her if she's not confused by two loyalties. Discussion over."

Seth pushed through the swinging doors, heading toward the living room. He saw Ronnie at the entrance to the hallway, and stopped.

He gave her a long look, then walked toward her. He crouched down and put a hand on her arm.

"Veronica, were you eavesdropping on us? Did you hear that?...Veronica?"

Ronnie could only stare at him. Her eyes turned toward the kitchen doorway where her mother had appeared, pain and defeat etched into her expression. Ronnie's lips began to tremble.

Her arm began to throb, and she realized that Seth had tightened his grip. He was gazing at her with a strange look, his eyes wandering over her face.

"Veronica, don't ignore me."

A dim voice from the kitchen. "Seth, don't."

"Veronica, I asked you a question. If you don't obey, there are consequences."

Her tongue was stuck. Even when he stood up and pulled off his belt, she was frozen. Even when he turned her against the wall and her tears dripped to the carpet. Her mind was numb.

Daddy

A shining figure bowed his head, his voice soft with grief. "The heavenly Father weeps for His child."

Another great being, his high-ranking garments glinting like the sun, stepped forward. "And another spirit is wounded. Loriel, she is now your charge. You have been chosen to lead this campaign."

"Yes, General." The first angel nodded his acceptance, but his eyes remained fixed on the scene before him. Then he sighed, repeating the man's words in a low voice. *"If you don't obey, there are consequences."* He shook his head. "If the Father's children don't obey *His* heart, there are indeed consequences. But the consequences fall not just upon themselves. The sins of the earthly fathers truly are passed down for generations."

"But God has promised that the righteous will inherit His blessing down to the thousandth generation! His mercy triumphs over judgment."

The two angels watched the little girl retreat to her bedroom and crawl under the covers.

Loriel's eyes darkened as he felt again the pain of the One he was created to serve, the Father's grief over a child's suffering.

"Loriel, this cycle must be broken. The consequences of this campaign are great, greater perhaps than we have seen since the battles for the establishment of this one nation under God. The enemy's plan is massive, but he is prideful, assured of his success in twisting the hearts and minds of men to destruction. He is expecting opposition, but he is not prepared for the war to be fought apart from his usual front. And on that front lies our hope."

Loriel looked back to the small girl sniffling under the covers. "If only they will listen."

The General smiled and laid a strong hand on his arm. "That, too, is your charge." He stepped back and gave the traditional salute. "It is time, Commander. You must be strengthened for this journey. Clothe yourself in the armor of God!"

Loriel lifted his head and opened his arms wide. A melody of praise poured forth from his lips, catching him up before the Throne. He lost himself in the beauty and the power of worship before his Maker, captivated by the glory of the Ageless One. He could feel himself growing strong with the power of the Spirit, his wings unfurling with sparks like lightning.

How long he reveled in worship he did not know, but the time came—as it always did—when he felt the Lord's release. He was created for the fight, but still he longed to stay before the Throne, longed for the day when all creation would bow before the humble King.

And his purpose was to hasten that day. Loriel bent his knee and heard his call.

As I set aside My glory and dwelt in the land of the shadow, so must My servants also go. The darkened lands are thirsting for My living water. I am calling to My bride, My church! Carry My message! And minister…minister to My precious lambs.

Loriel closed his eyes at his Master's longing for those He had died to save. A heavenly resolve began to burn in his breast, and he lifted his head, his eyes fierce with determination. He was created to serve and protect these who were so precious to his King!

He launched himself upward, a great cry on his lips as a shining host rallied to his call. They wore no weapons, for the Prince of Peace was their standard. This campaign was not yet a battle against the enemy. This campaign was to awaken a sleeping bride.

ONE

High school. Ten years later...

Ronnie ran her last lap with the other girls, grateful that the physical effort spared her from thinking. A girl in front glanced toward the stands, and despite herself, Ronnie's head jerked sideways. The two men in the stands were still intent in conversation with their coach.

All three pairs of eyes were fastened on her.

Ronnie looked forward and tried to keep an even pace. She could hear her heart thudding, feel her ponytail swinging at her back. *Please...please...*

The pack reached the stopping point and tailed off, each girl slowing, walking, hands on hips, taking subtle gasps of air and trying to look as if they ran that pace every day before breakfast.

Ronnie leaned forward and stretched her back and legs, then kept walking, moving easily in the warm-ups each cheerleader wore on cool days. It would be December soon. The end of the season; no more Friday-night games.

She glanced toward the stands again, her skin prickling in the cold. She tried not to fidget. She'd made it this far; maybe fate would make a way.

There was a sudden murmuring among the girls. The coach was climbing slowly down from the stands, her face shadowed. Ronnie hardly listened to his words. "Each of your routines was great, but at this time..."

The two men gathered their things and headed toward the parking lot, taking her college dreams with them.

The other cheerleaders shared disappointed chatter as they collected their books and clothes from the locker room. One or two patted Ronnie on the arm as they passed. "If anyone would've made it, it would've been you..."

Ronnie exchanged pleasantries, unable to remember a moment later what she had said. She slung her backpack over her shoulder as her friends climbed into the cars waiting in the parking lot; their parents', their boyfriends', their own.

She started on the long walk home, thinking of Tiffany's e-mail that morning. Maybe a blond ponytail and blue eyes could do what fate couldn't.

☆ ☆ ☆

A brassy car horn broke Ronnie out of her reverie as she waited to cross the street.

"Hey, Ronnie! Need a ride?" An elderly grocer she'd known since childhood was leaning out his pickup truck's window.

"No thanks, Mr. Dugan." She smiled at the old man. "I'm almost home."

"Come on, Ronnie. I know you better than that. You still got two, three miles yet." He leaned over and swung the creaky door wide.

Ronnie hesitated, then sighed and clambered up into the truck. "I am pretty tired. And I do have to work tonight. Thanks."

"I'm heading past your place anyway. As long as you don't mind if I take five minutes to drop off some equipment on the way."

"No problem." Ronnie sank back into the cracked vinyl seat with a sigh of gratitude.

They rode in silence as they approached the center of town. There wasn't much traffic. The McDonald's and the liquor store were doing a brisk evening business, but few cars lined the strip of other storefronts. Even the parking lot of the local supermart—once, the town's main attraction—was sparsely populated. A sheet of plywood had recently gone up over the entrance to the dance studio where she had spent so much of her time.

"So you just come from cheerleading practice?" Mr. Dugan asked.

"No...not exactly."

"You look like you did."

"Yeah." Ronnie looked out the window.

"I've known you since you were born, child. What's wrong?"

Tears crept into the corner of her eyes, and she kept her head turned so the old man couldn't see her face.

"I just..." She took a deep breath and tried again. "I just lost my last chance at a college scholarship." She saw Mr. Dugan look sideways in silence, giving her time to form the words. "One of the big state schools has this famous cheerleading team, and they hand out scholarships every year. They just had tryouts. None of us made it."

"Ronnie, I'm sorry. I didn't realize you wanted to go to college."

"Well, I do." Tears threatened to erupt again. "I have to. I *have to*. Look at this place, Mr. Dugan!" She jabbed her finger toward the windshield. "Half the storefronts are boarded up. And all my classmates want to do is hang out in the McDonald's parking lot and smoke weed."

She caught herself and glanced sideways. "Oh—I probably shouldn't say that in front of you."

He gave her a sad smile. "It's not like it surprises me, Ronnie."

"And then they'll have babies too early, or get stuck in some minimum-wage job at the factory for the rest of their lives." She closed her eyes. "I want *more* than that! I want to get out and do something important, something that helps people."

"Like what?"

Ronnie didn't answer for a moment, then she continued in a quiet voice. "About three years ago, I hurt my back really bad in that car accident."

"I remember. You had that cast thing on for a while."

"Yeah. Well, it only got worse, even though I saw a couple of doctors about it. Finally, someone referred me to this physical therapist. She worked with me for a whole year, until I was back to normal. And she didn't even charge me the whole fee, only what the insurance would cover from the jerk that hit me. That's the kind of thing I want to do. That therapist knew so much cool stuff, and she could help people with it! I don't want to work at the pizza place for the rest of my life. I don't want to end up stuck here like—"

She caught herself before the words slipped out. *Like my mother…*

Mr. Dugan glanced at her and then looked back at the road. The wheels of the truck bumped over the entrance to a small parking lot, and he steered the truck to a gentle stop.

"I'll be back in a jiffy."

Ronnie watched in the rearview mirror as the elderly man began hauling a heavy industrial cooler out of the back of the truck. She jumped out and ran around to the back.

"That's so heavy! Can I help—"

Mr. Dugan braced the chest against the tailgate and lowered it to the ground. He grinned at her as he slid a dolly under its base, secured it with a few straps, and wheeled it away, whistling to himself.

She watched him go, heading toward Big Al's Fix-It Shop. The other storefronts had worn signs proclaiming Shepherd Christian Books—*All Your Christian Needs for Less*, Oasis Tanning Salon, and Guns Galore—*Guns Guns Guns!*

She rolled her eyes and climbed back into the pickup. Maybe she should think about changing jobs. Tiffany had hated working at the tanning salon, but sure had loved looking sun-bronzed in the dead of winter.

Ronnie made a face. Just another dead-end job. Why was it that she was the only one of her friends who wanted to look beyond the next paycheck, the next boyfriend? Last year when she'd had her final back checkup, she had sat in her doctor's private office and stared, transfixed, at the diplomas on the wall, the books on the shelves behind his desk. She listened, envious, as he rattled off the dosage and instructions for patients' medicine from memory. Now *he* was making a difference, and was helping people and making great money at the same time. Just like her physical therapist. They weren't trapped: they could do anything they wanted to do.

Why on *earth* were they doing it in this town?

The driver's door creaked open and Mr. Dugan settled in behind the wheel. "Okay. We're out of here."

He started the engine and feathered the clutch just so. As the old pickup got underway, he continued their conversation as if they had never stopped.

"You know, my daughter-in-law—Angela Dugan—is a guidance counselor at your school."

"I've seen her a couple times."

"Why don't you go talk to her tomorrow? Maybe she'll have some ideas for you. I know she'll appreciate your desire to go to college. She went to college, you know. The only one of us to go."

"Really? Where?"

"Georgia State."

Ronnie's eyes widened. "Georgia State! That's where—I mean, I had been thinking about Georgia State, too. But if I don't have a scholarship, I'll have to put myself through school."

"Atlanta isn't cheap, you know."

Ronnie looked down at her hands. "Yeah, I know."

A few minutes later, the pickup pulled up a narrow side road and stopped. Ronnie gave Mr. Dugan a quick hug and hopped out by a row of mailboxes down the road from her house, glad that excuse had come to mind.

She waved as the truck drove away, collected a short stack of mail, and headed down the road for home.

"Well, I don't *care* what you think!" Ronnie's eyes snapped across the kitchen. "I can finish high school by GED and start at Georgia State in the fall if I work enough."

Her mother shook her head, grinding a cigarette into an ashtray on the counter. "You can get a job here and start college next year if you're still so wild about it. It's not like you've got anything special to offer an employer. So there's no need to go so far for work."

Ronnie made an exasperated noise. "Give me a break. You know how hard it is to find a good job these days! And I'm a hard worker, but there's certainly no work in this town that would pay enough for me to *live* on, much less save for college."

"You can live here."

"No, I can't. And you know that." She tried to hold her mother's gaze, but the tired eyes flickered down and away. The kitchen was silent a moment.

Her mother reached for the half-crinkled pack lying on the counter beside her, and turned slightly to light another smoke.

Ronnie opened the refrigerator door, looking for something to eat. "At least the beer is still here from this morning," she muttered. "That's something."

"Seth bought a new six-pack before you got home."

Ronnie pulled a lone apple from the crisper drawer, then set about searching the cupboards for the box of macaroni and cheese she knew was there somewhere. She made and ate her dinner silently, sitting at the kitchen table and staring out at the lawn. Her mother retreated into the living room to watch television, leaving Ronnie alone.

Could she do it? Did she have the guts? Would her friends miss her? She looked down at her plate, her stomach sinking. Did she have any choice?

The sound of a souped-up engine broke her spell, and she moved quickly over to the sink, rinsing her plate and putting it in the dishwasher. She heard the screen door slam shut, and Seth's heavy steps into the kitchen.

"I thought I told you to clean the kitchen this morning."

She kept her back to him, rinsing a few of the dishes stacked in the sink. "You did. But I had school, and then the cheerleading tryouts. I just got back."

He walked over and gripped her arm, swinging her unsteadily around. "Don't you get lippy with me, young lady."

She yanked her arm out of his grasp and glared at him, her breath catching in her chest. "You've been drinking, Seth. Why don't you just go sleep it off?"

"Why you—" He slapped her across the cheek. "Why don't you just sleep *that* off?"

Ronnie stepped back, her face stinging, then pushed past him and headed down the hall. Her mother never looked up from the television.

She swept into her room, closed the door and locked it, then turned and kicked it with her foot, hard. She flopped down beside the bed and pressed a hand to her cheek, trying not to cry. Just another day in the Hanover family. If you could call this a family.

She pictured her coach addressing the rejected cheerleaders, and a wave of despair swept over her. Was she *ever* going to be anybody? Maybe she was just fooling herself. Maybe she should just accept the fact that there was nothing special about her.

She scooted over to her nightstand, opened the bottom drawer, and lifted out a weathered shoebox. She leaned back against the bed and opened the lid. A white teddy bear, well-loved and worn in patches, stared up at her.

Ronnie smiled and pulled him out. Teddy had a lot of secrets on him, a lot of comforted tears. She set him aside and felt in the box for the folded paper she knew was there.

It was yellowed with age, soft and brown and worn from many creases, many foldings and unfoldings. Ronnie carefully spread the page on her lap, pondering the familiar words, surrounded by little drawings and stickers; perfect for a second-grade child.

Ronnie, I'm very glad you and your father joined us at church today! Although you just came to my Sunday school class for the first time, I can tell there is something special about you. You have a kind heart. I watched you help and comfort that little boy when he cut himself, and it is clear that you have a gift. A gift of healing, of helping people. Just like in the story of the Good Samaritan, you care about other people and it shows.

I don't know how long you and your dad will be with our church. I'd love to have you every week. But just in case, I wanted you to know that you are a special girl, and Jesus loves you very much. Don't ever let anyone take that away from you.

A chime from the computer made Ronnie turn, and she carefully refolded the page and stowed it in its hiding place. She checked her e-mail and smiled. Now here was another person who had believed in her…even if some of her crazy plots were a little unorthodox. Including the one she was pushing at the moment. Ronnie clicked on Tiffany's e-mail.

Where are you, girl? I've been trying to instant-message you all afternoon!

Listen, you need to stop thinking so much and just do it. Now that your man is history, you've got no reason to stay. I'll be back in town on Friday to close my bank account and all that, so you can come back to Atlanta with me. Otherwise, you'll just have to find a ride or pay for the train, and I know you don't have the money.

One look at the car I'm driving, you'll wonder why you waited so long. I told Marco and the others that you're finally considering it, and we can set up

*an interview as soon as you arrive. I know they'll love you. I'm only worried
that once they check you out, I'm history!* ☺ *Just kidding. Sort of.*

*Anyway, you know you need to get out of there, so make like Nike. I'll see
you Friday.*

Ronnie laughed when she reached the end of her friend's message. Well, why
not.

She stood up from the computer and started rummaging in her closet for a
duffel bag. Tiffany was right. She thought too much, worried too much, planned
too much. There was nothing for her here. Not one of her girlfriends really knew
her. And her former boyfriend was pretending she wasn't even there. She finished
loading up her duffel bag, stowed it out of sight, and got ready for another night
at her busy, dead-end job.

There was no more reason to stay, and—she shuddered slightly at the thought
of Seth's probing eyes—every reason to go.

"Here you are." Ronnie slid the round serving tray onto the table. "It's hot, so
watch it."

The foursome at the table reached for the slices of pizza. One woman looked
up. "Oh, can you refill my soda?"

"Sure thing." Ronnie put on a cheerful face. "Anyone else?"

The others shook their heads, their mouths full of pizza.

As she turned away, a customer at another table caught her eye, motioning at
his watch. She hurried over.

"Sir?"

"Remember, I need to be out of here by seven-thirty."

"Of course, sir. They're moving as fast as they can in the kitchen."

"I've been waiting for fifteen minutes already."

"Yes, sir, I know, but it *is* a large order."

A man at the next table motioned at her, and she held up a finger, indicating
she'd be right there. The first man was still talking.

"Well, just see what you can do."

"I will, sir."

"And refill my Coke?"

"Certainly, sir."

She grabbed his glass and stopped by the next table. The customer jabbed his
finger toward the pizza in the center of the table.

"This is sausage, and we asked for pepperoni."

"Oh, I'm so sorry." Ronnie reached to grab the tray. "It'll take them just a few minutes to get a new pizza out."

The customer looked annoyed. "I wish you'd checked before you brought it out."

"I should have, sir, but we are very busy tonight. I really apologize."

"We're short on time, and this is going to cost us. I need to talk to the manager."

"I'll get him right away."

The man nodded and turned back to his family's conversation. Ronnie hustled toward the kitchen, the faulty pizza in one hand and the two empty glasses in the other. A minute later, she had fresh glasses on the first two tables, and had stopped by the third to reassure them that their pepperoni pizza and the manager would be out shortly.

The front door chimed, and she headed that direction. Too few waitresses tonight, and the customers kept arriving. At least she'd make some good tip money if she didn't make too many mistakes in her rush.

She saw two grade-school-age kids and slowed. "Are you eating here or take-out?"

A young girl looked up at her. "Here. Mom's right behind us."

Ronnie grabbed three menus and looked up as the door chimed again. Her face lit up with astonishment.

"Susan!"

"Ronnie." A woman in her thirties came toward her, arms outstretched for a hug. "So good to see you."

"These are your kids?"

"Yes, they are." Susan introduced them, then gave Ronnie an intent stare. "I didn't know you were waitressing. You look terrific. How's your back?"

"Wonderful, thanks to you! I was just telling someone about you today." Ronnie heard a patron calling to her from a nearby table. "Let's get you seated, and you can look at the menu for a few minutes, okay?"

"Great. Maybe we can catch up if you have time."

Ronnie laughed as she headed toward the beckoning table. "Time is a bit hard to come by, but I'll find a way."

For the next hour, Ronnie sped around the restaurant, taking and filling orders, smiling at the customers, refilling glasses, making change, and stashing her tips safely in her apron. The irritated family man left her almost nothing, but everyone else seemed to think she'd done a good job. In the midst of the rush, she brought Susan and her kids their calzones and drinks, but had time for nothing but passing pleasantries.

Later, as Ronnie cleared Susan's table, Susan said, "Well, you certainly seem to be doing well. Is it always this busy?"

Ronnie nodded. "It's finally slowing down, thank goodness. Long day."

"So, how long has it been, Ronnie?"

"I think my final appointment with you was over a year ago."

"That long?" Susan shook her head. "Time flies. So you graduate from high school in…?"

"In June. I'm a senior now."

"Any thought about what you want to do afterwards?"

Ronnie set her tray down on the table and crouched down a bit, lowering her voice. "Actually, I've decided I want to become a physical therapist."

"That's great!" Susan exclaimed. She winced and looked around. "I guess you don't want your employer to know."

"No. The owner thinks I'm going to be here forever. I'm going to have to have a difficult conversation with him pretty soon."

She wiped an imaginary spot off the table, nervous at the thought of *how* soon.

"Have you decided where you want to go?"

Ronnie grinned. "Where do you think?"

Susan returned the smile. "You'll love Georgia State, I promise."

"I know. You convinced me. After all your two-hour brainwashing sessions—disguised as physical therapy—what choice did I have?"

"Well, it's not just a matter of opinion, you know. They have the best program. And since you'll get the in-state tuition…" She shrugged.

"It's a no-brainer, I know. For the first time in my life, I feel like I have a direction." Ronnie swiped the table for the fifth time, then caught the owner/manager beckoning to her. She sighed. "I have to go. I didn't even get to hear how you're doing."

"No biggie. The kids have a pizza party here next Saturday, so I'll see you then."

No, you won't. Ronnie tried to smile. "It was good to see you."

"You, too. If you ever have any questions, give me a call, okay?"

Ronnie nodded as the little family waved and left. She headed back to the restaurant's cluttered office, where she found the owner sitting at his desk, making up the work schedules for December. He glanced up as she appeared in the doorway.

"Hey, Ronnie. Listen, we've got a couple big holiday parties in the next few weeks, which of course I want you to do, so I moved your shift from—" He broke off as he saw her expression. "What's wrong?"

She took a deep breath and gave him a rueful smile. His expression changed from cheerful to apprehensive as she took a seat on the other chair in the office.

"I—uh—I have to talk to you."

Ten minutes later, she walked out of the office, grabbed her coat, and headed for the door. She smiled and said good-night to the others.

As the cold night air hit her face, she straightened with renewed determination. The hardest tie had been cut. One more to go.

"Thanks, Ms. Dugan." Ronnie gave her guidance counselor a quick hug. She juggled a stack of papers in one hand as she reached for the doorknob. "You've been great. Just like your father-in-la said."

The counselor gave a short smile and placed a gentle hand on Ronnie's arm before she could open the door.

"Before you go, may I ask you something?" At Ronnie's perplexed nod, the counselor smiled again. "May I pray for you?"

"Uh, sure." Ronnie felt her cheeks growing pink. "I guess. That would be nice."

Ms. Dugan kept her hand on Ronnie's arm and closed her eyes. Ronnie peeked sideways, then shut her own eyes tight. She felt awkward, standing in the cramped office like this, holding her exit papers. No one had ever prayed for her before.

"Lord Jesus, I ask that You watch over this girl as she goes. I pray that You would be with her as she travels, as she finds a job, and as she makes friends in a new place. Keep her close to You, Lord Jesus, and never let her go."

The counselor paused, and Ronnie was astonished to hear emotion cloud her voice. "Lord…just…please protect her in her new life. I ask this in Jesus' name, amen."

Ronnie looked up to see tears in her counselor's eyes. She stood still, not knowing what to say.

The woman took a breath and gave a self-deprecating smile. "God loves you very much." She reached across Ronnie and opened the door. "I will pray for you. May the Lord bless you and keep you."

Ronnie shuffled through the door. "That, uh, that means a lot to me. Thank you."

As she walked away, clutching her high school records and GED materials, she shook her head slightly. What was *that* all about?

The school bus groaned to a stop at the end of the little road and Ronnie made her way down the bus stairs, balancing a stack of school materials. She gave the driver a brief wave and watched him drive off, swamped by a sudden feeling of unreality.

That was it. In another hour, Tiffany would be in her driveway and she would be gone before anyone got home.

Ronnie trudged down the street, her backpack straps cutting into her shoulders. She had loaded up as much as she could from her locker, and was carrying the rest. A few feet shy of her driveway she stopped to get a better grip on the load.

"Well, I told you twice, Linda!"

Ronnie's head snapped up in alarm. The sound of Seth's slurred shouting came clearly through the flimsy kitchen door. She could hear her mother's protests, then some sort of scuffle.

Ronnie looked around, then crouched behind the unkempt row of hedges that lined the street, her heart pounding. Why were they home?

"You better go get it!" There was the sound of a blow, and Ronnie clenched her fists at her mother's familiar pleading.

"Okay, okay! I'll go now, Seth. I'll get it. Stop! I'll go!"

Ronnie heard the kitchen door bang open, and the sound of her mother's little car starting up. She hefted her load and scurried around the hedge so she couldn't be seen from the road. The decrepit car backed down the driveway and sped off.

How on earth was she going to get out of here now?

Her back ached from the strain of the backpack and her awkward hiding position. Carefully, she set down her stack of materials, then lowered the cumbersome pack to the ground and pushed it under the hedges as much as she could.

She hurried along the edge of the yard to the side of the house, wincing as a carpet of fallen leaves crackled under her feet. She paused in the shadow of the house and caught her breath, listening for any clamor from inside.

Nothing. Seth was probably too drunk to notice anything. But that would just make it worse if she were caught.

She rounded the corner and slipped along the back of the house, then reached up and released a catch on a window screen. With a practiced yank, she pulled the screen off, then stopped to listen. Again, nothing.

It took only a moment to step up on the old tree stump and get inside—many a boyfriend had gone this route—and she clambered down atop her desk, carefully avoiding the computer that had already been disconnected. She had saved for more than a year to buy it. She couldn't leave it behind.

She grabbed the cordless phone and slipped into her closet as she punched the buttons, closing the door as much as she could.

"Hello!" The cheery voice rang through the receiver.

"Tiff!" She spoke in a stage whisper. "Tiff, can you hear me?"

"Ronnie?" Her friend's voice dropped a few notches. Ronnie could hear traffic in the background. "That you?"

"Yes. Just listen. Seth is *home*. He doesn't know I'm here. I snuck into the house to call you."

Her friend let out several curses. "There's no way I'm driving up–"

"No, no, I don't want you to. He might— Well, anyway, you shouldn't." She hesitated. "Do you still want to take me?"

"Don't be an idiot. We just have to find another way to do this."

"There's really only one option." She outlined her idea in a hoarse whisper, her ears alert for any noise in the hallway. "The only problem is, we have to do it right away. My mom will probably be back soon."

"Okay. I'm already heading toward you. Give me ten minutes."

"I'll meet you in the other driveway."

"Deal."

Ronnie clicked off the phone and dragged a heavy suitcase out of the closet. She pushed the window open all the way and shoved the case up and out, listening to its soft *thump* on the ground below. It was just too bad if some things broke. No way around it. Next went her fully loaded duffel bag. She frantically stripped her bed, tied the sheets and pillows inside her blanket, then stuffed her phone, alarm clock, and a few other electronics inside the loose bundle.

She clambered out the window, the soft bundle cumbersome in her arms, and dropped to the ground below. As her feet hit the dirt, she tripped and fell, the electronics ringing and clattering. She held her breath.

"Linda, that you?"

She could hear heavy feet tromping down the hallway—passing her bedroom and heading into the master bedroom at the side of the house. The side of the house she would have to sneak around in order to meet Tiffany. She lay motionless, heart pounding, listening to curses and mutterings as the heavy feet headed back down the hallway to the living room. She tried not to picture what would happen if her drunken stepfather looked out the back window.

Shaking with tension, Ronnie gathered her bundles and dragged them around the corner of the house and toward the deserted house next door. She pushed through a cluster of trees and a small thicket, scratching her face and arms, before stepping onto the quiet driveway.

A shiny yellow convertible was already stopped there, its engine off, its driver looking nervously in the rearview mirror. She jumped from the car when she saw Ronnie, and ran to help.

She grabbed the suitcase from Ronnie's hand and gave her a brief hug. "What can I do?"

Ronnie was out of breath. "You can—you can load the trunk while I bring the rest out. And if you're feeling brave, you can go get my backpack and school stuff from over there." She pointed.

Tiffany didn't look thrilled, but set off without a backward glance. Ronnie crept back the way she had come, mentally reviewing the things she still had to bring.

Finally, just her computer was left. Tiffany stood on the old tree stump, helping Ronnie leverage the heavy monitor out her window, when she suddenly froze.

"Your mother! I just heard her drive up!"

Ronnie worked frantically to gather up the rest of her computer equipment, passing it out to Tiffany in pieces.

Knock, knock! "Ronnie, you in there?"

Ronnie stared into Tiffany's wide eyes. Her friend vanished under the windowsill.

"Ronnie?"

Ronnie stood by the door, trying to make her voice sound normal. "Yeah, Mom. What do you want?"

There was a hand on the doorknob. "Can I come in for a second?"

"Uh, no, Mom…I'm changing. You need something?"

"Yes, I need something. Can you come out when you're done?"

"Okay."

She listened as her mother moved away, then she hefted a box of computer accessories and clambered out the window. Her speakers and CDs still lay on the desk.

Tiffany was already hustling around the side of the house, the heavy monitor in her arms. Ronnie clutched the CPU to her chest, strung the mouse over her shoulder, and hurried in her friend's wake, leaving the last bits and pieces in a box under the window.

"Yeah, baby!"

The wind blew past at eighty miles per hour, and Ronnie yelled in explosive relief and delight as the yellow convertible sped onto the expressway. She threw back her head, her ponytail whipping in the breeze, and raised her arms in triumph.

Tiffany glanced over from behind the wheel and grinned. "I can't believe we made it!" She punched a button on the CD player and out blared their favorite song. Tiffany began singing along, moving with the beat behind the wheel.

Ronnie laughed, almost giddy. The weight of the world was lifting off her shoulders, rising, rising with every mile behind her. The sun was low and vivid on the horizon, her best friend beside her, and she was *gone!* She was embarking on an adventure to finally have a life!

She put a hand to her head, trying to keep flying strands of hair out of her eyes. Despite her efforts, she could feel her ponytail loosening.

"Give it up!" Tiffany shouted sideways. "Caution to the wind, baby!"

Ronnie hesitated, then looked at Tiffany and let her hand fall away. With deliberate exuberance she tilted her head back and shook her hair in the wind. The ponytail holder blew away down the road behind them as the car sped toward Atlanta.

TWO

T wo kilos for you. No more," Tyson barked at the man beside him as he watched his underlings distribute their load.

Three other senior members of the group came and went, slipping out the side door with their briefcases and backpacks, heading for their own rendezvous. And still the little man stayed, standing off to the side, belligerence in his eyes, relying on his unique position to give him this access to the top echelon of the organization.

Finally, Tyson gave a signal and his men jumped down from the truck and shut the back door, the clang reverberating around the empty bay. He turned to go, only to find Snoop in his face again.

"You said I could have—"

"I said," Tyson hissed through his teeth, "*if* you could handle the last shipment, we'd *think* about giving you that run. Instead, you got two mules arrested, dropped your nine, and left federal agents crawling all over the plane." He turned and headed for the office. "Not the most successful trial, all things considered."

Snoop shoved his kilos in his duffel bag, and trotted beside the second-highest-ranking man in the organization, gold chains thumping against his chest. "Not my fault, bro! Look here, you know—even Proxy knows—that we was set up. And no way the feds found the gun. But I got contacts all over south side, man, and y'all need me. And since I hear that y'all are getting into some new business, well, as I see it y'all need me even more."

Tyson ignored him, trying not to seethe. Snoop aggravated everyone, but his information was valuable enough to warrant patience. Until last week's debacle, at least. He wished Proxy would just let him blow the informant away, but that wasn't his call. After a moment, he smiled to himself. Snoop didn't know that once the new business line was secured, the old lines were history. Maybe then.

The two men pushed through a door and up a series of narrow stairs, legacy of the forties-vintage trucking depot they had recently purchased. On the third floor, Tyson strode through a wide, empty space and entered a large but cluttered office furnished with a sturdy metal chair and desk, remnants from the original WWII-period furniture.

Snoop poked around. "Man, what happened to your old spiffy digs? Don't Proxy and them like you no more?" He turned back to Tyson and guffawed, slapping his thigh.

Tyson clenched his jaw and stood behind his desk, entering some notes in the log.

Snoop stepped across the desk from Tyson. "Look, I just messin' with you. I know the big man dig you." He slapped Tyson on the arm.

Tyson narrowed his eyes. "Snoop, you better get out of here."

"Okay, man, I'll go." He grinned slightly and crossed his arms. "I'll go just as soon as you cut me some slack and tell me when the next run—"

The phone rang on the desk, making Snoop jump. He started to open his mouth again, but Tyson held up a hand and picked up the receiver.

"Tyson Keene."

Snoop began to wander around the office again, muttering to himself.

Tyson listened for a moment, then jerked in surprise. "You're certain?" His eyes flickered to Snoop, and he bent to open and close a few drawers, looking for something. A flat smile appeared on his face as he listened. "I concur, sir…Where?… Okay, sure…"

He talked quietly for another few minutes, then put down the phone and continued to rummage in his messy drawers. Across the room, Snoop gave a derisive snort and meandered back to stand again in front of Tyson's desk.

"So, noisy man, you gonna tell me when the next run is, or do I have to find out where Proxy lives and go ask him?"

Behind Snoop, the door to the office silently opened, and a man in an elegant black wool coat slipped inside. He looked at Tyson over Snoop's shoulder, and nodded.

Tyson stopped his drawer searching and leaned across the desk, his face close to Snoop's. "You want to ask for a promotion from Proxy himself, do you?"

"Sure thing. For two years I been dying to meet the big man. I don't even know his real name." Snoop cocked an eyebrow. "Say, why do they call him Proxy, anyway?"

"Because," the man at the door spoke softly, and Snoop whirled around, "I do all my work by proxy." He nodded at Tyson.

Snoop swung back toward Tyson, who lifted a gun from the desk.

"Recognize this?"

He smiled as he pulled the trigger. Snoop stumbled backwards and landed in a heap at Proxy's feet.

Five minutes later, Tyson watched as two other men shoveled a sheet-wrapped bundle into the back of the truck in the empty bay. Proxy was leaning against the wall, arms crossed, as Tyson gave brief instructions to the two helpers.

Tyson walked over to his boss as the truck rumbled out the massive doors and into the quiet dusk. "That's one problem solved."

"And one created." Proxy detached himself from the wall and stretched. "But necessary, of course. Let me know what you hear through your channels, and I'll see you next month before the gathering. It's imperative that this transition goes well."

Tyson hesitated. "Of course. But…if I hear something urgent…?" He let the unspoken question hang in the air.

Proxy smiled slightly. "Just give me an e-mail or voicemail report as usual. The rest will have to wait until a regular contact point."

"Certainly, sir."

The two men went their separate ways in the growing darkness, and Tyson studiously avoided watching which streets Proxy's small car took as its lights faded from sight.

Proxy checked his rearview mirror and backtracked several times, then headed onto a packed main road, convinced no one was following. On the thoroughfare, he kept a cautious eye on the cars around him, more out of habit than concern.

The Atlanta rush-hour traffic was heavy as usual, and he fiddled with the knob on the radio, hoping that this little rattlebox would even pick up a signal. Surprised by the clear reception, he listened to the local traffic report and made his decision.

One mile up the road, he abruptly turned left just as a traffic light was changing and pulled into a massive mall parking lot. He drove around the perimeter of several high-traffic department stores, then cut right and made his way up the ramp of a parking deck. He wound his way through the structure and out the other side, swinging back into traffic on a facing street. Five minutes later, after a few more maneuvers, he turned into a hotel entrance and drove up to the valet stand.

An earnest-looking young man stepped forward and opened his door, handing him the valet ticket stub. Proxy nodded his thanks, pulled his briefcase off the seat beside him, and stepped out with a dollar in his hand. He pressed it into the young man's palm, discreetly returning the ticket stub, and stepped into the hotel.

Tyson's people would retrieve the car, clean it, and dump it, and he would have new wheels before their next meeting. Proxy smiled to himself. He had chosen his top lieutenant well. Tyson was still learning the ropes, but he had the business acumen to properly manage their unique new opportunity.

He walked quickly through the elegant lobby and took the elevator down to the hotel's underground parking deck. He settled into the leather of his Mercedes 600SL, and enjoyed the tamed purr of the three-hundred-horsepower engine. Much better than that rattletrap Tyson had found for his use today.

The preprogrammed entertainment center came to life, and with a soft command, the strains of Mozart's *Don Giovanni* filled the car. He hummed to himself as he pointed the car toward his next stop.

THREE

Ronnie applied her lipstick for the second time and fumbled to put the cap back on the tube. It slipped from her fingers and rattled onto the smooth marble of the bathroom countertop.

Tiffany's towel-wrapped head poked around the corner from the shower. "Girl, you need to chill. There's nothing to be nervous about. You want some weed before we go?" Her head disappeared, and Ronnie could hear her toweling off.

"No, I won't be able to think. It's not that. I just…" Ronnie looked at herself in the large mirror. "I just wonder if I'm doing the right thing."

"Hey, it's a job, right? Finding a good job these days is really tough. And it's so glamorous; you'll love it. It's also great money…the best money you can make anywhere as a waitress at least."

Something in Tiffany's voice made Ronnie turn.

A moment later, the sound of the phone made her start. She put her hand to her chest. Maybe she *should* smoke some weed before the interview.

Tiffany hurried from the bathroom. "That'll be Marco. I forgot to tell him whether you were coming in today or tomorrow. You're good to go, right?" A pause. "Ronnie?"

Ronnie took a deep breath and smiled into the mirror. "Right."

Thirty minutes later, the two girls piled into the yellow convertible and headed out.

The air was cold, the sun high in the sky. Ronnie pulled some sunglasses from her purse. She watched as well-appointed strip malls and leafy subdivisions sped by, her mind a bit blurry but her sensations enhanced by the quick toke Tiffany had offered. The high was already wearing off, but at least she felt less jumpy.

"It's so green. Even in the winter."

Tiffany nodded. "Yeah, lots of trees. It's even better in the summer. The whole metro area is really pretty, and these suburbs are my favorite."

They turned onto another road, lined with residential areas under construction. Ronnie peered at the presale signboards.

Affordable homes from the $300s…

Ronnie's mouth fell open. "Three hundred thousand dollars is *affordable!*"

"Yeah, those houses aren't even the really big ones. In a couple days I'll drive you around Buckhead. That'll make your eyes pop."

"Why is the club in this kind of area instead of…you know…"

"A seedy downtown neighborhood?" Tiffany glanced sideways, amused. "Where do you think the customers are?"

Ronnie looked down at her hands. "Good point."

A few minutes later, Tiffany sped down Tenth Street—one of the busy arterials that ran for miles through the Atlanta suburbs—and steered into a strip mall parking lot. A dozen cars dotted the pavement here and there in front of a rambling, stand-alone building.

"Lunchtime. And late lunchtime, at that." Tiffany pulled into a staff space at the side of the building. "Very few customers. Come on."

The building was actually kind of pretty and—well—*almost* classy. It had no windows, of course, and was painted a dark plum with shiny silver trim. A neon signboard advertised *The Challenger* to passersby on the nearby highway.

It was very dark inside. Music was pulsing in the background as Ronnie followed Tiffany through a foyer and into a main room lined with tables. The primary light came from colored neon tubes high up on the walls or from the stages scattered around the room.

There was a woman on one of the stages, and Ronnie glanced up at her. She quickly looked away. She was going to have to get used to this.

"You must be Ronnie." A man was approaching, hand outstretched. "I'm Marco."

Tiffany made the introductions, and Marco ushered them to a booth near the door. "So, Ronnie. Tiffany tells me you're interested in a wait-staff position." Marco smiled and gestured a waitress over. "This is Maris. Maris, Ronnie is going to be joining us shortly."

"Oh, goodie."

Ronnie looked up quickly at the acerbic tone in the woman's voice, but the woman winked, her eyes twinkling.

"Good to meet ya, Rennie."

"Ronnie," she said. "Short for Veronica."

"Well, then, *Veronica,* what should I bring ya?"

"A Diet Coke would be great."

The waitress took the others' orders and sashayed away without a word. Bemused, Ronnie looked at Marco and then Tiffany, who started laughing.

"Maris is from the Bronx. You'll get used to it. It takes her a while to warm up to the competition."

"The comp—"

Marco's voice was smooth. "Just a figure of speech, Ronnie. Wait-staff jobs are coveted positions. But we're all glad you'll be joining us. Now I know we have some questions for each other, so let's get down to business, shall we?"

For the next few minutes, Marco asked about her background, and described the club's operations. Ronnie gradually began to relax. Despite the atmosphere, maybe the managers and staff weren't as sleazy as she thought.

"And what sort of experience do you have?"

"Well, for three years I've waitressed at the local pizza place, so I know the job." Ronnie hesitated. "At least…I know a restaurant job."

Marco smiled slightly. "You'll find that being a cocktail waitress isn't so different. You'll have a bit of a learning curve, of course, and you'll need to learn all the drinks—" He paused. "And, of course, I have to ask…are you at least twenty-one years old?"

Ronnie held his gaze as Tiffany had instructed her. "Yes, of course."

"Of course. Anyway, as I was saying, you'll need to be comfortable with all the different drinks, as we tend to serve far more alcohol than food. At least at night. Lunchtime is more the business-lunch crowd."

Ronnie risked a glance around at the few patrons scattered throughout the room. She saw the woman who had just been onstage—now wearing a stunning gold dress—weave her way toward one table, stop and chat for a moment, and then take a seat with the three men.

She turned back to Marco, gesturing at the table, her voice rising slightly. "We have to *eat* with the customers?"

Tiffany snickered. "No, silly, at least not the waitresses. When it's slow, the dancers sit down with them so the guys get to know them and come back as regulars."

Ronnie took a deep breath and looked at Marco. "Just one thing. I need to know if there's anything I should be aware of about what goes on…you know… behind the scenes."

"Ronnie!" Tiffany turned to her, aghast. "You can't be implying that—"

"Look, I'm not implying anything, and I'm no prude. I trust you, Tiff, but this is all really new to me and I just want to know if I—"

"It's a legitimate question," Marco said. "This is a valid, law-abiding business and we will not tolerate any illegal activities of any kind. We pay our taxes and comply with all government regulations. We provide legitimate adult entertainment for those who choose to access it, and have the strictest procedures to ensure that the legality of our operation is not compromised." He looked across the table, his eyes intense. "Does that answer your question?"

Ronnie straightened. "Yes, sir, it does. Sorry for asking."

"It's understandable." Marco stood, and the girls joined him. "We'll check your references, but based on what Tiffany has said, I don't foresee any problems. We look forward to having you on board, Ronnie."

"Thank you, sir."

"And call me Marco."

"Okay, Marco."

"We'll see you tonight for your first shift at seven, then. It'll be a busy time to be trained, as Saturdays are our highest-volume night. But I'm confident you'll be able to handle it." He gestured to Maris, across the room. "Maris will be working a double shift, and she'll handle your training tonight."

"Maris?" Ronnie looked at Tiffany, confused. Tiffany looked away. "But I thought Tiffany would—"

"I've assigned Maris to train you, for various reasons. She's been a waitress far longer than Tiffany, and essentially functions as an assistant manager." He looked at his watch. "I'll see you in four hours."

Ronnie started to thank him, but Marco was already weaving his way through tables and vanishing behind a "staff only" door at the far side of the large room. She let out an explosive breath, and heard Tiffany chuckling beside her.

"You did great. He digs you."

"*That* was digging me?"

"Yep." Tiffany put her arm around her friend and gave her a little squeeze. "You'll get used to all this soon, and you'll love it. I'm really glad you're here."

"Well, *I'm* glad *you're* here, as I certainly wouldn't be doing this by myself!" She took a surreptitious glance into the darkened room, where a lone woman again danced onstage, then looked away, embarrassed by her own curiosity. For the briefest moment, she wondered what it would be like to be up there. "Come on, let's get out of here."

They stepped from the gloom into the light, and Ronnie winced and shielded her eyes. "Wow, that is bright."

"You'll get used to it. You'll get used to a lot of things."

Ronnie shook her head as she climbed into the car. "It's going to take me a while to adjust to this, I can tell."

"You'd be surprised. After two weeks, it'll seem the most normal thing in the world." Tiffany pulled out of the parking lot. "So what did you think of Marco?"

"He seemed okay, and I'm glad he was patient with me."

"Yep. He liked you. Be prepared for The Question."

"What do you mean?"

"The 'are you ready to try it?' question."

"Try what?" She looked sharply at her friend. "Stripping, you mean? Forget it!"

"That's what I thought before, too. But I'll tell you…after being around for a couple months, you won't have any problem with it. I'll bet you're asking for a try-out within four weeks."

"No way."

"Yes way."

Ronnie crossed her arms. "Tiffany, I can't believe what I'm hearing. I came all the way to Atlanta for this. You promised me it wasn't anything weird."

"And I'm telling you," Tiffany sounded impatient, "it's *not* anything weird. You're just not used to it right now, but just give it a few weeks."

"A few weeks—a few years! There's no way anyone is going to convince me to take my clothes off in front of a bunch of people!"

"You'll convince yourself. Once you get acclimated, and once you see the difference in your income, you'll get into it." She hesitated. "And…it's fun."

The greenery was a blur as the car sped toward Tiffany's apartment. Ronnie didn't look at her friend.

"When did you stop waitressing?"

Tiffany's voice was light. "About four weeks ago."

"So that's why you aren't going to be doing my training tonight."

"That's why."

Ronnie was silent as the car turned into Tiffany's apartment complex. She saw the security gates, the well-tended landscaping, and the elegant lighting in a whole new light. Her mind flickered to the plush furniture in Tiffany's apartment, the marble countertops, the brass doorknobs…the new convertible.

"And how long have you had this car?"

Tiffany pulled into a private garage and brought the car to a slow stop. "Just two weeks." She smiled at Ronnie's expression. "In just the last month, I've made twelve thousand dollars."

FOUR

Ronnie stepped into the neon darkness and followed Tiffany around the perimeter of the main room. A curving chest-high wall separated the walkway from the tables and the three stages beyond. She felt herself drawn by the colored lights, the pulsing music, the mysterious dusky atmosphere just beyond the wall.

The tables were half empty, but the stages weren't. Ronnie took her eyes off the lights and focused them on the Staff Only door.

Once through it, Tiffany led her to a staff break room. Maris was slouching on a well-worn sofa, her feet up on a coffee table, smoking a cigarette and absently fiddling with a Palm Pilot. Her gaze was fastened on a small television set mounted high in a corner of the room.

"Our Tel Aviv correspondent has more on the latest attack..."

She turned her head slightly as the two girls came in, then turned her attention back to the news. She jabbed her cigarette into an ashtray beside her on the couch.

"Hey, Mar, what's up?" Tiffany walked over to a water cooler and glanced back at Ronnie as she filled a paper cup. "Want some?"

"No, thanks." Ronnie looked up at the newscast and then back at Maris's face. "Uh…are you okay?"

Maris took a shaking drag on her cigarette. When she blew out the smoke, her voice was so soft Ronnie could hardly hear her. "Another terrorist bombing."

Tiffany swung around, her eyes wide. "Here?"

"In Tel Aviv. Hamas retaliating for Mossad's raid last week."

"Oh." Ronnie had no idea what she was talking about.

"The president just announced that we're sending more troops overseas, *and* calling up more troops for domestic response. Thousands of them. What do you want to bet we'll have people in fatigues on every street corner before this is over."

Tiffany sipped her water and motioned for Ronnie to join her at the cooler. They turned their backs to the room and Tiffany slowly filled a cup of water, talking in low tones.

"Her brother was killed back when the World Trade Center collapsed. One of the hero police officers. Her sister is a customs agent or something here in Atlanta.

They follow this terrorist stuff pretty closely."

"You should, too, you know." The weary voice made Ronnie turn. Maris was rising from the couch and stretching. She stuffed the Palm Pilot back into her apron. "It's not going away any time soon."

Tiffany made a face. "I don't want to think about it. Too depressing. If they get you, they get you." She grinned and tossed her hair back out of her face. "And our job is to take their mind off their troubles, right?"

"No, *your* job is to take their mind off their troubles." Maris gestured to herself and Ronnie. *"Our* job is to get them plastered so they spend as much money as possible. So, shoo. Your shift is on. Go get yourself all dolled up. I'll show Ronnie the ropes from here."

"Yeah, okay." Tiffany winked at Ronnie. "Can't be late for the money train."

Ronnie rolled her eyes, but laughed slightly. "Get out of here, you idiot."

As soon as Tiffany was gone, Maris put her hands on her hips and looked Ronnie up and down, her eyes intent. Ronnie stepped back, uncomfortable.

"What—"

"Size six."

"What—yes, that's right. How'd you know that?"

"That's my job, dear. Come on."

Maris hustled out of the room and down a hallway, saying a short hello to several people as she passed the kitchen. Ronnie hurried to keep up.

Maris made an abrupt turn into a large walk-in closet and ran her finger over a chest-high shelf stacked with uniforms.

"Six…six…SIX. Here you are."

She pulled out a plastic-wrapped packet and handed it to Ronnie with one hand while pointing toward a rest room door with the other. "You can change in there."

Ronnie poked her head inside the rest room, and looked back at Maris. "Is this where the others change?"

"The dancers? Nope. Their changing room is their own territory, not the waitresses'. And never the two shall meet."

"Why?"

Maris gently pushed Ronnie into the ladies' rest room and followed her inside. Ronnie glanced around, then headed toward the handicapped stall to change. She could hear Maris chuckling.

"That won't last long."

"What won't?"

"Modesty."

Ronnie shook her head. "Try me."

"Oh, they will. Trust me."

Ronnie ripped open the plastic packet and took out a little black sleeveless dress and a body-hugging silver cocktail apron, just like the one Maris wore.

"Well, answer me this, Maris. Why haven't *you* become a stripper then?" She paused, then continued when Maris didn't answer. "If the money's so good and it's so *normal* like everyone says, why aren't you up there? And why's a girl from a police family working in a strip club anyway?"

The silence lengthened as Ronnie finished changing and zipped up her dress.

"Maris?"

"You don't know this business yet, Ronnie." The other woman's voice was flat. "I'm not pretty enough to make it up there."

Ronnie winced and slowly pushed open the stall door. Maris was standing in the middle of the room, frowning at her reflection in a mirror.

Ronnie cleared her throat. "What do you mean, you—"

"And secondly, I'm the black sheep of my family. And since they really don't give a rip where I work, I might as well make as much money as I can, even if I can't make the big money onstage. Are you ready to get started?" Maris headed for the door.

"I'm sorry—" The door closed on Ronnie's apology. She sighed, then slowly followed in her trainer's wake.

"Our clientele is up 10 percent again this year." Marco's eyes gleamed as he swung his chair around to look out at the club floor. His one-way window had a prime view of the action. The place was getting packed. "That's *new* clients, gentlemen. Very promising for the future."

A slow drawl answered him. "And revenues?"

Marco hesitated, then turned back to the two men sitting in front of his desk, their backs to a regular window that overlooked the staff hallway.

"Flat, unfortunately. Patrons are holding more tightly to their wallets these days."

"So revenue per patron has dropped off. Well, that has to change." One of his guests steepled his fingers, his menacing tone at odds with his good looks. "Once the next phase begins, we'll need to funnel a lot of cash and we'll need a good cover. A failing club won't cut it."

Marco narrowed his eyes. "Who said anything about *failing*, Tyson?"

"And furthermore, Proxy was in here just a few weeks ago. He said we need to recruit a lot more candidates."

"Proxy was here?"

"Yes. He was highly complimentary of the dancers, but said there just weren't enough that will work. We need more; more than the usual bimbos. We need more of the right *kind* of girl."

"You know that we've been steadily recruiting, Tyson."

"I know and he knows. But you know what we're looking for, and so far you don't have it."

"I disagree. We have two new girls that started just last month who are prime candidates. They're bright, well-spoken, tall, and have all the right assets." Marco motioned out the one-way window to the stages, where the activity was beginning to heat up. "One of the girls is out sick tonight, but Tiffany—excuse me, her stage name is Sasha—is on. We have, of course, held you a table where you can evaluate her potential for yourselves."

A small smile appeared on Tyson's face, and he leaned back in his chair. "Excellent. You know I won't pass that up."

"I thought not."

"But…" Tyson steepled his fingers again. "It's not enough. We need more. We have to have them active as soon as possible, and there's no way we'll make our schedule if this element lags behind."

Marco stood up. "I'm well aware of the plan and our needs. You stick to worrying about your side of things, and I'll worry about mine. I know how my industry works. There'll be no problem delivering on schedule."

A passing movement in the staff window caught his eye, and his lips pressed together in a flat smile.

"Why don't you let me show you to your table, gentlemen?"

He ushered them out the door, took two steps along the hallway, then raised his voice slightly. "Excuse me, Maris."

Maris and her trainee turned from the door of the kitchen, surprised looks on their faces. Maris stepped forward. "Hey, Marco. What's up?"

"I'm just showing these patrons around the back and wanted to introduce them to some staff members."

"Gee, why am I not surprised?"

Marco gave her a quelling look and made the introductions. "Maris and Ronnie, I'd like you to meet…"

He watched Tyson's eyes as the man shook hands with the new girl, watched the flicker of a smile that came and went as they made small talk. With satisfaction, he noted the expression on Tyson's face as the waitresses turned away and continued with their duties. Marco waited a few moments, until the two visitors dragged their eyes back to him.

Marco smirked and leaned forward slightly. "Told you so."

☆ ☆ ☆

Maris gestured Ronnie forward to meet the kitchen staff. She showed her the electronic system used to place the orders and take payment, and described how to serve the customers and clear their tables.

"Keep in sight as much as possible, and ask regularly if they want more drinks. Be sweet and pushy and keep 'em spending. That's how you'll make your money. It's all about your take. The sassier you are, the more they like you."

"I wouldn't have guessed."

"Yeah, good, just like that." She was through the swinging kitchen doors and halfway down the hallway before Ronnie caught up.

Maris pushed open the door to the main room and strode around the back. Ronnie forced herself to look at the stage as they passed.

A young woman in a bright pink dress and high heels strutted on the main stage, accompanied by a pulsing beat and cheers and applause from the audience. Ronnie started, and looked closer. It was Tiffany!

She slowed her step, staring at her friend. She looked beautiful! Ronnie stopped and watched, transfixed. By the time Tiffany was done, she had collected a garter full of bills and pranced offstage with a cocky grin on her face. The crowd yelled for more, but soon another girl came on and the audience turned its attention to her.

Ronnie leaned against the wall that separated the walkway from all the tables, her intended task all but forgotten. Tiffany really did look like she was having fun. How was that possible?

She felt a touch on her arm and gave a start. Maris was standing next to her, a sad smile on her face. She started to say something, then held up her hands. "I won't say anything. Come on, we're running behind."

She led Ronnie to a sunken bar area on the other side of the walkway, and introduced her to a middle-aged man with long hair pulled back in a ponytail. "This is Nick, our bartender. One of them anyway."

Nick winked at Ronnie. "The best one, babe."

"Ronnie's new and I'm showing her the ropes. Will you give her a crash course in the different drinks when I'm done?"

"Will do." Nick winked and his voice grew silky. "We can even arrange a private tutorial later if you'd like. I can show you everything I know."

Ronnie snorted. "Great, that shouldn't take long."

Nick laughed and went back to shaking a silver tumbler. "You'll do. Come back whenever you like."

Maris pulled Ronnie along the back of the room and said under her breath,

"Always get in good with the bartender. You've got to pony up part of your tips to them, and how fast they serve *you* is how fast you serve the customer. And that equates to your overall—"

"My take, I know." Ronnie paused as they neared a glass door set in the wall. "What's this?"

"The gift shop."

"The what?"

"The gift shop. You know—porno movies, that kind of thing."

"Gross."

Maris laughed and gestured her onward. "You *are* a sweet young thing, aren't you?"

They circled to the opposite side of the main room, passing behind one of the stages and into a circular foyer lined with doors. "This area houses our V.I.P. rooms. These are smaller rooms used for private parties, that kind of thing."

Ronnie walked across a plush carpet to a door that was standing slightly ajar. She pushed it open. The room housed a few low tables and a private bar.

"Do I really want to know what goes on in here?"

"Not what you're thinking, obviously." Maris leaned past her and firmly shut the door. "Our regulars often request private dances, but that's *all* that happens."

"Whatever you say."

"I'm serious. The customers aren't allowed to touch the girls. The bouncers are pretty darned serious about enforcing that rule."

"I haven't met the bouncers."

"Really? Well, come on. You need to meet more of the staff anyway."

She led Ronnie back to the front door and walked her around the room, introducing her to the bouncers and several other staff members.

Ronnie nodded and smiled and shook hands. The names were a blur. At least everyone seemed nice. What were such normal people doing working in a strip club? She shook her head in exasperation. *She* was here, wasn't she? Everyone had her reasons.

"Maris, there you are! Are you two ready to start?" A young woman in a waitress uniform was hurrying toward them, cocktail tray in hand. "I should've been out of here ten minutes ago."

"Oh, Tina, I'm so sorry!" Maris took the tray from her. "Tina, this is Ronnie. I was just showing her around. I completely forgot about your son!"

"That's okay. I just need to get out of here." Tina ducked behind the bar, took off her silver apron, and retrieved a small carryall bag. "If I hurry, I can get to the clinic before it closes."

"Go." Maris gave the girl a gentle shove toward the door. "We'll cover here."

"Thanks!"

Maris grabbed an order pad and several pens from the bar and gestured for Ronnie to do the same. "I can't believe I forgot! I promised Tina we'd start a bit early so she could take her baby to the doctor. He has a fever or something."

"She has a baby?"

"Two. One's a toddler, the other's just a month old."

"Wow. She looks great for having just had a baby."

"Yeah, there's a gym around the corner. She's getting back in shape to go back up."

"Up where?"

"Up there." Maris gestured at the stages and shoved the order pad in her apron. "Come on, we've got to hustle." She strode onto the floor and made her way among the tables.

"Well, Mr. Travis, nice to see you tonight. I'm taking over for Tina. Can I bring you anything?…Hey, honey, welcome to The Challenger. What can I get ya?…Bob, you and that beer getting married or are you gonna want a fresh one any time soon?"

Ronnie watched and learned, ferrying away dirty plates and glasses and bringing out fresh ones. She was astonished to find that she was sweating from the pace her trainer set. At least this job would keep her in shape.

On her third trip out to the tables, Ronnie delivered a round of Tequila shots to a rowdy group of Japanese men wearing conservative business suits. They knocked the shots back and began cheering and clapping as a girl appeared at their table. Ronnie hurriedly collected the empty glasses as the girl started to dance beside the table.

One of the businessmen pounded on the table, pointing to the girl and then to the table. The others joined in, gesturing for her to climb up. The girl caught the eye of one of the bodyguards, who nodded and moved closer. The businessmen went wild, hooting and gesturing.

Ronnie glanced at the girl's face, and was astonished to see her roll her eyes in private annoyance. Just as quickly, the exasperated look was gone, replaced by a dazzling smile. The girl nimbly stepped on a chair, then to the tabletop, and continued her dance.

Ronnie backed away and served another group, watching as the girl finished her dance to appreciative yells, climbed down from the table, and walked away, her smile vanishing.

Ronnie hurried to place an order with the kitchen, her mind whirling. That girl didn't look like she was having fun at all.

She checked the order with Maris, got it to the cooks, and was starting back toward the door when Marco came in.

"Maris, table twenty-two needs two orders of nachos and another round of rum-and-Cokes on the double. They asked for Sasha ten minutes ago, but she must not've gotten the message. They want the Platinum Room for a large party next week, and they aren't happy." He looked at his watch. "I've got a call to make. Take care of it, please." He vanished inside his office, closing the door behind him.

Maris yanked the empty tray from Ronnie. "I'll get the drinks and nachos out to twenty-two. Go find Sasha on the double and get her out there."

Ronnie grabbed her arm. "Wait, which one is Sasha?"

"Your friend Tiffany. Snap to it, girl. Two of our best customers are at that table, and if they walk out, heads will roll. The dancers' changing room is down that long hallway and to the right. Green door." She vanished inside the kitchen, her voice raised.

"Priority order, two Nachos Grande!"

Ronnie half-jogged down the corridor, her eyes frantically searching for a green door. Why did they call Tiffany, Sasha? She could hear female voices and hesitated. Cracking the door open, she poked her head inside.

"Tiffany?"

A girl standing in front of a floor-to-ceiling mirror turned toward her, lipstick in hand, a confused look on her face.

"Uh—sorry—Sasha?"

The girl gestured toward the back of the room. A long, low mirror and countertop littered with makeup bags, hairspray, and other accessories ran the length of the room. Several girls were clustered at the far end.

Ronnie spotted Tiffany's distinctive dress in the group and hurried back there. The girl who had just danced for the Japanese businessmen was seated before the mirror, reapplying mascara with violent jabs of her wand, her voice raised in agitation.

"And if they think I'll do a bunch of table dances for them for a lousy twenty bucks, they've got another think coming! I can't *believe* I've only made two hundred dollars tonight! And not even that, once I cough up twenty to the DJ."

Another girl was spraying her hair as she talked. "Girl, did you see my table earlier? Dan and his buddies were slobbering all over themselves as usual, but hardly coughed up a twenty."

"What idiots." The other girls chimed in. One girl told a crude joke mocking one of her customers and the others laughed.

Ronnie quickly circled over to Tiffany and tugged on her arm.

"Table twenty-two wanted you. Ten minutes ago. Marco had me come get you."

"Oh, my gosh."

They hurried toward the door and down the hallway.

"I thought you said this was fun."

"It is fun. Just not when you're making no money."

Ronnie slowed to a stop as Tiffany pushed on through the door. "Oh, is *that* how it works? Yeah, great job, *Sasha.*"

FIVE

The third floor of the old war-era building was no longer empty. The vast room was packed with people, mostly men, sitting on rows of folding chairs. Weak sunshine filtered in through windows set high in the twenty-foot walls. A low rumble of quiet conversation rolled around the room as the clock ticked toward ten.

Tyson finished his phone call, made a few quick notes, and left his cluttered office. He chuckled as he looked over the rows of people. It wasn't every day these men were asked to sit on plastic folding chairs. Too bad he couldn't take a picture.

He worked his way to the front of the room, casually greeting several people by name. Proxy had previously identified a few key players, and Tyson had his eye on one or two others. If he could recruit a few leaders for Proxy's plan, it would solidify his standing in the boss's eyes…and propel him into the elite financial strata he had been aiming for his entire life.

His Ivy-League MBA had given him financial means, but he was limited, always limited by the system, by the egos in the corner offices, by the overzealous regulators of capitalism. The system was broken and needed to be fixed. True capitalism needed to be refreshed, restored. And Proxy's plan provided just the means to do it. It would come at a price, sure, but history would admit it was for the best.

Tyson stood for a minute by the platform, watching the hardened faces in the room—all hardened, but not all clever. All bold, but not all skilled. Dealing with people like that had been the story of his life. But not for much longer.

It was always for the best when the weak made way for the strong; when those who had the true skills and ingenuity were not hampered by the leeches of capitalism—the unskilled and uneducated, politicians and regulators, those who did not understand the proper use of economic power. Survival of the fittest was as old as the primordial soup, and it needed to be restored. It would be restored. And in the meantime, Tyson would gain wealth beyond imagining. All true innovators deserved their rewards.

Tyson carefully hid his disdain and stepped up to a small platform at the front of the room. He tapped on a microphone. The conversations stopped and all heads turned his way.

"Good morning. Thank you for coming and for your flexibility with this location. I know we had originally agreed to hold this gathering at the beach compound, but I think you'll agree the change is more than worth it. Allow me to demonstrate."

Tyson picked up a small box and pressed several buttons. Shades came down over the windows, plunging the room into near blackness. Two giant panels on the wall behind Tyson slid smoothly sideways, revealing a massive, state-of-the-art multimedia screen.

He allowed himself a careful smile as murmurs rippled around the room. It had been a long wait, but his value was finally being recognized. He *would* succeed where others had failed.

"Gentlemen, many of you may be concerned about our prospects in the current environment. I've heard as much in many private conversations. However, I have to tell you that I'm not concerned. I'm enthralled. I'm invigorated by the possibilities. The turmoil in our country provides us with opportunities that are virtually unprecedented. Allow me to set before you a vision for the next year."

He clicked the remote and the screen came to life. He clicked through his presentation as he spoke, outlining strategies that most of these parochial captains would never have had the foresight to recognize.

After a few minutes, a silent video clip appeared, showing police patrolling a major airport.

"Many of you have been worried about the ever-increasing presence of law enforcement on our streets, at our borders, and in the air. You are right to be concerned, which is why we've revamped our procedures over the last few years. But I have news for you." He leaned forward. "This time presents our greatest opportunity thus far."

The next slide was a comical drawing of a police officer barely visible under a stack of paperwork. The audience chuckled.

"As you know, gentlemen, for the foreseeable future, law enforcement will be fully preoccupied with bolstering homeland security against foreign intrusion. They're looking for terrorists, not traffickers in substances that shouldn't even be illegal to begin with. Their technology is outdated, they're overloaded with new demands, and their abilities lag far behind their new requirements…much less their old ones. A longtime informant recently confirmed that our law enforcement agencies have been given official—if confidential—orders to prevent violent terrorist actions even *at the expense of* pursuing other illegalities such as drugs, prostitution, and the like.

"Given this reality, Proxy believes the time is ripe for this organization to expand its activities. At first, we contracted, intimidated by the visibility of law enforce-ment. But now we believe distribution and profits can be increased by at least 20 percent with very little increased risk. Here's how we foresee using your networks in the coming year."

Tyson outlined the plan, step by step, and he could see the faces before him changing. Several still looked confused, but most grasped the possibilities. And a few savvy businessmen asked astute questions, carefully considering his answers. Good. Good.

An hour later, Tyson turned off the screen. "We recognize that more analysis is needed before we decide which markets and distribution channels hold the least risk and the most promise. Therefore, we're putting together a special task force to con-sider all the options and will present our findings and recommendations to you within the month."

Several of the captains began to raise their hands. Tyson pretended not to notice and busily tapped his presentation papers together on the podium. "As you leave, please remember to pick up the latest CD-ROM with the quarterly spreadsheets and your new codes. Thank you for coming."

As he stepped down off the stage, he was besieged by several of the leaders.

"What do you mean 'a special task force'?"

"If you think you're going to push me aside…"

"Who will serve on this thing? If it's Magnus instead of me, I swear—"

"Gentlemen, *gentlemen!*" Tyson held up his hands and gave his best placating smile. "This task force is merely an administrative formality. We need to crunch the numbers and ensure that our market recommendations to you are accurate. After all, we're here to serve you."

Several voices rose again. "But you can't…"

Tyson heaved an exaggerated sigh. "Okay, listen. If you feel that you have a head for statistics and really want to spend several weeks doing regression analyses of pur-chasing trends, then by all means let me know." He made a pained face, and several of the captains chuckled and relaxed slightly. "But otherwise, we'll appoint just a few people who have a track record in this sort of thing and get back to you soon on our recommendations. Sound fair?"

As the group nodded and turned away, Tyson went looking for his intended tar-gets. Within a few minutes he had discreetly invited all five of them to attend a private meeting in his office after the others had left. As expected, no one declined the invitation.

He stepped into a quiet corner and pulled a cell phone out of his pocket. Proxy was expecting an update, a message in his anonymous, internet-based voice-mailbox.

Tyson flipped open the phone and pushed a few buttons. He glanced around to ensure he would not be overheard.

The electromagnetic wave signal from Tyson's phone left the third floor of the building, sped to a nearby cell tower, and was relayed to a switching office, where the signal was instantaneously routed into the nation's vast telecommunications network. The signal—like the millions of others being handled at that same moment—raced through multiple relay circuits and was beamed to a communications satellite five hundred miles above the earth.

The geostationary satellite's transponder received the uplink, and its electronic brain checked the ultimate destination—an internet voice mailbox hosted by a foreign company. The electronic intelligence amplified the signal and bounced it to the next satellite along. The signal raced through the sky network just as it had been passed on the ground, side-by-side with hundreds of thousands of other digital telephone signals, television broadcasts, and credit-card transactions.

Less than two seconds after the call was initiated, the final satellite downlinked the original signal—intact and undamaged—to a ground station outside the United States. It was quickly passed to the appropriate, anonymous voice mailbox, where a quiet, satisfied message was left.

The message would be picked up later that day via another telephone call, one that would find another random routing through the edge of space, along with a cacophony of other signals.

Purely by chance, one of those signals originated from a ground station outside Washington, D.C., where a satellite engineer was testing a connection with a colleague in Silicon Valley, California. He stared at the data on his computer screen, let out an exasperated expletive, and rapidly typed something on his keyboard. Hundreds of lines of code flickered across his computer screen, but the necessary program didn't run. It was his colleague's turn to swear.

The engineer had to fix this problem with the LEOSAT repeaters, and do it fast. Reprogramming a ton of old code wasn't the most enjoyable job in the world, but it was necessary and he had been working around the clock. His company's satellites were tasked with passing billions of bits of sensitive data for major television networks, banks, and airlines—as well as for several homeland security defense contractors, such as the one he was on the phone with now. Those applications were secret, of course. None of the engineers knew the full story—they just programmed their pieces of the puzzle.

Both the engineer and his counterpart were exhausted, but kept working. These low-earth-orbit satellites were not just used to grease the wheel of commerce—they were used to catch the bad guys. With the right tracking technology, their satellites could see through walls and into corners.

Too bad that no satellite, no matter how sophisticated, could peer into the human heart.

Tyson perched on the edge of his desk, an aide hovering nearby. "First of all, I'd like to thank you for interrupting your plans in order to stay for this meeting. I think you'll find it to be a profitable use of your time."

An elderly man with thinning hair chuckled. "Any time Proxy has a new idea, it's *always* profitable."

"That's right, Waggoner. You've been in on quite a few of Proxy's brainstorms, haven't you?"

"Yep. That's why I've stayed in this network, even though some of these young 'uns don't have the work ethic of my kitchen cabinets. All they want is a quick buck. No effort, no vision." He gave a sharp nod. "But Proxy—now he's got vision. Picked you. Picked us. Now he's got something new up his sleeve. Can't wait to hear it." The old man sat back in his chair and crossed his arms.

"Good." Tyson pursed his lips a moment. "Before I begin, let me ensure that each of you wants to be involved. The 'statistical market analysis' was just a smoke screen. This task force will be creating a business model that'll make your current levels of wealth look like peanuts. We've chosen you because we believe you share the core philosophy behind our plan and are willing to leave sentiment behind. We've chosen you because we believe you're capable of the total commitment this plan will require; in time, you must be willing to drop your current operations and perhaps even leave the country. Therefore, once I outline Proxy's plan, there's no turning back." He gave a matter-of-fact smile. "You all know the penalty for disloyalty or mismanagement. If you're uncertain about whether you want to hear the plan, the time to leave is now."

He paused and scanned each face before him. No one moved.

"All right then, here's the deal. We believe that our largest underground business opportunity to date comes out of the most popular, most *above* ground industry that we've seen in years: the domestic security industry."

☆ ☆ ☆

"So it begins." A giant figure with shining features straightened from his vantage point, his expression somber. "Sinful man has put into motion what we are directed not to stop. Only the obedience of the Redeemed will determine the outcome."

Loriel turned and addressed the group before him. "For now, our orders are clear: protect the young woman and stir the Body of Christ. We must keep an eye on the machinations of those who have given themselves to the darkness, and stir up those who can cast a great light. If only they will."

Loriel cast his gaze over the ranks of the heavenly host. In earthly time, ten years had seemed to pass in the blink of an eye. The preparations were over, and the time had come for a battle that carried vast consequences. He began making his assignments, taking comfort in the certain knowledge that his Master was in control.

As he often had since being given this command, he could feel the Lord's deep love for His wayward children, His longing for fellowship with them…and His boundless pain at their preoccupation with so many things other than Him.

Six

H oney! Where are my shirts?"

Doug Turner stood in his walk-in closet, frantically flicking through his hangers. He brushed past the half-full garment bag that hung nearby and leaned out the closet door.

"Honey!"

"I can't hear you!" A distant voice sounded from the kitchen. "Hold on, I'm coming."

He ducked back into the closet, jamming his work shoes into the slots in the garment bag. He had his suits, his ties, his toiletries, but—

His wife appeared in the doorway, a dish towel in one hand and frustration on her face. "You know I can't hear you all the way in the kitchen. What did you say?"

"Where are my work shirts?"

Sherry's face went from annoyed to ashen. "Oh my gosh, I forgot to pick up your dry cleaning!"

He brushed past her and grabbed his tennis shoes. He quickly sat on the bed and pulled them on. "I'm going to miss the plane."

"No, hold on. You keep packing and I'll run and get them. It'll only take ten minutes, tops. I'm so sorry; the kids were crazy after church yesterday and I just—"

"Sherry, I keep telling you that I can pick up my own dry cleaning. You know that."

Sherry dropped the dish towel and grabbed a jacket from her closet. "I know, but I *want* to help you out."

"But it doesn't help me if you keep—"

"Keep forgetting. I know, I know." Sherry trotted down the hallway after him. She grabbed the keys before he did. "Seriously, let me make up for this. I can just run in and out. It'll only take ten minutes and—"

"Fine, just *go!*" Doug made an exasperated motion with his hands. "The more you explain, the later it'll get!"

He caught a glimpse of the hurt look on her face before she raced out the door. His conscience niggled as he headed back toward the bedroom. But if she kept forgetting these things he might as well just do them himself. And he was already working too hard as it was. He hadn't even been able to go to church yesterday because of that Tokyo deal, and that was the second time this month. Unacceptable.

He grabbed the garment bag from the closet and threw it on the bed. Everything else was packed. There wasn't much he could do but wait.

He headed for the kitchen. He had skipped lunch to come home and pack his things, at Sherry's insistence. He knew she wanted to spend time with him before he left, and he wanted to accommodate her, but next time she offered to drive him to the airport, he was going to have to say no. It was just too stressful. He'd leave straight from the office instead. And he'd get his dry cleaning himself from now on.

The refrigerator was cluttered with diet sodas. Doug pushed them aside, looking for something to eat. Diet this and diet that. Why couldn't Sherry buy *normal* food?

He grabbed a jar of peanut butter and stuck a spoon into it, his conscience niggling again as he ate. He knew his wife hated the extra weight she had carried around since the kids came along. And it was nice that she wanted to slim down, just for him. Why couldn't he be more supportive these days? It was like every little thing set him off.

Peanut butter and spoon in hand, Doug wandered out to the living room and turned on the television in their built-in entertainment center. He settled into the corner of the comfortable sofa and picked up his remote control. Maybe he could at least glance at the regional weather forecast before his flight.

The channels scrolled by as he bounced from station to station. He found the news, but didn't stay long; the usual details on the war on terrorism, blah, blah, blah. Unused to being home during a weekday, he was amused by the images from soap operas, infomercials, and syndicated reruns that flicked by.

Whoa, what was that?

He backtracked a couple of channels and paused. A bikini-clad model posed on the beach. Now she was under a waterfall. The camera pulled back to show a host of make-up artists, lighting equipment, and producers surrounding the waterfall shot. A male announcer's voice described the long hours and technical effort that went into creating a series of popular college co-ed calendars.

Doug's eyes drank in the parade of pictures. Wow. That next girl actually looked a lot like Sherry…like Sherry had looked ten years ago when they were in college together. The girl shook her head and her glossy, dark hair cascaded over her eyes and around her shoulders. The camera panned down a bright yellow bathing suit over a perfect tan.

"And we'll be right back with Calendar Co-Eds after these messages."

Doug looked at the remote in his hand. What was he doing? He lowered his head and shut his eyes tight. He could still see the waterfall, still see the long view of the perfect tan. That last five-second glimpse would probably stay in his mind for an hour. He heard the soft music of the calendar show returning, and changed the channel.

He changed the station several times, but his eyes weren't focusing. They were seeing the pictures in his head.

After a minute, he clicked the remote quickly backward. It would just be a couple minutes, and then Sherry would be home so he'd have to stop.

When he heard their SUV pulling into the garage, he quickly turned the channel to CNN, and then turned the television off. He hurried into the kitchen and put the peanut butter back where he found it, then met his wife at the door. She was trying to open the door with one hand, while holding a mass of plastic-wrapped clothes with the other.

"Here, honey, let me do that." Doug took the dry cleaning out of Sherry's hands. "Thanks for doing this."

Sherry was out of breath. "I drove—I drove as fast as I could."

"I'm sure you did."

"What? You don't believe me?"

"That's not what I said!" Doug tightened his grip on the mass of hangers and headed back to the bedroom. He could hear his wife's sigh all the way down the hall.

"Why do you always run away from me when I'm upset?"

He shut his mouth tight, not trusting himself to answer. He jerked at the hangers, trying to pull some shirts free, his fingers clumsy with anger and haste. If he missed this plane—

Sherry appeared in the doorway. "I'm sorry. I really want to help. And I think you're still fine for the flight if we leave right away, so stop going nuts."

Doug felt his face going red. He forced himself to calmly detangle the last hangers and pull three shirts free.

"I should've left from the office. I don't think coming back home really works."

"I was just trying to get a little time together. I've hardly seen you since you came home from the *last* trip. You've been working late every night—"

"Please, Sherry, don't start."

"Well, I can't help it. What am I supposed to think? I feel like you enjoy work more than me and the kids."

Doug bit his tongue at the common refrain. He slotted the shirts into his bag, zipped it up, and headed toward the garage. He threw the bag into the backseat of the SUV, picked up his laptop case and stuck it behind the front seat, then climbed into the driver's seat.

Sherry appeared in the doorway, her purse over her shoulder, looking confused. "I can drive."

"Please hurry, Sherry."

"Fine." Sherry climbed into the passenger seat and shut the door, a little too hard. She buckled her seat belt and sat stony faced as Doug raced out of their neighborhood and onto the highway.

The silence crackled between them.

Why did she always start nagging him about his work hours when he was the most stressed? Did she think he *liked* working this many hours? Why didn't she trust him, that he tried everything he could to get home to her? He was working his tail off to support this family!

Sherry had her head turned firmly toward the window, and he could hear her sniffle. Hadn't he shown that he cared by trying this ridiculous plan of coming home to pack and having her drive him to the airport so they could spend some time together?

He sighed to himself. Some time together.

Sorry, Lord. I guess I'm being a jerk. Forgive me.

He took a deep breath. "Sherry."

A pause. "What."

"I'm sorry."

Another pause, then she reached over to take his hand. "I love you, Doug. I just want to be with you more. That's all."

"I know. I'm sorry. I just—I just wish you were able to recognize that I *do* want to be with you, and Brandon and Genna. It makes me feel terrible that you somehow don't think that I do."

Her voice was very small. "Well, what am I supposed to think? I wouldn't mind the long hours so much if you'd really *be home* when you're home. But you've just been so stressed that…" She sighed. "I don't know."

"You know it's not going to be forever. We went into this with our eyes open."

"Look, I know that! Anyone with a technology-related company works long hours these days—and I want you all to succeed as much as you do! But can't you leave work at work? Instead, you come home grumpy and snap at the kids."

He took a deep breath. "I know. I'm sorry. I'll try to be better about that. I really will."

"And we hardly ever…you know…do it any more."

"Yeah, I know. I just—" he felt awkward, searching for the right words. "I guess I'm just preoccupied."

"That's true—you have been."

"Well, it's not just me, you know! You're tired a lot, too."

Sherry looked down and didn't respond. In the uncomfortable silence, Doug sighed to himself, feeling deflated. It *wasn't* only his fault. And with the pressure of his job, it would be nice to regularly have that means to de-stress. Every now and then he couldn't take the pressure, and that bothered him. But he didn't tell her that. It would hurt her feelings.

He looked at the clock on the dashboard and sped up a little. If he missed this plane, the new deal would go south and she'd see even *less* of him.

Twenty minutes later they pulled up in front of the airport. He dragged his bags out of the SUV and set them on the sidewalk. Sherry slowly climbed down from the passenger side and gave him a tremulous smile.

"Sorry I made you late."

"That's okay, honey." He gave her a quick kiss. "As long as the security checkpoints aren't too bad I should be okay."

"Call me as soon as you get there."

"I will. Pray for my flight."

"I will."

He walked toward the nearest entrance, then looked back over his shoulder and mouthed *I love you*.

She didn't see him. A policeman was urging her to move along. She climbed into the driver's seat and slowly pulled away.

Doug walked into the terminal, feeling alone.

Sherry merged with the traffic, emptiness swamping her. She had so looked forward to having her husband all to herself for a solid hour or two. What on earth had gone wrong? Maybe it was too much to expect, that Doug would ever be able to relax and connect during a preflight rush.

A decrepit car with one taillight missing swerved in front of her, barely missing her bumper. Sherry stomped on her brakes, then leaned on the horn. Someone in the backseat of the car turned around and made an obscene gesture. Sherry watched as the old vehicle turned off at the next exit and sped onto a rundown street, tires squealing. Why did some people think they owned the road? She would never treat anyone like that!

The rest of the midday traffic was well-behaved as Sherry merged onto the main highway and headed north through downtown Atlanta. Her eye was drawn to a billboard that advertised a local church's Christmas show: *Bring the whole family!*

She gave the sign a sad smile. Doug wouldn't be back for their church's Christmas show this weekend. He had explained to Genna that he couldn't get back from California in time, and the four-year-old had seemed to understand. But as Sherry had watched her daughter prance around the house in her little angel costume, her heart ached at what her husband was missing.

And it wasn't just the time away from his family. Sherry wanted him to be *happy* in his work, not exhausted, not stressed. She remembered his delight in his first job out of business school, how he whistled in the shower on Monday mornings. Now, he was quiet and withdrawn on Sunday evenings, thinking about what was coming in a few hours.

They had a great house, two beautiful cars; the kids were in their church's expensive Christian school...and it wasn't worth it.

She drove around a curve, and another billboard jumped out at her. This one was larger, emblazoned with the name of a gentleman's club and a woman in a suggestive pose.

Ugh. Who would go into one of those places? They were dirty, in run-down neighborhoods, and reeking of alcohol. She glanced again at the woman's smoky-eyed picture as she sped by. What kind of person would do that sort of thing?

A moment later, Sherry let out a sigh. Who was she to ask that question? Before her life was transformed, she hadn't exactly been an angel. She had grieved God's heart many, many times. Why was it that a decade of distance made it difficult for her to remember that? It was as if those memories were pictures of a whole different person—a whole different life that she could somehow judge from afar.

She sat up straighter in her seat. Those memories *were* of a whole different person—in a way. She was a new creation.

Her voice was small in the gently humming car. "Thank You, God, for reaching out to me, for transforming me. Thank You for giving me this wonderful husband and family. Please, please forgive me for my snippy attitude." She gave a snort, annoyed with herself. "I'm probably overanalyzing everything again, like always. Lord, help me leave it in Your hands and not be so stressed. Help me learn how to be the wife that Doug needs me to be."

Her mind went to the decrepit car and to the woman on the billboard, and she sighed. "And help me love the unlovable as You do."

SEVEN

"Hey, Jordan." Doug set his laptop case on the tiled floor of the vast foyer and shook hands with his boss.

"Glad you made it. Your phone call about gave me a heart attack. I thought you were going to miss your flight."

"I nearly did. Had a problem getting out of the house, and then getting through security nearly torpedoed the whole thing. I ran up to the gate just as they were closing the doors."

"Been there." Jordan smirked. "I've had a few of those getting-out-of-the-house problems, too. Probably why I've been divorced twice. Well, time to go make money."

Jordan picked up his briefcase and walked toward a transparent wall that separated the foyer from a large office area. Doug could see frenetic activity in the cubicles beyond, harried people carrying papers and equipment, lots of people on the phone.

Jordan paused just shy of the office entrance. "I know you've never been here before—have you met the principals yet?"

Doug shook his head. "I only took over the deal after one of the managers went on maternity leave a few weeks ago."

"Maternity leave is the pits, isn't it? Makes you want to tell 'em to not bother taking the job if they're just going to leave for three months."

Maybe that's *the reason you've been divorced twice, you bozo.*

"Well, just remember that we've put a lot of time and effort into building this relationship."

"Jordan, I'm not going to eat them."

"Yes, I know, but—"

"Look, I'll give it a fair hearing, chief. I really will. I know you want this deal, and that they want this partnership. I'll do everything I can to find a way to structure it so that it works financially."

"Fair enough." Jordan chuckled. "With you, that's all I can ask."

He led the way into the office teeming with ringing telephones, raucous chatter, and clattering carts laden with equipment. Doug followed his boss around the edge of the large room, heading toward an open staircase. He resisted the urge to plug his ears.

They climbed the gently circling staircase to a catwalk that overlooked the clamor. Doug shook his head. He would go stark raving mad in this environment, but some people must thrive on it. There was no way he could live in Silicon Valley.

The catwalk led to a second-floor suite of elegant executive offices, visible behind another transparent wall. They stepped inside and shut the door behind them. Doug looked around the quiet waiting area and let out a sigh of relief.

He heard a chuckle from a nearby doorway.

"Gets to you, doesn't it?" A rotund man with a ready smile stepped forward, hand outstretched.

"Gavin Gilmore, I'd like you to meet Doug Turner, our CFO," Jordan said.

"Just call me Gil. Welcome, both of you." He shook Doug's hand, then led them toward a conference room. "Let's get started, shall we? I'll let you get settled in, and we'll get our executive team in here in a few minutes."

He looked at Jordan and paused, hesitating. "Jordan, I haven't told you—I was sorry to hear about your brother."

"Thank you. It was for the best, really. He'd been sick a long time."

"Hmm." Gil made a noncommittal noise in his throat, picking his words carefully. "So...you're running the company on your own now, correct?"

"Correct. But we have the same management team, same board of directors, same company structure." His eyes flickered for a moment. "The board feels it's important to demonstrate consistency."

"Ah. Well. Just wanted to know the new lay of the land before we got started." Gil headed out the door, then poked his head back in. "Want anything to drink? Coffee? Coke?"

"Coffee would be great."

Gil's head disappeared, and Doug could hear his voice outside the door, presumably talking to his secretary, asking her to round up both the coffee and the leadership team.

Doug raised an eyebrow, pondering Gil's question. The man's affable attitude was deceiving—he was more astute than many of their contacts. Most didn't realize how much was subtly changing under Jordan's solo management.

Ten minutes later, the small conference room was full, neat white briefing reports in front of each chair.

Gil was seated at the head of the table. "Well, Doug, we've spent a few months fleshing out the options from our end, and we also know what your company can bring to the table. Now we have to see if we can afford what you're suggesting, and vice versa. As much as we want this deal, we all know it needs to be a win-win for both sides. So we've put together all the partnership proposals for our different departments; defense contracting, telecommunications, and so on. Our department heads will give you the rundown."

He turned to the only woman at the table. "So, Jill, let's start with satellite systems."

"Sure." The redhead stood up and walked toward the whiteboard on the wall. She was wearing a slim jacket and stylish, but short skirt, and no wedding ring.

Uh-oh. Doug's eyes narrowed. He felt the familiar tightening in his gut. He forced himself to look away briefly and took a subtle breath. He looked back as she began her presentation, briskly laying out the various options. She turned from marking on the whiteboard to look at him from time to time, explaining what their department proposed.

She's not as pretty as Sherry. He wanted to glance at her legs, and forced himself to stare at her face.

She made a joke and briefly smiled in his direction. He could feel his ego stirring. *She knows that I'm the key man here. And I'm in better shape than these middle-aged guys she works with.*

He broke the eye contact and looked down at his yellow pad, scribbling a few notes, forcing his mind in another direction. *If their margin is so small, that pricing structure wouldn't work...*

By the time her presentation wound up, he had pages full of notes and fifteen minutes of battling the subtle thoughts that fought for his attention.

If the GPS package is two hundred thousand, then we may have to outsource. Does she find me attractive? Stop it. Concentrate on the numbers.

Their testing schedule won't allow enough time. I bet I'm a better husband and father than whatever guy she's dating... Cut it out. What was that product timeline?

Look at her face, look at her face, look at her face...

As she turned and walked back to her seat, he snuck a swift peek at the view. He forced his eyes away and swiveled his chair toward Gil.

"So, Doug, any questions?"

"Nope." He scribbled a last few notes, hoping he hadn't missed any key facts. "I want to hear all the presentations before I start trying to contradict your numbers."

Low chuckles sounded around the room.

"Fair enough." Gil gestured to the man sitting next to Jordan, and he walked over to the whiteboard and erased Jill's scribblings.

Doug found his eyes flickering in her direction. She was sitting back in her chair like every other executive, waiting for her colleague's presentation.

Doug wrenched his attention back to the man at the whiteboard outlining a defense-industry proposal in a low monotone.

Doug stifled a yawn and reached for his coffee, very aware of Jill's presence down the table.

Sherry poked her head out the door of the church pantry, checking on the kids for the fifth time. The half-dozen rambunctious youngsters hadn't burned down the playground yet. Thankfully, a teenage girl appeared to have the madness under control.

As Sherry stepped back inside the small room, one of the other volunteers broke off from a conversation and glanced at her from beyond a shelf of canned goods.

"Everything still okay?"

"All limbs still attached," Sherry said as she returned to cataloging the latest holiday contributions.

The questioner turned back to her sorting job and her conversation with another volunteer. "So anyway, I just think they're embarrassed. I doubt either of them will come back."

"What a shame." The second woman's voice was clear, although she was out of sight behind several food racks. "You'd think *one* of them would want to come. It's a shame for both to lose their church and all their friends."

"Especially during a custody battle. How dreadful."

Sherry worked silently, torn between a desire to eavesdrop and her annoyance at the women's gossiping.

The second woman continued. "Pastor tried to talk them out of it but they were bound and determined. So they'd probably just feel guilty if they did come back."

"Awful, just awful. It's reaching epidemic proportions. You know, I just found out that the Silvertons were divorced, too."

"You're kidding!"

"Nope. It's the second marriage for both of them. You know, I really wonder whether it's appropriate to have him on the worship team."

There was a pause, then Sherry heard the second woman continue her sorting of food cans. "You know, I never thought of that, but it's a good point. Are we condoning divorce if we place a divorced man in a leadership position?"

"It's not like he's a pastor, of course, but still."

"Well…then again, there could've been good reasons for their earlier divorce, biblical reasons. Maybe his former spouse cheated on him. If that's the case, you certainly wouldn't want to limit the poor man."

"I imagine the worship director must've taken that into consideration."

"If he even knows."

Sherry saw the first woman straighten, a jar of peanut butter in her hand. "I wonder if he does know. Not many people do. I would hope the Silvertons would have told him privately, but maybe not."

"Well, you know the worship director best. Why don't you quietly pull him aside one Sunday and ask? That way you don't stir up a fuss, but you check to see whether we need to address the issue."

Sherry finished her cataloging and wove her way across the small food pantry, clipboard in hand.

"Melanie, those boxes are done. Anything else?"

The second woman stood up from her chair and stretched, smiling. "Thanks so much, dear. It looks like we're almost finished. You're very sweet to volunteer today."

"Well, I'm sorry I haven't had a chance before. It's certainly an important cause." Sherry looked across the shelves and boxes. They weren't exactly sagging under their load. "Will this be enough food?"

"I'd imagine so. We generally don't have a flood of direct requests after all; we usually just hook up with an inner-city ministry that needs the holiday contributions, and they take care of actually getting the food to the people that need it. Much more efficient."

The door opened, and all three women turned as a young man shuffled in. Sherry wrinkled her nose at the rank smell.

Melanie set down the clipboard and moved forward. "Can I help you?"

The man turned his glassy eyes toward her, and Sherry noticed that Melanie flinched back from his breath.

His voice was sluggish. "I need food and stuff. I saw your church from the street." He looked slowly around the room packed with cans and supplies. "Your office folks said you was back here."

Melanie pulled a sheet off the clipboard. "Before we can give you anything from the pantry, we need to get your name and contact information."

The man took an unsteady step back, his voice belligerent. "Why?"

"Because we like to know who we're helping."

He stared at her for a long moment, then began spelling his name in a too-loud voice. "And I don't have no home address right now."

"Okay," Melanie jotted the information down. "We can give you a bag of canned goods, if that will help."

He just stared at her with his glassy eyes. Clearly disconcerted, she put her hands on her hips.

"Will that help you?" Another pause. "Sir, you are drunk. Maybe it's best if you take a couple of hours to—"

"I need a place to stay, too."

"We, ah, we don't have a ministry like that. We can refer you to a church that does, a few miles away."

"I don't have no car."

Melanie looked at the other two women, flustered. "Well, we don't offer a shuttle service, sir. You can probably walk there in less than an hour." She moved to a small cabinet and pulled out a brochure. "There's a map right here. You just walk straight down Tenth Street out front, and turn right at the second light. It's another mile and a half down. You can't miss it."

The man took the brochure and squinted at it, standing still in the middle of the room. When he hadn't moved a full minute later, Melanie began bustling around the room arranging a sack of groceries for him.

Sherry sidled up next to her as she set a stack of canned vegetables into a grocery bag. Sherry kept her voice low.

"If he doesn't have a car, how is he going to carry that big bag three miles?"

Melanie swiveled around. "Sir, how much food would you like?"

He looked up, his face vague. "Maybe just some peanut butter and bread. I like peanut butter and bread. They may let me keep it at this shelter."

"Oh, sir…" Melanie hesitated, and then quickly loaded the rest of the bag, adding an extra jar of peanut butter and setting a fresh loaf of bread on the top. She hefted the bag and placed it into the drunken man's arms. Melanie wrinkled her nose in distaste, but duty called.

"Sir, I'm going to drive you over there. It'll only take me five minutes."

She stepped back, screwing up her courage to brave the man's smell, and then ushered him out the door, glancing backward with a roll of her eyes before the door closed.

The first volunteer looked at Sherry in astonishment. "Good heavens. That's something you don't see every day!"

Sherry stared in the direction Melanie had gone. "Good for her. It was the right thing to do."

"I guess. I don't know. I'm of a mind that people have to be willing to stop drinking and taking drugs and get themselves on a good track first, or we risk aid-ing and abetting their habits. Otherwise, if we give them food, they'll take the money they would've spent on food and use it for drugs instead. That's not a good idea."

"I suppose—"

The pantry door slammed open, and the teenage girl stood in the doorway, surrounded by kids.

"Where was Mom going? Who was that man?"

"That man was someone who came to the church for help, and your mom was helping him," Sherry said.

"But what was she *doing?* They drove away together!"

"She'll be right back. She was taking him to a nearby shelter for the night."

"What on *earth* was she thinking? That has to be dangerous, and he has *got* to smell up our car!"

The other volunteer spoke up. "I'm sure she's fine. Now why don't you let the kids keep playing. We're almost done here. Five more minutes, tops."

The kids ran back to the darkening playground, followed closely by the frowning teenager.

The other volunteer turned back to Sherry. "You were saying…?"

"I guess I was just saying that although you've got a good point, how are we ever going to help anyone if they have to be cleaned up first?"

"I'm not saying they have to have their life totally in order first—"

"No, no, I know. But if we require them to be off drugs and straight first, don't you think we'll miss a lot of the people that Jesus would've helped when He was walking the earth?"

The other volunteer smiled. "You've got a good heart, but we need to be able to counsel and monitor the people who're seeking help, and we're just not equipped to do that kind of ministry here. It's too complicated, and we could do more harm than good trying to find our way through the maze. We should leave it to the people who know what they're doing."

Sherry's mind flickered again to the drive back from the airport; to the decrepit car and the strip club billboard. A well-known adage suddenly overtook her thoughts. *There but for the grace of God go I…*

After refereeing a lively, two-hour financial negotiation, Gil closed his briefing book.

"Well, we could go on for a couple hours, but I think we have a handle on the parameters. Doug, thanks for coming. I know this could be beneficial to both parties, and we've got hundreds of man-hours invested, so I hope we can make it work."

"It would be nice." Doug could feel Jordan's frosty glance at his side, so he held up the briefing book. "I appreciate the tremendous effort you all have put into this. Now from our end, I'll just have to take a couple of days and crunch the numbers a bit."

Gil stood, and the others followed suit. He leaned to shake Doug's hand. "Give us a call if you need to clarify something before our meeting on Friday. We've listed the phone numbers and e-mail addresses for each of the executives, so you can get back to them at any time."

Doug nodded, forcing himself not to look down the table again. "Fine. I'll also be busy on another deal in town, but I might be able to call a few people to nail down additional details. You all have my contact info as well."

Gil glanced at his team, then back at their guest. "Well, Doug, what are your plans for dinner? We'd talked to Jordan about taking you both out to one of the local places. You've got to be starved by now."

"Yeah…Okay, well—"

"Great, great." Gil turned to his leadership team. "Who's going?"

Before Doug knew it, he and Jordan were ushered out the door, heading to a local eatery.

As Gil led the way toward an empty table for eight at an upscale Tex-Mex restaurant, Doug felt his cell phone buzzing in his pocket.

He checked the display and gave a start. "I forgot to call my wife!" He grimaced at his forgetfulness and heard Gil and Jordan chuckling beside him, joking about pesky wives.

"I'm going to take this outside." He turned to go, pressing the Receive button. "Hi, sweetheart."

"Hey, honey, you didn't call me! I was worried about you."

Doug stepped outside the front door of the restaurant. "I'm sorry. I've been in one long meeting right up until a few minutes ago."

"You could've called me as you were driving to the meeting."

"Yeah." Doug's shoulders drooped with fatigue. "I'm sorry. I just forgot."

"Don't you care that I'm worried about you?"

"Sherry…" Doug closed his eyes, struggling for patience with the woman he loved, "of course I care. I'm just exhausted right now, honey. I'm not thinking all that clearly these days."

"But—"

"Honey, I don't mean to put you off, really I don't, but I'm at a business dinner here. I just don't have time to hash this out right now."

He paused. No response.

"Honey?"

"I'm still here."

"I want to talk to you but I just can't right now. And I'm sorry I didn't call earlier."

"I don't mean to bug you, honest." Another pause. "I love you, Doug. Go back to your meeting."

"Thanks for understanding. I'll call you later."

"It *is* later, Doug. It's already ten o'clock here."

"Of course. Sorry. I'll call you in the morning, then."

"That would be great. Since you'll be out there all week, is there any way we could connect at least once a day?"

"I promise I will. I'm sorry. I love you, you know."

"I know. I love you, too."

Doug walked back toward the table, his steps heavy. Maybe he wasn't so great a husband and father after all. Maybe he just wasn't being to Sherry what she needed him to be. Did he even have it in him? She was acting so insecure these days, but she wasn't naturally an anxious person. Maybe if he was a better man, she wouldn't be—

"Doug?"

He turned his head to see Jill coming toward him, her gaze friendly. She raised her eyebrows. "Anything wrong?"

"No. Just tired." Doug lifted his cell phone. "Missing my wife."

"Of course."

Jill wove her way toward their table, now full except for two adjacent seats. She pulled up one chair, and Doug slowly took the other.

Gil caught the eye of a nearby waiter, then looked toward Doug and Jill. "We just put in our drink order. What do you two want?"

Jill pursed her lips as she scanned the drink card. Doug had to look away, the mental refrain starting all over again. He could feel the warmth of her arm next to his. As they gave their drink orders to the waiter—beer for her, soda for him—Doug scooted his chair sideways.

She was probably brushing up against me on purpose. I bet she's attracted to me. Better let her down easy.

Jill leaned on the table and looked toward him. "So what's your wife's name?"

"Sherry. We have two kids."

"Must be hard to be away."

"It is."

"Do you have a picture?"

"Sure." Doug opened his wallet and showed her a snapshot of the family in front of a blazing fireplace. "This was just a few weeks ago."

Jill's eyes lit up. "Oh, that's so sweet."

She gave him a respectful smile, and he felt a warm glow. *She's impressed with what a good family man I am.*

Doug started to slot the photo away, but the man on his other side looked interested. Before he knew it, the happy family picture was passed around the table. He spent the next hour comparing notes with the others about families and activities.

One of the thirty-something executives talked about a recent marathon he'd run.

Jill turned to him. "I didn't know you were a runner. I ran that marathon, too."

That accounts for those legs…

Doug wrenched his thoughts off that dangerous track and looked over at the other man. "Um, so how hard was it to get a spot in that marathon? I did my first one in Atlanta last year and was thinking of doing another."

"Not too hard. So you're a runner, too?"

When Doug nodded, Jill turned sideways. "I thought you looked like it. What was your time?"

"Three hours, thirty-nine minutes."

"Wow." The other guy sat back in his seat. "Three-thirty-nine for your *first* marathon? That rocks. I just got down to three-forty-five after seven tries."

Doug gave a self-deprecating laugh. "There's no way I'll make that time again. I must've caught a good tailwind. Besides, anyone who can run *seven* marathons kicks my tail all over the road."

As the other man shrugged, Doug caught a glimpse of Jill glancing at him in admiration.

Now she realizes I'm humble, too.

He batted the thought away, disgusted with himself. He turned to look down the table.

"So, Gil, how long has your company been around?"

☆ ☆ ☆

Twenty minutes and another long battle later, Doug found himself yawning into the restaurant's signature dessert of fried ice cream.

"Well, it's been nice to meet you all." The others stood as he rose to his feet. "I'm on Eastern time, so I better go or I won't be any good for my meetings tomorrow."

Gil came around the table and shook Doug's hand. "Thanks for coming. We'll see you Friday. Call us if you have questions."

Doug kept his eyes turned away from Jill's affirmative nod. "I'll do that." He smiled and turned to go. Out in the air, he let the chilly wind wash his face. *Whew. Obstacle course completed.*

He drove the short distance to his hotel with his mind on autopilot. For just a moment, he replayed his first glimpse of Jill's sleek figure in that suit, then her admiring glance as he talked about his family, her respect for his marathon time. He straightened in his seat. Now *that* was affirmation.

He pulled up at the hotel, grabbed his suitcase from the trunk, and went to check in. Ten minutes later, he closed his room door behind him, hung up his garment bag, and pulled on a comfortable pair of sweats. He settled on the bed and grabbed the television remote. It was late, but he was too wired to sleep. He had to unwind.

That was another thing Sherry never wanted him to do. She wanted him to talk as soon as he got home from work or back from a meeting, when it was all he could do to form two coherent words in his own head, much less get them past his lips.

He clicked on the remote, and the television came to life with a scene from a recently released movie.

He and Sherry hadn't seen the movie yet, and he hated starting in the middle. As he began to press the "change channel" button, the thought crept in: The *reason* they hadn't seen the movie was Sherry's concern about the amount of nudity, especially by the famous female star. Doug had agreed that it was best not to expose themselves to that, but now he held the remote in hand, wavering.

The movie had been wildly popular at the box office, and he'd talked to several friends from church who had liked it. One of the men had even joked about how hot the actress's love scenes were.

I wonder what she looks like naked? Nah, I shouldn't.

He pointed the remote at the television and changed to a sports channel, watching the evening's NBA highlights, then the hockey scores. Yes! The Red Wings won again. He grinned. You can take the guy out of Michigan, but you can't take

Michigan out of the guy. When a commercial came on, he changed the channel again.

It's been fifteen minutes. I wonder if one of those scenes is on yet.

Doug wavered, then clicked back to the original channel. The famous actress was giving the newcomer-hunk star a slow backrub. What timing.

He sank back into the pillows behind him and settled in for the rest of the movie. After all, it was only R-rated; how bad could it really be?

EIGHT

The palm trees swayed overhead as Tyson settled back into his beach chair. He let out a satisfied sigh.

One of the others chuckled, a tall beer in his hand. "Sure beats that warehouse in Atlanta."

Tyson smiled, his eyes closed behind his sunglasses. "Yes, but the warehouse does serve a purpose. We're sure it's clean, which your homes and offices may not be. However, there's always the chance that one of the larger group would stumble into something if we were nearby. I think it's safe to set up the staff in the building, but I don't want the principals there. I figured if we had to meet off site, it might as well be offshore. No American police here."

"Any police at all?"

"Only those loyal to us. We pay them more than the local government does." He shrugged. "And since the local government wants our business, they're willing to see nothing, hear nothing, and conveniently forget our presence when working with the state department. And if they don't want to forget, then the fish get another meal."

He paused. "After lunch we have some business to attend to. I need to brief you on my last instructions from Proxy. He has an 'in' to a top defense manufacturer. We've already got one likely target in the works, so we need to analyze their product lines and prioritize our opportunities."

He looked beyond the circle, catching sight of his local chief of staff hovering nearby. "Ah, Manuel, lunch is ready?"

The little group relaxed through a leisurely lunch, served to them on the beach by the local discreet staff. One of the young women—no more than sixteen—had smooth bronze skin and long hair falling to her waist.

At the end of lunch, Tyson pulled the chief of staff aside and whispered something. A few minutes later, Tyson watched as Manuel approached the girl and spoke in low tones. There was some sort of an argument. When she tried to jerk away, the man grabbed her arm. The girl began to cry, and she was yanked inside a small hut, out of sight.

A smile played on Tyson's lips. The others would like this impromptu show. And if they were pleased with her, with what came after.

"No...no...don't. Please...you can't..."

Ronnie thrashed in bed, whimpering, her eyelids flickering. She curled up into a tight ball against the images that played in her mind. It never worked. She could always feel the groping hands, the secret shame.

If she told, he would take her away from her mother. Or she would be put in jail. Or worse would be done to her. Her childhood brain rang with the reasons, all the reasons for her silence.

As always, he stood from her bed and gave her a warning lash—a single lash—from his belt. The first time, she had cried out, and her mother had come running. And had been beaten unconscious. Ronnie never cried out again.

"No...*NO*...!"

There was pounding this time as he lay down beside her, a pounding on the door. "Ronnie? Ronnie?"

She bolted awake, aware of a voice in the dark. She sat up, panting, as the voice called out again.

"Ronnie?" Tiffany's worried face peeped in at her. "You okay?"

"I'm sorry." Ronnie looked at the clock on her nightstand. 4:13. They'd been asleep only an hour.

"The same dream again?"

Ronnie could only nod.

Tiffany gave her a long hug. "I'm sorry. Life stinks, doesn't it?"

"Thanks, Tiff. I don't know what I'd do without you. Sorry I woke you up."

"No problem." She stood. "You okay?"

"I'm okay. It won't come back tonight."

"Good. And if it tries to, you just flip your stepfather off for me."

Ronnie had to chuckle. "I'll try to remember that."

She settled back into the bed as Tiffany slipped out the door. She pulled the covers up to her chin, clutching them like a frightened eight-year-old-girl. She closed her eyes, hoping she could sleep, hoping she wouldn't be yawning at work all the next night.

Ronnie hurried out to her largest table, balancing her laden tray on her shoulder. She laid down the final steak platter, and waited while the customer cut into it.

"Is that acceptable, sir?"

The man's words were slurred. "It's acceptable, sweetcheeks. And so are *you*. I'll give you a hundred bucks if you dance for me."

Ronnie crossed to the other side of the table and filled a few water glasses. "I'm just a waitress, honey, but thanks for the compliment." She forced herself to give a saucy grin. "But I'll take whatever tip you want to give me."

The other men at the table laughed as she turned away. The sloppy man raised his voice.

"The name's Ron, sweetcheeks! And I'll keep tipping you until I get a dance. One of these days!"

Ronnie saw a new group sit by a table against the wall and hurried over, muttering, "Don't hold your breath, sweetheart."

Farther along the wall, behind a one-way mirror, several men sat in a room resembling a television production booth. Electrical equipment and control boards formed a horseshoe around them. One ran the many cameras, the other the control boards and computers. The third stood behind them, arms crossed, giving direction as the cameras scanned the room from all angles.

After a few minutes of silence, something on the control panel beeped, and the camera operator focused in tighter.

The man standing, uncrossed his arms and leaned forward. "Right there—who just sat down?"

"Hold on." The computer operator tapped a few keys and waited while several face-prints and paragraphs of text flashed across the screen. "Name of Wayne Jackson. The other man is…wait…Darrell Hardy." A few more clicks, and then a slow sound of satisfaction. "Ah…They're both with that big electronics manufacturer Marco mentioned yesterday. The one Proxy's looking at as a possible target."

"Good. Good." The first man nodded, pleased. "Are their positions helpful?"

More clicking on the keyboard, then the computer operator raised an eyebrow. "Jackson is just a midlevel manager, but…Hardy is apparently the chief operating officer."

"Excellent. Tab those, get the necessary data, and notify Marco right away." He straightened and his eyes turned to the next table along. "Let's see if we can make this night a two-fer, shall we?"

☆ ☆ ☆

Outside of Washington, D.C., a similar operation was taking place. Behind one-way glass, another camera scanned the crowd, capturing another face, another screen of data.

This one generated even more excitement. The data was compiled and transmitted to a control room in Atlanta.

Within five minutes, Marco was behind closed doors, staring at the promising data on his computer screen. He took a few cryptic notes and tapped his pen rapidly on the desktop. He would need to move even faster than expected; some of these targets were too good to waste. This Washington, D.C., satellite engineer would have access to some critical systems they needed.

But...would he be able to deliver the targets? As unsettling as it was, he forced his mind to run through the various scenarios. What if he *wasn't* ready yet?

He coldly replayed his cocky assurances to Proxy's lieutenant. Proxy didn't suffer fools lightly. Just last year, another man had held Marco's current position in the organization. He'd had a drinking problem and despite repeated warnings, became garrulous when smashed. In the crowded club one night he had held forth about masterminding the idea behind a very profitable—and until then, very secret—underground tunnel that had permitted an undetected flow of drugs and people into the country. Waving a drink at a fascinated crowd, he described how the tunnel originated on a small island off the gulf of Florida and ended inside a false fireplace in a house on shore. The next morning, he hadn't even remembered his late-night loquaciousness, but someone else sure had.

One week later, twenty million dollars' worth of cocaine and heroin had been captured in transit. A few hours later, Marco's predecessor had been found floating facedown in the Gulf, not far from his marvel of now-useless engineering.

Marco had been promoted the same day. He grimaced at the memory. An undercover cop must have been among the customers in the club, but no one had ever figured out who it was. Unsettling, but inevitable.

Marco looked again at the screen before him, planning his strategy. Even if he had to move prematurely he could still deliver. Despite Tyson's pointed concerns, they already had enough assets to do a credible job. Heck, he could even move a girl from Atlanta to Washington, D.C., if he had to. But he was pretty sure they wouldn't have to.

He was careful, and he was good at the game. He would not trigger Proxy's wrath. He looked out his darkened window into the neon-lit club and smiled. Quite the contrary. Soon…very soon…he would be indispensable. And Proxy rewarded loyalty well.

He picked up the phone and made a quiet call.

In the club outside Washington, D.C., the local manager put down his phone and went in search of one particular dancer. He found her reapplying her makeup, and pulled her into his office for a chat. She left the office with a small smile and went in search of the target.

Within twenty minutes, a lonely satellite engineer was leaving the club with a very beautiful girl on his arm. He couldn't believe his good fortune, couldn't believe that she had noticed *him*, had *wanted* him!

He knew he was breaking every rule in the book, breaking all the regulations surrounding his security clearance. His higher-ups would condemn his actions…if they ever found out. Which they wouldn't.

He looked at the gorgeous girl beside him and hurried to usher her into his car. He was sick and tired of long nights in front of his computer. It was his personal life and the security freaks would never find out. An opportunity like this didn't come along very often.

NINE

I s Mr. Woodward's secretary available, then?"

Ronnie tapped her pen nervously against Tiffany's kitchen table. The bay window alcove was a light-filled oasis, but Ronnie's eyes weren't focusing on her surroundings. She was concentrating all her positive energy on the woman at the other end of the phone. Maybe if she willed it hard enough—

The secretary came on the line. "I'm so sorry, Miss Hanover, but he just isn't available for a conversation right now. I know this is your third call, but he only takes phone calls from prospective students by appointment. As I said before, if you'd like to schedule a fifteen-minute phone call, we'd be happy to arrange that for you, as you seem like a motivated young lady."

"I don't—see, my schedule is just so crazy it's hard to *schedule* something. Especially since he only takes these calls in the afternoon, when I'm working."

"You're a waitress, you said?"

"Yes, that's right." *Please don't ask where, please don't ask where...*

"Well, could you perhaps schedule it during a break time?"

"Huh." Ronnie straightened slightly. "You know, I didn't think of that. Yes. Yes! I usually have a break around three or three-thirty...as long as he doesn't mind me calling from the restaurant."

"Oh, he's had people call from Chinese rice paddies before, Miss Hanover. I'm sure a restaurant won't faze him." Ronnie heard the clicking sounds of a keyboard, then the sound of pleasant surprise. "Actually, he had a cancellation tomorrow, believe it or not. I'm scheduling you for tomorrow at three o'clock. Will that do?"

"Yes, that would be great. Just great."

"Don't be late now, you hear? He only has the fifteen-minute slot, and he's a stickler about punctuality. He equates being on time with how much an applicant appears to care about their schooling. And that impacts his perception of their admissions application."

"Oh yes, of course. Thank you...Thank you so much!"

☆ ☆ ☆

Across town, a computer hard drive whirred slightly as the latest contact was captured, digitized and filed for retrieval. An hour later, after careful encryption and
multiple routings, an automatic report was sent to an e-mail inbox.

The computer was emotionless. The person who reviewed the files was not.
Marco smiled as he read the report. Everyone had a lever. It was just a matter of
finding it.

Ronnie jammed the last few pieces of lunch debris onto her overloaded tray, gave
the table a few perfunctory wipes with a cloth, and hurried toward the kitchen. A
moment later, she headed down the hallway toward the break room, fishing for the
coins in her apron. She jangled the quarters with nervous hands.

Would the admissions officer truly not mind that she was calling from a pay
phone with the din of a loud restaurant in the background? Maybe he would agree
to a face-to-face meeting if she could convince him it was worth his time to meet
with a high school dropout who hadn't even gotten her GED yet. If someone would
just give her a chance, she *knew* she could make a better life for herself. She was
working double shifts almost every day, and her bank balance just wasn't growing
enough. Maybe this Mr. Woodward would understand and give her the break she
needed.

She was almost at the break-room door when she heard Marco step out of his
office behind her. "Ronnie, can you come in here a moment?"

"Oh—Marco—I have an important phone call to make at three o'clock. Can I
come by in—"

"You're on duty. I need you in the office."

Ronnie stopped and turned around. "I'm actually on break now, and—"

"You're in my office now." He vanished back inside the door.

Ronnie clenched her fists and stomped down the hall and into his office.

"Sit down." Marco was holding out a chair, a small smile on his face.

Ronnie didn't walk across the room. "I'd like to stand, thanks. I want to get to
my phone appointment."

Marco's eyes narrowed. "I'd like to know what is more important than your job,
Ronnie."

"You'd like—! Well, fine, I'll tell you then." Ronnie jabbed her finger toward the
break room. "I'm supposed to be on the phone right now for a Georgia State interview at three o'clock. You have no idea how important this is to me."

"But for now, you work here, and I—"

"The only reason I *am* working here is to get the tuition for school!" She looked at the clock on his desk and blinked back tears, furious at herself for her weakness in front of her manager. "I was supposed to call the admissions director by now. What's he going to think when I stand him up? What chance do I have of being accepted?"

Marco's voice was calm. "Why didn't you schedule the call for your off-hours?"

"Because I don't *have* off-hours, Marco!" She stepped forward, her voice raised. "Or at least not when this admissions officer could talk to me. All I do is work, and I still can't get ahead. I have to save two thousand dollars by the time I start school and that seems as remote as the moon right now!"

"There's an easy way of solving that problem, you know."

Ronnie stared up at her boss's face, and took a step back. "No. *No way,* Marco. I've already told you..."

Marco shook his head. "Fine. Don't listen. It's not what you think—not exactly, anyway." He turned away. "Go make your call. We'll need to talk at the end of your shift tonight."

Something in his voice made Ronnie hesitate. "I'm sorry, I—"

"Go make your call."

Ronnie paused, then turned and ran for the break room. Shaking, she fumbled the coins into the slot and dialed the number.

"Is Mr. Woodward there?"

An interminable pause as the call was transferred. "Mr. Woodward's office."

"Hi, listen, this is Ronnie Hanover. I'm so sorry, I—"

"Oh, dear. I'm afraid he couldn't wait any longer. He got on another call just a minute ago."

"Oh no." Ronnie couldn't hide the tears in her voice. "Please. Is there *any* way to reschedule? My boss grabbed me just as I was going to call, and—"

"I'm sorry, Ronnie. He generally never tries twice for someone who doesn't seem to care enough the first time. He's too busy as it is."

"Can you...can you tell him that I tried everything I could to make the call, but that my boss canceled my break at the last minute? I might even lose my job over this. Georgia State is the only school I'm applying to. Is there *any way* he would allow me to make it up by taking a vacation day and coming down to meet with him?"

"I'll tell him, but I can tell you from experience that he's unlikely to agree. Besides, you probably don't have vacation days yet, right?"

Ronnie clutched the phone. "I'll figure something out."

A sigh. "I'll tell him, dear. But don't get your hopes up."

The secretary hung up, and Ronnie threw the phone against the wall.

Behind his closed door and his one-way mirror, Marco dialed a phone number and waited, idly looking out at the all-but-deserted tables in the club and the bored dancer making the minimum effort on stage. He jotted a note to himself to fine the girl. He couldn't afford any sloppiness at this point in the game.

The ringing stopped, and a jovial voice came on the line. Marco spoke in measured tones and allowed himself a thin smile as the heartiness was instantly replaced by tension.

After a few minutes, Marco replaced the receiver and walked over to a small side bar to pour himself a cup of coffee. He settled back into his leather chair and swiveled toward the one-way mirror. During this afternoon lull, he might as well take a break and enjoy the show.

"Good afternoon, Mr. Woodward's office." The secretary sat straighter in her chair, listening. "Yes, sir. He's in the office with a prospective student right now...Of course, sir, I'll get him right away."

The secretary pressed the hold button on the phone, then dialed an extension. A moment later, a confused-looking young man stepped out of the inner office and closed the door behind him. The secretary gave him a placating smile as she transferred the call.

After a few minutes, the admissions officer appeared in the doorway. He looked at the young man. "John, sorry about that. Thanks for being so accommodating. Come on back in."

As the prospective student shuffled back inside the office, the admissions officer caught his secretary's eye. "Call Ronnie Hanover back and see if she'd still like to schedule a meeting."

"Sir? But you—"

"I know I said not to, but she must know someone high up in our administration. The dean's office is pressing me to give her a full-fledged interview." He shrugged before vanishing back inside the office.

"A screwdriver, a scotch on the rocks, and two martinis. Thanks, Nick." Ronnie set down her cocktail tray and leaned against the bar, averting her eyes from where

Marco stood a few feet away. He was surveying the club, his arms crossed, a scowl on his face.

Her mind raced ahead as she picked up and delivered the drinks, smiling and accepting tips, hardly noticing a word that was said. Was it possible she might actually be fired? She could impose on Tiffany only for so long. What then?

No way would she go back home. She'd risk homelessness first.

"Hey, Ronnie, I'm so late!" Tiffany hurried up next to her and took a couple of deep breaths. A grin broke out on her face. "I just wanted you to know that someone from a Mr. Woodward's office called. She said Georgia State wanted to talk to you after all, and that you should call at your earliest convenience for an *in-person* interview."

Ronnie squealed. "Are you kidding? Really?"

"Ohmygosh." Tiffany was looking over Ronnie's shoulder. "Marco's going to kill me if I don't hustle. I'll see you later."

TEN

As the night wore on, Ronnie went about her business, serving the customers, refilling drinks, and averting her eyes from the stage and the girls that appeared beside her tables. For as long as she worked in the club, she had told Tiffany privately, she intended to watch as little as possible.

She didn't know that she herself was being watched. On every side, unseen eyes peered through a thick darkness, a fog of oppression and torment. Of fear and lust. Most of the eyes were filled with hate and a twisted desire. The dark beings used the very people they despised. The humans were created in the image of the great Enemy, the One who had banished them forever. That He would move heaven and earth to win back His wayward children was enough reason to despise them, to damage them with great precision. It made the dark beings stronger. They reveled in the destruction of a soul. They wanted each human child tormented on earth...and in the hereafter. They wanted them lost to their heavenly Father.

But there were also agents of the Father in the room, and He was not willing that even one should perish. The very presence of the messengers of light was painful to the seething, dark masses. They flinched away from the searing brilliance, enraged that they had no choice but to comply and allow the dreadful beings among them.

Their snarls hid their anxiety as they watched where their newest adversaries directed their attention. Their upcoming plan was brilliant in its construction, fiendish in its strategy, and massive in scope...so the influx from the Enemy was not surprising. But what did they want with the girl? She was theirs.

They did not know about the prayer.

Hundreds of miles away, a young woman crawled into bed beside her husband, her face grave. He took one look at her and laid down his book.

"Honey...what's wrong?"

"Do you remember that girl I told you about, the one who dropped out of school a few weeks ago?"

"The cheerleader? Ronnie somebody?"

"Ronnie Hanover. I don't know why, but I can't get her out of my mind. I keep thinking about her. I pray for her, but this *feeling* doesn't go away."

Her husband gave her a confused smile. "Sweetheart, you have kids drop out of school practically every week."

"I know." The woman sat up again. "I don't know why, but I feel like she's in danger. I've got such a burden for her."

"Well, if it won't go away, I guess you should just keep praying." He sat up also, and pulled his wife to his side. "Let's pray right now."

The shining messenger appeared by Loriel's side, his manner taut, expectant. Loriel continued scanning the dark and teeming room. When he finally spoke, his gaze remained watchful and he did not turn to look at his lieutenant.

"Report, Caliel."

"Commander, some of the saints are listening and obeying. The prayers are beginning. But it will probably be some time before a true army beseeches the Throne of Heaven."

"You know how critical our mission is; we dare not move too early. The next phase will soon unfold—the phase you have been chosen to shepherd. Meanwhile, we must wait and we must work as the Lord has directed."

Caliel nodded, his eyes grave as he watched Ronnie go about her rounds. "I fear for her."

"I, too. We do not have as much time as we had hoped." Loriel straightened and turned to face his lieutenant. "The campaign is growing urgent. And this will be your first command."

"I am ready, Commander."

"Then choose a contingent and go. You know your posting well, and you are released to return; not just as watch-carer, but with the authority for the next critical stage of this campaign. I will see that you are not followed, and I will join you later. The Lord has said it: in the end, this war will likely rest on your outcome."

Caliel gathered his troops and lifted his hands in worship. "May God grant us strength!"

The dark forces watched the sudden, swift departure of their adversaries. There was a moment of pure consternation. Where were they going? What was going on?

They had been expecting an all-out battle to steal the girl away. They had been strengthening their defenses and sharpening their weapons. But the enemy had gotten cold feet. Now all they had to contend with were a few sniveling remnants of the enemy host, weak in their isolation.

Several demons sauntered up to the highest-ranking angel, taunting him with their graphic plans for the girl he seemed to care so much about.

He stared them down, and they backed off slightly. But they could see the pain in his eyes. So much the better. The owners and managers in the club had been perplexed by the girl's resolve. With the enemy host gone, it was just a matter of time.

"Time to talk, Ronnie." Marco appeared at Ronnie's side as she wiped her last empty table for the fourth time. "No more stalling."

Ronnie followed her boss, reluctantly entered the office, and waited as he closed the door behind her.

"Have a seat."

Ronnie complied, as she hadn't earlier that day. What had she been thinking?

Marco walked around behind his desk and leaned on it. "You and I both know that I could fire you for your attitude earlier today."

Ronnie looked down at her hands, biting her tongue against any retort.

"But I'm not going to. You're young, but I believe you have the makings of a valuable employee."

"Thank you." Her voice was tired and she didn't look up. "I don't know what I'd do if—"

"But I'm going to ask that you seriously consider several options for increasing your productivity with us."

"What do you mean?"

Marco pushed back his chair and settled into it, propping his feet up on his desk. He stifled a yawn. "Well, from what you said earlier, you need to make more money. There are many ways to do that, but you have to be open-minded, willing to try new things. You can't be so set in your ways, especially if you want to earn enough money for school."

"But stripping—"

"Listen, Ronnie." Marco gave her a rueful smile. "You've made it clear that you don't view dancing as appealing. Fine. I'm not going to force you into anything. But there's a reason for the saying, 'try it, you'll like it.' I believe that you would come to enjoy it very quickly—and would *really* enjoy the money. I hope you'll change your mind eventually because, frankly, I think you'd be a big draw for the club."

Ronnie looked down again. "You implied that stripping wasn't the only thing you wanted to suggest."

"That's true." Marco swiveled in his chair and looked out at the deserted stages, his voice oddly distant. "You probably don't realize it yet, but our club is well-connected. Not only in this city—we're well connected in the world of magazines, movies, and other media. Movie producers are in here all the time, and you served one of them recently without knowing it."

"I did?"

"And as he was leaving, he approached me to ask if you'd be interested in speaking with them. They want to give you a screen test."

Ronnie's mouth dropped open. "You're kidding."

Marco laughed. "I'm serious, Ronnie. This could be a big break for you. Several of our girls have been approached over the years, and I will tell you that for those who've made it, this is a lucrative way to supplement your income."

"Would I have to move to California?"

"No, no." Marco waved a hand, chuckling. "These are independent producers that work from everywhere. The one I spoke to is based here in Atlanta. They put out dozens of movies a year, and the average shoot is only a few weeks. We'd work out a schedule to grant you leave during those weeks, as we like to see our girls succeed in this area."

"A few *weeks?* What kind of movie can be shot in a few weeks?" Ronnie stared at the look on Marco's face, and comprehension flooded her. "Give me a break, Marco! Do you really think that if I'm not interested in stripping, that I'd be interested in porn movies?"

"Ronnie, Ronnie, these aren't hard-core porn films. These are independent adult-entertainment productions. Don't judge them so quickly—they may not be at all what you're thinking."

"You really had me going there for a second."

"Just check it out." Marco wrote a name and number on a slip of Challenger letterhead and handed it across the desk. "Don't be so judgmental before you know what it's really about."

"Yeah…" Ronnie studied the paper and let out a long sigh.

"What's wrong?"

"It just seems like…like everyone wants to push me into this stuff. I wish someone would recognize that that's not the reason I'm here. I'm here so I can go to college. I wish you all would consider what's right for *me*. But you just don't care. You don't care about me, or my plans, or what I want for my life."

"Ronnie, who do you think got you the interview at Georgia State?"

Her head shot up, her mouth opening in astonishment.

Marco smiled and leaned forward. "I told you, we're very well-connected in this city." He stood and walked over to her chair. "We want to help you, Ronnie. We *do* care about you. We consider our employees a family, and that's what a family does."

ELEVEN

Tiffany slung a small purse over her shoulder and cocked her head. "Are you sure you don't want to come with us? You've been talking about seeing this movie for weeks."

Ronnie didn't move from the kitchen table. The noontime sun was flooding in the bay window alcove, beckoning her. She forced herself to shake her head. "I can't. I have to work tonight, and this afternoon is the last free time I'll have to fill out the paperwork before the deadline."

"Oh, come on. You can do it tomorrow. You have until five." Tiffany playfully tried to push her out of her chair. "Stop being so serious and get out and *live* for a change!"

Ronnie laughed but clutched the tabletop in a vise grip. "And I've got to save up for a car, Tiff! I can't afford to go to lunch and the movies and go shopping— I can barely afford to pay my share of the rent for this palace you call an apartment, much less get my own near the school."

"It's just a cheap matinee, and you don't have to buy anything if you don't want to. Just come *with* us." Her voice grew plaintive. "It's been more than a month, and we haven't done anything fun since you got here."

"I—I can't, Tiff. I *have* to get my GED. And tomorrow I have that big interview at Georgia State. That's why I'm here at all, remember?"

"Yeah," her friend sighed, "I know. I know. But promise," she wagged her finger in Ronnie's face, "as soon as you get that paperwork filed, we go out and get dinner somewhere or go downtown and have some fun. And you have to stop being so stubborn and just let me pay."

Ronnie lifted her hands in surrender. "Okay, okay. Once isn't going to kill me."

"Good." Tiffany leaned over and hugged her friend. "Good luck with all the paperwork. See you tonight at the office." She grinned and sashayed out the door.

"What did you call this thing again?" Ronnie looked over at Tina, who was also applying her makeup at the women's powder room mirror. The room was crowded. Two other waitresses gushed over another young woman, who was perched on the edge of a lounge chair, her hands clenched in nervous fists.

"Amateur night."

"But if they're actually on stage, how can they be—"

"Think of it like a talent contest. Teachers or secretaries or lawyers—whoever—go onstage for two minutes, and just try it out." Tina turned back to the mirror. "Whoever wins the contest gets five hundred bucks. Half a grand for two minutes ain't bad."

"So it's just for fun?"

"Some people just do it for a lark…for kicks, you know? But this is how the managers find a lot of new talent. You win the contest, you *definitely* get hired. Probably here, but also sometimes at one of their affiliate clubs."

"It sounds nerve-wracking." Ronnie eyed the other girls, who were heading out the door. "How do people even hear about it?"

"That girl," Tina nodded in the direction the group had gone, "knows two of the waitresses, and they convinced her to come try it."

"Well, if the other waitresses are so eager for their friend to try it, why aren't they going up there themselves?"

Tina capped her lipstick with a click and gave Ronnie a look. "Oh, honey. They are."

Ronnie sat in the sparse waiting area of the admissions office, reading the multipage application, brochures about student activities, the college catalog.

"Ronnie Hanover?"

She looked up as a very tall man stepped toward her, a welcoming look on his face.

"I'm Vance Woodward. Why don't you come into my office?"

"Okay." She moved toward the door, surprised that he politely waited for her to enter first.

Inside the office, she stopped short and found herself smiling in delight. The walls, tables, and bookshelves were laden with vintage Americana—trinkets and collectors' pieces from dozens of companies that had been around for years. Even the chairs in front of the standard-issue desk looked as if they were from an old soda parlor.

The admissions officer seemed amused at her reaction. "I probably go overboard as a collector."

"No, no, I love it!" She ran her hand over an old gramophone by the door. "I've never seen—I mean—how did you *get* all of this?"

Mr. Woodward gestured her toward a seating area around a coffee table. She perched on the simple sofa, while he pulled up one of the vintage chairs.

"Oh, I started collecting when I was a kid and just never stopped. It finally drove my wife crazy, so she insisted I bring most of the stuff to the office. We hit a bad financial patch a few years back and had to downsize to a smaller house, so I guess I can't blame her."

He sat back and reached for a pad of paper on a nearby table. "Now, Ronnie, let's get one thing out of the way. You missed the call that we had scheduled last week, and I'd like to know why. There's a passage in the Bible that says 'out of the fullness of the heart, the mouth speaks,' and, similarly, I believe that what is in someone's heart will be shown by their actions. When you don't make a scheduled appointment, I can only assume that you're either careless or unmotivated—neither of which characterizes the students we're looking for."

Ronnie's mouth was dry. "I do care, Mr. Woodward. I want to go to college more than anything. That's why I wanted to meet with you. And thank you for taking the meeting."

"You're welcome." The admissions officer inclined his head. "So what happened?"

"My boss stopped me as I was about to make the call, and insisted I come meet with him that minute. I did everything I could to get him to wait—I really did—but I was worried he would fire me. And there's no way I'll earn the money for school unless I keep this job."

"Can your family help you?"

"No. No, my family isn't...helping me."

"Do they live nearby?"

"No." Ronnie took a deep breath. "They live a few hours south. I'm here on my own."

"Have you graduated from high school yet?"

"No, I had to drop out. But I'm going to get my GED in the spring, so I'll be ready for school by the fall. I'm living up in the suburbs with a friend, and I have a good job so I can pay the tuition. I'm going to make this happen, one way or another."

Mr. Woodward sat back in his chair and nodded slowly. "It sounds like you're a very motivated young lady."

Ronnie looked down, suddenly close to tears. "Thank you."

"Well, remind me to get you some financial aid information when we're done. I think you might be able to get some grants to help with the costs. Now—"

"Grants? I was assuming I'd have to take out a loan."

"Perhaps not—or not as much of one. The school sometimes gives grants to those in financial need...such as those whose parents can't afford to help pay for school." He smiled. "We'll get you that information shortly. Now, if you don't mind, I have a few standard questions to ask about your academic record and activities, and then I'd be glad to answer anything I can for you."

Twenty minutes later, he looked at his watch and rose to his feet. "It certainly sounds as if you are the sort of student we're looking for. I can't promise anything until the applications are reviewed, but I'd say you have a very good chance of admission." He smiled down at her. "And frankly, I'd say you have a very good chance of success in life, as well."

"Thank you, sir."

He walked her out the door of his office and asked his secretary to get her a packet of financial aid materials.

"Please call me if you have any further questions, or need help in the process. That's what we're here for." When Ronnie nodded silently, he gave her an intent look. "I'm serious, Ronnie. It sounds like you're swimming uphill, and you might need a boost from time to time. Don't hesitate to call."

"All right...and thank you." Ronnie turned as the secretary approached.

"Here you are." She handed over a large manila envelope. "That should have everything you need. You might want to go relax in the library for a few minutes and look through the materials. If you have any questions, you could just run over to the financial aid office. It's not that far away."

"I'll do that." Ronnie slotted all the papers she'd received into the envelope and hugged it to her chest. "Thanks for all your help, really."

"My pleasure." The brisk demeanor melted into a smile. "Good luck, Miss Hanover."

The campus library was nearly deserted for the holidays, as Ronnie pored over catalog after catalog, flyer after flyer. So many classes! So many activities! Her eyes soaked in the pictures of international skylines: Paris...Shanghai...Sydney. An international exchange program—now *that* would be an adventure.

She flipped through the course catalog. To work in physical therapy, she could concentrate in premed...or maybe physical fitness... Four years of it! Maybe she'd even go on to get a masters degree! The tingle of excitement made her jumpy. She wanted to start classes now. She gave a little snort of amusement. Yeah, except for that little hurdle called a high school diploma.

She turned to the next booklet, and her smile faded. Well, she would have to face reality at some point. Maybe if Mr. Woodward was right, she'd be able to get some grant money and take out fewer loans. She ran her fingers down the costs of tuition, materials, room and board, jotted some notes in her notebook, and pulled the financial aid materials from their envelope.

Ten minutes later, her note taking slowed, and then stopped. Ronnie read the fine print again, and again, then laid the packet on the desk and buried her head in her hands.

Parental agreement! She more than qualified for a "financial need" grant, but there was no way that her family would cooperate. Seth would never allow her mother to disclose their finances to the financial aid office, much less cosign a loan application so she would have enough to live on while she completed her degree.

She squeezed her eyes shut tight as the full reality hit her. She was going to have to be a part-time student. No four-year degree for her. She was going to have to keep working at The Challenger, and juggle day classes with night work.

If only she could find a way to get one of those grants.

TWELVE

S herry pulled into the church parking lot and stopped the minivan in a spot by the front door.

"Okay all of you—out!"

Her voice was cheerful but firm. Five hours of raucous grade-schoolers was about all she could take. The science museum was kid-friendly, but still...thank goodness the parents took turns on field trip duty.

The chattering kids—all but Brandon and Genna—wrenched open the mini-van doors, and scattered to the cars and vans dotting the parking lot. Several parents that Sherry didn't recognize were standing or sitting on the church steps.

One woman glanced toward Sherry's minivan, did a slow double take, and headed her direction.

Sherry rolled down her window, shivering a bit as the December air crept into the toasty vehicle.

The woman had an incredulous smile on her face. "Sherry—Sherry Rice?"

"I'm sorry, do I—"

"I'm Jo Markowitz, Sherry! From Harvard?"

"Jo!" Sherry jumped out of the minivan and hugged her old college friend. "I haven't seen you in—gosh—eight, nine years?"

"Not since homecoming that first year out."

"Right, right! What're you doing here?"

Jo glanced at the church building behind her, a tinge of disbelief in her voice. "I could ask you the same thing."

Sherry gave a small laugh. "Yeah, I bet you could."

Jo watched a Volvo station wagon pull into the parking lot. A red-haired boy sat in the rear fold-down seat, his hair poking out at wild angles.

"Well, that's my son. Hopefully he didn't electrocute himself at SciTrek."

"Um..." Sherry smiled. "I did see him try that electrostatic demonstration one too many times."

"Well, that accounts for the hair. Plus, he's a boy."

The Volvo doors swung open and the kids bounded out. The redhead caught sight of Jo's waving arm and ran up to her, nearly knocking her over with an enthusiastic hug. He immediately started chattering about all they had seen and done during the day, until Jo gave him a good-natured "noogie," pressing his face into her side to silence him. He howled and batted at her hands.

She released him and pointed toward Sherry. "Blake, this is Sherry Rice, one of my old friends from college. Can you say hi?"

He looked down at his toes, suddenly shy. "Hi."

"Hi, Blake. I have a son about your age. His name is Brandon."

The little face lit up. "I know Brandon! He's on my basketball team. But...his last name is Turner."

"That's my Brandon. My married name is Turner. You know, Brandon's in the van...why don't you say hi?"

Jo gave her a direct look. "We have a lot to catch up on."

"Yes, we do."

"Listen, what're you doing now? Could you take the time for coffee?"

Sherry hesitated, covering her indecision by looking at her watch.

When Sherry nodded, Jo pointed down Tenth Street. "You know that coffee shop in the bookstore? The kids could amuse themselves in the children's section while we talk. I've got a commitment in a few hours, but until then..."

Sherry shivered again. "That sounds great."

Ten minutes later, the kids were happily exploring the latest electronic wizardry in the children's section, clearly visible from the coffee shop, with firm instructions not to venture into the rest of the bookstore. Sherry found an empty corner with two plush chairs and sipped her hot tea, watching Jo fix her cream-and-sugar at a nearby countertop.

"There we are." Jo settled into a cushiony chair with a contented sigh. "I love this coffee."

Sherry barely nodded. The silence lengthened as they sipped their drinks.

"So Blake is in the Trinity Chapel School with Brandon? First grade?"

"Yes."

"Are you married? Have other kids?"

"Yep, I'm Jo Woodward now. My husband's name is Vance. We met right after college, at our church in New York City, while I was in nursing school. He's a great guy, I'd love for you to meet him."

"That would be nice, sometime. So no other kids."

"Nope, just Blake. But he's a handful!" Jo leaned forward, perched on the edge of her seat, her eyes gleaming. "Sherry...I know I haven't seen you in years, so forgive me if I just cut through the polite chitchat and ask you a question. Have you come back to the Lord?"

As Sherry nodded, Jo's eyes filled with tears. She reached out and gave Sherry a fierce hug, whispering "Praise God!" over and over again. Sherry returned the embrace, and tears filled her own eyes. It had been so long…

Jo released her and gripped one of Sherry's hands. "You don't know how long I've prayed—" She broke off, her eyes watering again. "I can't believe it. It's so awesome of God to let me find this out. I've lost touch with your old roommate—does she know?"

Sherry laughed. "Are you kidding? Claire was the first person I called."

"I'll bet! So—what happened?"

"Well, you know what happened at school…and everything." Sherry looked down, and she could feel her face turning red. "When you and the others came to Jesus, I turned further away. I know it makes no sense, but I was so furious and confused, I felt like I had to go against the pack and run as far from God as I could. Claire and I didn't room together after that first year, and I pretty much spent the rest of college partying and living it up, and…well…you know all about the rest of that."

"I remember. We were all praying for you, you know."

"Yeah." Sherry gave a short laugh. "Claire told me that several times, and I just yelled that I didn't want any part of her or her God, and to stop praying for me. I'm so glad you all didn't stop."

"Me, too." Jo gave an incredulous shake of her head. "God is so good."

"So…after all that other stuff that happened, when I graduated I decided to pull it together a bit and move back down here."

"You're from Atlanta? I didn't know that."

"Well, not from Atlanta but from Georgia. My folks live a few hours away. But I really didn't want to stay there; no good job prospects. And since Atlanta was the best market, I jumped right in, found a great job in marketing and lived the life of a swinging single woman."

"Oh."

"Yeah." Sherry sighed. "'Oh' is right. And what was supposed to be so fun just didn't appeal to me anymore. It was like I was going through the motions. I started to get so lonely, I even began to return Claire's e-mails. I found myself just wishing God would either kill me or prove to me that He was real."

"But hadn't you made a commitment to Christ when you were a teenager?"

"I thought I had, but I went through such a long rebellion it was hard for me to believe any of it anymore. None of my so-called friends or boyfriends bought it, and the only ones I knew who did, were people from college like Claire and you…and Doug."

"Ah, now we're getting to the good part! You're married to Doug Turner!"

"Yes, I am."

"Well, don't torture me…how on earth did *that* happen?"

"Well, I have to tell you how I came to the Lord first. Believe it or not, I finally lost it one night in front of the stupid television. There was a cheesy show by a local pastor, talking about how no matter what we had done, God would forgive us and take us in. He told the story of the prodigal son, and about the transforming power of the father's nonjudgmental love. I called Claire, sobbing that I wanted to be transformed, that I didn't want to live this empty, shallow life anymore. She prayed with me on the phone."

"Oh," Jo held her hand to her heart, "that must've just made her so—"

"She was sobbing, too. I know it sounds stupid, but I was almost as joyful for her as I was for me. I know how much she prayed for me, all those years. The next day, she called me back and told me that I had to get plugged in to a good church, and to Christian friends. So this time, I really did it. I broke off my relationships with the men that I was seeing—"

"Men? Plural?"

Sherry looked sideways. "Does that really surprise you?"

"Uh…no…not really. Sorry."

"So anyway, I broke off those relationships, and really pulled back from the other friends. I was pretty lonely for a few months, but I knew if I went back to that crowd, I didn't have the resolve to stay the course. I had no idea how to find a good church, so I called a Christian man that Claire said was also working in Atlanta— our old college buddy, Doug Turner."

"Oh, *now* we're getting to it."

"So he suggested that I go to his church with him on Sunday."

"Let me guess—Trinity Chapel?"

"Trinity Chapel. I get plugged in, start growing in my faith, and then I notice that Doug starts looking at me across the sanctuary on Sunday mornings."

"And the rest is history. What an amazing story." Suddenly, Jo started and swiveled in her seat. "Oh my gosh, I completely forgot about the kids!"

"They're fine. See?" Sherry pointed to where the two boys and Genna were squabbling over a book set. "I've been keeping an eye on them. So what about you? I didn't know you were even in Atlanta. You don't go to our church…do you?"

"No, we don't, although we love the church's school for Blake. We go to Good Shepherd Church."

"Just a couple miles away."

"That's the one."

"I've always wondered why some folks who have their kids in our school don't go to our church."

Jo swirled the coffee in her cup and studied it closely. "Well...we found a church that fits us better."

"What do you mean, fits you better?"

"We wanted a church that focused on service. There's so much need in Atlanta, and it just breaks my heart. The people at Good Shepherd are really loving, and pretty much everyone is involved in the ministry somehow. Our family volunteers downtown a lot. It's good for Blake, too."

"Yeah," Sherry pursed her lips. "Trinity Chapel does some of that, but I don't think it's a huge priority."

"That's sort of what we felt, too. And Trinity just— Well, never mind."

"No, what were you going to say?"

Jo looked up. "Let me ask you first: What do you like most about your church?"

"Well...it's been my first real church, where I've learned about my faith. It's a strong, biblical church."

"That's great, obviously. Anything else?"

"The kids like the children's program, and the pastor is really nice."

"You've made a lot of friends there?"

"Not as much as I'd like. That really would be nice, especially once Genna's fully in school and I've got more time on my hands. But...well...it's just hard to really connect with people." Sherry gave a self-conscious shrug. "And there aren't a whole lot of folks who would understand my past."

"What does your past have to do with anything?"

Sherry looked up, surprised. "You've seen our church. It's full of these perfect, happy people who grew up in Christian homes and have walked with the Lord for years. It's nice to be in that environment—it keeps me on the straight and narrow—but they'd never understand."

"But everyone's made mistakes. We're—"

"Not these folks. I mean, yes, we're all human, but I'm telling you, these are good Christian people and they'd be shocked."

"Well, okay, maybe...but you think they wouldn't accept you?"

"I know they wouldn't."

Jo shook her head. "It's funny you say that. When we moved here, we visited your church two or three times because we really liked the pastor. But we just never connected with anyone at Trinity. It was like everyone was good-looking and well-dressed and had on their 'happy faces,' but it just seemed a little…shallow. Sorry if that offends you."

"Is your church any different? About being surfacey, I mean?"

"Well, last week this guy came forward afterward and cried all over the altar, asking for prayer for his addiction to drugs and illicit sex. And there were quite a few people praying for him. There's a reason they named our church Good Shepherd, after all."

"Wow. That would never happen at Trinity. It's too pristine for that."

"And that doesn't seem strange to you?"

"No—it would seem strange to see anything else. I'm telling you, the people at Trinity just don't have those problems." Even as she said the words, her brain was turning to the drunk that had stumbled into the food pantry. *Maybe that's because we don't let them in the door…*

She frowned to herself, feeling her defenses rising. "Surely, there are things you would change about Good Shepherd, too, right?"

"Oh, of course." Jo waved a hand. "Sometimes, I think we get so wrapped up in trying to change the world that we don't worry about changing hearts. I mean, I know how important it is for people to accept Jesus as Savior and Lord, but I'm not sure everyone in the church does."

"But, see! That's the whole *point* behind a church. What's the good of having a loving church if it's not preaching the gospel and getting people saved?"

Jo didn't respond for a second. When she did speak, she looked at Sherry directly, her voice tight.

"I could ask a reverse question—what's the point of having a Bible-teaching church if all the saved people just stay in their holy huddle and don't follow Jesus' command to get out in the darkness and love 'the least of these' in His name? The book of James wonders whether such people are even Christians at all."

"Well, at least we're preaching the Word."

"Well, at least we're living it out."

The two women stared at each other, tense. Then suddenly, their lips twitched and they started laughing.

"What an argument!" Jo said. "I'm sure Jesus is rolling his eyes right now. I'm sorry. I just get a bee in my bonnet about the whole social justice thing, and sometimes I don't know when to stop."

Sherry shook her head. "No, you make some great points. I think we *should* be concentrating more on caring for the 'widows and orphans.'" She chuckled. "I've got it—let's solve this problem in one fell swoop by giving all the standoffish Christians a glimpse of earthly life without money and giving all the loving pew-sitters a glimpse of eternal life without Jesus!"

She looked beyond the coffee shop railing to check on the kids, and gave a start. "Where'd they go?"

"What do you mean?" Jo's eyes widened and she jumped to her feet. "I'm sure they're here somewhere."

The two women hurried back to the children's section. No Brandon, Blake, or Genna. No kids at all, in fact.

"Where'd they all go?" Jo was looking around, her voice tight. "There were ten kids in here just a few—"

Giggles sounded from the other side of the bookstore, back toward the coffee shop. They wove their way among ranks of bookshelves and arrived at a sunken reading area. The floor was littered with children. A puppeteer was reading a book and acting out the story with a series of hand puppets.

Brandon, Blake, and Genna were seated near the back. A teenage girl was sitting beside them, her eyes watchful.

Sherry turned to see a well-dressed woman come around the corner at brisk speed, followed closely by the store's manager. She stopped abruptly when she saw Sherry.

"Oh, *there* you are."

"Hi, Melanie." Sherry turned to Jo, who had gone to hug her son. "Jo, I'd like you to meet Melanie, from my church." She looked back toward the manager. "What's going on?"

Melanie shook Jo's outstretched hand, then pressed her hand to her chest. "Well, dear, your kids were unsupervised, so of course I called the manager."

"These your kids?" the manager asked.

Sherry and Jo nodded.

"Please don't leave them alone in the store again."

Jo put her hands on her hips. "We didn't. We were just a few feet away, in your coffee shop."

"Still, I'd urge you to use greater caution next time. These days, vigilance is always warranted." He turned to Melanie. "Has the situation been resolved to your satisfaction, ma'am?"

"Yes, sir. Thank you for your kind help."

Sherry tried to contain her annoyance as the manager disappeared around the corner. "You reported us to the manager?"

"Well, dear, I recognized sweet little Brandon and Genna, and didn't see you anywhere. So when all the other kids trooped over to the puppet show, I had my daughter bring them over here to keep an eye on them."

"But we gave them strict instructions to stay in the children's section, where we could see them," Jo said.

Melanie looked over the top of her small glasses. "Well, sorry, dear, but I didn't know you were there."

"Well, thank you so much for looking after our children," Jo said. "We really appreciate it."

Melanie inclined her head. "Perhaps next time you can bring your coffee over to the children's section."

"Perhaps we'll just do that."

Once Melanie and her daughter were out of sight, Jo let out an explosive exclamation under her breath.

"Sorry about that," Sherry said.

"No problem. Oy. How do you *stand* that?"

Sherry drove back home, her windshield wipers working overtime against the sudden winter rain. Somewhere in her purse, she could hear her cell phone ringing. She jerked to a stop at a light and fished it out.

"Hello?"

"Hi, sweetheart."

"Doug!" Sherry smiled as she pulled away from the light. "I miss you. Are you okay? I missed your call earlier. We had the field trip."

"Yes, I'm fine. I miss you, too." Doug's voice sounded hushed. "I'm in the middle of meetings, but we just took a short break. I thought I'd try to get you since by the time we're done tonight it'll be too late to call."

"I'm so glad you did. Are your meetings going okay?"

"They're fine. Some challenges, as usual."

"Is Jordan pushing you too hard? Don't let him push you around."

"It's fine, Sherry. You have to stop worrying about that. I won't let him push me around."

"Okay. Sorry."

"Well, I just thought I'd touch base—"

"You're not going to believe who I just ran into!"

No response. She could hear him talking quietly to someone. After a second, he came back on. "Sorry about that. The meeting's reconvening. What was that you said?"

"I said you're not going to believe who I just ran into today."

"Who was that?"

"Jo Markowitz, from school."

"No kidding? That's amazing. I can't wait to hear about it."

"But not right now, right?"

"Sorry, honey."

"That's okay. Have a good rest of your meeting."

Doug tossed his car keys on the nightstand, loosened his tie, and sat on the bed. He reached to pick up the phone. Room service wasn't his favorite option, but he just didn't have the energy to go to a restaurant.

He puttered around the room, changed into sweats, and spent a few minutes organizing various documents from the day's meetings. The food arrived with unusual speed, and he sat on the bed, watching the news and trying not to cram every bite into his mouth at the same time.

When he was done, he pushed the room service tray aside, collapsed back into the pillows and picked up the remote control.

The screen came alive with the opening credits of another first-run movie. As he watched, half-seeing, his mind did a guilty gallop around the steamy scenes from the previous night's film. Several images of that actress had stayed with him all day, despite his halfhearted attempts to push them away.

Discordant music interrupted his thoughts, and he watched the screen more closely. This was a recent horror movie. He made a face. No thanks. He should just call the front desk and ask them to turn the pay-TV system off.

I wonder if...

No.

Just check...what's the harm?

No. Pick up the phone and tell the front desk to turn it off.

I wonder if...

He pressed a movie station button once, then twice, then three times. At the fourth click he stopped.

The flickering images pulled at something deep within him. He knew he should change the channel, but the screen filled his tired senses, his burdened mind. He laid the remote beside him on the bed, and lay down his resolve.

THIRTEEN

Doug awoke in the hotel room, feeling dirty. Shame washed over him as his mind leapt to the images of the last night. It wasn't fair to Sherry. He loved her. *He loved her.*

He went to take a shower, his steps leaden. As he passed the silent television, he tried to push back the alluring images in his brain. All the way through his shower, all the way through breakfast. Again and again, the struggle. Over his cereal, he read the paper without really seeing the words.

He retreated to his room, the television looming large near the bed.

Turn it on.

The remote control was right there on the tousled bedsheets. Right there. Doug swayed from the effort to avoid picking it up. And his meeting wasn't for two hours.

God, help me.

He forced himself to walk to the closet, to dress in his business clothes, to pick up his laptop briefcase and walk out the door. He closed it behind him, feeling a flood of relief.

And the pictures came again. He whimpered slightly and half-ran down the corridor, heading for his car. But where could he go to escape the parade? It went with him.

Other memories accompanied him out to the car, and out on to the highway. He was thirteen years old, playing backyard ball with his buddies. A wild pitch landed in the neighbor's garbage can. When he ran to retrieve the ball, a familiar logo peeped out from behind an empty pizza box.

That night, he offered—much to his mom's surprise—to take out the trash. On the way back, he stashed the ragged men's magazine under his shirt. He knew he shouldn't, knew God didn't want him to, but *he* wanted to. Up in his room, he studied the images, his young eyes wide, a primeval urge pulling at him. That was his first time. And if he closed his eyes, he could still see Miss September.

Miss September had been a problem his whole life.

Doug pulled off the highway at the appropriate exit and coasted into the parking lot of a popular coffee shop. He still had ninety minutes to kill before his meeting.

He settled into one of the comfortable couches with a tall latte, then pulled out his cell phone, anxious to hear his wife's voice.

Doug furrowed his forehead when he heard the familiar sounds of his home voice mail.

"Sherry, it's me. I miss you so much. I've got over an hour before my next meeting, so if you get this message by noon your time, please call. I can't wait to talk to you. I love you."

He read another paper, then, on a whim, redialed his home.

Sherry picked up on the fourth ring, sounding agitated.

"Hello?" A wailing noise filled the background. "Hello?"

"Hi...sweetheart?"

"Oh, Doug, I—Genna, you stop that now. I told you to *stop that.*" Doug could hear a smacking noise and then more wailing.

Sherry came back on the line. "It's been a rough morning."

"Sounds like it. What's going on?"

"Genna wasn't feeling well so I kept her home from preschool, but she's disobeying me at every turn. I've already had to spank her once."

"I'm so sorry. I wish I was there to help."

"I wish you were too. Bad timing for her to get all headstrong—no! She just dumped her juice on the floor."

"On *purpose?*"

"It's like she's two years old again. Hey, Genna—Genna, go to time-out. Now." Sherry sighed, and Doug could hear her mopping up the spill.

"Let me talk to her."

"I don't know if it'll help. She—"

"Just let me try."

Sherry handed the phone to their daughter, and Doug tried to sound as solemn as he could, when all he really wanted to do was give her a huge hug.

"Genna, this is Daddy."

A small, angry voice. "Where are you?"

"I'm in California, sweetheart. You have to be good for Mommy, okay?"

"No, Daddy, no!" He heard the phone clattering to the floor, and his four-year-old daughter throwing a two-year-old temper tantrum.

What on earth?

Sherry retrieved the phone. "She ran upstairs. I better go."

"What's wrong with her?"

"She's mad at you."

"What?"

Sherry heaved a sigh. "She's just really realized that you won't be there on Saturday for the play, and she started trying to rip the wings off her costume."

Doug couldn't speak for a minute. He felt like he'd been punched in the heart. "I've never seen her like this."

Another sigh. "She's been like this a lot lately."

"I haven't seen that."

"Well…you haven't really been around much."

I'm just a worthless idiot. I can't even do right by my own family.

Doug started to open his mouth when he heard Sherry trying to talk to their daughter. She came back on the line.

"I've got to go, honey. Lisa called a few minutes ago about our year-end tax stuff, and when she heard all the commotion she suggested I come over. Maybe that'll take Genna's mind off the whole thing."

"Is there anything I can do?"

"I wish there was."

Doug closed his eyes. "I'm sorry. I'm sorry."

"Yeah. Me, too. I've got to go."

The phone went dead. Doug stared at it for a long time, his mind dull.

Sherry grabbed Genna's arm in one hand and knocked on her friend's garage door with the other. It opened slightly, and she stuck her head into the kitchen. A teapot was whistling on the stove, and two mugs stood ready on the counter.

"Hellooo? Lisa?"

A distant voice sounded around a corner. "Come on in! I'll be right there."

Sherry turned to her daughter, who was hopping up and down with anticipation. "Okay, you can go. But *be careful.* And if I see you doing tricks I'm going to come out there, and you'll have to sit quietly while I talk with Mrs. Elliott. Understand?"

Genna nodded, trying to pull her coat sleeve free, her eyes focusing on something out the window.

Sherry crouched down and looked into her daughter's eyes. "Understand?"

"Yes, Mommy."

"Okay." Sherry released her arm and gave her daughter a pat on the behind. "Go have fun. Maybe you'll get some of this crabbiness out of you."

Her daughter raced around the corner of the garage, to the enticing pleasures of their neighbor's backyard.

"Hey, come on in." Lisa was standing in the doorway, twisting her hair into a clip.

Sherry stepped over the threshold and gave her friend a hug. "You're a lifesaver."

"You sounded like you *really* needed a break. And since a morning of tax returns has made me want to jump off a cliff, I figured tea with a friend was a much better idea."

Sherry gave a genuine laugh for the first time that morning, starting to relax. "Where's Genna?"

Sherry pointed out the kitchen window. "On your trampoline."

Lisa handed her a mug of tea, and the two women sank into the comfortable chairs surrounding the kitchen table.

"So." Lisa looked into her eyes. "Tell me."

"Oh, I don't even know what to tell."

Sherry took a sip of her tea, wondering how much she should say. Lisa just waited patiently.

"Well, like I said, Doug left Monday on this business trip. He's got meetings all week, including one on Saturday for brunch. So by the time he gets back he'll miss the kids' Christmas play. We thought Genna understood, but I think it just sunk in today and...well, she's just missing her daddy. She's had a rough few hours."

"Bless your heart." Lisa's Southern twang was gentle as she looked at her friend. "And how are *you?*"

"Well...you want to know the truth? It's getting hard. I don't know how you and Eric do it, with all his traveling. Ever since Doug started flying around so much this summer, I feel like we never connect any more. How *do* you do it?"

"It's a little easier for me, since all the kids are a bit older and in school until three or four o'clock. I can occupy my mind with work or whatever, but it's never *easy.* You just miss your man."

"What if...what if you're worried he's not missing you?"

Lisa sat quiet for a second, then looked up, her eyes concerned. "What would make you think that?"

"I don't know." Sherry got misty-eyed. "It's just that every conversation seems to end up in an argument these days." She told Lisa a little bit about the last few conversations with Doug, and then hesitated. She saw Lisa at church every Sunday. How much could she really say?

The kitchen was quiet for a minute, the teapot simmering on the stove.

Lisa finally stirred in her chair, her face thoughtful. "How are you and God doing?"

"How are—" Sherry sat back, startled. "I don't know what you mean."

"Well, truthfully…it just sounds like you're lonely and stressed. God longs to fill those voids, if you'll let Him. But sometimes when we most need His presence, we drift away."

"Look, you know a little about my story, right? You're probably the only one at Trinity who does. I spent a lot of years not just drifting but *running* away. So I know what you mean. But I pray—" she looked up at Lisa, her eyes concerned—"I never want to fall away again. Never. But I guess it's pretty easy to let things slip."

Lisa set down her mug and leaned forward. "Sherry, can I be honest about something?"

"Uh…sure."

"This might sound trite, but the only way to let things slip is if *you* let it happen. God is the perfect Father, the perfect lover, the perfect friend. Just like your relationship with Doug or any other person, your relationship with God requires tending to. But the difference is that He is always there, always ready, always up for a chat…and even more wonderful, is always longing to spend time with you."

Sherry looked down. "I know that."

"I know you know that. So here comes a challenge for you. Right now, you're sad because you think Doug hasn't been tending to your relationship. Well, maybe there are two sides to the story, but let's just assume for the moment that you're completely accurate. I want you to think about the fact that just like you feel the distance, feel ignored, and are saddened because of what Doug is missing out on— and what *you* are missing out on!—realize that your heavenly Best Friend is saddened by what you're missing out on whenever you don't tend to your relationship with Him."

"But there's no time. With the kids and doing all the work around the house and volunteering at the school, I'm just exhausted all the time." She felt tears near the surface. "I feel like if I add one more thing, I'll just…"

"Look, I really do understand. And God has great grace in our lives, and He knows when you're so tired that you can't see straight. He created us; He understands all that. However, there are ways to solve this problem. And you have some options that others might not, especially since your kids are already in school. Send the kids off to school, or hire a babysitter for Genna if it's not a preschool day, and spend an hour with the Lord each weekday."

"An hour?"

"That's my suggestion."

"I can't imagine what I'd pray about for an hour."

"It might take some getting used to, but I promise you—after a few days your spirit will start to crave your time alone with Him. You'll soak up that prayer time like a dry sponge soaking up water. Although even ten minutes is something, you'll really be amazed what a difference an hour makes."

Her eyes were kind. "And you'll also have more to pour out on others. Because right now," she turned her empty mug upside down, "you're trying to pour out from a dry cup, and it's not working."

Sherry looked into her own nearly empty mug. *I can't imagine trying to pray for an* hour. *I'd be bored out of my mind.*

"And you know, as you pray—for Doug, for your marriage—you'll find that a lot of the issues that are so worrisome to you now, will be worked out."

"You're probably right."

Lisa walked over to the stove and brought back the teapot for a refill. "Look, we aren't miracle workers, but God sure is. As long as both partners in a marriage have a soft heart and a teachable spirit—which both of you have—and are trying as best they can to follow God, I have to think that God will be faithful to solve whatever problem they're praying about."

Lisa returned the teapot to its place, and Sherry watched her daughter happily bouncing on the trampoline. She'd been doing that one thing for well over half an hour, and she didn't look like *she* was getting bored.

"So, where is Doug this week?"

"California."

"That's funny, so is Eric. He's in San Francisco all week for a convention."

"Doug's in Silicon Valley, land of a zillion microchips. Will Eric be back in time to see Rebekah in the church play?"

"He's flying out at three o'clock on Friday. It means he's going to miss the last half-day of the convention and will get in after midnight, but at least he'll be sure to be back. He didn't want to risk flying out Saturday morning and maybe cut it too close if they got delayed or something."

"Understandable these days. I wish Doug could've done that."

"Well, I suppose he would have if that brunch meeting wasn't really important."

"Yeah."

"Listen…are you all in a small group?"

Sherry looked up. "Yes. Well…sort of. We have one that we try to go to when we can, when Doug's in town. Haven't been there much lately. It's on a weeknight, which is tough for the kids."

"You know, we have a home group that meets here on Friday night for that very reason. We'd love you to visit sometime."

Sherry gave a noncommittal smile. "Thanks, that would be nice." She stood up, restless. "I don't want to take too much of your time, Lisa. You were sweet to ask me to come over, and to let my daughter exhaust herself on your trampoline."

"Anytime. It's a standing invitation. You live so close, it seems a shame that we don't get together more often."

Sherry gave her friend a quick hug and hurried into the backyard. She helped her daughter down from the trampoline and headed back toward home, her mind turning over the radical, hour-long-prayer idea.

She ushered Genna into the warmth of their home, then stood for a long time at the kitchen window staring out at trees bare of leaves and flowers without the warmth of spring.

FOURTEEN

S unlight pierced the room through a gap in the thick hotel curtains. As consciousness returned to Doug's sleepy mind, shame rushed in alongside. He groaned and pushed his head into the pillow.

It had him in its grip. Again. He'd been free of it for years, and now the barrier had again been crossed. He sensed a familiar dark chasm pulling him in, years of struggle looming. Why was he trading a few minutes of pleasure for an open door on years of pain?

He grabbed his Bible from his bag and tried to turn his mind to his morning prayer routine. The images intruded even as he tried to pray.

How can I ask God to bless my family, protect my family, when I'm such scum? God, forgive me. Forgive me for...for that sin that I engaged in. Let me be free of this! Don't let this be another two years of struggle.

He showered and changed, going through the motions with no heart. He was such a fool. How could he do this to Sherry? To God? He knew it was harmful, knew he could not control it once he got started, and yet he had again allowed it in. He felt like throwing up.

God, help me!

He forced himself to read his Bible, sitting in an armchair with his back to the television. The pages of the Word of God became blurred with images from the previous night, images that had haunted his dreams.

Doug crumbled into tears.

God, forgive me.

How many times could God forgive before his pleas became hollow, meaningless? Several years ago he had asked, *begged,* for forgiveness every single day before again repeating the cycle every single night. Or every single afternoon.

Sometimes he'd stay clean for a few days at a time, until something triggered the memory of an image on the Internet, and within minutes he'd be on-line, his office door closed, spellbound in front of the computer monitor. He knew how to erase his electronic tracks so the systems administrator would never catch his use. But it wasn't like anyone at the company would care anyway, not like some companies where they'd fire you for a first-time infraction. Jordan himself had shown him some of his favorite sites. And now after two years of freedom, the cycle was starting all over again.

Doug slapped his Bible shut. God would *have* to help him this time, would *have* to. This could not happen again!

He shrugged into his jacket and picked up his laptop briefcase. He had to call Gavin Gilmore and ask some additional questions before the big meeting Friday. In the back of his mind, he wondered which members—or member—of the leadership team Gil would refer him to.

He pushed that thought away, feeling useless and inept. He was too weak for this.

Sherry hugged her kids good-bye, and watched as Brandon and Genna scampered off to play with the friends milling about the courtyard. The morning bell at Trinity Chapel Christian School would ring in just a moment.

She saw the volunteer coordinator approaching with a smile, and wavered for a second.

"So, Sherry," the coordinator pulled up by her side, looking at her clipboard, "what would you think about library duty today?"

"Um…actually, I left you a message yesterday. You must not have gotten it."

"No, I haven't had time to check. What was it?"

"Just that I'm going to need to cut back on my volunteering for a while."

The woman's eyes widened with surprise. "Do you mind my asking why?"

"Well…we just have a lot going on right now. Some…uh…difficult things we're dealing with. I have to readjust my time priorities. I'll still be available to help. Just not as much."

The coordinator looked down at her clipboard. "I'm sorry to hear that. We've relied on you a lot. This will leave a hole."

"I'm sorry. You know I want to help. But it *has* been a volunteer thing; I've never been paid."

"Well, yes, but—"

"Listen, I feel terrible, but I just can't commit to as many hours as before, especially in the morning. In fact, I need to head out right now."

"I guess you need to do what you need to do. Let me know when you want to go on the schedule again."

"Well, I'll be back this afternoon. I can probably fit in an hour or two before Genna is done with preschool."

The woman made a notation on her pad. "See you later, then." She gave a brief smile and turned away.

Sherry drove home and pulled the van into the garage, sitting for a moment as if gathering her courage. Then she ventured upstairs as if it was new territory.

There was a little nook by the window that would do fine. A little corner with an overstuffed chair and reading lamp that were rarely used. The only time she read anymore was in bed, after the kids were asleep, while Doug—propped up on the pillows beside her—perused the latest spreadsheets from work.

She pulled out her Bible, a pen, and a simple journal, and sat in the comfy chair. She looked at the clock, and then bowed her head and spoke aloud, feeling somewhat foolish.

"Lord, for the next week, at least, I promise that I'll spend an hour with You each day. Help me to be faithful. Come visit with me now, and help me learn more of You. Help me to know how to pray for Doug, for our family, for our marriage."

She opened the Bible to the beginning of Acts and began to read. It suddenly felt like coming home.

The conference table was littered with papers, charts and spreadsheets peeking out from under haphazard piles. The other offices were dark, the frenetic activity of the operations floor stilled for the weekend. Inside the small conference room, the few remaining people sipped lukewarm coffee and soda. It was getting late on a Friday night, and no one wanted to let exhaustion influence promises that would get them fired on Monday morning.

The whiteboard at the side of the room bore the scattered marks of multiple scribblings and erasures. Standing beside it, Doug finished his last statement, yawned, and capped his pen with a definitive click.

Gil rose and slapped Doug on the back. "Good man! That eliminates the UNIX cost-sharing problems. I would never have thought of that structure. I see why Jordan calls you a miracle worker. Thanks for all the effort you're putting in on this."

Doug glanced sideways. Jordan didn't look over, but kept pecking at his laptop. Doug cleared his throat.

"I'm just doing my job, Gil. Just remember that there are still a few big hurdles to cross."

"Yes, yes. Of course. Ever the cautious one, eh, Jordan?"

"Um-hm." Jordan nodded, intent on his computer. "I'll be done here in just a second."

"You two are a regular Laurel and Hardy," Gil said. "Well, since we're almost done here, I say we think about getting some dinner."

Doug's tired mind went to his lonely hotel room. And the looming TV. "Good idea. You want to know the truth? I'm tired of room service."

"Anxious to get back to the wife and kids—what, Sunday?"

"Actually, I'm hoping to get home before then if I can reschedule my Saturday meeting." Doug noticed Jordan's sideways look. "My little girl is in the Christmas play at church, and I'd really like to be there."

"Aw, that's sweet." Gil clasped his hands over his full paunch and rocked back and forth on his feet. "That'll be a nice little surprise."

"That's the idea. I don't want to tell them ahead of time, in case I don't make it. But it would be great to surprise them if I can."

Jordan raised his eyebrows, his gaze still on the screen, and made a crude joke about what reward Doug would be expecting from his grateful wife.

Gil slapped Doug on the back again. "Let's think about food, eh? Anyone have a preference?" Gil elbowed Jordan in the side. "I believe I have a hankering for some buffalo wings tonight."

"You *always* have a hankering for buffalo wings, Gil," Jordan said.

One of the other men spoke up, grinning. "Sign me up!"

Gil clapped his hands together, still enjoying his private joke. "You like buffalo wings, Doug?"

Doug cocked an eyebrow. "What am I missing?"

"Trust me. You'll love it."

Following Gil's Suburban through the busy Friday night streets, Doug heard his cell phone ring somewhere down in his bag. He kept one hand on the wheel and fished for the phone with the other.

"Doug Turner."

The caller introduced himself and said, "My secretary said it was urgent—I hope I'm not calling too late."

"No, not at all." Doug sent up a silent, urgent prayer. "Listen, I'm sorry to ask you this so late, but I'm wondering whether you'd be open to rescheduling our brunch meeting tomorrow. Actually, I'm wondering whether it would be possible to do a Monday conference call instead."

He held his breath, waiting through a long pause.

"Anything's possible, I suppose, but it'll be difficult to work through all the details via phone. And of course I did want you to meet my colleagues." Another pause. "I've expended some considerable effort to coordinate this meeting, you know."

"I understand, and I'm sorry to do this at the last minute. A personal matter has come up that makes it important for me to fly back first thing in the morning. But I know you've put a lot into getting the parties together. If you feel it's too late to cancel now, I could of course keep the meeting, but I'd strongly prefer to head back to Atlanta if at all possible."

"It certainly sounds important. I hope it's not a family emergency."

"It's not exactly an emergency, but it's important for me to be there."

He stopped talking, but his caller didn't respond. "I have a little girl who's four years old. She's having a tough time with the fact that I'm going to miss her big performance in a Christmas play on Saturday evening."

"A Christmas play?"

"Yes, a Christmas play. And if I do our meeting and take the three o'clock flight, I won't get home until after eleven at night, given the time difference. I thought she was okay with it, but she's apparently rather distraught. I feel that I owe it to her to be there, if I can."

"Did you not know about the play before you scheduled the meeting?"

"Actually, if you want to know the truth, I plain forgot about it. My wife says she told me what date it was, but I just didn't remember when I was scheduling the meetings out here. I didn't realize the problem until my wife saw my flight itinerary."

He heard chuckling on the other end of the line. "I bet you were in big trouble."

"That's one way of putting it. I told her I really couldn't change the meeting— as you'd already started arranging it—but now after hearing how upset my little girl is, I thought I'd try to surprise them if it's at all possible. I do apologize. You deserved better."

"Well, it'll be a pain in the rear end, I'm not saying it won't, but you go home to your little girl. I'm sure my colleagues won't mind having their Saturday morning back."

In the lonely rental car, a grin lit up Doug's face.

His caller continued before he could respond. "And as long as we can do that conference call by noon on Monday, we should have time to complete the deal by close of business. Even though my colleagues haven't met you, I'll vouch for your word. You've never steered me wrong. Straight as an arrow, I told 'em. Straight as an arrow."

Doug sent up a heartfelt prayer of gratitude. "I'm glad you think so. And thanks so much for understanding."

"Ach." The gruff voice lightened a little. "It's not the end of the world. Maybe I'll do some secret Christmas shopping for my wife and kids while they think I'm at the meeting."

Doug laughed, suddenly feeling light as a feather.

He followed Gil's car around another few sharp turns as he signed off the call, promising to set up the conference call Monday morning, first thing, California time.

Ten minutes later, Doug stepped out of the car in front of a low building with neon lights, a busy front door, and no windows. An aqua sign, "Blue Oasis," rotated slowly above the building.

The other cars pulled up and the drivers climbed out, their faces eager.

He walked over to Gil and Jordan, who had ridden together.

"This wasn't exactly what I had in mind."

"Oh, come on." Jordan waved a hand. "Get some food, have some of Gil's favorite buffalo wings, and kick back for an hour."

The others were waiting with impatience a few feet away, their collars turned up against the chill.

Doug knew he should just beg off, but he really didn't have the energy for another "I-know-I-said-I'd-be-there-but…" conversation. So he wavered. He hadn't been in a strip club in years, not since a similar business trip to Bangkok, when he was right out of business school. Jordan had tried to get him to join the other executives on a few client nights, but he always had a convenient excuse. Now, he not only had no excuse, he wanted to join the gang rather than sit alone in his hotel room, staring at the television and fighting a battle of wills with the remote control. Especially now that he knew he'd be going home to Sherry tomorrow night.

Here, at least, there was a group of people, ready to kick back, relax, and have a good time. They'd be eating and talking of other things, not staring in lonely compulsion at the stage. Not indulging in a solitary, shameful craving. Here, the battle would be out in the open and therefore have less power. Much better.

He nodded his acquiescence and joined the group as they headed for the front door.

FIFTEEN

Loriel came to a stop twenty feet above the teeming airport security gates and scanned the crowd, waiting. His troop crowded into the area, their eyes watchful but not troubled. The Spirit had given them no heightened level of caution tonight, and the usual team was well on duty.

Loriel watched idly as a young woman walked through the scanner directly below him. The intent-eyed, middle-aged woman at the security station scanned the traveler's bag as it passed through, and began to turn to the next one. Within moments, a shining being was at her side, speaking to her.

She paused, and ran the scanner back, staring more closely at the shot of the young woman's bag. Suddenly, she sat up straight and pressed a button beside her console. Two security officials converged on her station, and she pointed at the screen, her voice low.

The officials pulled the traveler aside, did a hand search of her bag, and came up with nothing. Loriel watched the young woman's tension grow as they made a call on their walkie-talkies. Within minutes, another official with a dog appeared. The dog sniffed the bag and began whining, pawing at the underside.

One of the security officers clamped the young woman's arm in a vise grip. "You must have a fair amount in that false underside, young lady. Why don't we just take a walk over to the narcotics squad station and see what's really under all that leaded shielding?" Loriel could hear him chuckle as they took her away.

Loriel felt the Lord's gentle nudge, and rapidly turned his attention back to the thronging lines of people below him. He zeroed in on a middle-aged man who was approaching the frequent-traveler security checkpoint. He was pulling a small rolling bag and looking at his watch, his face bored.

The man presented his driver's license to the official on duty, who greeted him with familiarity. The guard made a joke as he swiped the traveler's credentials through his card-reader. Instantly, a red light came on at the security station, and a low alarm sounded. The man and official both looked up, surprised.

Loriel made a motion with his hand and one of his troop disappeared. A moment later, a very large security officer appeared from around a corner and began questioning the traveler, rather roughly pulling him aside.

The other people in the line looked on, curious, as the officer began demanding to see the traveler's identification, ticket information, and bag. The traveler glanced around, embarrassed, as the officer set the bag on a table and began searching it, pulling out each item one by one and slowly inspecting it.

Loriel watched, amused, as the officer held up a small pink packet. "And just what is this?"

The man stammered. "A gift—That's a gift for my wife. That's her favorite sort of cosmetics—"

"Open the packet, please."

The man complied, sneaking a peak at his watch. He held it up. "See? Just lipstick and stuff—"

The officer held out his hand. "May I see the lipstick, please?"

Bemused, the man handed it over and watched as the officer uncapped the lipstick and took his time manipulating the tube, tugging it this way and that, pressing on the metal seam, and closely inspecting the lipstick balm itself.

"What—"

The large officer spoke without discontinuing his efforts. "You see, sir, we've had warnings of people smuggling illegal substances in fake cosmetic cases." He finally recapped the lipstick and turned back to the packet. He held out his hand. "May I see the eyeliner pencil, please?"

Loriel laughed to himself. His colleague was having a little too much fun at this. Hopefully, the faithful servant below would honor his Lord and keep his temper. He'd understand, in time. Loriel's thoughts ran ahead and he gathered other members of his troop and gave careful instructions, dispersing them to their other assignments. The timing had to be just right. Too much was hanging on it.

Eric Elliott stared at the implacable gate agent and could feel his temper rising. Through the massive window behind her, he could see his plane still sitting there, preparing to depart.

"I'm sorry sir." Her brassy voice carried no twinge of regret. "But that's our policy. If you're not here fifteen minutes before the flight, we reserve the right to—"

"Look, I understand that, okay? You don't have to keep repeating it." Eric's normally calm manner was vanishing as quickly as his prospects of getting home to his family. And all because of some stupid makeup. "But I even called ahead that I was stuck at the security checkpoint, and someone *at this gate* promised they'd hold the seat. I'm a good customer, and—"

"Sir, I don't know who you talked to, but the fact remains that all the seats are—"

"What seems to be the problem here?"

Eric turned as a red-jacketed supervisor walked up to the desk. The agent cleared her throat as the supervisor went behind the desk and began scrutinizing the computer record.

"I was just explaining to Mr. Elliott that it will probably be tomorrow morning before—"

The supervisor held up her hand and spoke directly to Eric. "I apologize for the inconvenience, sir. I do see a note here in the record that you were in the terminal and stuck at the security gate. Per our policy for top customers such as yourself, your seat should have been held. I apologize. However, since your seat was released, and the plane is now completely full, we're going to have to make other arrangements."

The gate agent broke in. "I told Mr. Elliott about the weather front—"

The supervisor gave her a quelling look and continued speaking to Eric. "As you have no doubt heard, all our other flights have been delayed and will probably be cancelled once this front gets here. In all honesty, our first flight out of here in the morning will have a significant delay due to all the backups." She tapped on the computer keys. "I show an 11:30 departure that will get you into Atlanta at 6:30 P.M. I can give you priority seating on that flight."

Eric clenched his fists. *After all I've done!* He caught himself and shook his head. *Well, Lord, it's in Your hands.*

He watched the bank of windows as his intended plane pulled slowly away from the gate. He turned back to the supervisor. The brassy gate agent had somehow disappeared.

"Listen, I'm supposed to see my little girl in a children's Christmas play tomorrow night at my church. It'll break her heart if I'm not there on time. Do you have any other ideas for me?"

"Oh, sir." The supervisor tapped furiously on the keyboard as she spoke. "I want to try to help you, but even if we put you on another airline—which we'd be very willing to do—you'd have the same problem. Hold on...no...the other flights are booked solid, too, and in another twenty minutes or so, nothing's going to be leaving here until midmorning tomorrow."

Eric sighed. "Well, thanks for trying. I appreciate your willingness to help."

"Sir?"

He looked up as she paused, hesitating. "Yes?"

"If you don't mind a personal question...are you a believer?"

Eric gave her a tired smile, noticing for the first time the small gold cross pinned to her lapel. "Yes, I am."

"I thought so. Me, too. I appreciate that you were gracious under pressure, instead of yelling at my gate agent."

"Well…" Eric gave a short laugh. "I still have to work on what was being said in my *head.*"

The supervisor grinned. "I understand. And frankly, you can't always tell believers by how they behave. It's sad, but I've had many a fervent churchgoer get exercised and take it out on me or my staff."

"I'm so sorry. You must have to put up with so much."

"Sometimes. I just smile through gritted teeth and keep repeating Matthew 5:41 to myself over and over."

"And that is…"

"If an unjust person demands that you carry his burden for one mile, carry it for two…if an unjust person demands that you carry his burden for one mile, carry it for two…"

Eric laughed outright. "That's good. I've been in a few business deals where I could've used that Scripture."

As she smiled back, he felt the familiar caution. She was a nice woman; best to be careful. Especially with a sister in Christ.

"Wait!" She slapped her head and swung back to her computer. "What about—?"

He heard the keyboard clicking again. "San Jose! That's it. It's only an hour south, but the topography is completely different and it has very different weather. Yep…sure enough, their flights are going out tonight." She squinted at her watch. "Hmm. By the time we put you on a shuttle bus and get you down there, you're going to miss the regular flights. There's a red-eye to Atlanta at ten o'clock, but it's packed. If you can't get on that flight standby, we'll give you a hotel voucher and book you priority on the first flight out in the morning. Even if there are delays, you should still make it in plenty of time. Will that do?"

"Doris," Eric said, reading her name tag, "you're a miracle worker."

"We both know who the miracle worker is. God willing, we'll get you home to your baby girl in time."

SIXTEEN

The sky was still pitch-black outside as Doug Turner checked his belongings one last time, locked the rental car, and dropped the keys in the return drop box. He stood at the deserted curbside, waiting for the airport shuttle bus. If he stood any chance of going standby on the eight-thirty flight he would need to be the first one on the list.

Lord, please get me home on time!

After a few minutes of waiting, he looked around for a bench and then sat on the curb, pulling his trench coat around him. Too few hours of sleep last night. And not because of a movie, either. He shivered inside his coat and stared out at the darkened streets. Should he tell Sherry he'd gone to the strip club with the guys? It wasn't a huge deal, not a shameful problem like—well, like the other stuff was. He didn't want to hurt her feelings.

He wondered whether he should have gone at all. What kind of a Christian example was that to the others in the group? But it wasn't like he'd witnessed to them or anything. Of course, Jordan knew of his faith and sometimes gave him sideways jabs about being too straight-and-narrow, and why would he want to be a Christian and give up all his fun. It couldn't be *all* bad for Jordan to see that he could loosen up a little and still stay under control. Doug hadn't had any alcohol, and of course hadn't asked any of the girls for a table dance. He'd been thankful that only Gil had asked for a dance, and since the girl had been around the other side of the table, Doug had been able to ignore her. Well, mostly ignore her.

He saw the distinctive silhouette of the airport shuttle and stood up, grateful to have something else to think about.

The ticketing line for Doug's airline was long but moving fast. Through the crowd between him and the ticket counter, he idly watched the ticketing agents go through their routine as each passenger approached. Suddenly, Doug straightened. That woman looked like... He craned his neck, trying to see over the crowd.

At the meeting last night, Jill *had* mentioned a flight today. He hadn't even thought of it until now. But, no—it couldn't be her. And why did he even care?

Annoyed with himself, he continued to peer through the crowd. The woman collected her tickets and departed without looking back. Couldn't have been her.

He tried to stuff back an image of Jill at the whiteboard from their first meeting. It popped back up several times. And then an explicit memory from one of the movies he'd watched intruded as well. He tried to clear his mind, frustrated. He must just be too tired this morning.

He forced himself to think about business, about his family, about how excited everyone was going to be when he walked into the church that night—assuming he made this flight. The ticket agent assured him he'd have a good shot at one of the few standby slots, and sent him on his way, admonishing him to check in with the departure gate regularly.

Please, Lord . . .

Nearly an hour later, after clearing security, he went straight to his gate and conferred with the agent, smiling at the woman and trying to make friends with her. She tapped the keyboard a few times and looked up, her expression apologetic.

"If we can get you on, you're going to have to take a middle seat. Just make sure you're in the gate area twenty minutes before departure, and we'll try our best to get you a seat assignment."

Doug thanked her and started to walk away.

"Doug?"

He turned to see a middle-aged man walking toward him. Doug grinned in surprise.

"Eric!" Doug gave his friend a hearty handshake. "What a surprise! What are you doing here?"

"I'm on the eight-thirty flight to Atlanta."

"No kidding? I'm on standby for the same flight."

"What a coincidence." Eric Elliott cocked his head, smiling slightly. "I was just going into the club here. Why don't you join me?"

Doug followed Eric a few feet down the concourse and through the door of the airline's private club for frequent travelers. The door opened into an elegant marble-floored entryway with a reception desk. Eric showed his club badge to the man behind the desk, gesturing to Doug. "And he's with me."

"Thank you, Mr. . . . Elliott. Go right ahead."

The two men made their way past a counter where three ticket agents were helping short lines of passengers, and into the quiet, stylish seating area. A curved bar graced one wall and the other was floor-to-ceiling glass, overlooking the airfield. Eric set his bag and coat down by a small grouping of plush sofas and gestured toward the bar.

"I'm going to grab some orange juice. Would you like anything?"

"Coffee would be great."

Doug surveyed the club with its many amenities for the busy traveler. He pursed his lips, impressed. Maybe he would get a membership.

Someone walked up by his chair, and he stood to help Eric with the drinks. Instead, he came face to face with Jill, a bag slung over her shoulder, wearing a black turtleneck and blue jeans. He felt his breath catch in his chest.

"Hey, Doug. I thought that was you." She shook his hand, a friendly smile on her face.

"Good morning, Jill. Where are you heading today?"

"Just down to Los Angeles. I go down to see my boyfriend most weekends. They just called my flight."

Doug saw Eric walk up, and he made the introductions. "Jill's company is one of our clients, and she's on the big deal I've been working with this week."

Eric shook her hand. "Nice to meet you, Jill."

"Likewise." She turned back to Doug. "During the meeting yesterday, I didn't get a chance to mention several other synergies in the communications area, but I should run them by you soon."

"Give me a call next week."

"Will do. I know a couple of the other executives were dicey on the numbers, but in my department there are some real financial benefits so I hope the deal works out. Thanks for spending a week on this. I know it's a pain living out of a suitcase, but I think we made some progress."

"I agree. We'll see."

"Well—" she looked at her watch, "see you later. I've got to catch my plane."

"Thanks for stopping by."

She waved good-bye to the two men and headed for the door.

Doug tried not to follow her back view with his eyes. He turned to see Eric also wrench his gaze away. As the two men sank into the small sofas, Eric looked at Doug's face and gave him a rueful smile.

"Whew, brother, I don't envy you."

Doug laughed. "Are you kidding? I thought you were going to say you *did* envy me."

Eric shook his head, chuckling. "No way. I know myself. Working away from home for a week under those circumstances would be a huge exercise in mental self-discipline. My brain gets tired just thinking about it."

Doug nodded, suddenly somber. "That's true. " He sipped his coffee, wondering how much to say. "It hasn't been...an easy week."

The two men sat in silence for a moment. Doug wavered, his pride warring with his conscience. After a bit, Doug stirred and looked up at his friend. "So what brings you to Silicon Valley?"

"Actually, I was in San Francisco for a convention, but missed my flight home." He told Doug about being detained at the security check and about the airport shutting down because of the weather. "Thankfully, God seems to have worked it out. I was really worried about missing Rebekah's play tonight."

"Genna is in the play, too, you know."

"No kidding? I didn't know that. What does she play?"

"She's one of the angels."

"That's sweet. Not exactly theologically correct, but sweet."

"Yeah, the heavenly host that proclaimed Jesus' birth to the shepherds were probably mighty warriors, not cute little cherubs." He grinned. "We looked all over for fifteen-foot-tall four-year-olds, but we couldn't find any."

Eric gave a hearty laugh. "I can't wait. It'll be a fun night."

"What's Rebekah's part?"

"She's Mary."

"How perfect for her."

"Yes, she's a gentle spirit. It's weird, isn't it? She's only twelve, but probably not that much younger than Mary was when Jesus was born. Probably only a few years' difference."

"That's such a strange thought! Such a different time and culture."

"Yes. But think how unfamiliar our society would be to them. They may have started their families early and may not have lived past their forties, but here we have these long lives filled with so much trash and trouble that they couldn't even conceive of."

Doug shook his head slowly. "I wonder if it was easier to deal with the threat of disease and a grueling lifestyle; or today's threats of drugs, immorality, and all these other things in the middle of a comfortable lifestyle."

"It's not even so much a matter of something like drugs, which most people recognize as harmful. Today, we have these subtle attacks that don't even get acknowledged as harmful in our popular culture." Eric slapped his hand against his knee. "I mean, get this! I'm watching television last night, and this commercial comes on for this movie that was just released—I forget its name, but it's the one with that really pretty half-Asian, half-black actress…"

"You mean Hannah Perry?"

"Right, right. So anyway, within seconds into this commercial, there's a shot of Hannah Perry standing in front of a backlit window, undressing down to her lingerie. This image hits me in the face at eight o'clock at night—prime time, family hour! It was there and gone in two seconds—no chance to avoid it, no chance to look away. And now I can't get it out of my head."

"I know what you mean, man."

"And if I as a mature Christian man can't get it out of my head, how on earth is my fourteen-year-old son going to handle that X-rated image? At least years ago, you had the option to avoid pornography. Now it assaults you even when you don't want it. It makes me furious."

"I agree."

Eric was shaking his head. "So anyway, I don't know that there's an easy answer to your original question. Every time has its challenges—we live in a fallen world. But I almost wonder whether it was easier to live with the physical risks that you couldn't do much about—that you might die of a disease or be thrown to the lions or something—than to live with today's emotional and spiritual risks that you feel like you *should* be able to do something about, but can't really avoid."

Doug stretched and stood, coffee cup in hand. "I'm going to get a refill. Can I get you more orange juice?"

Doug saw a flicker of surprise cross Eric's face. He nodded and handed over his juice glass. "That would be great, thanks."

When Doug returned, Eric pulled out his ticket. "So where are you sitting on the plane?"

"I don't have a seat yet—I'm on standby." He told Eric about canceling his big meeting in order to surprise his family at the play. "I'll just be happy to get *on* the plane, even if I have to squish into a middle seat somewhere."

"Listen, let me check with these ticket agents over here and see if they'll allow me to give you one of my upgrades on your standby ticket so we can sit together in first class."

Doug raised an eyebrow. "First class instead of a cramped middle seat by the engine? No argument from me. Are you sure? I don't want to use up one of your upgrades if—"

"Please." Eric waved him off. "I've got zillions. Let me check."

He walked toward the agents, stood in the short line, and a few minutes later was waving Doug over.

"They want to see your driver's license so they can find your record."

Doug handed it across the elegant black desktop. This was *much* nicer than the ticketing throng out at the concourse gates.

The agent looked up and smiled. "They just updated the standby numbers, by the way. You've been confirmed for the flight."

Doug sagged in relief. "Thank God."

"So let me see what we can do with Mr. Elliott's upgrade certificates…" She tapped quickly at the keyboard. "Normally, passengers aren't permitted to transfer their upgrades, but as I told Mr. Elliott…" She peered at the screen then nodded. "Yes. His certificates are transferable. And wonder of wonders, there are two first-class seats together. I'm glad both you men got here early or that would never have happened."

She completed the transaction and handed Doug his boarding card. "Seat 4B. Thanks for flying with us."

As the two men walked away, Doug put on a mock scowl. "So *you* get the window seat, huh? Some friend you are!"

Eric turned toward him in surprise, then broke out laughing.

SEVENTEEN

Doug awoke as a flight attendant reached across him to collect a plate and utensils from Eric. He gave a startled grunt as he realized he'd missed lunch. He cracked an eye open, shielding his face from the sun blasting through the small window. "What time is it?"

"It's eleven-thirty California time, two-thirty Eastern time," Eric said. "You've been out for two and a half hours."

"Well, that's one way to make the trip pass quickly."

Doug sat up straighter and shook his head. His hand brushed his face, and he realized he had creases on his cheek from the patterned leather seat. He rubbed his face, embarrassed. "Some friend I am. You give me an upgrade to first class, and I conk out on you."

"You must've been short on sleep."

"You could say that. I got way too little shut-eye on this trip."

"I hate that. Especially with the time change. Early meetings aren't a big problem since my body clock has me up anyway, but—*whew!*—those late nights. By the time I get through with the dinner meetings, I'm out of it. Stick a fork in me, I'm *done.*"

"Especially when you don't have a choice to avoid the dinner meeting. Everyone else is fine and you're—well, you know." He drew circles in the air by his temple. "The night I arrived, I had a dinner with all the executives from this company that we're negotiating a deal with. They were drinking and having a great time, but I was pretty loopy even without drinking!"

"Is that the company your acquaintance—the woman you just introduced me to—works for?"

"Jill. Yeah."

"So out of curiosity, how'd you handle that? She go to the dinner?"

"Yep."

"How'd you handle that?"

"Honestly?" Doug gave a snort. "I struggled the whole time."

"Man." Eric shook his head, smiling. "You couldn't pay me to put myself in that situation. It's just not worth it. If I found her attractive, I mean. My thought life

119

would be a mess all night—or all *week.*"

The two men sat for a minute, and then Doug spoke up, his voice casual. "I'd be curious to hear how you handle those situations with all the traveling you do. I'm in a male-dominated field, so it's not as much of an issue, but I was in meetings with Jill several times this week, and…well…" He shrugged and looked at his friend. "You know."

The flight attendant approached from the first-class galley. "Mr. Turner, I'm sorry you missed lunch service." She bent down by his chair. "Would you like something to eat?"

"If lunch is still available, I would appreciate that."

"Yes, sir, it is. What would you like to drink?"

"A Coke, please."

She nodded and turned to Eric. "And a refill for you, Mr. Elliott?"

Eric handed over his glass. "Thanks."

Within moments, she was back with a linen-covered tray laden with turkey, fruit, bread, and salad.

Doug bowed his head over his meal, then took a slow bite of the large roll and sighed with appreciation. "I was starving." He glanced over at Eric. "You were about to tell me your thoughts."

"Well, I was just thinking about times I've been in a meeting with a woman I find attractive. It might sound stupid, but I was actually pondering an analogy to your bread, there." Eric gave a self-deprecating chuckle. "Okay, don't laugh, but here goes. You like bread, but you like it even more hot and buttered, right?"

"Sure."

"Well…forgive the crude analogy, but let's just say that guys in general are usually 'hungry,' so to speak. We're visual and tend to have these images in our heads. For whatever reason, God just built us this way, even if we have the best home lives in the world."

"Okay."

"So I'm hungry, and when I see that bread, I'm attracted to it. And if it's 'hot,' I'm even more attracted to it."

Doug laughed. "Okay."

"I can't do too much about either of those two things—I'm a guy, so I'll notice an attractive woman. And if she's got a great body or nice legs or whatever, I'll probably notice that, too. I can't do much about noticing it. But what I *can* do is take control of my reaction to her or—even better—do something that'll remove me from the temptation entirely. If I don't remove myself from the environment, I'm still hungry, and that hot roll is still sitting there, calling my name. It's awfully hard to ignore it. My mind is going to go back to it again and again and again."

Doug smiled ruefully. "That pretty much describes the meetings that Jill was in."

"Right, but sometimes I can't change my environment that much. I've got a business meeting that includes someone like Jill. She's an executive, probably a whiz at what she does, and I can't *not* deal with her just because she happens to be a really attractive woman. I can't just leave the restaurant, so to speak. So that hot roll is still going to be sitting there, calling for my attention.

"But even if I can't remove myself from the situation, I can do something about my reaction to her." Eric picked up Doug's crumpled butter packet. "No matter what, I can avoid 'buttering the roll'—I can avoid doing anything that will make it even more attractive to me. Going that next step or not is up to me. I may not be able to do anything about the fact that this woman is attractive, but I can sure avoid anything that will make her even *more* attractive. If I'm ruthless about not giving those thoughts or images an audience, I've avoided buttering the bread. But if I leave that mental door open even a crack, and allow myself to entertain those images for even a few seconds, now I'm hungry *and* I've just purposely buttered that bread. Now it's my fault that it's more tempting and more difficult to avoid."

"Well, yeah, but it's not like you're going to act on it or anything."

Eric raised his eyebrows. "No, but it doesn't matter if it even gets that far, right? I don't want to commit adultery in my heart."

"Of course. I was just making the point."

"Well, but see, that *is* the point. If I'm tempted—and *let* myself be tempted—I'm desiring someone other than Lisa. You'd be desiring someone other than Sherry. Not only is that a sin against the Lord, it undermines my relationship with the person I love most in this world. I've heard of many men—mature Christian men—who kept buttering the roll more and more and eventually it turned into an affair."

Doug paused, then shook his head. "We would never let that happen."

"You're so sure? What do you think happened to the former pastor and his wife?"

"Of Trinity Chapel? They retired and moved to Florida."

"No. He had an affair with a thirty-year-old parishioner, and when it was found out the church asked him to resign. He and his wife are living in Florida, but separated."

"That's terrible." Doug's head was swimming. "I never heard that."

"You were away getting your MBA, and they kept it as quiet as they could." He grimaced. "As quiet as they could given the church gossips who spread the news faster than an e-mail chain letter."

Doug sat there, trying to pull his fractured thoughts together. Their former pastor had been a tremendous man of God, a good friend of Doug's, one of the main people who helped grow Sherry's relationship with the Lord. He had been a rock for the church, the main reason it had grown from several hundred members to several thousand in just a few years. And because of his humble spirit and gift of evangelism, many of those new members were new believers.

Doug looked up, shaken. "I can't understand what happened."

"What usually happens." Eric sighed. "He looked great on the outside, but inside he must've allowed something that undermined him. You don't just wake up one day and decide to throw away a wonderful thirty-five-year marriage and a devoted church flock. It had to have been something that happened over time. He allowed the door to crack open just a bit…just a few more thoughts…just a few more conversations. He allowed himself to butter that tempting bread. And one day, he just stopped avoiding that temptation. The same exact thing could happen to you, could happen to me, if we don't guard our hearts. I'm as vulnerable as the next guy."

The flight attendant came by to clear away Doug's empty plates, and he reached for a magazine in the seat pocket in front of him. Eric sat back, staring out the window. Doug reread the same page three times before he sighed and closed the magazine. His voice was low.

"So what do you do?"

Eric didn't turn his head. "When?"

"When it's turned into a struggle—more than the norm, I mean."

There was a long pause, and then Eric turned back. "I have to get away from it as soon as I can. Lisa and I have a rule, for cases when I'm really struggling, when I've gone further in my thoughts than I should have."

"Glad to hear it's not just me."

"Good heavens, man, no. Anyway, what was I saying?"

"Your rule."

"Right. Well, I promise Lisa that I'll have no private meetings with the woman who's causing that mental struggle—causing *IT*, so to speak. And no going out to dinner."

Doug looked up, surprised. "With just that woman, you mean?"

"Nope. If *IT* has arisen in my mind during a meeting, I don't even go out with a group. If *IT* is going to dinner, I'm not going."

"But isn't that unfair to her? What if she needs to keep discussing business with you?"

"Then I can discuss it at a scheduled meeting the next day in an office setting."

"But that is condescending to her as a businesswoman." Doug gave an incredulous laugh. "How can you justify treating another executive that way just because she's a woman?"

"It has nothing to do with her personally, you know." Eric was looking at him, curious. "It has everything to do with *IT*—my response to her. This struggle has now arisen, and I'm in danger. I need to get myself out of danger."

"But what about her feelings? It just seems so *rude.*"

"Well, obviously I don't do it in a rude way! There are ways to be fully businesslike, where no one knows I'm trying to avoid her company."

"I'm just surprised that you would risk hurting her feelings just to avoid a few struggles over dinner."

"Well, first of all, of course I don't *want* to hurt her feelings. And as far as I know, I never have!" Eric leaned close and caught Doug's gaze. "But if any woman is going to get her feelings hurt, *it's not going to be my wife.*" He raised one eyebrow slightly, and sat back, shrugging. "That's just the bottom line for me."

Doug's mind drifted to the Silicon Valley meetings with Jill. He gave a mental snort. *Eric is way too paranoid about this. I'm not going to go out and have an affair just because I have a group dinner with a woman I find attractive. I'm happily married. I love Sherry.*

He looked back at the news magazine in his lap, and opened it again, giving it a firm shake. "Well, thanks for sharing your thoughts, Eric."

"Sure thing. You know, we need to do lunch after church with you all. It would be fun to get together when we're both home."

Doug gave him a polite smile. "Any time."

As the "final descent" announcement came over the loudspeaker, Doug took his coat from the overhead bin and stored his bag under the seat. On impulse, he pulled out his wallet and stared at the recent picture he had shown Jill at that first dinner. He loved Sherry so much. He would never do anything to hurt her or their marriage. Sure, he got annoyed with her at times, and things had been a bit tense the last few months, but none of that changed the big picture. She was the best thing that had ever happened to him—other than his salvation, of course—and he was so blessed to have her. And the kids. He tucked the wallet into his coat pocket, a prayer of thankfulness going through his mind. God had been so good to them.

The plane wheels touched down with a squeal, and the aircraft began the long taxi back to the appropriate gate. Doug leaned toward his friend and grinned.

"I can't wait to see the look on Sherry's face."

Eric cocked an eyebrow before comprehension dawned. "Oh, that's right—she thinks you're going to miss the show."

"They all do. I'm trying to figure out how best to surprise them."

"Hmm." Eric's eyes twinkled. "We should coordinate somehow. I'm going straight to the church after I pick up my luggage. Do you need a ride?"

"That would be great. I figure we'll be there about thirty minutes before show time."

The plane pulled up to the gate, and the passengers disembarked. The two men walked together along the crowded concourse, developing their plan as they headed for the underground tram that would take them to the baggage claim.

As they rode the down escalator, Doug's phone rang. He glanced at the readout and made an amused grimace.

"Doh! It's Sherry. I didn't call her today. She's probably furious with me." He grinned as the ringing stopped. "I'm supposed to be on a plane right now, so she probably just wanted to leave a voice mail berating me for not calling her."

Eric looked at him, curious. "Why didn't you?"

"Because I'm not that good an actor. I was in the airport really early today. I thought I might give it away if she asked where I was and I had to lie through my teeth."

"Good point."

Five minutes later, the tram got stuck underground, the automated voice apologizing every minute. "We are experiencing technical difficulties. Please stand by."

By the time they were done "standing by," both men were looking anxiously at their watches. They ran up the escalator and raced to the baggage claim.

EIGHTEEN

Sherry Turner hurried up to the house and rang the bell, admiring the festive holly and ivy that festooned the walkway. The front door opened, and Lisa Elliott gave Rebekah a big hug before shooing her out the door.

Rebekah trotted down the walk toward Sherry's van, clutching a bag filled with her costume and makeup. Lisa gave Sherry a quick hug as well.

"Thanks so much. I'll be along in an hour or so. Would you save a seat for me and Eric?"

Sherry smiled. "Sure thing." Without warning, she was overtaken by a huge yawn.

"Goodness. Are you okay?"

"Sorry." Sherry put her hand over her mouth, trying to stifle another yawn. "Brandon is sick, and he's been up a lot the last few nights. He's staying home with a babysitter." She gave a rueful laugh. "I wish *I* could stay home with a babysitter!"

"You sure you're okay to take the girls to the warm-up? Why don't I—"

"No, no, I'm fine. I'll see you there."

She climbed back in the van and sped off toward the church.

A voice piped up from the backseat. "Thanks for picking me up, Mrs. Turner."

"No problem, Rebekah. I'm glad to do it. Genna had to be there for the warm-up, too, you know."

In the rearview mirror, Sherry saw Genna tug on the older girl's coat sleeve, heard the small voice.

"Are you nervous?"

Rebekah's voice was also quiet. "A little, I guess."

"This is my first ever show."

"Really? It gets easier the more you do it. You'll be great. When I did the show last year, I…"

Sherry listened in amusement, thankful as Rebekah stepped into the "big sister" role.

"Is your daddy going to be there?" Genna asked.

"Yes. He's flying home tonight. He may be a little late, but he'll be there."

There was a long pause, then a quavering whisper. "I want my daddy to be there, too."

Sherry started to respond, but Rebekah leaned over and patted her daughter's arm.

"I'm sorry, Genna. Why don't you tell God how you feel?"

Immediately, the little girl clasped her hands together, fingers tightly intertwined. She scrunched her eyes shut.

"Dear God, this is Genna. I'm sad my daddy is in California. Please bring him home tonight to see my show. Amen."

Sherry grimaced. Rebekah had meant well. But the four-year-old had no concept of how far away California was. She probably thought that her dad could change his mind at the last minute and show up after all, if he really wanted to.

Sherry looked in the rearview mirror and roused a bright smile. "Sweetheart, God hears your prayer. Your daddy will be home tonight, but *after* the show. He'll be there at breakfast in the morning. Okay?"

Genna still had her hands clasped. She looked down at them, then back at Sherry, her eyes wide. "But I prayed, Mommy."

"I know, sweetheart. And God heard you. And He loves you and wants what's best for you. But sometimes He asks us to wait for things we want. Daddy will be home later. He'll be so excited to see you, and you can tell him all about your play and show him the videotape in a few days. How about that?"

Genna settled back in her seat, her hands firmly clasped. "Okay, Mommy. But I'm still going to pray."

Sherry dropped the girls off at the front door and found a parking space. She walked with tired steps up to the church and took a seat, fighting to keep her eyes open in the deserted sanctuary.

She rested her head on the back of the pew in front of her and tried not to cry. She knew Doug cared about his family, but here she was again, lonely, without him. She was tired of feeling like a single parent, up all night with sick kids. And why was she always having to apologize to the kids for their father's absence? And now, her little girl was not only going to be heartbroken, she was going to be confused about prayer, about whether God really heard her cries.

Sherry gave a sad laugh and sat back in her empty pew. She'd wondered the same thing a few times.

She fished her cell phone out of her purse and started to dial Doug's number. She hesitated, clicked the phone shut, then picked it up and dialed again.

"Doug, this is Sherry. I wish you had called me today before you got on your flight. How many times do I have to ask you to keep in touch when you're traveling?" The words gushed out, and somehow she didn't want to stop them. "It makes me wonder whether I really matter to you at all. And just so you'll know before you see your daughter in the morning, Genna prayed that you'd be here tonight for her show. I told her we don't always get what we want, when we want it, which I'm starting to realize myself." She paused, then added, grudgingly, "I love you. I hope you make it in safe tonight."

She clicked the phone shut. Instead of feeling better after unloading her anger, she felt worse.

Great. Now I'm a nagging wife, too. She forced her mind away from that thought. *He deserved it.*

The two men hurried to Eric's car and exited the airport. For the next thirty minutes, Doug could hardly sit still. He watched the clock, anxious at every traffic slowdown, every stoplight.

For the next half hour, Sherry sat in the pew, fighting an internal battle as the church gradually filled up around her. The more she tried to convince herself she'd done the right thing in leaving that message for Doug, the worse she felt. She had to find a way to distract herself.

Several people she knew took a seat right in front of her, chattering about something. She leaned over and tapped their shoulders. "Merry Christmas, you guys."

They turned, surprised. "Oh—Merry Christmas, Sherry." They gave her a quick smile, and then turned back to their conversation.

So much for Christmas cheer. She greeted others as they found their seats, answering the question "Where's Doug?" with a saccharine smile, over and over again.

"He's in California on business. He couldn't get away."

"Oh, what a shame." The inevitable pat on the shoulder. "Well, he can see the video."

Each time, Sherry nodded and murmured her thanks, forcing herself to smile. She looked up in relief when Lisa rushed in.

"Where's Eric?"

"He got hung up at the airport. He'll be here soon." She laid her coat across a long space next to her, by now the only free space on the row. "Apparently he's bringing someone with him. A friend he ran into at the airport or something." She looked over, and her smile faded. "Are you okay?"

"I'm fine."

Lisa was silent for a minute as she set her purse under the bench in front of her. She spoke without looking over.

"Sherry, one of the things that drives me crazy about this church is this surfacey 'everything's fine' thing. I can tell something's wrong. If you want to talk about it, I want to listen."

Sherry sat on her hands and gazed up at the church's graceful ceiling.

Where are You, God?

She looked back at Lisa. "It's nothing earth-shattering. I'm just upset with Doug."

"You feel like he should've been here?"

"I feel like he *could* have been here! It's not like he didn't know about it. He just forgot!"

"But he had his meetings—"

"He scheduled those meetings after I told him about the show date. He could've arranged everything differently from the start, in time to be home—like Eric did— but he just plain forgot. It just wasn't *important* enough to remember. He just didn't care about his own daughter's show!"

She caught a curious glance from the people in front of her and fell silent. Great. Now *her* marriage was fodder for the gossip mill.

Lisa reached over and gave her a hug. She kept her arm around Sherry for a few moments, then gave a gentle squeeze and released her.

"Doug loves you all a lot. Are you sure he truly doesn't care, Sherry?"

Sherry gave an exasperated sigh. "He cares. I know he does. He's pretty upset about missing tonight, too, especially once he heard how upset Genna was. But it doesn't change the fact that it's his fault and he could have been here."

"Yeah, I know. But can I make a suggestion?" At Sherry's nod, she wrinkled her nose a bit. "I don't…I don't think it will help to berate him about it. Husbands walk a fine line all the time, trying to please both work and home, and he's working awfully hard to support your family."

"But home should be his first priority—not his last!"

"I know. I know. Believe me," she gave a short laugh, "I've been there, babe. Eric and I have been around this mountain multiple times over the years. But…well, what I've found is that Eric truly wants to be home with me and the kids, and honestly feels that he tries to be home as much as he can be, given the constraints of his job. The only other solution would be to get a different job. And for the moment, I just couldn't ask that of him—he's so alive with this one, he loves it so much. I want him to love what he does for a living. That is so important to a guy, you know."

"No more so than for a woman." Sherry looked sideways, affronted. "I loved my job, too, and I gave it up in order to be home with the kids for a few years. Why can't he make the same kind of sacrifice?"

"Well, of course he *can,* if that's what you both decide is best for all of you. But it's different with men. Their work is a part of them—a part of their manhood—in a way that's just different from women." Lisa looked sideways, curious. "Surely you know that."

"I don't know that I buy it. Granted, you may be catching me on a bad day, but I don't know why it would be any bigger of a deal for him to make that sacrifice than for me."

The lights dimmed and Lisa leaned over and lowered her voice. "We'll have to talk more about this at some point. I'd like to continue this conversation."

Sherry sat back in her seat, feeling energy ebb away like the fading lights. The screen above the stage came alive with the words of a Christmas carol, and the congregation eagerly rustled to its feet. She forced herself to peel off the pew and stand with the others, trying without much success to enter into the Christmas joy so evident all around her.

> *Hark! The herald angels sing, glory to the newborn King!*
> *Peace on earth and mercy mild, God and sinners reconciled.*
> *Joyful all ye nations rise, join the triumph of the skies!*
> *With th' angelic hosts proclaim, Christ is born in Bethlehem!*
> *Hark! The herald angels sing, glory to the newborn King!*

Genna filed out of the music room with the other kids, costumes rustling, holding Rebekah's hand tightly. They walked quickly down a long hallway toward the lobby and the entrances to the stage and the sanctuary.

Her lower lip quivered as she approached the empty lobby, and she began to sniffle.

Suddenly, their music director was by their side, her music sheets clutched in her hand. "Genna, dear, what's wrong?"

"My daddy's not here! I prayed, and my daddy's not here!"

The woman gave her a soothing pat on the back, her voice comforting. "There, there. I'm sure he's just in the sanctuary with your mommy."

Genna caught Rebekah giving their director a quick shake of her head, and she began to bawl.

"I want my daddy!"

"Oh, sweetheart." The woman picked her up, and Genna wrapped her arms around her, sobbing into her shoulder.

The director quickly put her down again and looked into her eyes. "Genna, I'm sorry your daddy isn't here, but we need you to be an angel tonight, okay? We can't have a sad angel up on stage, can we?"

"No." Genna wiped her nose with her white, filmy sleeve.

The woman winced, then gave her a bright smile and chucked her under the chin. "We're celebrating the birth of baby Jesus tonight, right? That's a happy thing. Baby Jesus!"

Genna sniffled and gave her a small smile. "Baby Jesus."

"That's my girl. So we're going to be joyful tonight, right?"

Genna sniffled again and perked up slightly. "I'm still praying for my daddy to be here, you know."

"You do that, dear." The director patted her on the back again and stood to call the group to attention.

Eric's car pulled up in the crowded church parking lot as the sound of a Christmas carol poured from the windows.

The two men scrambled out and ran up the steps and into the lobby, slowing to catch their breath as they approached the area near the sanctuary.

Joyful all we nations rise, join the triumph of the skies!

Costumed kids milled around the lobby, chattering in nervous tones. Several men from the congregation held elegant banners on long brass poles, depicting nativity scenes and the songs of the heavenly host. Doug craned his neck, his eyes searching the small throng.

A woman's voice was raised slightly above the excited hubbub.

"Okay, kids, listen up!"

"Daddeeeee!"

Genna came hurtling out of the crowd and leaped straight for her father, her face radiant.

Doug caught his daughter, smothering his face in her filmy costume, and knelt on the floor. He held her tight, surprised by his own tears, rocking her back and forth.

"I love you, Genna. I love you, little girl."

He could feel her little fingers clenching and unclenching the coat on his back, hear her smothered voice.

"I prayed, Daddy! I prayed, and you're here! God is *magic*, Daddy!"

Doug laughed through his tears and looked into her shining face. "He *is* magic, sweetheart—He's *miraculous.*" He tried to pull himself together, aware of Eric standing by, grinning from ear to ear, then crushed his daughter in another hug. He lowered his voice. "Oh, God, thank You."

A woman hurried over. "Doug, how thrilling that you're here. I hate to take you away from your daughter, but we've got to get started or we're going to miss our cue." She turned back to the group and raised her voice.

"Okay, everyone. Listen up. As the next song starts, the ushers will go in the front door and carry the banners along the front of the sanctuary, turn and process up the aisle to the back of the church." She turned to the men. "You'll place your poles in their holders, and then you can rejoin your families for the remainder of the show."

She turned to the mass of children. "Where are my angels? Okay, kids, remember, you follow the men in, but instead of following them up the aisle, turn to climb the stairs and go all the way to the top of the stage. Just like we practiced!"

She got a chorus of eager nods, and Doug patted Genna on the bottom, scooting her toward the other kids.

"I'll be out there watching you. I love you!"

Doug looked around for Eric as his daughter scampered toward the other kids. He had slipped over to the director and was talking to her in a low tone, grinning. The woman looked up, raised a mischievous eyebrow, and beckoned Doug over.

O come, all ye faithful, joyful and triumphant,
O come ye, O come ye to Bethlehem.

As the second carol resounded around the sanctuary, Sherry closed her eyes.
Father, forgive my bitter spirit tonight. I'm sorry.

She looked up to see the side doors at the front of the sanctuary open. A procession of majestic banners made their way along the front of the room. With so many people standing, all she could see were the banners as they made the slow turn and began their march up the aisle.

Come and behold him, born the king of angels,
O come let us adore him, O come let us adore him.

Sherry watched as a dozen small children in angel costumes climbed up the steps on the stage, holding their arms in careful ballerina poses. She craned her neck to see Genna find her place and turn toward the audience, a wide grin on her face. She was almost dancing on tiptoe.

O come let us adore him, Christ the Lord!

Sherry lost sight of her daughter as the banners approached, blocking her view. She craned her neck to look around them. A soft murmuring began in the crowd, growing louder as several people turned to watch the procession continue up the aisle, their faces registering surprise. It almost seemed as if they were looking at her—

She heard Lisa's soft gasp, and her friend clutched her arm.

"*Sherry.*"

Sherry turned—and there was Eric, his face alight, carrying a banner at strict attention.

"What…?"

As Eric pulled near their pew, he looked sideways and winked at the two women, then stared straight ahead and solemnly continued up the aisle. Several people standing nearby began grinning and pointing, giving Lisa and Sherry the thumbs-up sign.

Sherry gave them a polite return smile and started to whisper to Lisa, who clutched her sleeve for silence, her eyes dancing, her tone exasperated.

"*Sherry.*"

Doug forced himself to stare straight ahead, his back ramrod straight, looking every inch the regulation banner-carrier as he processed up the aisle.

> *Sing choirs of angels, sing in exaltation*
> *Sing all ye citizens of heaven above!*

He heard the murmurs, saw the pointing fingers, the wide eyes. How many people had Sherry told that he was gone, anyway? No matter. He wasn't much one for scenes, but in about three seconds this would all be worth it.

3…2…1…

His wife's face screwed up in that adorable way she tried to keep from crying, and her hands flew to her mouth. In that instant, she looked like their little daughter, her eyes as wide as saucers.

Doug kept both hands firmly on the banner pole and turned his head as he passed her pew. He mouthed *I love you* as he marched on up the aisle. He could practically hear those around her sighing *awww* on cue.

> *Glory to God, all glory in the highest*
> *O come let us adore him, O come let us adore him,*
> *O come let us adore him! Christ, the Lord!*

Doug joined the other men at the back of the sanctuary and placed his pole into its permanent holder. Then he and Eric slipped down the aisle and joined their wives just as the carol ended.

Sherry grabbed his hand so hard that he gave a gentle wince and loosened her grip. He ran his finger down her cheek, wiping off the wetness. She burrowed her head into his chest, and he wrapped his arms around her and closed his eyes. This was his calling as a husband, a father.

Lord, thank You.

> *Yea, Lord, we greet thee. Born this happy morning.*
> *Jesus to thee be all glory given.*
> *Word of the Father, now in flesh appearing.*
> *O come let us adore him, O come let us adore him*
> *O come let us adore him, Christ the Lord!*

The music died away, and the congregation took their seats. As the lights dimmed to black, one spotlight focused on the side of the stage. A preteen boy in a shepherd's cloak stepped into the light.

"'God sent the angel Gabriel to Nazareth, a town in Galilee, to a virgin pledged to be married to a man named Joseph, a descendant of David.'"

He turned toward the main stage, where the lights rose, revealing Rebekah, in a simple costume. She was sitting on a low stool and sewing. Another tall young man wearing a bright garment and wings stood behind her.

"'The virgin's name was Mary. The angel went to her and said…'"

In the darkness at the back of the sanctuary, Loriel appeared, watching as the children reenacted the eternal story. Dozens of other shining beings also hovered nearby, their faces turned toward the stage, their eyes intent. Loriel felt the touch of the Spirit. He, too, never tired of the recounting.

"'And there were shepherds living out in the fields nearby, keeping watch over their flocks at night. An angel of the Lord appeared to them, and the glory of the Lord shone around them, and they were terrified. But the angel said to them, 'Do not be afraid! I bring you good news of great joy that will be for all the people. Today in the town of David a Savior has been born to you; he is Christ the Lord. This will be a sign to you: You will find a baby wrapped in cloths and lying in a manger.'"

"'Suddenly a great company of the heavenly host appeared with the angel, praising God and saying, 'Glory to God in the highest, and on earth peace to men on whom his favor rests!'"

Loriel heard a soft rustling by his side, and turned to see Caliel watching him in the dim light from the stage, curiosity on his face.

"Were you there?"

"Yes, my friend. I was."

"To have seen the coming of the King! To have proclaimed our Lord made flesh!

We all watched in awe. But to have been there…" His voice died away, his eyes staring into the past.

Loriel put a hand on his shoulder. "Caliel, I was honored to be one of the great host above Bethlehem that night. I was honored to observe the birth of a tiny child." He stopped for a moment, overcome, and his voice came out as a whisper. "But the joy was bittersweet. It was not easy to comprehend that our magnificent King was a tiny babe, helpless before those who would eventually betray Him."

"As much as I would have wanted to be there," Caliel said, "I do not know whether I could have handled such a mission."

"You could have, if our Lord entrusted that task to you. The event was beyond the full comprehension of *any* of us—even Gabriel himself—for we knew there could be only one reason why our King would choose this course—to sacrifice Himself as the spotless lamb. All glory to our God, and peace to men on whom His favor rests!"

He looked over at the young lieutenant. "And that, of course, is why you were called here. My charge during that time was similar to yours at this time—to help prepare hearts to receive and to reflect His love. I went to a stiff-necked people who thought they sought God but whose hearts were ill-prepared to receive Him." He gestured at the intent congregation spread out before him. "You go to a complacent people who think they have God, but whose hearts are ill-prepared to reflect Him— or receive Him in His lost lambs.

"The bride *must* awaken, must reflect the love of her Lord. There is so little time—" Loriel's brows furrowed and he broke off. He was still not released to share the full import of their charge.

Caliel paused in silence for a long moment, staring at the stage before them. He slowly straightened, and gave his commanding officer the traditional salute. "I still do not know why I was chosen for this charge, and I know there is much I do not yet see. But the Lord's ways are good and I am created to serve Him."

Loriel clasped his shoulder again. "You were chosen with a purpose here." He gestured to the many other angels nearby. "Be watchful and stay in close contact until—God willing—we join forces again."

He saluted and was gone.

NINETEEN

Doug stretched and retied his running shoes, then quickly put his gloves back on. How had he let Jordan talk him into this?

"Ready to go?" Jordan and his right-hand man—the company's chief operating officer—bounced up next to him, running in place.

At Doug's nod, the little group set off around the large park. He tried to ignore his freezing nose. He looked over at Jordan. "You're crazy, you know that? One of the coldest days of the year and you still—"

"Hey, we all decided we were going to get in shape, right?"

"Yes, but haven't you ever heard of a gym?"

The COO laughed. "It's good to get some fresh air. We've all been working too hard on this Silicon Valley deal. And we might as well make it a working lunch, eh?"

He laughed at his own joke and Doug rolled his eyes.

"So, Doug…" Jordan was breathing easily, and his voice was casual. "What is it looking like? You've had a few days to look over the numbers."

"I don't know, Jordan. I'm trying everything to make it work."

Jordan ran a few paces without comment, then his voice came out calm and cold. "You know this is one of the biggest market opportunities we've had. Everyone knows that the security industry will be booming for the foreseeable future. And these folks are leaders in that industry, especially when it comes to their hardware. We don't get in on the ground floor and partner with them on their information-processing packages, they'll find someone else who will."

"I understand that, chief, but I'm having a hard time taking such a big loss on a partnership at this stage of our growth."

"You said you'd find some tax loopholes that would—"

"I said I'd *try*. I can't promise anything. If the IRS doesn't go for the structure, there's nothing we can do. And even if they do allow it, it would still create a big hole."

"Not if we can get the right terms from Gil's people, though, right?" the COO said.

"I'll keep working on it."

"Good man." Jordan didn't smile, and the encouraging words suddenly carried a hint of menace. "You just do that."

The three men ran in silence for a few minutes and entered another section of the park. Two women runners approached from the opposite direction. They smiled as they passed, ponytails bobbing. Jordan turned to admire the view and whistled, his countenance back to normal. Then he snapped his fingers.

"I almost forgot. We've got those possible new clients coming in tomorrow. We'll need to get the whole executive team to take them out to dinner. Especially you, Doug, since their CFO will be here."

"Where to, boss?" the COO asked.

"It's been a while since we've been to the Challenger, hasn't it?"

Doug had passed the neon sign for the place every day for several years. The last time he'd been sucked into his sinful black hole, he'd even been in the club two or three times. Well, maybe more than that.

"You know me, Jordan," Doug said. "I'd prefer to just find a good restaurant. Maybe Ray's—"

"C'mon, Doug. You went to the club in Silicon Valley with us, so none of that religious nonsense. It's the perfect place for a good night out. The only executives coming are men. No 'liberated women' to get their delicate sensibilities offended. And I know the principal dealmaker, and I *know* he likes the Challenger. He even mentioned it last time. So that's where we're going. And we need you there. End of discussion."

Doug gritted his teeth. As a younger man, he would have just said no and taken his lumps. But now he had a wife, a nice house, two cars, two kids in private school and fifty thousand dollars left on his student loan bill. He couldn't afford to lose this job. And it wasn't like he'd never been in the club before.

He sent up a silent prayer for protection, and kept running. One thing for sure: he would not tell Sherry.

The Elliotts' den was alive with chatter, the fireplace providing a friendly crackle in the background.

Sherry and Doug had been ushered into the cozy room and introduced to everyone in the home group. Now some people stood by the fireplace, sipping hot chocolate and catching up, while others clustered on the sofas or chairs Lisa and Eric had placed around the room.

Doug already knew one of the men in the group, and they were soon off in a corner, talking technology. Sherry retreated into the kitchen to help Lisa bring out some snacks.

Lisa laughed at the look on her face. "You look a little overwhelmed! What's wrong?"

"Nothing's wrong. It's just that…" Sherry made a face and lowered her voice. "I had no idea how many people I'd never met in our own church! I only recognize one or two of the folks here. And we've all been going to Trinity for years."

"It really is hard to get to know people in a church our size. It's so important to get plugged into a small group—that's where community is built." Lisa handed her a tray laden with savory breads, fruit, and veggies, and pointed toward the den. "Why don't you take this in there and make yourself popular with everyone? We'll start up in just a few minutes."

Ten minutes later, each member of the group took a moment to tell the new couple a little about themselves. Sherry tried to keep all the names straight, but she forgot half of them within seconds of their introduction. There were the young newlyweds, the single mom with three kids, the technology manager Doug had been speaking to, an older husband and wife that had just returned from three years on the mission field, and several other people that lived within a few miles of the Elliotts'.

Finally, Eric turned to Sherry and Doug. "Why don't you tell us a little about yourselves? What you do for a living, where you live, about your family, how you came to know the Lord…all that sort of thing."

Doug glanced at Sherry and took her hand. "Well, I'm Doug Turner, and this is my wife Sherry. I guess I'll start. I'm the CFO of an information and technology services company downtown…"

For the next few minutes, he and Sherry shared some brief details about their lives. They held hands and neither gave any indication of the distance that had grown between them. For tonight, at least, they would act as if everything was normal. And suddenly, Sherry realized, it *felt* normal.

As Eric led the group in a discussion time, Sherry could feel herself relaxing in the warmth and candor of those around her. She actually heard the newlyweds share how tough the last few months had been for their marriage, how many expectations had been shattered, how each had come from broken homes and were terrified of the same thing happening to them.

An older wife leaned over and patted the young woman on the knee, speaking words of encouragement.

Sherry found herself wishing that someone knew her well enough to reach out and comfort her, encourage her, and support her in what she was going through.

What do you think Lisa is there for, silly?

Sherry looked across the room and caught Lisa's eye. Her friend smiled, and

Sherry felt almost as if Lisa could read her mind. She felt her cheeks turning pink, and turned her attention back to the discussion at hand.

Doug held Sherry's hand and listened with veiled interest to the advice the newly-weds received. He could not, of course, let on that he was worried about the tension in his own marriage. But he could listen.

Ten minutes later the topic turned to fathering. Eric asked everyone to describe how their experience with their father had affected their view of God as the ultimate Father. When it was Doug's turn, he could feel Sherry grow still by his side, could feel her support in the way she leaned against him, the way she squeezed his hand.

"Well…" Doug gave a self-conscious laugh and rubbed his hand over his hair. "This is actually a bit hard for me to share, since I don't know you all very well."

"You don't need to share anything you don't want to, Doug," Eric said. "I should've made that clear."

"Well, I'll just say this. As you can probably guess from my reaction, I didn't have a great relationship with my father. He was never abusive or anything like that, he was just distant. He worked all the time, was traveling all the time. And when he did come home, he would be so critical. My grades were never good enough, that kind of thing. I spent all of my childhood trying to please him, hoping that this time he'd give me a hug and say 'well done.'" Doug shrugged, feigning a nonchalance he didn't feel. "But that never happened. I finally just learned to accept it, so it would stop bothering me."

Lisa gave Doug a sad smile. "That must've been so hard. Did that affect your view of God at all? You said you'd been a believer since childhood?"

"I was a believer, but yes, I guess that did affect my view of God. It took years before I could grasp the concept that God loved me whether or not I did things right. I guess you could say I had a real works-oriented view of the Lord. I did good, He loved me; I did something wrong, He didn't."

"I know that happens a lot," Eric said, "but it still hurts to hear it. God is so loving toward us no matter what we do!"

"I know that now." Doug shrugged again. "But it took a long time."

"Well, thanks for being so honest."

Doug could feel embarrassment rising. They probably thought he was a phony.

After a time of group prayer to close out the meeting, people began talking in animated tones, looking in no hurry to leave. It was a Friday night, after all.

One couple with a new baby excused themselves, but the rest continued to chat while Lisa went to make a new round of hot chocolate and decaf coffee. Sherry found herself laughing along with the many stories and jokes. Doug even chipped in a couple of quips about the vagaries of the technology world, drawing chuckles.

A few minutes later, one woman was finishing a story about all the problems they'd found with their new house, once they moved in.

"And the downstairs sink didn't work, the bedroom windows wouldn't open, and all the support beams on the deck were rotten! We were beside ourselves, trying to figure out how to fix everything, until two investigators showed up at our door asking questions about our inspector. It turns out, he was the contractor's brother and both had been under state investigation for a year! Thank goodness, once we knew it was fraud, our home insurance covered all the repairs."

Sherry put a hand to her head. "It's amazing you can laugh about it."

"I can now. You should've seen us a couple of months ago!"

"I know what you mean. Last week our kitchen sink and dishwasher shut down. No water where it was supposed to be, but lots of flooding where it *wasn't* supposed to be. So Doug decides he'll crawl under the sink and try to fix the problem." Sherry laughed. "Now this is the man who doesn't know a screwdriver from a socket wrench, but that doesn't phase him! He wouldn't even look at a book to figure out what to do. He just gets the toolbox—actually he had to borrow our neighbor's—and starts banging away. But Doug was in *way* over his head. His dad can fix anything, but Doug's just the opposite. He's a great businessman, but when it comes to home repairs, he's totally clueless."

She flashed Doug a teasing grin,

"So anyway, he tried his best, but nothing worked. And then he couldn't figure out how to put all the pieces back together! We finally had to call a plumber who charged us this insane amount to fix the original problem, *and* all the things Doug had broken, banging away for three hours."

Doug waited until Sherry finished the story, afraid that she might say something even worse. When she was done, he excused himself to find the bathroom.

His back was ramrod stiff. Fine. That was the last time he tried to figure out a homeowner project, get soaking wet, and make his back ache for three hours to try to get his wife a working sink. They could spend all their money on contractors from then on, for all he cared.

☆ ☆ ☆

Sherry watched as Doug left the room. Couldn't he take a little teasing?

The missionary wife gave Sherry a short smile. "You know, my husband wasn't much good with tools either until a few years ago. But out in the field, we had no other choice. So by trial and error, he learned how to fix all sorts of things—even our car!" She looked around at the group, her voice proud. "He's amazing now. You should see him. He can poke around with his tools and almost always have the car fixed in no time."

There were plenty of pats on the back for her husband, who looked embarrassed.

She glanced again at Sherry, her eyes kind. "I bet Doug would be the same way if he had the chance to make his mistakes. Trial and error is sometimes the best way to learn."

Sherry suddenly felt about two inches tall. Her face flushed again.

"I'm sure you're right. I didn't mean to imply—"

"Dessert everyone!" Lisa walked in with a tray of cookies.

Sherry watched, glum, as Doug returned to the room, but stayed away from her. She rose and edged her way over to him. "I'm sorry. I just realized that I—"

"You made me feel so stupid." Doug had his arms crossed over his chest. He kept his head turned toward the room and away from her. "Great first impression. I can imagine what everyone thinks of me now."

"I'm so sorry, honey. I wasn't thinking."

"You think about everything. All the time!"

"I know." Sherry put a hand on his arm, but he didn't budge. "It was just a joke, though. Just a joke about plumbing. I can't believe it would make *that* much of a difference to anyone."

"Then you're the one that's clueless this time." He stalked off without another word.

Doug went into the kitchen to get a drink. Eric passed him on the way back out to the den. "Hey, Doug, can you go grab another pack of napkins from the pantry?"

"Uh—sure." He found the door to the walk-in pantry, fumbled around for a light, and stood in the small room, staring at the shelves laden with canned goods, drinks, paper products. He could hear two women enter the kitchen and rinse their cups in the sink.

"Wow, it sounds like it didn't go well at all." Doug recognized the voice of the missionary wife.

"No. I really liked him, but if the kids don't, it's sort of a moot point." That was the single mom talking. There was a sad sigh. "I guess I was just trying to make something happen."

"I'm sorry. It must be so hard sometimes."

"All the time. It's especially hard to look around the home group and see so many happy couples—so many wonderful husbands. Why couldn't *my* ex-husband have been like them? I mean, look at Eric. He adores Lisa. And Doug—I've seen him at church with the kids. He's such a wonderful father. And he even tries to help around the house. I mean, Sherry doesn't know what she has! If my ex had ever tried to do anything to make my life easier, I would've just keeled over from shock." There was a long sigh, and the sound of the women moving away. "Why can't I just find someone like Doug or Eric?"

The older woman's reply was lost as their voices faded into the general ruckus in the other room.

Doug emerged from the pantry, napkins in hand and face flushed. He stood a little taller, shaking off his previous anger and melancholy. At least other people appreciated him.

TWENTY

Ronnie Hanover brushed past the last group of customers heading out of the gift shop, their purchases in plain brown bags. The neon stage lights were extinguished and the overhead lights were coming on as the group straggled toward the main door.

Once all the men had left, she slipped into the gift shop to exchange some of her Monopoly-like "club cash" tips for real bills. She waited for her change, glancing around the small room lined with racks of adult videos, magazines, and paraphernalia. She yawned and turned back to the counter. How funny that all that stuff used to shock her.

The gift shop door chimed as Maris headed in on the same errand. They chatted for a moment, then headed for the bar.

Nick saw them coming and pointedly looked at his watch.

Maris clucked her tongue. "Honey, keep your pants on. We're doing the best we can." She counted out her bills and laid the required percentage in front of Nick. Ronnie did the same.

Nick gathered in the money and gestured to a group of staff lounging in the main club area. "The gang is partying at my house tonight. Don't want them to beat me there. Especially since some of them are half-wasted already." He tucked the bills into a money belt. "You two coming?"

Maris shook her head. "I'm asleep on my feet." She gave a jaunty salute as she walked away.

When Ronnie also shook her head, Nick rolled his eyes. "You gotta get out, girl. You work too much." He closed up the bar and walked toward the front door, jangling his car keys.

The sound of laughter caught Ronnie's attention, and she glanced across the darkened room to where Marco was holding his weekly staff meeting with the dancers. Several of the girls were counting out their night's earnings as he talked, separating out the tips for the bouncers and the disk jockey. She noticed that their stacks of money were significantly thicker than the one she had just used to tip Nick. Marco said something amusing, and the group laughed again.

142

Ronnie sat on one of the deserted bar stools, waiting for Tiffany. This not-having-a-car thing was getting old.

Tiffany was kidding around with one of the bouncers, who suddenly picked her up and slung her over his shoulder. Tiffany shrieked, upside down, and pounded his back in mock protest until he set her down.

Ronnie leaned against the bar and set her chin in her hand. The dancers had all the fun *and* made all the money. What was her problem? Why shouldn't she be in the elite group? She was a great dancer. She could probably do the job better than most of them.

By the time the meeting broke up, Ronnie just wanted to go to bed. Tiffany approached but walked straight past her, chattering with another dancer about a party.

Annoyed, Ronnie hopped off her bar stool. "Hey, wait up."

Tiffany turned, surprised. "Oh, hey, Ronnie, I thought you'd left already."

"How could I, silly? You're my ride."

"Oh...yeah." Tiffany glanced at the dancer beside her. "We're heading over to Nick's party. You want to come?"

"No way. I really need to get some sleep."

"Well...can you get another ride back to the apartment? I really want to go to Nick's."

Ronnie sighed. "I think everyone I know well enough to ask for a ride left while I was waiting for you to finish your meeting. Can you drop me off and then go?"

Tiffany hesitated, then looked up. "Look, Ronnie, if I drop you off, it'll be at least forty-five minutes before I get there, and it's late already. Most of the others are already there. I don't want to miss a good party just because you're too uptight to go."

Ronnie pressed her lips together. "Is that the way everyone thinks of me?"

"Well...yeah. I mean—*I* know you're not, but all you ever do is work. You need to come out with us."

"I'm not uptight, Tiffany. I'm tired."

She waited for her friend to speak, but Tiffany just looked at the door.

"I guess I'll just have to get a cab, then."

"That's probably best." There was a long pause, and then Tiffany looked back up at her friend. "I don't want to do that to you, but honestly...I'm getting a little tired of being your limousine."

Ronnie sighed. "I guess I can see that."

"You really need to get a car, girl. You've *got* to have saved up enough in a month for a down payment."

"I guess." *There goes my college deposit.* "It's just that I don't know *anything*—"

"Oh, don't be so hard on yourself!" a boisterous voice broke in.

The bouncer who had thrown Tiffany over his shoulder stopped beside the two girls. He was digging at his teeth with a toothpick and smacking his lips. He grinned sideways at her. "From what I can see, you're not, like, a total idiot. Maybe a half idiot—or a quarter idiot."

Ronnie rolled her eyes and tried unsuccessfully to keep a straight face. "Brian, you jerk, that's not what I was saying. I was trying to say that I don't know anything about cars." She shoved Tiffany sideways, breaking their tension. "And now I have to go out and buy one just because my *friend* here simply refuses to cart me around like royalty wherever my little heart desires."

"Well, I'll help you," Brian said.

"Yeah, right." Ronnie tried to shove him, too. It was like trying to move a wall.

"I'm serious."

"Sure you are." When he didn't respond, she looked up at his face. *"Are* you serious?"

"Sure." Brian tossed the toothpick into a nearby trash can. "I have all morning and afternoon off tomorrow. Why don't we drive around and look for a new vehicle for you. I didn't have anything else planned."

Ronnie took a deep breath. "You know what, Brian? You're really sweet. I think I'll take you up on that."

Tiffany grabbed his arm. "Since you weren't going to the party, would you maybe take Ronnie home?"

"Tiffany! I don't want to inconvenience—"

"Boy, you really are uptight, aren't you?" Brian clapped a hand against Ronnie's back, steering her toward the door. "Just accept the help, for Pete's sake!"

Ronnie allowed herself to be ushered through the front door and toward Brian's Lexus. She saw Tiffany, laughing, wave good-bye as she climbed into her convertible.

Ronnie rode in silence as Brian made one correct turn after another. After a minute, she spoke up, her voice casual. "I guess you know your way to Tiff—uh, Sasha's apartment."

"I helped her move in."

They approached the security gates, and Brian punched in the access code. Ronnie's eyebrows rose, but she kept her mouth shut. When Brian pulled up in front of her darkened building, she gave him an awkward smile.

"Thanks so much."

"No problem. How about I pick you up at ten tomorrow? It's sort of early, but when you're comparison-shopping it's best to get an early start."

"That'd be great." Ronnie climbed out of the car. Before she shut the door, she said, "I—well, I want to thank you for driving me home. But, listen, don't feel like you have to help with the car."

Brian held up a hand and shook his head at her. "You need to stop selling yourself short, Ronnie. You're a nice girl. Let me be a friend, okay?"

Ronnie nodded, warmth rising in her cheeks.

"So, like I was saying, I'll see you here at ten."

Ronnie bounded up the steps to the second-floor apartment. As she entered the cozy space, she realized she was still smiling.

Brian pulled into a parking space in front of the dealership, and Ronnie smiled as several salesmen made quick tracks in their direction. Every dealer that morning had been eager to help the man in the luxury Lexus—only to discover that his female passenger was looking for a cheap preowned vehicle, thank you very much.

Even better, it turned out that Brian was a whiz at cars and could see through a sales smokescreen in a second. Fifteen minutes later, as Brian lifted the hood and examined her latest find, Ronnie thanked her lucky stars that she hadn't had to do this alone.

Brian shook his head at the salesman. "I thought you said this car had never been in an accident."

"That's what we understood from the woman who traded in this vehicle. We can only go on what the original owner has told us."

Brian grunted. "Then you all aren't doing your job."

He gestured Ronnie over and turned his back on the salesman. "See here…and here…classic result of a front-end collision. Probably had to replace the hood and the front bumper, and it might've thrown other things out of whack. Who knows what that might mean for you in a year?"

Brian started a heated discussion with the salesman, and Ronnie moved on down the rows. She'd been excited about finally buying her first car, but all the cars she liked, she couldn't afford. She'd wanted to look at cool SUVs and convertibles like Tiffany's. Within the first ten minutes, she'd downgraded to sensible, five-year-old sedans in unpopular colors. The down payment on some ugly lemon was going to cost her the precious advance she'd saved for tuition. She resented the car already.

She stopped in front of a champagne-colored Civic and shaded her eyes from the sun. She squinted toward the price tag in the front windshield. She looked closer and called Brian over. He took one look and raised his eyebrows at her. The salesman approached, and Brain began the usual discussion while Ronnie circled the car, trying not to appear anxious.

It was beautiful. A four-door sedan, sure, but a nice sporty line and a great color. She peered inside. Simple upholstery, with all the usual amenities. And only twenty-one thousand on the odometer. It *was* higher than her intended price range...but only by a few thousand dollars.

Brian fiddled under the hood and seemed to like what he saw. Ronnie crossed her fingers. After a morning of finding no cars even close to her price range, this little number seemed like a bargain. But why the great deal...what was wrong with it?

The salesman's voice drifted in through the windows. "Former rental cars sell back to us at twenty thousand miles, and since they've been driven harder we lower our price."

Ronnie settled behind the wheel. It fit her perfectly. If Brian said the engine looked okay, she would buy it. It would be more than she wanted to pay—even after she haggled the salesman down—but at least she would enjoy the car she was driving.

Forty minutes later, the salesman and his manager shook hands all around and ushered Ronnie and Brian out of the office.

"Congratulations. We'll fix those few items, and you can pick the car up tomorrow."

Ronnie smiled and thanked them, suppressing the butterflies in her stomach. Had she really just signed a loan agreement for that high of a monthly payment?

She settled into Brian's passenger seat and thanked him quietly. As he pulled out onto the highway, she laid her head back against the soft leather and closed her eyes.

"Hey, Ronnie, don't worry, seriously." Brian sounded like he was grinning. "It's always a little nerve-racking to get your first car, but—"

"It's not the car I'm nervous about—it's the car loan! I've never been on the hook for a monthly payment like that, ever."

"Ahh, don't worry about it. I bet you'll be trading it in for a luxury model in a few months. You'll have no trouble making the payments once you get onstage."

Ronnie's eyes flew open. "What did you just say?"

"I said it would be easy to make the payments once you go onstage. Heck, *you'll* probably earn enough to pay for a full trade-up within a few weeks."

"What makes you think I'm going onstage?"

Brian jerked in surprise. "What—you don't want to?"

"I keep telling everybody—"

"Look, no offense, Ronnie, but it just seems silly, that's all. You're an attractive girl, you've got a great figure, and you'll make a ton of money. No one understands what your problem is. I know you're young, but you're in the real world now and you have bills and obligations. You at least have the ability to make a good wage, unlike some others. Trust me, I've seen girls go through this for several years now, and once you get up there, you'll wonder what the big deal was. Trust me."

Ronnie sat in silence, her monthly expenses parading on the screen of her mind. Even working extra shifts, it was going to be tight. And there was still the advance payment for her tuition. Assuming she even got in.

Ronnie groaned and bent double, her head near her knees, her hair hanging down around her face. "Have you ever felt like you just wanted to crawl into bed, pull the covers over your head, and keep the world at bay for about a week?"

"All the time."

Ronnie felt his hand find her shoulder and give it a gentle rub.

"It'll be okay, Ronnie. Honest."

Brian watched as Ronnie waved good-bye and bounced up the stairs to her apartment. Two hotties in one place. Maybe she'd be even better in bed than Tiffany was. *Sasha,* he reminded himself. And Ronnie would get a stage name, too—soon, if he had anything to do with it. She was so silly to keep protesting such an obvious step.

He turned out of the complex and onto a nearby tree-lined parkway. The subdivisions got bigger and more elegant as he passed, and his gaze lingered on the sweeping, gated communities.

Someday. Someday soon.

He slowed and pulled into a circular entrance with a discreet guardhouse. A uniformed man leaned out the window.

"Yes, sir?"

"I have a meeting with Marco Navarre."

"Just a moment." The guard scanned his computer screen, then peered at the monitor that showed Brian's license plate number. In front of Brian, the tall gate began to open. "Okay, sir. It's your fourth right, up the steep hill and—"

"I know where it is, thanks."

Brian drove along several wide, hilly boulevards, admiring the view. Several new houses had gone up since he'd been here last. Well, *houses* wasn't quite the word for it. By any definition, these were mansions. Not the sprawling manor homes of the "old money" elite in Buckhead, but certainly all the understated elegance of the new money South—entrepreneurs who owned blue-chip businesses, technology companies…and adult-entertainment empires.

He turned into a cul-de-sac. At the far side, a long driveway led upward to a graceful building hidden among massive trees on the side of a hill. Brian drove into one of the many bays under the house and took an elevator to the main level. The elevator opened onto a wide front porch with a dizzying view of the steep hill below. He stayed close to the wall and rang the doorbell.

At the first ring, Marco himself answered the door.

"There you are!" Marco waved him inside and shut the door. "The others will be here soon, but I'm dying to know."

"Everything went fine."

"And she…"

"She bought a nice little Civic—about three thousand dollars higher than her top price range."

"Excellent! Well, sit down, sit down. I'll get you a drink and you can tell me all about it."

Brian ventured into the seating area near a wide sweep of windows. Glass doors led out onto a large deck that seemed designed to induce acrophobia. Brian had been out there only once, and even during Marco's parties, which had a way of dropping one's inhibitions, he had never been out again. Before Proxy came on the scene, stoned loyalists had sometimes been dared into walking the banister, and Brian had no intention of joining that group. One girl—there for the men's amusement during a bachelor party—had fallen and broken her back. They'd given her a generous sum to keep her quiet during two years of rehab.

Proxy had heard about it and supposedly demanded an end to the frat-party shenanigans, but Brian wouldn't chance it. There were far better ways of proving his loyalty.

"So." Marco came around the side of a wide couch, handed him a glass, and took a seat nearby. "How'd you arrange it?"

Brian shrugged. "I made her think that all the cars she could afford were wrecks under the hood. Once we finally saw a nice-looking car close enough to her price range to seem feasible to her, I gave her the green light."

"And that one…?"

"Actually, that one wasn't too bad. No obvious problems." At Marco's grunt, Brian made an apologetic face. "You can't have everything. But it was a rental car so it'll probably require some expensive repairs within six months or so. And if it doesn't, we can always arrange something."

"Excellent. Well done."

"The other thing is—I think she may be easier than we think to get up onstage. I got the impression that her money worries were working overtime way before the financial burden of the car. I don't know what other hooks you're pursuing, but I'd keep 'em active."

"Good." Marco had a pensive look on his face. "With your typical waitress, we could expect her to ask for a stage audition in—what—three and a half months?"

"Three and a half or four."

The doorbell buzzed long and loud, and Marco stood up, looking down at Brian. "We can't wait that long."

Outside Washington, D.C., a satellite engineer received a good-bye kiss and was shooed out the door. He climbed into his new car and gave his girlfriend a little wave before he backed down the driveway.

His heart pounded as he watched her blow him a kiss, saw her eyes darken with a smoky promise for their next encounter. That very evening, if he was successful in his task. Oh, he was a lucky man.

He drove the few miles to his office, his mind turning over the job set before him. He shouldn't do it…but he couldn't help himself. And what harm would it really do, anyway? The lazy financial sharks of the world made hundreds of times what he did for working so hard, day after day, without complaint. Why shouldn't someone settle the score a little, skim off some of their profits? He didn't mind receiving some of the windfall.

Especially—a little shudder passed through him—when it came via her. And she really loved him, too; she had told him so. She couldn't imagine her life without him.

He was proud that he had gotten her out of the club, convinced her to stop stripping. It was worth it, this business proposition, since it helped her, too. And it was so easy for him. She had made it clear how admired his skills were in certain circles.

Even on a weekend, the security checkpoints were busy—no rest for low-paid, overworked government contractors these days—but soon he was in his office, the door closed behind him. His colleagues knew he needed to rework the satellite code again, and would leave him alone with his boring, arduous task.

His breath came faster as the minutes stretched on, his fingers busy on the keyboard. He was skilled at writing programs that took up little space and ran invisibly in the background. He also knew a thing or two about erasing his tracks. There was no way anything but the most direct search would find the changes he had made.

He queued up the program, tested it to ensure it would run properly, and relaxed back in his chair, smiling. Two hundred thousand dollars for creating a simple electronic "back door." One afternoon's work. Not bad.

By the time he left the office that evening, he had already been fantasizing for hours about his planned rendezvous, and was impatient with the usual exit-security procedures.

He waited in a short line, watching the guard scan the woman in front of him. Both faces were serious, intent. What went on in that building was too important to national security to take lightly.

When it was his turn, he submitted to the same process, his conscience prickling. Thank goodness the scan couldn't read his mind. They had assured him—*she* had assured him—that it was purely a moneymaking venture, that they needed access to the communications satellite network for bank wire transfers and the like. It was just by chance that *his* satellites were used for homeland security purposes as well. She had been offended at his "allegations," his nervous questions, and had pulled away.

He never brought them up again.

TWENTY-ONE

T he sun sent long beams through the tall glass walls as Ronnie sank into the bubbling Jacuzzi. Thirty minutes of swimming laps and she was ready for a little pampering.

For once, she was glad for the amenities that upped the rent in Tiffany's complex. A heated indoor pool and Jacuzzi were almost enough to make her forget the craziness of the last few weeks. She had a new car, was working constant double shifts to pay for it, and was almost finished with her GED. And if she didn't hear soon about her early admissions application to Georgia State, she would keel over and die.

Last week, she'd taken a chance and called Mr. Woodward's office. He hadn't been available, but his secretary told her that although they couldn't commit to anything yet, things were "looking positive."

Looking positive? What does that mean? That you can't find any reason to reject me yet?

Under "employment history," Ronnie had not mentioned her current job. She'd listed the pizza place and included a glowing recommendation from her former boss, but nothing from her current one. Maybe they wouldn't notice.

She sank down into the bubbling water, buried up to her nose. Why was she so ashamed of her job? Her coworkers were nice people, and even though Marco was pushy he was a good boss. She didn't know the strippers very well yet, but Tiffany said they were a nice group. They were former schoolteachers, real estate agents, stay-at-home moms, students, high school dropouts…people just like her. The club treated her well, and she made a better wage than she would flipping burgers. So why the hang-up? Did she think she was somehow better than everybody else?

She saw a gleam of blue and red through the wall of glass. She watched as the little truck pulled up at the mail pavilion, and the mailman began slotting his load into the boxes.

Fifteen minutes later, Ronnie pulled on a comfy pair of sweats and headed for her mailbox. She took one look at the large envelope from Georgia State, and breathed out a sigh of relief.

Inside her apartment, she read through the cover letter.

"We are pleased to inform you…"

A month ago, she would have been jumping around the room. But admittance seemed a minor hurdle now. She flipped through the pages, and there it was.

"An advance tuition payment of $750 is due by…"

Ronnie shook her head and shuffled through the papers, looking for a financial aid application. Was there *any* chance that Seth would share the family's lousy financial information so she could get that scholarship? If not, how could she come up with seven hundred and fifty dollars so soon?

It would only take one weekend onstage…

Ronnie started to bat the intruding thought away, and then stilled. She knew she could probably make that much in just a few nights as a stripper. But she had protested the idea so much and so publicly that it had become a point of pride. She couldn't change her mind now; everyone would rag on her for weeks.

Shouldn't your college dream be worth a few weeks of teasing?

For the first time, Ronnie allowed the thought to take shape in her mind. But as soon as she pictured herself onstage in front of her panting, hooting customers, she felt sick to her stomach. And she'd also have to entertain them at their tables, endure their intent eyes searching every inch of…

No way.

The ring of the phone startled her.

"Hello."

"Ronnie! I wasn't sure you'd be around. You've been working so much."

She sat up in surprise. It had been so long since she'd heard her mother's voice. "Yes, I have been."

"Is it going like you'd hoped? I—I'm worried about you, you know."

You've got a funny way of showing it.

"It's going okay. Work is keeping me busy. I bought a car."

"Really? What kind? Can you afford it?"

"It's a great car. You'd love it."

She gushed about the deal she got, and what the car looked like. She described the excursion with Brian, playing up her amusement at the salespeople falling all over themselves to help him only to regret the hard bargain. She talked about Tiffany's great apartment, the gym, pool, and Jacuzzi.

"Wow, sweetheart, it sounds like you're really thriving up there."

"Well, it's a lot of work—but I have the best news of all." Ronnie paused. "I got into Georgia State!"

There was a gasp on the line. "You got in?"

"I got in, Mom! I'm going to college!" She hesitated, then plowed ahead. "But there's just this one issue..."

For the next five minutes, Ronnie explained the financial aid application process. She could get loans and maybe even scholarships, but the family would need to disclose their financial statements. Her mother grew quiet.

"Please, Mom. Please don't say no. I don't think I can do it otherwise. I'd need to pay cash, and there's no way I can make that much."

"You know how much I want to support you, sweetheart."

"Don't say that! Either you support me, or you don't. Either you tell Seth you have to give the school our financial statements, or you don't care about me and my dreams. There's no middle ground."

"Ronnie, that's unfair."

"What's unfair is for you to say you want to help, but to never actually do it." Tears prickled Ronnie's eyes. "I can't believe you care more about what Seth thinks than about my life. Especially after all that's happened."

There was a long pause, then Ronnie heard a defeated sigh. "I'll ask him. He's just in the next room. I'll ask him."

An image filled Ronnie's mind. The year before, she had walked in on a furious fight, with Seth holding her mother against a wall. She could still hear the slaps, the pitiful cries, all because her mother had asked Seth if they could advance Ronnie two hundred dollars for a cheerleading competition.

A year later, Ronnie heard the fear. "Mom, I don't want you to ask him if—"

"No, I'll ask him. I owe you that." Her voice grew stronger. "I love you, Ronnie. I'll ask him."

"Mom, I—"

"I love you, sweetheart. I'll call you back."

There was a click and she was gone.

Ronnie sat frozen, clutching the phone until the tinny error message came on. She set the receiver down and dialed the number. There was no answer.

TWENTY-TWO

A shining figure surveyed the dusky streets below, tracking with a small battered car as it made its way across town. He intervened when necessary, ensuring its progress. The timing would have to be perfect.

A sudden rustling caught his attention and he looked over his shoulder. Half a troop was following his route, eager to see the long-awaited meeting unfold. If he hadn't been so troubled by the events of the day, he would have grinned at them. As it was, he was sorely looking forward to this appointment. It had been ordained since before the foundations of the world.

Mr. Dugan pulled the new grille down over the door of the grocery store, and locked it with a snap. What a shame that the town had declined so much. Forty years ago, he didn't even have to lock the *door* at night.

He hurried across the parking lot to his truck and drove to the new drugstore, one of the few gleaming chain stores that had been added in this town.

The door chimed when he entered, and a bored-looking teenage boy eyed him from behind the counter.

"Yeah?"

"I need to get a refill. The last name is Dugan."

The teenager took his time walking to the computer and tapping a few keys. "It'll take ten minutes to get this filled." He disappeared into the back to find the pharmacist.

Mr. Dugan sighed, frustration near the surface. He'd called it in earlier in the day just so he wouldn't be late to his men's Bible study. He needed to say something!

Peace. They can wait.

He gave a rueful smile as he turned away from the counter. He wanted to get to know the drugstore staff, wanted to invite them to church. It would be ironic if he turned them off for the sake of a Bible study.

He wandered the cluttered aisles and stopped with knee braces and bandages on one side, baby toys on the other. Maybe he could buy a cute trinket for his grandson.

The door chimed as someone entered, trailing a cloud of cigarette smoke. He wrinkled his nose, annoyed. The woman wore a face-obscuring hat and sunglasses. She stopped in front of the ice packs and knee supports, and turned her back to him.

She took a long drag on the cigarette, and Mr. Dugan gave a pointed cough. Maybe she would get the picture.

The teenage clerk meandered over with an ashtray. "Uh, ma'am? You're not allowed to smoke in the store. Sorry."

The woman turned and awkwardly jabbed her cigarette out. Mr. Dugan looked over, and his satisfied smile died on his lips.

Her hands were shaking.

When the teenager walked away, Mr. Dugan spoke to the woman, startling her.

"Thank you for being willing to put your cigarette out. I sometimes have asthma, and it's hard to be around smoke."

"Sorry." She turned away again. For the first time, he noticed that she was cradling her left arm against her body.

"Excuse me. Are you okay? What's your name?"

A pause. "Linda."

In an instant, he knew. He touched her on the shoulder and turned her to face him. She tried to keep her head down, but it didn't matter. Under the glasses, her cheeks were puffy and red. A small welt laced her neck.

He lifted her chin, and she didn't resist when he pulled her sunglasses off. His breath caught in his throat as he saw the reddened eyes, the bruised cheekbone, the lines of pain on her forehead.

"Linda Hanover. I thought I recognized your voice." He sighed and shook his head. "Who did this to you?"

"I had an accident—"

"No, you didn't, Linda. Who did this?"

He waited through a long pause and realized he already knew the answer.

"Linda, can I pray for you?"

Tears sprang to her eyes. She pressed a shaking hand to her mouth and her voice was very small. "Yes."

"My church is only a couple blocks away. Why don't we go there? It's a better place to talk, and I'll pray for you, okay?"

Linda closed her eyes and nodded.

He reached to lay a hand on her arm. She gave a gasping cry and jerked away.

Mr. Dugan held up his hands. "I'm so sorry. I didn't realize. Let me take you to the hospital—"

"No!" She gave him an alarmed look.

He kept his hands up. "Okay. Okay. I just thought you might want it looked at. Let's go to the church and—"

The pharmacist called his name. He was going to ignore it, but Linda gestured for him to answer the call.

"Go get your medicine. I'm not going anywhere."

"Can I get you anything?"

With her good arm, she reached down to the display in front of her and picked up a small sling. She handed it over, wincing, not looking at him.

He hurried to the counter. As his purchase was rung up, he asked the teenager if he could use the phone.

From up near the rafters of the church, the angels watched the little group of three people in the front pew. Mr. Dugan and his wife talked with Linda and held her as she cried. They prayed for her, talked some more, and prayed again.

Mrs. Dugan went to make a phone call, and returned with a smile.

"It's all set, my dear. Our daughter-in-law is making up a room right now. You'll like her. She's a guidance counselor at the high school. And since we'll be out of town for a few days, I'll feel better if you're with her and her husband."

"What if Seth—"

"For the moment, we won't tell him where you are," Mrs. Dugan said, "and there's no way for him to find out. Let's get you safe and healed up first, and then we'll discuss the next steps. All Seth needs to know right now is that you won't be coming home for a bit. We have some clothes you can borrow, so there's no need even to go back to the house."

Linda shuddered, as she had many times in the last hour. "But when I *do* come home, he'll be so furious—"

"Linda, you have some new friends now," Mr. Dugan said, "and we care what happens to you. And God is watching over you. Let's let tomorrow worry about itself, and trust that God will work it out."

Mr. Dugan noticed Linda's fretful gaze settle on a pair of outstretched hands in a stained-glass window above the altar. The hands were battered and bloodied, pierced with the marks of nails.

Her anxious movements stilled and she sat for a long moment, staring at the window. Finally, she looked down at her hands and nodded.

"Linda." Mrs. Dugan's voice was gentle. "I also called over to the hospital."

Her head jerked up and she started to protest.

Mrs. Dugan reached over and took her good hand. "My dear, you need help. You need to get that arm looked at, for one thing. The hospital has some very nice staff members who are used to dealing with women in your situation. Okay?"

"I don't have health insurance. And no money."

From up near the rafters, the angels noticed Mrs. Dugan give her husband an anxious look.

"Linda," he said, "I believe that God brought us together, and He will provide. Let's take one thing at a time, okay? Let's get you to the doctor."

There was another long pause. Then a small voice. "Why are you doing this? You hardly know me."

"That's an easy answer, Linda." He opened a pew Bible and flipped through several pages until he found what he was looking for. "We're followers of Jesus, and Jesus loves you. Listen to His heart here as He talks to His followers. 'Come, you who are blessed by my Father...For I was hungry and you gave me something to eat, I was thirsty and you gave me something to drink, I was a stranger and you invited me in, I needed clothes and you clothed me, I was sick and you looked after me, I was in prison and you came to visit me.'

"Then the followers are a little confused, and they ask when they had ever fed or clothed Jesus! Here's what He says: 'I tell you the truth, whatever you did for one of the least of these brothers of mine, you did for me.'"

He laid down the Bible and looked straight into Linda's red eyes. "We may not know you well, but you are God's creation, and precious to Him. You are our sister. And whatever we may do for you, we know we're also serving Jesus, who loves you very much."

Linda looked uncomfortable. "But I'm not very religious..."

Mr. Dugan gave a great bark of laughter. "Religious! Neither am I! It's not about religion; it's about a relationship with God."

He fell silent, patting her hand. A church bell chimed.

"So, my dear," Mrs. Dugan said "Shall we get that arm looked at?"

She and her husband helped Linda up and to their small car. Mrs. Dugan drove the car, while her husband followed in his decrepit pickup. The angels followed, their eyes watchful as the Lord cast an impenetrable barrier over the little procession. The entire mission must be sheltered from enemy eyes. They knew the forces of darkness had lost the woman's track the moment she set out from the house that afternoon. And unless something unforeseen happened, they were never getting her back.

☆ ☆ ☆

The social worker parted the curtains to Linda's partitioned-off area of the emergency room. She hugged her clipboard to her chest and gave Linda and the Dugans a warm smile.

"The officer is here. Shall I bring him in?"

Linda nodded and watched the social worker hurry away before Linda changed her mind again. This was all moving so fast. How had these people persuaded her to do something she'd been terrified of for years?

She looked down at the fresh cast on her left arm. He'd never broken anything before. Well, nothing visible. He'd broken her spirit—and her daughter's—years before.

She heard the social worker talking to the policeman, and her mouth grew dry. If she filed this report, Seth would kill her. Terror crashed in on her and she gave a violent shudder, clenching the flimsy bedsheets in her fist. Seth had always been able to find her at the shelters, at the homes of their few friends. And what had come next…her stomach wrenched at the pain of the memories. Her heart beat faster. She had no money of her own, no saleable skills; no way to get away, to start over. What made her think anything could change now?

Something touched her arm, and she jumped. Mrs. Dugan was standing by the bed, deep understanding in her face.

"Linda, it'll be okay. You'll be safe. And we'll help you. There's nothing to fear."

Linda stared back into the clear eyes of a near-stranger who had dropped everything to help her, and saw…kindness. A deep kindness she had never known. It was as if the warmth of the sun shone through those blue eyes, straight into her frozen soul.

When the policeman finally entered, she was sitting quietly, waiting, holding Mrs. Dugan's hand.

TWENTY-THREE

"Hey, girl." Tiffany poked her head inside the break room, then gave a huge yawn. "I thought you'd left already."

"Wish I had. Took me forever to close out tonight."

Ronnie leaned deep into her locker, fishing for her things. She pulled out the folder bulging with college materials, still where she had shoved it after getting her acceptance days before. At this rate, who knew if she'd ever use them? She thought again—as she had all night—about her conversation with her mother. She never had been able to reach her.

Ronnie slid the folder into her shoulder bag and slammed the locker's metal door. Then the two friends walked out the staff hallway and into the quiet club. The tables were empty, except for a small group huddled around a booth where the DJ and a few bouncers were relaxing.

Tiffany headed that direction, then glanced back over her shoulder. "Why don't you wait for us? We're going to hang out at Nick's once we're done here. You should join us. It sounds like you've had a hard day."

"Well…"

"I'll just be a minute. C'mon."

"You are just bound and determined that I'll have a good time, aren't you? Even if you have to drag me into it?"

"Kicking and screaming, babe." Tiffany grinned. "Someone has to."

Ronnie started awake to the distant sound of a telephone. She fumbled on her nightstand, knocking over a picture frame and a half-full glass of water before she dimly remembered that the phone was in the kitchen.

Her head was heavy, her eyes unfocused. She squinted toward her nightstand, shielding her eyes from the light blasting in the bedroom window, and cursed under her breath at the sight of the water dripping onto her bag and apron, in a jumble on the floor. She grabbed a tissue and dabbed weakly at the puddle. That was the last time she let Tiffany talk her into partying on a work night.

Work night! She batted the clutter aside from the clock on her nightstand, and then groaned: 11:25. She was supposed to be at the club by noon. So was Tiffany.

She fumbled to her feet and headed for the door, taking it slow. It had been a while since she'd had a hangover this bad. Maybe she wouldn't wake Tiffany up, just to get her back.

She opened the door and shuffled down the hallway.

"Boy, you look terrible."

Ronnie squinted toward the kitchen. Tiffany was sitting in the nook, fully dressed, eating a piece of toast and reading the newspaper.

"You're up."

Tiffany raised an eyebrow. "Uh…*yeah*. Gotta go to work."

Ronnie closed her eyes. "In about fifteen minutes, I'm gonna be real mad that you didn't wake me up. Right now, I've got to shower."

"Have fun." Tiffany turned back to the newspaper and took another bite of toast. "I wanna see how fast you can move."

"Jerk." Ronnie muttered under her breath as she turned back to her room.

"That's jerk*ette* to you, babe."

Ronnie groaned and steadied herself against the wall. At this rate, she wouldn't get to the club until one o'clock, and Marco would dock her pay.

That thought sobered her enough to carry her through showering and changing, and a quick once-over of her hair. She'd have to do her makeup in the car. She glowered at Tiffany as her friend breezed out the doorway ahead of her.

Hadn't Tiffany drunk as much as she had? She couldn't remember. In fact…Ronnie stopped, momentarily confused. She couldn't remember anything about the night before.

She drove toward the club on autopilot, her mind racing. What had she done? She didn't mind a good buzz, but she hated being out of control.

As she entered the busy breakroom, she noticed Nick, the DJ, Brian, and several of the other bouncers elbowing each other. Maris glanced at her from beside her locker, then turned away. The men started applauding, hooting and cheering.

"Here she comes, Miss America!"

Ronnie blushed and tried to frown. "Cut it out. What're you doing?"

The DJ sidled up to her as she worked the combination to her locker. "Yo, sis— I think it's more a matter of what *you* were doing."

"What're you talking about?"

The DJ whipped off his shirt, put on a simpering face, and tiptoed across the floor. "Hi, I'm auditioning for Miss Naked America."

Ronnie leaned against her locker with a thud. She could feel the blood rising in her cheeks. "You've got to be kidding me."

The DJ grabbed her around her waist and pressed her into him. "Oh, baby, I wouldn't kid about that. I just want to know when I get to see the next audition."

Ronnie dug her fingernails into his chest until he broke off with a curse. She saw Nick sitting at one of the break tables, chuckling at the scene.

She turned back to her locker, forcing her voice to remain steady. "I'm not sure I believe you idiots, anyway."

Nick rose from his table, took a last drag, and extinguished his cigarette. "Oh, we all saw you, Ronnie. And don't take this the wrong way, but you looked good. There shouldn't be anything that stops you from getting up there, now."

"I can't—"

"Look." Brian stepped forward. "I know you're probably nervous about it. Who isn't, at first? But you already showed it to us. You might as well get paid for it."

Ronnie pressed her lips together and turned away.

As she fastened her apron around her waist, she realized Maris was looking at her out of the corner of her eye. She gave Ronnie a subtle shake of the head, a strange look on her face, and glanced around as if she wanted to say something without the others overhearing.

Nick eyed his watch and gave Ronnie a parting slap on the back. "I've got to go open the bar. Maris, you're opening, too. You coming?"

Maris straightened, and in an instant the strange look was replaced by her usual briskness. She clicked her locker shut and whisked out of the room without a backward glance.

Brian turned to Ronnie and shrugged, a brotherly smile on his face. "We aren't trying to embarrass you, you know. We're just looking out for you. Just think about it, okay?"

Ronnie kept her head down, trying desperately to remember her embarrassing actions at the party. What had she been *thinking?* She tried to dredge up the usual indignant thoughts that rose when someone suggested stripping, but they were nowhere to be found.

Marco stuck his head out the door and hollered down the hall. "Phone for you, Ronnie!"

Ronnie turned, confused. "For me?"

"Hurry it up!" Marco was gesturing her toward his office. "I've got a meeting in a few minutes."

Ronnie headed back up the hallway and sidled over to Marco's desk, staring at his face. She hadn't given anyone the club's number. If this was a setup...

"Hello?"

"Ronnie, is that you?" The voice was high-pitched, anxious.

"Mom! I've been trying to call you! Are you okay?"

There was a long pause. "Not really, baby."

"What happened? What—"

"Honey, it's too long to go into. But you can't reach me at home, not for a while. I wanted to give you a number where I'm staying and…and ask you a question."

Ronnie scrabbled on the desk for a sticky note and a pen, aware of Marco's curious gaze. "Go ahead. What question?"

Her mother read off an unfamiliar number. "I'm staying with a couple named Tom and Angela Dugan in town."

"Who?"

"You don't know them, baby. It's a long story."

Ronnie started to ask another question, then sat up straight. "Mom…how did you get this number?"

"Well, you'd said the Challenger Restaurant, so I called information."

"Oh." She heard a tapping noise and looked up to see Marco standing by the door, pointing at his watch. "Mom, I've got to get back to work. Can I call you later—"

"Ronnie, I need money."

"What?"

There was a long sigh. "I had to go to the emergency room. My arm's broken. I was…I was hoping you'd made enough money by now that you could send some home. The hospital bill will be several thousand dollars. Even five hundred will help."

"Mom, I—"

"I'd understand if you don't have it, I just—"

"It's not that, it's—" Ronnie broke off. The tide was rising, and she was about to be swamped. She had no choice. She squared her shoulders and stood. "Mom, I've got to go back to work right now. But I'll figure something out and call you first thing in the morning."

A small voice. "Thank you."

"And, Mom—don't go back to Seth."

"I got a restraining order, you know."

"You're kidding! You've never—"

"It's a long story. Go back to work, sweetheart. We'll talk in the morning."

Ronnie hung up the phone and turned as Marco bustled back toward his desk and sat down, making busy about his meeting preparations. When she just stood there, he looked up, irritated.

"What?"

"My mother needs money for some medical bills, and I need money for a tuition payment." She blurted out the words before she talked herself out of it. "I'd like to have an audition."

"Well…" Marco's voice lingered on the word. He sat back in his chair and steepled his fingers. "I'm glad to hear it. Sorry about your mother, of course."

Ronnie stood, stiff as a board. "Of course."

"We have an amateur night coming up on Monday. Will that do?"

Ronnie nodded, not trusting her voice.

TWENTY-FOUR

oney, you ready to go?" Sherry Turner leaned out the car window and hollered toward the open kitchen door. "We're going to be late!" A distant voice wafted through the doorway. "Hold on, I forgot my laptop."

Sherry groaned as her husband hurried back out the door, carrying case in hand. "And *why* do you need your computer?"

"Well," Doug's face was sheepish as he climbed into the driver's seat of the family minivan, "I have to make a final decision on this big Silicon Valley deal. So after church, I really need to run to the office for a couple hours."

Protests erupted from the backseat.

"Daddy, you promised!"

"But the picnic…!"

Doug turned in his seat, backing quickly down the driveway. "Look, it's only two hours. You can go and I'll join you after—"

"No way," Sherry said. "The picnic will be over by the time you get there. If you have to work, go in the evening. The kids haven't seen you all week. You can eat junk food with them, play a little softball, and then go into the office after dark."

"Well…all right…" Doug heaved an exaggerated sigh.

"Good." Sherry saw a small smile playing at the corners of her husband's lips. She whacked him on the arm, trying not to grin. "Hey! That's what you wanted all along, isn't it? Isn't it? You just wanted to get us all nervous so that we actually end up *glad* that you're going to the office tonight."

Doug shrugged, his eyes twinkling. "Hey—I'm under attack here. I'm taking the fifth for my own protection."

Genna piped up from the backseat. "So you're coming, Daddy? Right? You're going to watch my song?"

Doug looked in the rearview mirror and smiled. "Of course, sweetheart. I wouldn't miss it."

☆ ☆ ☆

Late that night, Doug set a stack of papers down on his desk and rubbed his temples. The numbers just didn't add up. No matter how he tried, he just couldn't find a way to make it work.

A letter from the IRS sat at the top of the pile. The nail in the coffin.

"Therefore, we cannot approve your requested tax structure..."

He stood and placed the spreadsheets back into a holder on his desk. Mary would organize all his evidence into nice, neat briefing books for the board meeting on Wednesday. Not that it would matter.

The board was expecting his sign-off, and Jordan was already planning two years down the road as if it were a sure thing. He snapped his computer bag shut with a little more force than usual. Why did he always have to be the bearer of bad news? At least he was keeping the company healthy and on track. Jordan would just have to understand that as attractive as some of these partnerships looked, they didn't make financial sense.

Doug tried to stretch out the tension in his neck and shoulders. He needed one of his wife's back rubs. He smiled ruefully to himself and reached for his coat. With the way this day had gone, he needed more than that.

He glanced at the bronze clock on his desk. Ten-thirty! Sherry was probably already asleep.

He headed for the elevator, his steps soft on the plush carpet. At ground level, he exited the elevator and headed for the door, his shoes clicking on polished marble. He stepped up to the security station and nodded to the guard as he handed over his employee I.D.

A few moments later, Doug steered his car through the parking lot. He pulled up at the darkened security booth and waited while the camera sent his license plate number through the verification system. He tapped his fingers against the steering wheel. It was a lot quicker when the guards were on duty. After a minute, the gate slid sideways. Doug's wheels bumped over the pressurized grating that would sound an alarm if someone tried to slip into the compound as he drove away.

The dashboard clock read ten-forty-five as Doug pulled onto the freeway and headed north. His stomach growled, and a thought entered his head. He pushed it away.

A few minutes later, the thought came back. *Just for a few minutes.*

He gripped the steering wheel tighter. *No.* He clicked on the contemporary Christian station. A few minutes later, he turned onto another freeway and saw the inevitable signboard.

Just for a few minutes, to unwind. The food was pretty good.

Doug shook his head and tried to block out the signboard, but the small thought had become a vise grip, pulling him toward the exit. Just like so many things in the last few months. He didn't want to resist.

He took the exit, made a right turn, and pulled into the parking lot. He had a feeling of unreality as he stepped out of the car, paid his cover charge, and entered the building.

The music was pulsing, and the darkness enveloped him. His legs took him toward the light, toward the thumping beat, toward the flashing lights on the stages. He slid into an empty table and waited a moment as the anticipation grew, then slowly looked up at the nearest stage. His mouth went dry.

Ronnie saw the new customer sitting alone and sidled up to him. "Hey there, what can I get you tonight?"

He jumped and turned away from the nearest stage, where Tiffany was dancing. Ronnie didn't glance up at her friend. It was all getting really old. And amateur night was tomorrow. Her mind shied away from that thought as she repeated her question.

"What did you say?" The man was clearly trying to gather his thoughts. "I'm sorry...what?"

Behind their one-way mirror, three men scanned the room as the camera operator did his stuff. The lead watcher leaned forward and tapped on a monitor. "Who is Ronnie talking to?"

The computer guy glanced at the picture on his monitor, and worked some magic on his keyboard. He frowned. "He could be a previous contact, but it's not a certain match. But if it is him...wow...we've got another bull's-eye. Should we send it in?"

"Yes." The other man watched his colleague press the buttons that would send the camera shot to the verification center. His eyes turned to the next table along. "Continue, please."

"Can I get you anything? You hungry or thirsty, or both?" As the words left her mouth, Ronnie realized her customer didn't have a menu.

"Um—" the man straightened and smiled briefly. "Sorry, yes. Both. I'd like your buffalo wings, a club sandwich with your house sauce, and a small Caesar salad."

Ronnie glanced over with a smile. "Gee, for a man with no menu, you certainly know your way around this place. What can I get you to drink?"

"Ginger ale, please."

Ronnie looked up from her order pad. "Would you like a beer? Drink special? Our Challenger Tooters are only five dollars tonight."

The customer shook his head. "No thanks."

Ronnie smiled and moved toward her other customers. A few minutes later, on her way toward the kitchen, she glanced back. The new customer was slumped in his chair, not looking at the stage, rubbing his temples. His blue shirt looked expensive but bore all the wrinkles of a long day.

Ronnie found herself feeling sorry for him.

Doug sat with his head in his hands.

Lord, what's wrong with me? Why can't I break this thing? I've even memorized the menu! I have a beautiful wife and children, a great job, a great church—why do I keep doing this?

The music was pounding, pressing in on his brain, making it hard to concentrate. He sensed someone nearby and turned his head.

The girl up on stage was gyrating right at the edge of the runway, her gaze fastened directly on him. He was trembling. A moment later, a ten-dollar bill was in his hand, then in her garter. He took several shallow breaths as she gave him a big wink and turned to the next man along. By now there was a crowd of men around the end of the runway, all panting for the slender, circling figure. Doug watched, captivated, as she collected dozens of bills, then finished her dance with a flourish.

He crept back into his seat, and his hand brushed something on the table. His buffalo wings and ginger ale had arrived. He picked up a wing and bit into it, only to quickly lay it back down.

He groaned and pushed the food away; then stood, threw two twenties on the table, and grabbed his coat off the other chair. He headed for the door, pushing past the bouncers, past a group of people waiting to enter, out into the cold air.

He jerked open his car door and tossed his coat on the passenger seat, then climbed in and slammed the door. He laid his head against the steering wheel and wept.

TWENTY-FIVE

The dressing room was a hive of activity. A dozen girls were staked out in their own little corners, holding whispered discussions with their supporters, glancing at the competition from behind heavily made-up eyes. The winner tonight would get five hundred bucks, cash, on the spot. Plus a guaranteed job offer. They'd heard the money only got better, and they wanted in.

Tiffany teased Ronnie's hair in front of the mirror, reminding her of all they had practiced. She'd had her roommate slinking and strutting around the apartment in one of her best outfits, getting her routine down pat. And then when Ronnie started getting nervous, she'd brought out the Valium.

When they'd arrived at the club, Ronnie had demanded two beers in quick succession. Several of the other girls in the contest had been popping Ecstasy and looked happy as clams, but Tiffany—her demeanor now crisp and professional—had advised against it.

"Wait until you win, then you can celebrate. Otherwise, the X will make you lose your focus. We can pop some later."

"It's only two minutes, right? You said it was just two minutes."

"Yes, just two minutes." In the mirror, Ronnie saw Tiffany roll her eyes. "Ronnie, you need to chill. I would say 'take a chill pill' but you already have!" She giggled. "You're going to have so much fun, you'll wonder why you haven't done it before. I don't know why this bothers you so much."

On one side of the two girls, two great beings stood, their faces solemn. On the other side hovered a small group of cackling figures.

A dark figure whispered the words to Tiffany, and out poured the earnest lies from her mouth. He gave his shining foe a smug look, and kept a crooked talon firmly hooked into Tiffany's head. Despite their pitiful efforts, the noble enemy would never keep the new girl from falling. And they certainly weren't going to touch the dark figure's existing prey.

Loriel stepped forward, as he had many times before, to put a hand on Ronnie's shoulder, to counter the enemy's words with the loving and gentle challenge of the Lord. His charge was still nervous, knew her path wasn't right, but looked determined to proceed. And once she did, her ability to be impacted by their message would again diminish. Loriel sighed, his eyes sad. He had seen it so many times before.

The door near Ronnie popped open, and some half-dressed contestants squealed in indignation as Marco poked his head inside.

"Two minutes! I need the first three girls in the wings now."

He vanished out the door, and Tiffany turned and looked at the girls, a teasing smile on her face. "He's going to see it all in a few minutes, you know."

One of the girls tossed her hair as she finalized her preparations. "Under *my* terms, Sasha."

"Yes, yes, of course. You're going to do great. You going up now? Well, good luck!"

The music started pounding onstage, and Ronnie could hear Marco announcing the start of Amateur Night. The audience whistled and hooted, and she clutched her costume in tense fists, picturing all the men she'd gotten to know, all her regulars, seeing her out there tonight. Maybe Maris had been right. She turned to Tiffany, her head clearing despite the beer.

"How can I *do* this in front of these people I've waited on?"

Tiffany laughed. "Listen, they're here for one reason only—to see the girls take their clothes off. And you're here for one reason, too—to take their money. They use you; you use them. It's an even trade. I don't know why Maris ever tried to talk you out of it. You've been busting your tail all this time, but you haven't been getting a cut of the real action. Now you can."

Tiffany glanced at the clock and helped Ronnie finish arranging her costume. "Remember what I said—from now on, you're an actress. Make them think they're the hottest stuff in the world and you are *unbearably* attracted to them. That you'd jump them in a second if it weren't for club rules." She snapped her fingers in Ronnie's face and laughed. "You'll get to be a darned good actress up there."

"Do you have another beer?"

"Yeah." Tiffany pulled one out of a small fridge at the side of the room. "Here you go. Cheers."

Ronnie guzzled it, feeling the warmth rising in her skin, the inhibitions finally melting away. She realized Tiffany had taken her hand and was leading her toward the stage.

"There you are!" One of the production guys grabbed her by the arm. "Ready,

Ronnie? The last one is just finishing."

He started to hustle her up a small flight of steps, then stopped and looked her up and down. He grinned and flinched as if he'd been burned by her touch. *"Yeow!* Ronnie, you look *hot!* Knock 'em dead!"

Ronnie pushed back the last fuzzy thought of retreat, and gave the guy a sweet grin. *Might as well start acting now.* She climbed the few stairs to the wings of the stage and straightened. Two minutes. Just two minutes.

She looked over her shoulder, to see Tiffany give her the thumbs-up. The last girl finished to the sound of whistles and cheering, and the stage went black.

"Did you see her at the end?" Brian waved a beer like the lord of the manor, one arm loosely about Ronnie's shoulders as an animated crowd surrounded her. "She had them eating out of her hand. A natural she is, a natural!"

The DJ chimed in with an admiring but crude joke, and the crowd roared with laughter.

"Make way, make way, best friend coming through!" Tiffany said as she pushed back into the throng.

She passed another drink to Ronnie and made another rousing toast to Ronnie's win. The crowd cheered again, drawing sideways grins from the other patrons of the all-night bar.

Ronnie was giddy. The Ecstasy was in her bloodstream, five hundred dollars was in her pocket, and all was right with the world.

Why *had* she waited this long?

Loriel hovered outside the pub, tears in his eyes, alone. He was laced with the desperate pain of the Father. The pain of *knowing* what was to come, of seeing the dreadful path looming ahead of a lost child…the road that so rarely gave up its willing prey. But if it didn't… Loriel closed his eyes and prayed. The consequences were too great to imagine.

TWENTY-SIX

L ook, Jordan." Doug Turner stood at his desk, one ear pressed to the telephone, sorting through some papers. "I get what you're saying; I've known all along. But the board needs my honest opinion tomorrow and I'm going to give it. That's what you hired me for."

He set a file folder down a little too hard. "Don't threaten me, chief. If you'll just calm down, you'll realize that we'll make *more* money if we don't take such a big loss on this deal for the next three quarters. Especially since the risk is so high and we're in such a vulnerable stage ourselves."

Doug listened to another diatribe and tried to unclench his jaw. His boss was going to give him a heart attack at the age of thirty-two. He broke in when Jordan's cell phone crackled, forcing Jordan to pause.

"Chief, I'll do everything I can to present it in the best possible light. I've got all the glowing revenue projections and the nice little color pie charts and graphs you wanted. But at the end of the day, they're going to ask for my honest opinion, and I'm going to have to give it. There's no guarantee all those big revenue projections will ever materialize. And if they don't, we're going to be out of business."

Jordan started to say something, but Doug forestalled him. "Since you're the majority owner now, I would think you'd have an incentive to listen to me." He forced himself to laugh, adopting a joking tone. "I don't know why you're holding on to this so tight, chief. You're like a dog with a bone, man. You've got to let it go."

There was a long silence on the other end of the line.

When Jordan spoke again, his manner was stiff. He thanked Doug for his advice and hung up. Doug slowly put down the phone and wondered if his life span at the company was about to be drastically shortened.

"So what's our first target?" Tyson put down his pen, sat back in his chair, and opened the floor for suggestions.

He and the others were spaced around a butcher-block table in the villa's expansive kitchen; papers, beer bottles, and coffee mugs littering every conceivable surface around them. The windows were shut against the cool breezes of the night, and flames flickered over gas logs in a nearby fireplace.

It was decision time.

The numbers had come in, the small group had convened in the islands, and the prospects were now identified.

Tyson stared around the circle, watching the firelight flickering on the hardened faces. He knew what they were thinking. No one wanted to be the first to step into the fray. Every suggestion had a consequence—an effect on a city, a military troop, a piece of infrastructure—and everyone knew that someone's extended family, someone's acquaintances, would end up being in the wrong place at the wrong time.

They had taken to calling themselves the Security Group—S-Group for short. None of them gave a rip that their decisions would mean the opposite of homeland security. They existed to create and then exploit the system's weaknesses. Once these deals went through, they'd be able to live for the rest of their lives down in these islands, immune to any wreckage at home. Besides it was all part of the inevitable cycle of destruction and rebirth. It was what made the economy grow, what capitalism was made of, what had increased American productivity during and after every war. The current system was broken, corrupt, choked by overzealous regulators of every stripe. It was time for a return to pure capitalism; survival of the fittest. Sure, there would be a few years of pain, but the nation would bounce back stronger for it. And it wasn't as if someone else couldn't come up with the same idea as they. If others were going to get rich, too, they figured they might as well get in on the action.

Sherry grabbed a roll of paper towels and mopped frantically at the kitchen table, which was a better option than strangling her son. She swept aside the neatly organized stacks of mail on the tabletop, trying to contain the spreading grape juice spill—perilously close to her checkbook and the expense reports she'd just spent an hour compiling.

Brandon was running around the kitchen with Blake Woodward, oblivious to the nightmare he'd just created. They had grabbed two flashlights and were stampeding out the door before Sherry trusted herself to speak.

"Brandon, Blake, grab a towel and come back here!"

They kept running, giving no sign that they had heard her. A door slammed as the two headed out into the dark.

Ring!...Ring!...

Sherry growled in exasperation and looked at the phone, which kept ringing. She pressed the speakerphone button with her elbow and went to dump the sopping paper towels in the garbage.

"Whoever you are, hold on a second!" A moment later, she was back, cleaning her hands on another towel. "Sorry. Who is this please?"

"It's Lisa." There was a pause. "It sounds like you're having quite a day."

"You could say that."

"I won't keep you then, but listen—were you all coming to home group on Friday?"

"I think so. Both of us have really enjoyed the last few weeks." She grimaced. "Well, after Doug forgave me for being so insensitive that night. We've enjoyed getting to know everyone."

"It's mutual, you know. Well, if you're going to be there, why don't you all come over for dinner ahead of time? It'll just be salad and pizza, but we'd love to have you."

"It's a deal." Sherry felt a genuine smile rising on her face. "That would be fun."

"See you Friday then."

"Okay." Sherry started to say good-bye, and then gave a strangled laugh. "Oh, and Lisa—"

"Yes?"

"Despite the craziness, I want you to know that I did still have my hour-long prayer time today…just in case you were wondering."

"Me? Wondering?" Lisa laughed outright. "That's great to hear. Imagine how you'd be today if you hadn't had your cup filled this morning!"

By the time Doug left the office, Jordan had returned none of his calls or e-mails. Jordan was working at his home office most of the day, so Doug knew he was choosing to ignore his chief financial officer. Not a good sign.

As Doug drove away, he replayed the tense conversation over and over again. It got worse each time. The phone was slammed down instead of simply hung up, and Jordan's quiet anger became vengeful fury. Doug's mind began to turn with memories of previous employees Jordan had fired—sometimes on trumped-up excuses simply because they didn't get along.

Doug pulled into his driveway and stared at his dream home. Would they be forced to downsize just because he insisted on telling the board the truth? What would Sherry say? He knew he and his family weren't materialistic—at least not too badly—but Sherry loved their beautiful home. They probably didn't have enough savings; they really needed to scale back their budget. Once the kids were in bed, he'd better go look through their expenses and see what they could cut.

He pushed open the kitchen door. Sherry was sitting stiffly at the table, surrounded by bills and papers. She got up and gave him a swift kiss, her body tense.

The kids came running, stampeding through the room, hollering. Sherry jerked around and hurried to the table to protect her work. Doug gave a private sigh when he noticed that Blake was in the mix. He liked Blake a lot, but on this night he would have preferred a calm home. He gave all the kids—including Blake—a hug, trying to hide his anxiety. They immediately started telling him about their day, talking over one another, their words competing for dad's attention.

"*Quiet!*"

The kids swung around to see Sherry standing by the table, her hands raised for silence. She pointed at the basement door.

"Downstairs! *Now.*"

The kids trooped out, their faces disappointed.

Doug and Sherry stared at each other for a minute, then Sherry frowned.

"What's wrong?" she asked.

"Oh…" Doug forced a laugh. "One of those days."

"Was preparing for the board meeting tough?"

Doug stretched his neck, hoping she'd just drop it. "Yeah, you could say that."

She stepped closer, staring into his face, her manner challenging.

"What's wrong?"

Why did she always have to make like the Grand Inquisitor when he'd had a hard day?

"Well…I told Jordan that I'm going to have to give the board my true opinion tomorrow. I think they'll probably reject the deal. Jordan's furious. He didn't return my phone calls all day."

"That's not good."

"No, it's not."

"Well, you know what you're doing. Jordan isn't a numbers guy; that's why he needs you. He's just going to have to realize that you're right and he's wrong."

So glad you *know how to handle my irrational boss.*

"Did you tell him he was wrong?"

Talk about a dog with a bone…

"I tried to, Sherry, but he didn't want to hear it. Remember, he wouldn't return my calls."

"Well, how unprofessional is *that?*" Sherry put her hands on her hips. "I can't believe him sometimes. He just gets a bee in his bonnet and won't listen to reason. Well, you just remind him that you've been working seventy-hour weeks to make this deal work—at the expense of time with your family—and that you've done everything he's asked you to do. I can't believe he'd be mad at you after all you've done for him!"

"I—"

"And another thing. You know the finances inside and out, and he's just going to have to stop micromanaging the company and trust you to have a clue what you're doing. You're just going to have to stand up to him."

"I'm not sure that—"

"That's why he made you the CFO after all, isn't it? Didn't Jordan himself tell you last year that you'd saved the company a boatload of money on bad deals? Didn't he?"

"Yes, he did."

"And the board trusts you, right? I mean, they specifically kept you in place when Jordan took over the company after his brother died. I bet they'll be glad that you're telling them the truth, rather than being a yes-man! *Somebody* has to look out for the interests of the company's investors, if Jordan isn't."

"Sherry."

"What?"

"Can we not talk about this right now?"

"What do you mean?"

"It feels like you're attacking me."

Sherry's face reddened. "I'm not attacking *you*, I'm furious at Jordan. He—"

"I don't have the energy to fight right now."

"But I'm not fighting you. I'm mad *for* you!"

Doug closed his eyes. "I need to go chill for a while. I'm going to go watch the news."

"But—"

Doug shook his head. "Please, Sherry."

"Fine." Sherry began moving the piles of paper off the table, her motions jerky. "Go watch TV. Dinner'll be ready in twenty minutes."

"Thanks."

Sherry watched Doug disappear into the den, her emotions roiling.

Why did he never want to talk about these things? Why was he always shutting her out? She wasn't stupid—she had a Harvard degree, too! She could see what was going on at the company, and had had it up to *here* with Jordan. The nice house and the cars weren't worth it. She wouldn't mind if Doug transferred to another job tomorrow. She just wanted her husband back—her fun loving, kind, generous husband who tossed the kids in the air when he came home and gave her a big kiss.

The man who came home these days was tense and worried, and kept things inside.

She stood at the stove, stirring a pot of spaghetti, tears leaking down her cheeks. She loved her husband, but what had happened to their fun, their little touches of love? They shared a house, shared a bed, but she hardly knew what was going on in his head anymore. Why would he never share it with her? Didn't he love her anymore?

Late that night, Doug lay awake, staring at the ceiling. He'd been unable to sleep over the sound of Sherry sniffling next to him. He knew she'd been crying, and felt helpless to know how to fix it. He knew he was at fault somehow, but didn't know what he'd done or how to change it back.

He had tried to move to her side of the bed, to stroke her hair, to run his hand over her back, but she had stiffened. He had retreated, hurt and confused.

Now she was asleep, and he was staring at the ceiling at one-thirty in the morning. The board meeting loomed like a large dead-end in the morning. He tried to pray, but his thoughts felt like lead.

He slipped out of bed, put on a sweatshirt, and closed the bedroom door behind him. A long bonus room downstairs had been converted to a home office the week they had moved in. He closed the French doors behind him.

Within minutes he was looking at a spreadsheet of the family's expenses, and wincing.

He went online to look at the last few months of credit card bills and shook his head. Why did Sherry feel the need to buy all this *stuff* with his hard-earned money? They were going to have to have a long, hard talk in the morning.

He still wasn't tired.

A small, buried thought kept trying to rise up, and Doug kept pushing it down. It knocked again, and finally got to the surface.

You're all alone, and everyone is asleep...

His stomach twisted in anticipation. He typed in a Web address, almost shaking when he heard the music, saw the first pictures. He quickly entered a credit card number. One of his credit cards; a bill that Sherry never opened.

He was all alone, and everyone was asleep.

The website was flooded with credit card numbers; tens of thousands a night. Each time a customer paid with plastic, a signal was routed to the credit card company.

But they also went somewhere else; a large prewar building in Atlanta staffed with a trusted team of analysts. Every transaction was captured and analyzed. Possible targets were profiled, reports compiled. It was tedious work, but every now and then there was an immediate payoff.

An analyst's computer chimed as several transactions came in, one right after the other. With a yawn, he opened the necessary screen, looked at the most recent transactions, and sat up straight. He looked again and called his supervisor over.

There were two credit cards listed: one was from a satellite engineer in the Washington, D.C., suburbs; the other was from Doug Turner. Both were on-line at that moment.

The supervisor smiled and picked up the phone. Sometimes, people just made it too easy.

Down in the islands, Tyson listened for a moment, a satisfied smile on his face. He clicked his phone shut and looked at the others, then pointed at the short list on the table in front of him.

"Well, we got two of our targets again tonight. We're now over 50 percent of our first target list. Since we have redundancies built in, I'd say we pull the trigger and get started. The timing's perfect."

One of the older men nodded. "I agree. We can alter the plan as we go, if a necessary piece is absent. We need to start bringing in cash flow now." His face was hard. "And there are many other means of achieving our objective, if simple persuasion is ineffective."

Tyson shook his head. "Maybe later. Other methods are likely to draw attention and suspicion. We *must not* trigger any profiling or any law enforcement activity, or our best customer prospects will disappear. The whole point of these operations is that because they are being set up under the radar, using domestic resources, that they will be a complete surprise."

The older man's eyes narrowed. "Then what happens if one of our targets refuses? Will that send a whole project down the drain?"

"Maybe not down the drain, but we might have to move to a different project for a while." Tyson held up a sheaf of paper. "Look, you've seen the list. Any customer would pay big money for any one of these projects; very few will care which one is actually triggered."

"And when is your big meeting with our first prospect?"

"Tomorrow at noon. They're flying in as we speak, using a regular courier run to the islands as cover. They need to be out by the usual departure time of five o'clock so as not to arouse suspicion. You never know who's watching."

"If someone could be watching, how will you be able to meet with them without drawing attention to *you?*"

"I don't know yet. I'll find out tomorrow." Tyson shrugged. "Proxy set the whole thing up. He put out the feelers and got the bite. He assured me it's been worked out."

There were a couple of raised eyebrows around the table, but nobody disagreed. Proxy's track record was almost perfect. It had become natural for these hardened operatives to place complete trust in someone they didn't know, and had never actually seen.

TWENTY-SEVEN

Doug rose in the morning, his eyes heavy with lack of sleep. Not a great way to go into the board meeting.

A parade of images from the dark hours accompanied him as he found his robe and pulled on a pair of slippers. He feebly tried to push them away, and headed downstairs for coffee.

Sherry was already in the kitchen, busy around the coffeepot. She turned when he walked in and gave him a long hug.

"I'm sorry." She rested her head on his chest. Her voice was soft. "I'm so sorry I made you upset last night. I didn't mean to be confrontational... I just get so mad at those guys sometimes. I'm so proud of you, and I just want them to appreciate what they have in you."

She gave him another squeeze, then looked up into his face. "I know you'll do the right thing at the board meeting today." She smiled and turned back to the coffeepot.

Doug straightened. He should tell her that he might be fired, should ask her advice. It wasn't fair to her otherwise. He stepped toward her and opened his mouth.

She turned from the countertop, two steaming mugs in hand. "So, sweetheart, how'd you sleep? I noticed that you'd gone downstairs."

"How'd you know I went downstairs?"

She gave him a curious look. "Well, you weren't upstairs and I assumed you were catching up on some work in your office."

"Oh—right. Actually, not just work but looking at our family budget. That kind of thing. Bank statements on-line; you know. All that stuff."

It was getting late. He needed to get a shower and get on the road. He took a few sips from the coffee mug and escaped up the stairs.

The chief operating officer was waiting for him when he got to the office. He was sitting in Doug's chair, his feet up on Doug's desk, smoking a cigar.

Doug hurried into his office and halted in surprise.

"Hey. What's up?"

The COO blew out a long breath and smoke curled around his head. "Come in and close the door."

Doug hung up his coat and glanced at his watch. "I've only got a few minutes, and I've still got a few things to do for the meeting."

"Close the door, Doug."

His voice was calm and cold, and Doug's skin crawled. He slowly closed the door.

"Sit down in that chair." The COO pointed at the chair in front of Doug's desk. "Good. Now. We need to have a little chat before the board meeting."

"Look, if Jordan put you up to this, I just want to go on record to say that—"

"There will be no going on the record here. What I have to say to you is between you and me. Nobody else will know."

His colleague calmly pressed a few keys on the computer's keyboard. "I'd like you to see something." He turned the monitor toward Doug and hit "enter." The screen went black then flickered to life. Sleazy music blared out. A video of the inside of a strip club began to play, and the camera focused in on one person in the crowd.

Doug grabbed the arms of the chair, sure he was about to vomit.

The COO watched him carefully as he pressed another series of keys.

Doug's voice came out husky. "Stop...please..."

Another scene was played, and then another. Dates and times flashed across the screen, dates and times when he was supposed to have been at work...when Sherry was in bed. Trusting Sherry. A wife he adored, who loved and trusted him implicitly.

O God, O God... Doug closed his eyes, but they flew open again when the music changed. A screen flew by, a graphic of a credit card—with Doug's name on it—being paid into an innocent-looking computer. The screen crackled to life with a date and a time, and Doug realized it was showing the wee hours of that very morning. A parade of images began—exactly as he had seen it downstairs in his office. Every scene, every picture in its ghastly, brutal explicitness. Every key stroke, captured. Every perverted desire, graphically laid bare.

O God, O God... Doug grabbed the trash can and vomited up his breakfast. What would Sherry say? She'd never understand. How could any woman understand? What would the church say? He'd lose his friends, his family. His kids. Everything he had.

O God, O God, have mercy...

A cold voice broke into his despair.

"No one has to see this, Doug." The COO was leaning back in Doug's chair again, watching as Doug cleaned off his mouth and sat back down, shaking.

"What do you want?" Doug forced his mouth to work. "Why are you doing this?"

"I'm doing this because I need you to cooperate. Because I have a lot of money at stake, and I don't intend to lose it. Because you and your stupid ideals are throwing a wrench into some carefully laid plans. And I don't intend to let that happen."

He leaned forward, lacing his fingers together on the desktop, the perfect picture of reason. "So here's what we're going to do. You're going to tell the board today that you fully approve of the Silicon Valley deal. You're going to tell them that it's the best thing for the company, and that we can't afford to lose all the money and time and effort that has already been expended on the project. You will fight off every objection, overcome every concern. They will listen to you and approve the deal."

Doug tried to sound calm. "What then?"

"You'll come back to your desk and work for the company like a good boy for as long as I tell you to. You will not quit, and you will not mention this little conversation to anyone—inside or outside the company. You're a highly skilled CFO, and I need you as long as you don't let your idealism get the best of you. I intend to ensure that that never presents a problem again. From time to time, I may ask you to approve a particular deal, green light a given project. You will squelch these nitpicky negatives you keep coming up with, look at the big picture, and stop trying to sabotage my efforts."

Doug closed his eyes again, and then tried to sit up straighter in his chair, grasping its arms for support. "You know that I can't...I won't...do anything illegal. It's one thing to approve a deal I disapprove of fiscally. It's another thing to get into an activity that could land me in jail."

The COO puffed out a few smoke rings. "Highly moral words, Doug." His eyes traveled to the now-blank computer monitor. "Funny that they come from the same man I saw on that screen, tipping a whore."

"What my personal problems are is none of your business."

"Oh, but I'm making it my business."

"Obviously." Doug clenched his jaw. "What I'm trying to say is that if I have a personal struggle that I'm dealing with, that's a matter of my conscience. It's another thing entirely to commit fraud or do something illegal. I will not do that, no matter what the consequences."

"Well, well. The man of steel comes out." The COO stared at him, a half-smile on his face.

Doug stared back, trying to relax. His colleague suddenly stood up, placing the cigar on his ashtray. He walked around to the front of the desk and perched on it, staring down at Doug. Without warning, his face relaxed into a smile.

"I'm glad I have your attention, but you're taking this far too seriously. I'm not talking about anything illegal. Not remotely close to it. I don't have the same moral qualms as you, but I don't want the cops hounding me. I stay within the law because it's too inconvenient not to. However, what I *am* talking about is you getting back to the job of being the kind of CFO that this company needs. I have my own side interests that depend on some of these deals, and I don't intend to let your idealism flush all my money down the drain."

Doug sat still for a moment, trying to force the words out. "What will you do with that…that…"

"That highly instructive video presentation has been made into a CD-ROM, which will remain in my possession indefinitely. If I find that you have talked to *anyone* about this—inside or outside the company—I will personally ensure that copies find their way to your wife, your church, your alumni association, your professional association, and anyone else that you care about."

"If all you care about is my green-lighting these deals, why the blackmail? Wouldn't it have been a lot easier for you to just fire me and hire someone to be your puppet?"

The COO stood to his full height. Doug slowly stood as well, waiting.

"It might have been easier, but it would've created too many complications. Jordan likes you; the board likes you. You've done a lot to get the company to where it is today. You have a lot of skills that cannot be easily replaced. It's in my best interest to protect my interests, and your presence is one key to that."

"What if I decide to leave?"

"Oh, didn't I make that clear? Unless someone else fires you, consider yourself part of the furniture for the indefinite future."

There was a sharp knock on the door. Doug swung around and stared at the computer monitor. It was dark. Doug reached across the desk and turned it away from the door, seething at the smirk on the COO's face.

There was another knock, and Jordan suddenly poked his head in, his face annoyed.

"Doug?" His eyebrows lifted in surprise when he saw the two men in the room. "The board is waiting for you both. What's keeping you?"

Doug forced his tongue to work, forced some semblance of normalcy.

"Sorry. Did Mary get the briefing books—"

"Of course she did. They've already been passed out. Everyone's waiting for you. Come on."

Doug finally began to move, and Jordan made "hurry up" motions with his hands. Doug dimly sensed the COO following as they hurried around corners. Jordan walked next to Doug and lowered his voice.

"I know you're set in your ways, Doug, but I'm asking you one more time to reconsider your position on the Silicon Valley deal. Even if you could be *neutral* for the deal rather than against it, that would help."

Doug slowed to a stop outside the conference room. He turned and looked Jordan full in the face, but saw only agitation. Doug glanced back at the COO and saw his face darken with threat.

"Jordan, you should know that I have reconsidered my position. I may have been too hasty in my criticism."

A flicker of surprise flashed across his boss's face, quickly replaced by delight. "Wonderful! That's all I can ask. Well, let's see what they say."

Several hours later, Tyson took another call in his island paradise. The deal was a go and not a moment too soon. Tyson looked at his watch and called his driver.

The car took him to a boat and a fairly smooth thirty-minute ride. From there he went on foot to a bustling five-star hotel and found the right elevator. He rode it down to the subbasement, stood in the corner of an abandoned kitchen area, and waited. Proxy's instructions had been specific.

There was no one down here; the corridors were deserted. The restaurant equipment was dated and covered with a fine layer of dust. Tyson could hear the distant rattle and hum of a busy kitchen above his head, but this level appeared to be completely unused.

It was a brilliant place to rendezvous. There was no way that any tail could follow without being seen or heard, and it would be difficult for a bug or tracer to penetrate so far below ground.

Within five minutes, two men appeared from nowhere. Their eyes were hard and they carried guns. They wore western clothing, but when one man spoke, it was with a thick accent.

"What are you doing here?"

"I'm sorry. This is a big hotel, and I appear to have lost my way. I'm looking for Mr. Mohammed."

"And who are you?"

"My cousin is an old friend of his. He suggested that we meet."

The two men lowered their weapons, but their faces remained watchful. The first one parked his gun in a holster under his jacket.

"Please to follow me."

The little group set off down the echoing corridors, which seemed to stretch forever. From time to time, they would reach a locked, rust-encrusted metal door, which would open smoothly to the guard's key and reveal another set of passageways beyond. The corridors were poorly lit and damp in several places.

After walking for about five minutes, they reached another subbasement lobby. A set of storage rooms were spaced along the passageway, facing a service elevator. The two men ushered Tyson into a small storage room lined with linens on ranks of shelves.

They closed the door behind them, blocking out the light. No one said anything.

After a long moment, Tyson heard an indecipherable noise and realized that the wall that had been behind the doorway was opening, shelves and all. It swung outward like a regular door and light flooded in.

He stepped into the light, and was instantly pushed up against a wall, the barrel of a machine gun pressed to his head.

He let out an alarmed exclamation, and heard a soft chuckle from the room beyond. Someone gave a short command in a foreign language—Arabic?—and Tyson felt rough hands searching him, as another person scanned him with an electronic device.

Just as quickly, he was released. He tried to catch his breath and still his heart's pounding.

"I am sorry."

Tyson turned to see a small, olive-skinned man approaching. He spoke with a trace of a British accent.

"I apologize for the rude treatment, but we had to be sure you were not bugged, or carrying anything dangerous to us."

Tyson tried to look indignant. "I wouldn't—"

"Ach." The man interrupted him with a wave of his hand. "You might be bugged and not even know it. We had to be sure. Please, sit down."

He led the way to a small conference table ringed with comfortable chairs. There were lush hangings on the wall, and the room was lined with silk flowers and greenery. An alcove in the corner hinted at a kitchen area beyond. The room was carpeted and the air smelled fresh.

Tyson took a seat, glancing around. "Quite a setup you have here."

The small man smiled. "It has proven useful."

"Are you Mr.…Mohammed?"

"You may call me that, yes." He turned and said something in Arabic to one of the guards, who disappeared into the kitchen and returned with a pitcher and glasses.

"Would you like some orange juice?" Mohammed said.

Tyson almost laughed. "Uh—sure."

Mohammed's gaze was serious. "It is the only drink I can offer you. We do not take alcohol, of course."

The guard poured two glasses and retreated. They were left alone.

Mohammed studied Tyson for a moment. "Tell me about yourself, please. You come highly recommended, but I like to know a little about the person I am dealing with."

Tyson gave the man a quick overview. Tufts undergrad, Wharton MBA, top-tier consulting…and then Proxy recruited him.

Mohammed interrupted, his eyes bright. "And do you know your Mr. Proxy well?"

"I'm afraid I cannot discuss him. That is his request. I'm sure you understand."

"I do." There was no trace of disappointment. "Most wise. Well, let us begin."

Mohammed stood and began a slow circuit around the room, as if the motion helped him form the words.

"I represent, as you know, a government that has a great interest in Proxy's proposal. We have reviewed your initial offer, and I have been given authority to negotiate programs and financial terms on their behalf. Subject to their final approval, of course."

Tyson nodded, as Mohammed continued.

"You, of course, have been authorized by Proxy to do the same. So let us not waste time. No one can hear us here. And no one is watching. We cannot have many such meetings, so let us discuss the choices you have presented to us."

"First, you must agree to one nonnegotiable condition," Tyson said. "If the condition is met, then we can continue our discussion. If you cannot agree, then I'm afraid this conversation must end and we will adjourn until your backers are able to reach agreement."

Mohammed's eyes narrowed in surprise. "And the condition?"

"Proxy must have a full 50 percent of our payment up front, nonrefundable, deposited in the financial institution of his choosing within one week of this meeting."

"But how can this be? This project will take some time. Months, even one or two years in some cases. You will not have delivered anything within one week."

"Our greatest risks will be taken during the setup phase, before a single project is completed. Our first payment is for the setup, whether or not the program is instituted and whether or not the desired outcome can be delivered. All sorts of things can go wrong, and we are taking all the risk on the front end."

The small man resumed his circuit of the room, nodding. "I cannot promise anything but—"

Tyson stood. "If you cannot promise anything, Mr. Mohammed, then I'm afraid this conversation must be postponed until a later date."

Mohammed stopped a few feet away and crossed his arms. He looked down at the floor, appearing to take his time thinking the demand through.

Tyson felt a surge of confidence. It was an act. He would never have been sent into this meeting without the full ability and authority to negotiate such details.

After a long moment, he looked up at Tyson. "Agreed, then. Fifty percent, non-refundable, in one week."

"Thank you, Mr. Mohammed. Now, let's get down to business. What project would you like to discuss first?"

His contact's eyes gleamed. "Next year. Superbowl Sunday."

TWENTY-EIGHT

The mall clamor stirred Ronnie's senses as she and Tiffany left one store and walked on, scanning the window displays. Ronnie had already spent more money on clothes in one day than she had in the past year, and yet hadn't exhausted the amount she'd saved from the last few weeks of dancing. And that was after paying her monthly bills, finishing her last GED payment, helping her mother with some medical expenses, and sending Georgia State her advance tuition payment.

She could get into this.

"Oh, you'll love this place!" Tiffany pulled her through the entrance of a trendy boutique.

Ronnie protested, but paused by a display rack, running her fingers over the soft silk of a nearby dress. "Really, Tiff, don't you think I have enough for now?"

"This isn't the part of the store I was talking about. Come on."

Tiffany wound her way to the back of the store and spoke quietly to the woman at the counter, who smiled and gestured toward a closed door.

Tiffany grabbed Ronnie's arm. "Come on, slowpoke. Only one person can use it at a time, so let's get in there before someone else does."

Ronnie hung back. "What—"

"You are such a party pooper. Just go with the flow and stop asking so many questions!"

She propelled Ronnie through the door and flipped on the light.

Ronnie stood in a good-sized room lined with mirrors on one side and shelves and drawers on the other. Directly in front of them a procession of mannequins displayed different lingerie styles.

Tiffany closed and locked the door behind them. "This is one of the few stores you can actually buy the kind of dancers' lingerie we need. You've got your outerwear; now you need the fun stuff!"

Ronnie tried to relax as Tiffany chattered on about what she'd recommend, forcing herself to act nonchalant as Tiffany prodded her to try on various items.

The lights were stark and glaring, not like the dark stage-show environment, and she was with an old friend with whom she'd shared junior high slumber parties, braces, and childhood broken hearts. It was easier to wear—and take off—these racy outfits when she was putting on an act, a persona, especially now that everyone was calling her by her new stage name, Macy.

Ronnie suddenly stopped and looked up. "You know something, Tiff. I've got to be honest. It is *really* awkward doing this with you in the room!"

Tiffany gave a start of surprise, then laughed. "I guess I can see that. I'll wait outside."

Ten minutes later, Ronnie left the store with her cheeks pink but head held high, a new bag dangling from her hand.

"You got some mail, Linda!" Angela Dugan came back into the house balancing a short stack of bills and magazines. She poked her head into the guest bedroom and waved an envelope. "Looks like another one from your daughter."

Linda Hanover tore open the envelope and a check fell out. She picked it up and stared at it, her mouth half open.

"What is it?" Angela was hovering in the doorway, curious.

"She sent me another check. For a thousand dollars! That'll finish paying off the hospital bill."

"Wow." Angela walked over to the bed and looked over Linda's shoulder. "That's a good daughter."

"But I don't know how she can afford it. I don't want her to put herself at risk, helping her old mom."

Her host laughed a little. "Don't worry so much. It's something to be thankful for! Remember, we prayed that God would make a way to pay those medical bills."

"Yeah, but—"

"Linda." Angela sat down and took Linda's hands in hers. "I'm sure Ronnie is fine with it, or she wouldn't have sent the money. And this provides a way to pay the hospital by the date the full amount was due. Isn't that *amazing?*"

"I guess so…"

"It's amazing." Angela gave a firm nod and stood back up. "God watches over our every need."

"It does seem coincidental, doesn't it?"

"There's no such thing as coincidence. God has everything in His control. Listen, why don't you come to church with us tonight? I'm sure pastor would love to hear about this answer to prayer, and the others have wanted to meet you."

"Well…okay. I guess I owe it to you."

Angela sat back down on her guest's bed. "Linda, you don't owe me anything."

"How can you say that?" Linda stared at her in astonishment. "You've taken me into your home! You've given me food and a place to sleep and clothes. I thought I was going to have to go to a shelter or something, but you've kept me safe from Seth, and given money for the doctors—even though I know you have as little extra as I do. How can you say I don't owe you anything? Of course I do. You and your family are amazing! Who else would do such a thing for a total stranger?"

"You're right that it's pretty unusual to take a stranger in," Angela said. "But Jesus said 'Whoever helps one of the least of these, my brothers or sisters, does it as if they are helping me.' How can we *not* help you, when Jesus said that it's like helping Him?"

Linda frowned at the blanket on her bed and sighed. "But I'm nobody. I don't deserve the help. You know it and I know it, and—uh—Jesus knows it. You heard it all at the hospital." She flopped forward, burying her face in the blanket. "What I allowed my own daughter to go through because I cared more about saving myself than saving her. I don't deserve your help. I deserve Seth; I deserve what he gave me."

"Don't say that! No one should be treated like that. Look, it's not whether you deserve the help or not; it's that God loves you, and He has asked us to love you, too."

The voice was muffled in the bedclothes. "But I'm not a good enough person."

"Ah." Angela felt a smile cross her face. "I see. Well, let me ask you something. When you die, what do you think determines whether you'll go to heaven?"

Linda sat back up, a confused expression on her face. "Well...just...whether the good things I did outweighed the bad things. And I have done good things, you know. I have. I stayed home with Ronnie all those years instead of working like I wanted to, 'cause I knew it was better for her. Especially with the divorces." Her face crumpled. "But I guess the divorces count against me, don't they?"

"Oh, Linda." Angela reached over and hugged her guest. She felt tears prickling her eyes as she sat back and stared into the childlike gaze. "I have some wonderful news for you. All that you've ever thought about how to be accepted by God is wrong. It has nothing to do with whether you've done enough good things to outweigh the bad. No one can earn their way into heaven."

"But I thought—"

"I know what you thought. It's a common mistake. We so much want to be in control; we somehow think that if we can be good enough, God owes it to us. But the Bible says that none of us can ever be good enough. Who do you think has been the best, kindest, most giving, most wonderful person in recent years?"

"Uh—Mother Teresa, probably."

"Well, despite all the amazing, good things she did, not even Mother Teresa was good enough to get into heaven."

Linda's eyes grew wide. "You mean she's not in heaven? Then who on earth can—"

"Oh, I'm sure she's in heaven. But what Mother Teresa knew was that God accepted her because she accepted His son, Jesus. God sent His only son into the world because God knew that none of us could ever be good enough. So Jesus came to live a perfect life—the only perfect person in history—and then die for us to take the punishment for all the bad things we will ever do. Mother Teresa did the wonderful things she did, caring for some of the poorest, most downtrodden people in the world, because she knew and loved Jesus so much that she couldn't *not* do those things. Because of what Jesus had done for her, God had saved her from hell, and she was overflowing with His love for the world."

Linda sat very still, her face confused. "But she deserved to go to heaven, didn't she? How could God have sent her to...to hell? She was such a good person. It wouldn't have been fair."

"I know this is hard to understand, but our idea of fairness and God's are very different. And it's not like God is somehow less fair than we are! After all, God subjected Himself to the most unfair thing in the history of the universe; sending His perfect Son to pay the penalty for our sins. That pretty much trumps any of our ideas of fairness, don't you think?

"And also, He created the universe and trillions of stars with a simple word of His power, and He created every atom in your body. If we could fully grasp God's mind and ways, we'd be God, wouldn't we? The Bible says that God is pure holiness—such wonderful, dreadful holiness that it would strike people dead just to catch a glimpse of Him—and since none of us are that perfect, that holy, we have to have someone be a mediator for us. Someone who *is* that perfect, that holy, who can bring us into God's presence, so we can live with Him forever."

A wonder was growing in Linda's eyes. She said the uncomfortable word. "Jesus."

"Right. Jesus." Angela again found tears near the surface. "God sent His only Son to earth to be born as a human baby and live among us. He was so perfect, so holy, that the self-righteous religious leaders of the day couldn't stand it and they killed Him. But Jesus allowed Himself to be brutally killed like that to take the punishment for all the bad things we've done. The Bible says 'the price for sin is death'—eternal death—and Jesus paid that price for us. Then He rose from the dead three days later, showing that He had conquered that sin!"

Angela reached over and took Linda's hand. "All the awful things you've done—

even those I don't know about—are washed away by Jesus' death and resurrection. God knows you'll never be good enough. All you have to do is believe what Jesus did for you, and accept His sacrifice for you, and you'll be with God forever. Invite Jesus into your heart, and make a commitment to live for Him, and it'll be as if you were born brand-new into the family of God. You'll be a new creation—all the old sin and heartache and depravity will be washed away."

"I want...I want to—"

"Well, let's do it right here."

"No." Linda sat up straight, then jumped off the bed, a strange light in her eyes. "I want to do this at your church. Can we go? Now? Can we?"

Angela hesitated, then stood up. "I don't see any reason why not. The Wednesday night service starts in half an hour anyway."

Linda sat ramrod straight all the way to the church. She felt as if she stood poised on the end of the highest diving board on earth, with the deepest unknown waters below.

She sat stock-still through the service, perched on the end of the last pew, hardly hearing the words the pastor said, staring into the deep blue. Could she do it? How could she not? Everything Angela had said had pierced her heart, and she could hear a Voice calling her. Calling her as a father would call to his child, to take the leap into the deep. Calling her to let go of her own life, to trust in the one who made her, who loved her, who had been longing for her for all eternity.

The pastor's voice grew louder. "Some of you here tonight may not have had an earthly father you could trust, but you can trust the Lord, the perfect, loving Father. He wants you to come forward tonight to accept His love..."

Linda closed her eyes, reeling on the high dive.

Trust Me, beloved.

She stood up, drawn like a magnet toward the cross at the front of the church, faster, and faster, the deep waters dark and mysterious and beckoning. She sensed Angela standing to follow her, sensed a murmuring from the pews. She didn't care what they knew about her, didn't care what they thought. Her eyes were fixed on the cross.

She reached the front and fell to her knees. And she jumped. Words came tumbling out of her, words pleading for forgiveness, words mingled with sobs, great tears that splashed into the deep and were swallowed up in the deepest most profound love. She dropped like a stone...and landed in His strong and loving arms.

She fell to her face. All around her she could feel strong and loving arms. They held her and rocked her and welcomed her into the family of God.

TWENTY-NINE

Ronnie circled the club, prowling, looking for her next customer. Some of the other girls were back in the dressing room, gossiping, drinking, and reapplying their makeup, but she—as usual—was on the floor all night. Underneath a glittery red dress, her garter was bulging with bills.

She passed Tiffany and winked. Tiffany pulled her off to the side, her voice low. "How you doing tonight?"

Ronnie pulled her slit skirt aside just enough so Tiffany could see her garter.

Tiffany whistled through her teeth, then flashed a wicked grin and did the same thing, showing off far more cash. She laughed at Ronnie's expression.

"You may be the newest hot thing, babe, but I'm still the top moneymaker, and don't you forget it."

Ronnie narrowed her eyes, her voice deadpan. "Just wait another few weeks and you'll have to be content with being number two. Eat my dust, Sasha."

Tiffany gave Ronnie her best mean look, and then both girls broke up in giggles.

The two friends separated, and Ronnie approached a customer who was all alone at a table. She leaned toward him, lowering her voice, putting on a sultry edge.

"You're here late tonight."

The man gestured her closer, his movements sloppy. "It's a special occasion, Macy. Special occasion." He held up two twenties, waving them in time to the pounding beat of the stage music. "I want a birthday treat."

"Oh, I think I can accommodate you, baby."

Ronnie stepped back and listened for a good starting beat, then went into her act. She knew he was probably a workman without a lot of money, but she wanted what he had and she knew all the tricks to get it out of him. It was all about making a man think she wanted him.

She kept up the act and turned her mind from the present when—as with every customer—the unshaven man began staring her up and down from just two feet away. She kept her gaze sultry, her body in motion, and her mind fixed on the two twenties in his hand. But it never quite blocked out the creepy feel of his gaze.

She knew he was probably spending his mortgage or his baby's milk money on her, and she didn't care. He was using her to get what he wanted, and it was an even trade.

You okay, boss?"

Doug Turner jerked his head up. His secretary was standing in the doorway, a concerned expression on her face. That expression had been an almost permanent fixture the last few weeks.

"Yeah, sure, Mary. Why?"

"Well...didn't the COO just leave? You usually have a pile of action items for me when you come out of a closed-door meeting with him or Jordan, but you haven't given me anything today. Just wondering if there was something I could get started on before I left for the night."

"Oh. No. Thanks. He was just checking in on something. No action items as a result."

Mary brightened. "Well, that's good then, isn't it?"

No, it's not. Doug could feel his pulse starting to race. He gave a halfhearted nod and a smile and shuffled a few papers on his desk.

"Why don't you knock off, Mary? I think we're all done for the evening."

"If you're sure."

"I've got to get going anyway. Sherry's having some friends over for dinner."

"Well, good. Have fun."

Doug nodded again and turned away.

He drove out of the security gates feeling he had escaped alive from a lion's den. But the lions—or lion—would still be there tomorrow.

The traffic on the highway stalled his progress home, and before he knew it, *the* exit was upon him, staring at him, an easy turn in the bumper-to-bumper right lane. He merged into a middle lane and drove past the exit ramp, trying to stifle the images that rose unbidden to his mind.

Until late tonight, maybe...

Doug forced himself to think about Genna and Brandon, about what their gleeful welcome would be when he came home.

An image.

Don't think about that.

Another image.

Stop it. Look at the clock, put on the Christian station.

Another image. *You could sneak out tonight after Sherry's in bed. She'd never know.*

Stop it. Sherry would know.

Come on. At least go on that site you found yesterday. You know you want to.

There was no answer to that. He did want to. Did and didn't at the same time. He pictured himself sneaking downstairs to his computer and an excited knot formed in his stomach.

If I'm already being blackmailed for it, what's the point of resisting?

He growled and clutched the steering wheel tighter.

Lord, help me.

By the time the traffic let up, Doug felt as if his head was ready to explode. He turned off the highway, drove a few miles through the back roads, and pulled into his street.

Eric and Lisa Elliott's van was already parked in their driveway.

Oh, great. Now I'll be in trouble with Sherry on top of everything else.

He parked on the street and strode up the driveway, muttering to himself. At the garage door into the kitchen, he forced a smile onto his face, and turned the handle.

After all the plates had been cleared, the kids ran off to play in the basement, and the wives ventured into the messy kitchen to clean up. Eric beckoned Doug out of the dining room and into Doug's nearby office.

Doug followed, curious.

Eric pulled the door half-shut behind them, then turned to face his friend. "What's going on?"

"What do you mean?"

Eric gave Doug a long look. "Something's eating at you, man. This whole month, you've been tense as a two-by-four. You hardly talk at home group anymore, and your prayer requests are always things for the kids or your sick Aunt Martha. Never for you. But whatever's eating at you isn't getting better."

Doug tried to give a casual laugh, waving the concern away. "Oh, it's just work stuff. You know how it is."

Eric crossed his arms. "What work stuff? What's going on?"

"Well, uh…well, I'm just having a problem with one of my bosses. That's all."

"What sort of problem?"

"Good grief, man! Are you the Grand Inquisitor now?" He turned on his heel and walked out of the office. "It's no big deal. I just don't want to think about it now that I'm home. This is supposed to be a party!"

☆ ☆ ☆

Sherry hustled down the hall in a robe, her hair in curlers, toward the sound of a full-blown cat fight. Why did *she* always have to be the enforcer these days?

"Kids!" She poked her head into Brandon's room, interrupting the two half-dressed squabbling children. She grabbed each one by an arm, giving them a little shake. "Stop that! What a way to start the Lord's day!"

"She started it!" Brandon whined. "She wiped a booger on me!"

Sherry tried to keep a straight face and turned to Genna. "Did you do that, young lady?"

"I did not start it, Mommy! He used my hair bow to hang Little Michelle! See?"

Sherry looked where she pointed. Genna's favorite doll was on the end of a pink satin noose, swinging from Brandon's upper bunk.

"Brandon!"

"But I only did it because she—"

"That's it, kids! You've been fighting all weekend, and I'm tired of it! No television this week."

"But, Mom!'

"But the dinosaur show is on tonight!"

Sherry held up a hand. "No television this week. That's the end of it. And I want you both to apologize to each other this minute. This is ridiculous."

She stood there, waiting. "Brandon?"

He turned toward his sister and sighed. "Sorry I hung Little Michelle. That was mean."

Genna looked down. "I'm sorry I wiped a booger on you."

"Okay. Thank you." Sherry hugged them both.

Whoever said that people are inherently good never had small children.

"Kids, we leave for church in ten minutes. You'd better hustle." She grabbed a shirt for Brandon out of the closet. "Here. This goes with your khakis. Genna…." She pulled the bow from around the doll's neck and deftly tied it in her daughter's hair. "There. Go get your shoes and socks on. I want you both downstairs waiting in the kitchen in five minutes."

"Yes, Mommy."

Sherry half ran back down the hall and into their bedroom.

Doug was sitting on the bed, fully dressed and tying his shoes. He looked up as she hustled in.

"Wow, you're not ready yet?"

"Aaaaargh!" She went for his throat, only half-joking. "Why didn't you come help me!"

"Are you kidding? Boogers and hanging dolls? I wasn't getting in the middle of that one!" He stood, grabbed her around the waist, and smiled. "I'm sorry, hon. I'll corral the kids and make sure their stuff is ready. We'll be in the car waiting for you, whenever you're done."

"Humph." Sherry pulled off her robe and ran into her walk-in closet. She tried to stay irritated, but found that she couldn't. How could she be mad when her husband smiled at her like that?

She pulled on a simple dress—the only thing she didn't need to iron—and ran into the bathroom, hurrying to undo her curlers. She hollered in the general direction of the hall.

"Doug, don't forget their Bible verse sheets! They need to turn them in today!"

A distant holler back. "Where are they?"

"Genna's is on her dresser. I don't know where Brandon's is. You'll have to find it!"

There was a pause. "Uh—okay."

Sherry picked up a brush and pulled at her hair. She was always the one that got the kids ready, got them to do their homework, organized their belongings. Doug probably didn't know where half their stuff was. He would just have to learn.

Five minutes later, juggling her Bible, her purse, and her makeup kit, Sherry ran down the stairs, through the empty kitchen, and out the garage door. She collapsed in the front seat of the van, and Doug turned, his face tight, backing at high speed down the driveway.

"What?" Sherry said. "What's wrong?"

"We're late."

"Well, you could've helped with the kids, you know! When you were basically ready and I wasn't, why didn't you go deal with them instead of me?"

"You never asked. You just ran and did it. I figured why should both of us get involved and make us even later?"

"Why should I have to ask? They're your kids, too, you know! You saw how unready I was…you should've stopped me and told me you'd do it so I could get ready!"

Doug clenched his jaw and didn't respond. Sherry turned her face and looked resolutely out the window. Sundays were always the worst morning of the week.

They drove for a few miles in silence, turning onto Tenth Street and speeding toward the church.

"By the way, I have to do some work today," Doug said, his voice a deliberate calm. "I'll go into the office later, after dinner, so we can spend the day together."

"Fine." Sherry didn't look over.

They pulled into the parking lot and climbed out of the car; a ragged little group hurrying silently toward the church building, where the strains of joyful singing could already be heard.

The hubbub in the church lobby after the service was loud and cheerful, as people mingled in the common area. Eric came up and slapped Doug on the back.

"The gang's going to McDonald's for lunch. Wanna come?"

"Sure." Doug tried to find Sherry amidst the madness. "I guess. I should ask Sherry…"

"No rush. Lots of folks in the home group are coming. We'll just meet over there in about ten, fifteen minutes."

"Sure, sure." Doug corralled Brandon as he ran by, chasing another boy. "Hey! Where's Mom?"

"Over there, Dad." Brandon pointed. Sherry was deep in conversation with Melanie and her husband.

Doug headed that direction and touched his wife on the shoulder.

She turned. "Oh, I'm glad you found us. Melanie was just asking whether you'd be able to head up the youth retreat again this spring?" Sherry gave him a long look, trying to convey something with her eyes.

Doug couldn't tell what it was. He turned to Melanie. "Uh, thanks. I hadn't given it much thought…"

"Well, didn't you get the e-mail we sent you last week, dear?"

"Come to think of it, I guess I did see your request. I've just been so busy—"

"Well, please think about it, Doug. And if you could get back to us soon, that would be good. We need to get started."

Melanie linked her arm through her husband's and lowered her voice. "Pastor was thinking maybe one of the other men on the youth team could do it this year, but frankly I hear that the one he's considering is having a bit of trouble at home. He and his wife are apparently in *counseling*. We need a good role model for our young people. Someone solid, with a stable marriage. Like you. So please do agree. It won't be that much of a time commitment."

Doug caught Sherry's frosty glance and turned back to Melanie.

"You know, I really appreciate the offer. But even if it's not that much time, it may be too much for me this year. It's been really crazy at work."

"Well, but, dear, where are your priorities? Surely, wouldn't the youth of the church be worth taking a little time off? Surely, they are more important?"

Sherry took Doug's arm, the same way Melanie held that of her husband. She gave the woman a sweet smile. "Melanie, I think what Doug is trying to say is that his family is even more important to him than the youth of the church. I think it's great that he's prioritizing me and the kids ahead of this project."

Melanie frowned. "Well, yes of course, dear. But you already have a stable family life. These kids need to see good role models. You know, some of these children actually come from broken homes, blended families, where the mother and father are divorced. They need to see people like you in leadership."

Doug could feel Sherry's fingers digging into his arm. He gave Melanie and her husband a short smile. "You know that I love these kids, and I'll gladly continue to serve on the youth ministry team. But this year, I don't think I'm able to commit to leading the retreat. The time commitment just wouldn't be fair to my family at this time."

"Well, dear, okay. But our next choice might just have to be the couple who is in counseling. And I don't know if it's *appropriate* to have someone with an unstable marriage in leadership."

Doug cocked an eyebrow. "Well, just because they're in counseling doesn't mean they have an unstable marriage, does it?"

"Of course that's what it means. That's the whole point of counseling, I would think."

Sherry spoke up, and Doug could tell she was trying hard to keep her voice even. "Perhaps they have a *better* marriage because they're willing to go into counseling to improve it. I know of a number of couples who look great on the outside, but could probably use some counseling if there wasn't such a stigma attached."

Melanie was about to speak, when another woman approached her with a question. Doug and Sherry politely excused themselves. Doug held tight to his wife's hand as they corralled the kids and headed for the car.

Sherry loaded the kids in the van, then gave Doug a big hug and held him tight for a long moment.

"Thank you. Thank you for not taking that project."

Doug put his arms around his wife, pressing her cheek into his chest, breathing in the fresh scent of her hair. "I love you, Sherry."

"I love you, too, Doug."

He held her for a long minute, then released her, aware of curious glances from the others streaming into the parking lot. He smiled. "Let's go to lunch."

The McDonald's near the church was large, colorful, and very noisy. The kids gulped their food and ran off to explore the playground equipment—for the hundredth time—while the adults settled in for a leisurely lunch.

Doug and Sherry had arrived last and were seated at the end of a long table, chatting with the people nearest them.

At the other end of the noisy table, one of the other home group members asked what Eric and Lisa were doing that evening. Eric made a face.

"I'm actually getting together with a friend from college, to go see some awful art-house movie." He gave an exaggerated shudder. "This guy's a real skeptic; a classic arty, depressed, agnostic kind of guy. I try to get together with him every couple of months, as I'm probably the only Christian he knows. But he always chooses these *awful* movies. We're going to the late show at some independent theater down the other end of Tenth Street."

Doug's mind was wandering. Next to him, Sherry and another wife were comparing the latest ideas in window treatments. He pictured the pile of work on his desk. He had so much to do; he'd be at the office until close to midnight.

And what about after midnight...?

He closed his eyes as the unbidden thought rose in his mind. He tried to push it away, but it was there. A stark, inexorable choice. He tried to reengage in the conversation flowing around his end of the table, but *it* was still there. And in his head, the clock began to race toward midnight.

THIRTY

Doug Turner leaned down and gave Sherry a kiss. "Don't wait up for me, hon. I'll probably be at the office until the wee hours."

Doug ruffled the kids' hair, grabbed his briefcase, and scooted out the door, leaving the rest of the family at the dinner table. Once he was on the road toward the office in the gathering twilight, he reflected on his casual lie. How smoothly he had set up the late-night sin he knew he would not avoid.

He was weary of fighting. It was easier to just set up the excuse in advance and let what would happen, happen. If he could avoid the temptation when his car reached the exit later that night, fine. If not…

Doug sighed. Who was he kidding?

Eric Elliott kissed his wife good-bye at the kitchen sink, glancing out the darkened window. "Don't wait up, sweetheart. It's a late movie, and Rocko and I will probably get some coffee afterwards. I'll try not to wake you up when I come in."

Lisa smiled at her husband. "Have fun. Uh—if you can."

"Yeah." Eric grimaced. "This movie looks pretty depressing, but it'll probably stir stuff up and give me a good opening for our talk afterward."

"That's all that matters."

Eric gave her a big hug and reached around to pinch her bottom. "That's my girl."

"Hey!" Lisa swatted him with a dish towel. "Get out of here, you big lech."

"You have no idea." He pulled her close. "Maybe I *will* wake you up when I get in."

Lisa winked at him. "Feel free. I'll be dreaming about you anyway."

"Okay, stop it!" Eric pushed her away, laughing. "Stop it or I'm never going to leave!" He turned and yelled toward the den, where he could hear the television blaring. "G'night kids! Time to do your homework!"

There was a pause. "Night, Dad!"

"Do your homework! Turn off the TV!"

He could hear a couple of groans, then the kids came straggling out of the den and up the stairs.

Eric winked at Lisa and headed out the door. As he drove out of his neighborhood and toward a less-familiar section of town, he prayed that God would steel him against the inevitable crud he would let into his mind during the movie that night. He sighed. Was it even worth going just to have another discussion with a friend who had heard it all before? Why had the Lord so specifically nudged him to go?

He took the highway and got off at the designated exit, then drove quickly past the windowless, burgundy-and-silver building with the neon sign that lured so many travelers off the highway.

He prayed for protection over his mind and spirit, and prayed for those inside. He'd gone into a club like that several times in college, and the images haunted him still. He drove quickly past the club, searching for the small movie theater his friend assured him was there somewhere.

He found the theater just a short distance away and got out of his car. He saw a young woman leave the club, a garment bag over her arm.

Eric wanted to stare, and several images from years ago rose in his mind. He forced himself to turn his back to the young woman, to the neon lights, and prayed for the Lord's help in taking his thoughts captive. Then he hurried toward the theater, looking for his friend.

Doug pulled into the packed parking lot and reached into his glove compartment. Feeling rather foolish, he pulled out the fake moustache, fake glasses, and shapeless fishing hat he had used ever since the COO had confronted him. For several days, distraught over the graphic blackmail video, he had managed to stay away from the computer, away from the club. But within a week, resisting became a torture. So he had improvised.

He stepped out of his car and hurried into the sprawling building, his mind warring between self-justification and despair.

The credits rolled against a black screen, and another edgy song with indecipherable, wailing lyrics began to blast over the loudspeakers.

Eric waited until his friend stood and stretched, then joined him, merging with throngs of people shuffling past the darkened rows toward a weak exit sign.

The feeling of emptiness, of hopelessness in that place was almost palpable.

Eric's heart hurt. These people needed Jesus so much. God would fill their void with life and hope. But what chance was there if the pulpit they chose was the sort of movie he had just watched, the songs he had just heard? It would not surprise him, once he got to heaven, to learn that Satan himself had had a hand in crafting those.

They stepped out into the midnight breeze, and Eric's friend gestured toward the next-door coffee shop. Eric nodded and prayed that he would have the right words to say.

An hour later, his friend thanked him for his time and left, saying he had a big audition in the morning. Eric wished him well, and went up to the counter for another coffee. It was way too late, and he had a bit of a drive to get back home.

Doug looked at his watch, yawning, as he stepped outside the club and pulled his coat up by his ears. There was a bustling coffee shop across the way, and he had to get some or he'd fall asleep at the wheel.

He hopped in his car and parked right out front of the little coffee bar, hurrying in with his head bent under his fishing cap, pushing against the sharp night wind. He took one step toward the counter where a man waited for his order, and froze.

Eric turned, the warm cup cradled in his hands, and brushed past a customer standing still in the doorway. He put a hand on the door, but it wouldn't budge. He pushed again, harder, and could feel his tiredness and irritation starting to rise. They must have locked the door while he was sitting there with his friend.

No... That other man had just come in. He turned, glancing at the new customer's profile. Suddenly, the oddest sensation crawled up his spine. A sense of certainty that made no sense. A feeling that the Lord was nudging him forward, to take the risky step. He took another look at the man, now standing rigidly at the counter, giving his order in a hoarse voice.

Eric took a step back toward the counter. "Doug?"

The man made busy about paying the cashier and didn't move.

Eric took another step, his voice stronger, more certain. "Doug."

The customer turned, his frame rigid, his mouth a thin-pressed line under an unfamiliar mustache. Eric took in the strange disguise on his friend's face, and suddenly he knew.

Doug sighed and pulled off the hat. "Hi, Eric."

Eric gave him a long, searching look. Then he pulled a chair out from a nearby table. "I think we should sit down."

"Uh, no…no." Doug shook his head. "I need to get home. Sherry will be wondering…"

Eric pointed at the chair. "Sit down, Doug."

"So what is the status of the infrastructure strategy?"

Tyson listened with half an ear, weary of Mr. Mohammed's questions. Tyson had been working eighteen-hour days and was ready to crash for the night, but it was bright morning at Mohammed's command center and he was only halfway through his list.

"Did I lose you?"

Tyson jerked back to attention. "No, no, I'm here. I was just looking at some data sheets with that information." He'd slip up if he wasn't careful. And Mohammed would notice. He stood, his secure phone in hand, hoping to get the blood moving. "The infrastructure project looks promising, though not certain. We have compromised a satellite system that will allow us to input false signals without detection—at least for a time. So when the primary plan is triggered, we may also have a window for disruption of emergency responders. It's a good avenue for your backers to pursue."

"And other areas?"

"The other areas are all just possibilities at this point."

The cultured voice was intense. "My backers want *systemic* disruption."

"I understand, sir, but remember the terms of our agreement." Tyson clenched the phone tighter. "Until they commit to half the cost of that project, we are unable to move forward."

Tyson heard a long pause on the other end of the line. Despite his fatigue, he grinned to himself. Mr. Mohammed's backers were probably already putting pressure on him to get more for their money. They were used to dealing with people who shared their ideology, who were willing to chip in for the cause. Well, too bad. They had their ideology; he had his. And his had to do with money—lots of it.

The coffee shop was emptying. Eric's coffee was half-drunk, but Doug's was barely touched.

Eric's mind was whirling. If Doug was telling the truth about the COO at his office, this was an even bigger thing than a Christian husband fighting sexual temptation. But that was still the first thing that had to be addressed.

"So that's the reason for the disguise," Doug said. "I can't seem to stop it, but I couldn't bear to give them more ammunition. I figured a disguise would solve the problem."

Eric gave a short laugh. "It worked, too. I almost didn't recognize you."

Doug shifted uncomfortably in his seat, looking at his watch. "I should get home."

"Have you told Sherry?"

"No! It would kill her. I can't tell her."

There was a long pause, then Eric looked Doug in the eye. "In a way, you've broken the covenant with your wife. You must tell her, and you must make it right."

Doug's face crumbled, and Eric thought he was going to cry.

"I can't, Eric, I can't. She'll be so hurt. She's been struggling so much with her self-image ever since the kids were born…it would kill her… I can't. I *can't!*"

"I'm sure there are a lot of things to consider, Doug—consequences you'll have to deal with. But it's not just Sherry that I'm thinking of. I'm thinking of *you*. You have a problem that you've kept hidden for many years, and you need to get it out into the light and deal with it."

"I'll stop. I'll stop right now and never go back. Maybe running into you was just the kick in the pants I needed. I promise you, before God—"

"Doug." Eric's voice was stern. "That's not going to work. Oh, I have no doubt that you mean it now, and may even be able to stay pure for another couple of years. But what about the rest of your life? What about three years from now, the next time something happens to trigger it? You need to figure out what drives you toward this addiction and deal with it, so it holds no power over you, ever again."

"Hold on a second!" Doug pushed his chair back and pointed his finger at Eric. "I'm not addicted to sex. I've *never* been unfaithful to Sherry, and never will be!"

"I know you mean that. But I bet you would've sworn, years ago, that you'd never be wearing a disguise, going into a strip club, either."

Doug was shaking with indignation, but he settled back into his chair.

"It's not the same thing. Not the same thing at all."

"Let me give you an example of an addict," Eric said. "A drug addict usually starts off small—something like marijuana to get high. It takes his mind off things, lets him blow off steam. Then one day he finds that the same amount doesn't do so much for him anymore, and he has to take more, and then more to get the same kick. Eventually, marijuana isn't enough, and he goes for the harder stuff. Crack, maybe, or a club drug. He escalates. These, too, work well for a while, but he again needs more and more. He starts arranging his life around the ability to indulge in his addiction, starts lying to those he loves, to arrange cover stories. He doesn't *want* to stop anymore.

"If he has a conscience—say, perhaps, he's a Christian—he feels bad about this and shame every time he indulges. In church on Sunday, he cries and asks God for forgiveness. He promises the Lord he'll never, ever do it again. And maybe he stays clean for a while; maybe even a few years. But whatever it is in him that led him to go for the drugs in the first place—a hole in his heart, a need for excitement, adventure, whatever—hasn't gone away. He needs to be healed, to be delivered from his bondage."

Doug stared at him, unspeaking.

Finally, Eric cocked an eyebrow. "What?"

"I never—" Doug cleared a hoarse throat. "I never thought of it like other addictions."

"Well, it can be. I don't know if your case is a true addiction or not; I'm no expert. But at the very least, from what you've told me, it sounds like you've been unsuccessful at changing on your own. You are, to use the Bible's term, 'a slave to sin.' We need to address this." Eric looked at his watch and winced. "But this is not the time or the place. Tell you what. I'm in town this week. Why don't you meet me for lunch tomorrow?" He named a place and a time. "I've got a couple of hours I can squeeze in."

Doug looked down at the table. "I don't know..."

"We have to talk, Doug. You need to do this. For Sherry's sake and yours."

Doug slowly stood to his feet and gave a brief nod. "Okay."

"Good." Eric reached over and clasped his friend's arm. "And don't forget to take off that silly mustache. You'll scare Sherry half to death if she sees you crawl into bed like that."

THIRTY-ONE

Despite a sleepless night, Doug was up and ready for work before Sherry or the kids woke, kissing her sleeping head on his way out of the bedroom. He didn't want to answer any questions, didn't think he could stand to watch her sleepy eyes search his soul.

His heart hurt as he drove toward the office, the roads swift in the early-morning darkness. He loved Sherry so much. What was he doing to her? What kind of man was he? He parked his car in the secure lot and rode the elevator to the executive floor.

He passed the COO's office, and waves of shame rose like bile in his throat. It was all his fault. Everything that haunted him was caused by his weakness, his sin, his spinelessness. He was nothing, was less than a man. He'd always known it, and now he'd been found out.

He approached the wide windows at the end of the hall by his office, and suddenly he saw himself wrenching them open and flinging himself into the blackness. What hope was there? He could never change. They would find out what manner of man he was. All his years of desperate pretense; trying, pretending to be a good husband, good father, good businessman, good Christian. He would be revealed as the imposter he was. He'd be put out of the church, would be ostracized from everyone he loved. And Sherry would leave him. And he'd never see his kids again.

He headed toward the window, picturing the long fall, the peace of death. It would be over so quickly. So quickly.

O God…

Another picture rose in his mind: his wife in his arms, giving herself to him willingly, gleefully. Tears sprang to his eyes. Her hair, her soft skin, her touch demonstrating that she loved him, *desired* him.

Doug veered into his office and closed the door, falling on his hands and knees on the carpet.

"But I've failed her, Lord." He was sobbing aloud and his tears wet the carpet. "I've broken our covenant. And I can't stop. O God, help me stop. Forgive me, Lord. Forgive me."

Distantly, he heard his phone ring, a surreal sound at six in the morning.

Answer it, Doug.

He looked up, almost expecting to see someone in the room, so clear had been the message. He reached toward the phone, dashing tears away, trying to sound seminormal.

"Hello?"

"Doug?" It was Sherry, her voice high with worry. "Doug, what are you doing? Are you okay? I just had the most horrible dream, and I woke up and you weren't here! What are you doing at the office? Are you okay?"

Doug felt great tears leaking from his eyes, and his voice came out very small. "I'm so glad you called, Sherry. I'm so glad you called."

"What's wrong?" She sounded near panic. "I had a dream of you falling from a window!"

Doug closed his eyes, thanking God for His mysterious ways. "Sweetheart..." He took a deep breath and forced himself to speak quickly. "Something *is* wrong, but I don't want to talk about it over the phone. Tonight can you maybe get a sitter so we can go out on a date to talk?"

There was a strained silence, and Doug could tell his wife was struggling not to ask, not to jump in with question after question.

"I would come home and talk about it now, but there are things I have to do first. I know it's hard to ask you to wait so long, but...will you do it? For me?"

"Okay." Sherry's voice was stretched, strange. "I'll wait until tonight. Just promise me, Doug...promise me..." He heard her crying on the other end of the line, heard the desperate love in her voice. "Promise me you won't do anything rash."

"I won't, I promise you. I never will. I love you, honey. I'll see you tonight."

"Okay." The small voice again. "I love you."

When she had gone, Doug sat on the floor for a long time, his mind turning.

An hour later, he heard the first sounds of the office coming to life. Secretaries bustled outside, phones started ringing. A normal Monday morning. For everyone except him.

O God, let this be the day of deliverance...

Doug left a message for Mary that he would be in and out of the office all day, had some important things to do, and did not want to be disturbed—no phone calls, no meetings. He asked her to cancel all his appointments and give the excuse that he wasn't feeling well.

That, at least, is the truth...

When the clock hit seven-thirty, he picked up the phone and dialed.

"Eric Elliott."

"Eric…it's Doug. You're in early."

"I don't know why. I just woke up earlier than normal and decided to get a head start on the day. What's up?"

"Can we…can we meet earlier than lunch?"

"We can meet whenever you want. This is actually a pretty light day for me, and…wait… Looks like one of my main clients cancelled a meeting this morning. I guess the Lord had other plans. When do you want to get together?"

Doug stood at his desk. "How about right now?"

For the next two hours, the two men walked around and around the nearby park. Doug confessed everything, including things he'd held back the night before. The shame was still there, but with every lap, every confession, it was slowly being superceded by an inexpressible relief. All the dark things were being brought to light, and he felt the first sense of freedom.

He fell silent, and the two men walked a full lap without speaking. Eric appeared to be deep in thought. Or deep in prayer.

Finally, he looked up and stopped walking. He faced Doug head-on. "I'm proud of you, brother."

Tears again filled Doug's eyes. He dashed them away. Why was he such a crybaby this morning?

"I've got nothing to be proud of."

"Yes, you do. You're taking the difficult step, the courageous step, of confessing your sins 'one to another,' as the Bible says." Eric started walking again, and Doug kept pace. "But I frankly don't know enough about this stuff to help you beyond being a sounding board and an accountability partner. And you need more help than I can give. You also need good advice about how to approach Sherry, and I just don't know the answer to that. But I know someone who does."

Doug looked down. "I just don't want everyone to know…"

"It's not 'everyone'; it's our senior pastor."

"What?"

Eric nodded. "Many years ago, before he was a pastor, he used to counsel married couples who were in trouble. And he is compassionate because he's had his own share of heartache."

"What do you mean?"

"Well…do you remember hearing about that first church he pastored? They had that horrible split because he wanted to start an AIDS ministry. He was tossed out of the church *he* started and poured his life into because some highly 'religious' people thought he was condoning a homosexual lifestyle."

"I remember someone talking about that church split." Doug's brow furrowed. "I didn't realize he'd been fired."

"Fired and humiliated." Eric walked a few paces, as if weighing what he should say. "Few people know this, but Pastor and I have had lunch every few weeks for the last two years. We've essentially become accountability buddies, and I've gotten to know him so much better. That event hurt him so deeply, it has taken him years to get over it. And to a certain degree, he still isn't over it. He has felt like he should just keep his head down, be a good shepherd to his flock, and not rock the boat. No controversy; just keep everything on an even keel." Eric's voice dropped a note, and he shook his head. "A shallow keel."

Doug was at a loss for words. "Then why do you suggest that I—"

"Because he's a good man, and a good counselor. Not all pastors are, you know. But he's been trained in marriage counseling, and I also know he's overcome his own personal…challenges in this area."

Doug's eyes widened, but before he could say anything, Eric held up a hand. "I can't say any more than that. What he chooses to share is up to him. But I think we should go see him. Right away, if he has the time."

Eric pulled a cell phone from his pocket and gave him a questioning look. Doug nodded, and Eric punched in the numbers and put the phone to his ear, his voice small as he turned away.

"Lord, he's so busy…let him be available."

THIRTY-TWO

The silence in the pastor's office was palpable.

Doug Turner had finished his story in a rush, rarely looking up, confessing to his senior pastor all the things he had kept hidden for so long. Now he sat with elbows on his knees, staring at the floor, uncertain what would come from across the silent desk.

When he could no longer stand the stillness, he looked up. Pastor Steven was no longer sitting in his chair. He was standing at a nearby floor-length window, looking down at the large playground that served the church school.

Doug could hear the distant chaos of recess in full swing. His children were probably out there. Sherry might be in this building at the same moment, helping with the school as she often did. He felt curiously detached, waiting for whatever censure was coming.

Pastor Steven turned from the window and sat down again at his desk.

"Doug, I'm so sorry."

Doug let out a breath he hadn't remembered holding.

"What do we do now, Pastor?"

"What do you mean?" His voice seemed far away, his gaze distant.

"I know you have every right to remove me from the youth ministry and all the other positions I hold. But none of that's important to me anymore. Nothing matters except Sherry and my kids. Please. Please, Steve. Can you help me? Can you help me keep my family?" His pastor's face became a blur as he dissolved into tears.

Steven stood and came around the front of his desk. He went down on one knee beside Doug's chair and put a hand on his shoulder. On the other side, Eric had a hand on his back. The two men waited while Doug regained control. Doug finally looked up and saw that his pastor's distant expression had vanished.

"Brother." Steven's voice was tight with emotion. "Are you under the impression that I'm going to impose some sort of harsh church discipline on you? No, Doug. You're a courageous man; courageous to admit to a problem that many of us never discuss; courageous to want to do something about it. And although I don't have all the answers, I do have some. I cannot tell you what's going to happen with your family; only the Lord knows that. And there *are* consequences to our sin. But I know that whatever happens, the Lord loves you—and your family—dearly and He will be with you through this journey. And I believe that He will honor your efforts to set things straight with Sherry. I hope He will also set you free from the prison of this blackmail, although it sounds like you may have already made some illicit choices that will need rectifying."

Pastor Steven pulled up another chair in front of his desk and sat close to the other two men.

"I need to make a confession to you. One that I have already made to Eric. The reason that I'm able to speak to this issue is because I've gone through the same struggle, and God brought me and my wife through it. Oh, every man is different, and so is each man's struggle. But yes, very much the same. I progressed from soft-core magazines that I could buy in the bookstore to driving to hard-core porn stores miles from where I lived and worked, always terrified that I would run into someone I knew. When I was away on business, it was movies on the hotel cable. I visited a few strip clubs, but for me it was the pictures, the magazines that were the trap to my mind, my heart. I was truly a slave to sin.

"And it wasn't just on my personal time, either." Pastor Steven sighed and looked up at the ceiling. "I snuck the magazines into this office, hiding them under stacks of paper in the locked drawer in my desk.

"When God delivered me and began healing me and my marriage, I resolved to keep my life an open book. No locked cabinets, no locked and cluttered drawers. Everyone—my secretary, my wife, my staff—has access to any of my things at any time."

Doug felt color rising as his mind leaped to a tally of his many locked drawers and cabinets.

"And look—see my computer?"

Doug stared at the pastor's computer monitor, and then glanced back at the closed office door. The monitor was positioned on the L-shaped desk so that anyone coming into the room could see the screen.

"If I could've put a big glass window in my door, I would have. But in my position, I do have closed-door meetings that must remain private.

"So, Doug, you asked where we go from here. Well, it's not going to be a simple process. You've broken Sherry's trust, and she will very likely feel betrayed. Especially with the complication of the blackmail, which has put your family at even greater risk. You need to be prepared to work very hard at regaining her trust and showing her that you're willing to do whatever it takes to show your love to her as she deals with the ramifications of this. I can walk you through some ideas, but in the end, it'll be between you, Sherry, and whoever you choose to be your accountability partners."

"Accountability—"

"Surely you're familiar with the concept?"

"Well, yes, it's just…I don't want everyone to know."

"Understandable. But I'm talking a small group of men; perhaps just Eric and another friend or two. Men who have the right to ask you anything, at any time, about what you are involved in and what you are doing. Men you can confess something to if you slip, so that they can pray for you. Just having a group like that will help a great deal in your motivation to stay pure.

"But your willingness to be honest isn't enough, Doug. You must realize that Sherry is probably going to want more than that. Let me give you some insight into how she might feel once you talk to her about this."

"I know how she'll feel!"

"Do you?" The pastor's voice was sad. "Remember, she'll be in a very different place than you."

"What do you mean?"

"Well, think about it. Confessing this is devastating to you, but you'll be feeling free from the dark secrets for the first time. You'll be sad that you've upset your wife, but you'll be thinking that you're finally honest, that you are finally able to share these things with her. You may wind up feeling closer to her than ever. She, on the other hand, will be feeling betrayed. She'll wonder if you love her at all, will be feeling like she's finally waking up to how little this marriage has meant to you. To you, you may have just been looking at pictures on a screen; to her, you were willing to defile her lifelong marital love with a five-minute prostitute."

"I never—I wouldn't cheat on her!"

"That's not what I mean, Doug. But God created us as sexual beings, and He says point-blank that when you engage in a sexual act with someone that you become one with her—that you are bonded with her in a spiritual way. Every sexual encounter will affect you somehow…even if it involves you, alone, staring at printed pictures. You're becoming bonded, becoming one in a way that God intended solely for the covenant marriage bond. Your spirit is creating oneness with someone other than your wife. In that way, you *have* cheated on her. And she may very well feel cheated on, even if you never slept with another woman."

Eric stirred, looking at his pastor. "If I could jump in…?"

"Please."

"It's not just an issue of looking at a few pictures, Doug. Many men—myself included—have nothing to be proud of in that area. And to a certain extent, sometimes we might, to our shame, take a peek and satisfy a natural curiosity without it having devastating consequences. But we cross a line when we go beyond that curiosity and come back for a second peek…for a third. That's when it gets even more dangerous, becomes closer to cheating, so to speak. If we somehow can't stop ourselves, if we go deeper and deeper, especially if we begin to keep secrets or deceive our wives, we've gone deep into territory that is hurtful to our marriages."

Doug heaved a sigh. "I've been deceiving myself for so long, thinking that it wasn't affecting us—just me."

"There's no way for it not to affect you both, Doug," Pastor Steven gave him a sad smile. "Trust me on this. It was only after I'd finally been delivered that I realized how much had been affected before that I couldn't even see. But that's a subject for another time. We'll need to get to it soon, but not today. There's too much else to do right now."

"So what do I have to do?"

"Well, you'll need to prepare ahead of time to carry the load that this news will place on her. For years you've been carrying around a heavy secret—picture yourself carrying around, everywhere you go, a huge suitcase stuffed with all the illicit magazines you've ever looked at."

Doug made a face, and the other two men were forced to chuckle. Doug gave them a rueful smile. "It would be a pretty heavy suitcase."

"Exactly. Now picture this: You tell your wife your secret, and suddenly…you're free of the load! The problem is, that suitcase hasn't gone away. It's merely been transferred to your wife. Now she's picked that dreadful burden up and is carrying it around. She's living every day under the weight of it. So you need to do everything possible to lift that weight. Show her that you're not only serious about change, but serious about doing whatever it takes to regain her trust. Getting accountability partners will be a good first step. But it may not be enough for you to promise to tell them everything. She may view you as having broken other promises. If she's anything like my wife—or the many other wives I know who've gone through this—she's going to want carte blanche access to your possessions. And she's going to want your accountability partners to have that access, as well."

"You mean…like my computer?"

"Like your computer, your drawers and filing cabinets—anywhere you might hide something you'd prefer to keep secret. You should probably start by installing both filtering and tracking software on your computer so your wife can see everything you've done on the computer, if she wants."

Doug could feel the color draining from his face, could feel the eyes of the other two men on him, watchful.

"Doug," Eric said, "it's all about honoring Sherry—and honoring the Lord—and doing everything you can to keep yourself pure. Sherry needs to know that you're serious about this, that you're willing to do whatever it takes."

After a long silence, Pastor Steven took back the floor. "She also needs to know that you're willing to do what it takes to rectify the blackmail situation—which in some ways may be just as difficult. It sounds to me like you may have been compromised into doing something illegal—or close to it—and we don't know what unforeseen consequences may come from that if it's not corrected."

"Okay." Doug heard the hoarseness in his voice, and he gripped the arms of the chair and forced the words out. "Okay. I'll talk to Sherry tonight. And Eric—" he turned to his friend. "Not to be a total wimp here, but would you and Lisa come with me? I feel like I can't do this on my own."

Pastor Steven nodded. "Actually, that's a very good idea. Sherry will need a girlfriend to lean on, and if Lisa's willing, I think she'd be wonderful. She's mature and compassionate, and I think she can handle it if Sherry wants to vent now and then."

Doug hung his head. "I can't believe I'm the cause of so much trouble for my family. This morning, I actually thought it might be better if I just jumped out a window and spared them the pain."

"That, my friend, is a lie straight from the pit of hell." Pastor Steven's voice quavered and his eyes flashed with anger. "Satan is called the accuser of the brethren, and he's doing it right this very minute! He uses every wile to tempt wonderful Christian men, Christian husbands, with these illicit activities, then he bombards you with shame for doing them! And then he plants the thought that it would be better to leave your wife and children than to go through the refining fire and come out the other side cleansed and forgiven."

The pastor stood, and he seemed suddenly taller, more powerful.

"Come here, Doug! If you're willing, right now we're going to pray for you to be delivered from this temptation, from all that the enemy has woven around you over the years, from any foul spirits that have tried to attack you. This is where it stops!"

Doug shot to his feet, and his pastor placed his hands on his shoulders and began to pray.

"Lord God, come be with us now and show us how to pray! We ask, Lord, that You do everything that is necessary to deliver our brother from his long struggle, and to heal him and his family. Right now in the name of Jesus, we come against any plans and purposes of the enemy over Doug Turner's life. We bind any foul spirits who have attacked him and command them to go, in the name of Jesus!"

O Lord, help me! I cannot do this on my own! Prepare Sherry's heart, Lord!

Doug sensed Eric step up behind him, praying in agreement with their pastor. He felt his friend's hand against his back, the unwavering support. He began to sob, shaking with wracking moans as his two friends held him, letting out years of grief, years of stoic independence, years of pride and secret shame. The pain passed through him like a storm as the Holy Spirit swept his house clean and purified him. And his sins were forgiven.

Doug was swept up in an eternal embrace. There was such kindness. Such gentleness. No rebuke. No condemnation. The exact opposite of everything the enemy had whispered to him for so many years. Doug felt wrapped in the purest, most unconditional love he had ever known. The presence of the Lord was so thick, he felt he couldn't breathe. But he never wanted to leave. He knew—perhaps for the first time in his life—he *knew* his Father loved him despite his faults, despite his sin.

That is why I died for you, you know. So that you would not have to bear the burden you have been carrying.

Doug groped for the mind of his heavenly Father, desperate to hold onto that precious touch. *Don't leave me, Lord!*

And into his mind, one after the other, came the Word. *I will never leave you, nor forsake you…I am father to the fatherless…My grace is sufficient for you, my power is made perfect in weakness…*

He came to his senses on the rich carpet of his pastor's office. He was on his knees, on his face, the soft weave wet with his tears. He could feel the steady hands of his friends, but their voices were silent. He finally stirred himself and sat up.

"He spoke to me." Doug's voice was thick with emotion. *"He spoke to me."*

"What did he say?" Pastor Steven asked.

Doug closed his eyes, repeating almost under his breath. "I will never leave you, nor forsake you. I am father to the fatherless. My grace is sufficient for you, my power is made perfect in weakness…"

Pastor Steven stood and pulled Doug to his feet. "The Lord knows what you need to be healed, my friend. It's not just a matter of praying for deliverance from the evil one. You must also be healed from whatever wounds have driven you to need these sinful actions. His 'power is made perfect in your weakness.' But that's a subject for another time, hopefully another time soon when both you and Sherry can come in for counseling. If she's willing."

Doug gripped Steven's hand. "Here's hoping, pastor. And I've kept you long enough. I guess I have a lot to do before I talk to Sherry this evening."

THIRTY-THREE

Sherry parked the van in Eric and Lisa's driveway. Doug's car was already there, parked right in front of her. She made no move to open the door but just sat there, listening to the soft popping noises as the engine cooled down.

Her mind had been racing through the horrible scenarios all day. He'd contracted incurable cancer. He'd been fired. He'd lost all their money gambling... He'd had an affair.

Sherry closed her eyes, praying a shapeless, desperate prayer. She walked toward the kitchen door and stopped five feet away, reluctant to knock.

Lisa opened the door with a smile and a big hug of welcome. Sherry couldn't smile back. She stared Lisa in the face.

"What's going on, Lisa?"

Lisa linked her arm through Sherry's. "The guys are in the den. The kids had dinner already, and they're sequestered upstairs for the night, with orders not to disturb us. We've got some time to talk in private. Come on."

Sherry would have hung back, but Lisa's gentle grip was firm. She pulled her through the kitchen, through the hallway, and into the small den, where a fire crackled.

Doug was sitting near Eric, deep in discussion. Both men broke off when Lisa and Sherry came in. Doug came to his wife, tense and nervous, and enfolded her in a hug.

Sherry tried to hug him back, tears of panic near the surface. Her voice was strangled against his shoulder.

"Doug—what—"

"Let's sit down, sweetheart." Doug gestured at the empty space on the sofa where he'd been sitting.

"I'm not so sure I want to." Sherry gave a nervous laugh. "I want to know what's going on first!"

"Sherry, it's okay," Eric said. "Doug has something he needs to tell you, and wanted us here for moral support."

Sherry looked at her husband. "Moral support? For—"

"Let me translate." Lisa's voice was wry. "He wanted someone around to make sure you didn't kill him."

Despite herself, Sherry laughed and allowed Doug to guide her to the sofa.

"Okay, I'm sitting down. Would someone please tell me what's going on?"

Doug reached over and took one of her hands, but didn't look at her.

"I…have to tell you something that I've kept secret for a while. Well, pretty much our entire marriage."

Eric cleared his throat, and Doug glanced his direction, and then sighed.

"Well, actually our entire marriage and long before." He looked up, and Sherry was stunned by the fear in his eyes. "I have a problem with pornography, Sher. I've had it almost my entire life, probably since I was thirteen or so. It started off harmlessly enough, I guess, as a lot of guys do. But I haven't been able to stop it. It's gotten worse and worse."

"What do you mean worse and worse?" She withdrew her hand from his. "You haven't…you haven't had an affair? Have you?" She put her hands to her face. "Please tell me you haven't—"

"No." Doug corralled her hands again and looked her straight in the eye. "No, I promise you, Sherry. I have never had an affair."

"Then what…I don't understand…"

"I guess I need to explain what…what it means."

Sherry listened, stunned, as Doug described how, in college, he would buy magazines and sneak them into his dorm room, where he lived with other Christian men. No one knew. He'd continued the practice after they were married, bringing the magazines and hiding them in his home and work offices, eventually escalating to hotel porn movies on business trips. He described how he had searched for sites on the Internet, seeking out films or pictures he'd heard about. How he'd gone from an occasional visitor to a compulsive one. How he would sneak downstairs when she and the kids were asleep, unable to sleep himself until he'd indulged.

Sherry pulled her hand away and wrapped her arms around herself, tucking her chin into her chest as if to protect herself from his words.

"And then I started going to strip clubs. I'd like say it was all Jordan's fault for forcing me to go with him when we were on a business trip together, but that wouldn't be true. I kept it up on my own."

Sherry closed her eyes, trying unsuccessfully not to picture her husband in one of those places, trying not to imagine her beloved, her best friend, reaching out to tip a gyrating girl with a perfect little body. She shivered. Was he thinking of those girls, those disgusting pictures whenever they were in bed together? Was that the reason their love life had become so stale? He was indulging himself with total strangers.

"Was this—" She cleared her throat and tried again. "Was this what you were doing all those nights you were 'at the office' so late?"

Doug was looking down, his voice tight. "Some of the time. Yes."

She finally looked at her husband straight on, and the tears welled in her eyes. "Do you not love me anymore?"

"No!" Doug's gaze shot up, and he reached for her. She recoiled from his touch. "I mean yes! I mean…of course I love you! You're my *life!* Why do you think I'm telling you about this?"

"I thought maybe you'd been caught, and you had no choice."

He stared at her face, and answering tears appeared in his eyes. "Sherry, I'm sorry. I'm so sorry." He hung his head, and she could see the tears fall onto his knees, wetting his khakis. "I had to tell you, not just because I got caught, but because I couldn't stand not to. You deserve to know."

"How'd you get caught?" Sherry's voice was hard. "Where were you?"

"I don't know if I should—"

"Doug." Eric spoke for the first time, his voice gentle but pointed.

Doug clenched his jaw and closed his eyes. "I was at The Challenger, that strip club off the highway on the way home from work. Afterwards, I went to get coffee for the way home, and ran into Eric."

"When? When were you at the strip club?"

"Last night."

Sherry felt as if reality had shifted, as if something had come and stolen everything she thought she knew about their marriage, their love for one another. She sat, silent and stiff, for a long minute, staring into the crackling fire. Then she spoke without looking at him.

"Why would you have to fantasize on those…pictures, those sluts! Why would you have to lie to me?"

His voice was broken. "I don't know why, Sher. I just can't seem to stop myself, and I hate myself every single time. I never wanted to hurt you! I've prayed; I've cried; I've asked God's forgiveness. And I've promised never, *ever* to do it again…but I always do. I'm hoping that by telling you, somehow, it will help me stop."

"Sherry."

Lisa's voice broke in, and Sherry stared at her, annoyed. Why did they have to have such a personal discussion in front of their friends?

"What?"

"I've read up on this a little bit since Eric called me this morning. And although I'm no expert, I have discovered one thing. A husband can love his wife and kids absolutely and with no reservations, and still be trapped by this temptation. It often has something to do with deep wounds and insecurities that drive him to it, wounds that need to be healed. Obviously, it's also a choice the man is making, a willful sin, but Doug is making a courageous choice here in baring himself to you and to us, asking for help in healing whatever it is that drives him to this destructive behavior. He wanted to tell you in order to *strengthen* your marriage, to *show* his love for you. I hope you can understand that."

"I guess…I guess I can understand that to a point." Sherry's voice was tight, a sense of loss threatening to swamp her. "But how could he have lied to me? How can I ever trust him again?"

"That's what this whole thing is about, Sherry," Eric said. "Doug wants to do everything possible to be open and honest with you, so that you *will* trust him again. That's why we agreed that he needed to answer every question you asked, no matter how hard." He looked at Doug. "And that leads to another issue that complicates this whole thing even more."

Sherry slapped the couch in exasperation. "Great. What is it?"

"I'm being blackmailed," Doug said.

"What?"

"I have no idea how, but the COO has a video of me at…at the strip club. And of where I went on the Internet. He sprang this on me a few minutes before that board meeting…remember that? He told me to give the board my okay for the Silicon Valley deal or he would send the video to you, to lots of people in our church, and to anyone else where it might ruin my life. I was so scared I'd lose you, I—I did what he said. I couldn't stand the thought of losing you, of losing the kids."

Sherry shut her eyes, trying to comprehend this new revelation.

"So you've not only started lying to your wife and kids, but now you've done something that places the family in even more jeopardy—something illegal?"

"It's not illegal, it's just—"

"Whatever you call it, it's underhanded and could get you into trouble."

"I don't know. I've asked myself that a hundred times. I just don't know. And I don't know what to do now."

For the first time, Sherry felt the barest flicker of sympathy. She pushed it away and stared at Eric. "This is way more than I can process. I don't know what we do now."

"I'd suggest you focus on the main issue—Doug's struggle, getting him healed, and your relationship. You can deal with the blackmail as you go. That'll frankly require more prayer, and probably more time. In the meantime, let's go back to how you can build up trust again."

Doug touched her arm, and Sherry reluctantly turned toward her husband, although she didn't quite look at him.

"I know you have every reason to doubt my promise—"

"You got that right!"

"But I want to make a new promise to you: I will do anything that I have to, to regain your trust and to never sin against you in that way again."

"But from what you all just said, you can't help it." Her voice was laden with sarcasm. "Good grief, you're even being *blackmailed* because of it! So how can you promise me that you won't do it again?"

"That's what this whole process is about, Sherry," Eric said. "There are things that have to happen in order to help Doug stop the behavior, to set him free from the bondage he's been in. All of that is part of what he means when he says he'll do anything he has to do to regain your trust."

"And I'm not just saying it, sweetheart." Doug's eyes were anxious and sad. "I spent all day trying to figure out how I could prove it to you tonight." He pulled a folded page from his pocket and glanced at it.

Sherry stretched forward as if to see, and Doug jerked the paper back.

Sherry jumped to her feet. "You won't even let me see your stupid list! How the heck can I trust you with anything else?"

Doug stood up also. "I'm sorry…I just wanted to *tell* you these things, that's all."

"I want to see the list." Sherry knew she sounded stubborn, and she didn't care. Suddenly, that stupid piece of paper had become a symbol of everything he had tried to keep secret and hidden from her over all the years of their marriage. "Show me the list!"

He held it out. "You might not understand my random scribbles—"

Sherry snatched it from him and glanced down the page. Her brow furrowed, and she sighed, feeling foolish. "You're right; I don't get it."

"Sherry, why don't you all sit down again," Lisa said. "Let me see if I can help, from a girl's perspective."

Sherry sank back to her seat, keeping several feet between her and Doug.

Lisa leaned forward. "What do you need in order to feel that you could trust your husband again? How could he prove himself and his intentions to you?"

"Well, he could—I don't know exactly." She thought a moment. "I guess one of the first things would be to promise never to do it again. But how would I know if I could ever trust your promise?"

"Well, one of the ways is that I'll have an accountability group, a few men like

Eric who have the authority to ask me anything, at any time, and that I can confess anything to. In fact, I already have it set up. Eric and one other man have agreed to join me in this."

"Who's the other man?"

Doug half-smiled. "Pastor Steven. This afternoon, he gave me permission to tell you that he went through the same thing many years ago, and the Lord brought him and his wife through it. So he knows just what to ask."

"Pastor Steven was into pornography?" Sherry put a hand to her head. "That's more shocking than you!"

"Shocking to you as a woman, maybe," Eric said. "But it probably wouldn't be all that shocking to most men—at least men who think about it for two seconds. Sherry, what you have to realize is that this is a very, very common problem. Maybe Doug got a little deeper into it than some guys, but it wouldn't surprise me to learn that half the men in our church struggle with this in some way."

"Half the men!"

"In our culture today, this kind of temptation is nearly impossible to avoid. You know how men are more visual than women, right? Well, that's one of the issues, right there. It used to be that a man had to go looking for things that would titillate him in that way. Now, those things are so ingrained in our culture, they are nearly impossible to avoid. We struggle every day with images that blast us from all sides. We can't walk down the street anymore, or even watch family TV, without something tempting us. And many men find that temptation pulling them into just one look…and another…and another. It takes an incredible effort to avoid that, and some men—especially if they have issues that haven't been dealt with—may *not* avoid it."

Despite herself, Sherry felt curiosity rising. "You've mentioned something a couple of times now—what do you mean by 'other issues that haven't been dealt with'?"

Eric looked at Lisa, and she picked up a book from the lamp table beside her. "I read this book today from cover to cover. It's by a Christian man who overcame the same struggle. It describes this whole thing. It's fascinating, and I think you should read it as soon as you can. You'll learn a lot about a man's secret insecurities and need for affirmation—something that we wives often don't realize. One of a man's common triggers for pornography addiction actually results from the self-image that develops years earlier, as a young boy."

Lisa flipped to a highlighted chapter. "This is pretty new to me, but it makes sense. One thing this author says is that a father calls his son into manhood. And if the father is distant or derisive or whatever, the son may not end up feeling like a man." Lisa puffed out her chest in imitation of a swaggering male, and Sherry gave a brief smile. "Doesn't feel like a man who protects and conquers and provides for his woman.

"It's a bit foreign to us women, I know, but men really have an inborn need to be the conqueror, the adventurer, the one who slays the buffalo to provide for his family. It's what makes them feel like a man."

Sherry glanced sideways at Doug, and a small smile flickered on her lips. "Slain any good buffalo lately?"

Tears welled in Doug's eyes. He reached over and gripped Sherry's hand. This time, she didn't pull away.

"Go on."

Lisa was scanning a page. "So now suppose that you're a fourteen-year-old, fifteen-year-old boy. Suppose your dad always puts you down, and you feel inadequate—something many guys feel inherently anyway, apparently—and rejected. So you go up to your room and lock the door and pull out an old *Playboy* you found in your buddy's locker or somewhere. You look at the pictures, and you're stimulated, and you suddenly feel like a conqueror, an adventurer. There's an illicit excitement. You feel masculine all of a sudden…like a man. You've just gotten an affirmation of yourself from looking at a picture instead of out hiking or playing ball with your dad.

"Well, guess what? That fourteen-year-old boy will do it again. And maybe again. He'll subconsciously say, 'I don't need you, Dad; I'm becoming a man on my own.' And that mechanism—of looking at a seductive woman and feeling that excitement, that pleasure—will become a common way of dealing with the stress and pain of life as the boy grows into a man."

Lisa glanced over at Eric, and Sherry got the sense she was choosing her words carefully. "In our years of marriage, I've been shocked to find out just how deep male insecurity goes. Just how desperately men need affirmation—from all corners, but especially from their wives."

Unbidden into Sherry's mind came a procession of times she had criticized her husband. Times she had joked about him in public, ignoring the pained, embarrassed look on his face.

"So what you're saying is—" Sherry paused, trying to get the words out—"I could've contributed to Doug's problem."

"This issue is never the wife's fault—don't get me wrong," Lisa said. "It has little or nothing to do with the way you look or how much you weigh or whatever. It doesn't mean he doesn't find you attractive."

"That's not what I meant." Sherry sighed and looked at Doug. "I was just thinking about some times that I teased you in public or made jokes at your expense. I was thinking—" She looked down, embarrassed. "At those times, I remember thinking that it wouldn't hurt to have your male ego taken down a notch or two."

"Oh, goodness!" Lisa gave a pained laugh. "Listen, one thing that I've learned without any book to tell me is that the whole stereotypical idea of the male ego is usually a farce. That's just their public demeanor. The real man, inside, has many insecurities. A man usually feels he's going through life as an imposter, that he really has no idea what he's doing and he's just trying to avoid being found out!"

"Is that the way you feel?" Sherry asked Doug.

"Every day."

"Wow." Sherry stared at her husband, reassessing the familiar face. "I thought I knew you so well. I had no idea—"

"No idea? You know how much I hate looking like a fool in public. How much I worry about whether I'm doing a good job at work."

"I guess I just never…believed it. You honestly feel inadequate?" Sherry watched his slow nod and put a hand to her face. "I mean, you're so *good* at what you do. You're a great worker, a great husband, a great father—you're great at your church responsibilities, and you know your stuff. I guess I just thought that you *knew* all that about yourself."

"Why would I think that? I'm always sure someone's going to expose me for the imposter I am. And I'm not talking about blackmailing me because of my actions, either! I mean exposing that I'm an idiot who really has no idea what he's doing." His eyes flickered briefly to her face. "And frankly I'm surprised to hear you say that you think I'm a great husband or father. I'm not sure I believe that you really mean that."

Sherry stared at him. "Why wouldn't I mean it?"

"Well—I disappoint you so often. That's what you say, anyway."

"I—I—" Sherry stammered. "But you *are* a good husband and father. I would never want you to feel inadequate! I just get upset and—oh, I don't know." She gave up and turned back to their friends, her mind whirring. "I'm feeling pretty clueless all of a sudden. What do we do?"

"Well, we've been talking about that." Eric walked over and stirred the dying fire with a nearby poker. He picked up a couple of logs and set them on the blaze. "I think there are two tracks we need to pursue. The first is anything that will help you fully trust Doug again. We've made a list of things you might want, but frankly I'd like to hear it from you. The second track—which will need to happen at the same time—is anything that will help Doug work through the emotional issues that led him to this point. But first and foremost, I know Doug wants to know what he can do to satisfy you, to regain your trust, to help heal the hurt and damage that's been done to you."

Lisa looked at her, curious. "It's really your call, Sherry, as to what you need."

Sherry turned slightly, her back to Doug, staring at the fire. What did she need? She needed her husband back, that's what she needed. She needed the security of marriage without wondering and worrying that Doug was off somewhere watching another woman undress on stage. She shivered, repulsed, trying to push the thought away, unable to recapture the warmth she had felt a few minutes before.

"I don't know. I don't know what I need. And I don't know when I'll know." She stood up, talking to Eric and Lisa. "I can't think right now. There's too much in my head. I have no idea what I need, and I don't understand why that should be laid on me."

"Sherry, we didn't mean—"

"And I'm tired and drained and confused. I'm going home now. We're just going to have to talk about the solution some other time."

"I was thinking that if we got to the solution," Eric said, "that you'd be better able to sleep tonight, that you'd have more peace with this whole thing."

"Well, maybe I don't want to be at peace about it. I need to work through some of this. And I need to pray about it. I just can't process any more tonight."

"Okay, whatever you need," Lisa said. "But...um...you knew that Doug came tonight with a whole set of steps he was prepared to take to help you trust him. He doesn't want to dump the solution on you. I'm sorry if we didn't communicate that well. Sorry if there was a misunderstanding."

"Okay. Whatever." Sherry started to move toward the door. "I've got to get the babysitter home. Her parents didn't want her out too late." She didn't quite look at the others. "Maybe we can go over the other stuff tomorrow."

Eric ushered the silent couple out of the house, waiting in the doorway as they climbed into their separate cars and backed out of his driveway. He stepped back inside and closed the door. Lisa was right beside him, her face somber.

Eric pulled her into a fierce hug, burying his face in her hair, feeling the tenderness—the surety—of her arms around his waist.

He kissed her hair, resting his cheek against her head, and closed his eyes.

"God, help them."

THIRTY-FOUR

A sharp knock interrupted Doug Turner's thoughts, and he scowled at the door. He'd told Mary he didn't want to be disturbed today, either. "Yes?"

The COO came in and closed the door behind him. He stopped a few feet shy of the desk, staring down as if at an amusing prey.

"Hello, Doug."

Doug rose to his feet, feeling every bit of his height, and glared down at his shorter colleague.

"What do you want?"

The COO took a seat as usual, and propped his feet up on the desk, toppling a stack of file folders and a container of paper clips.

Doug clenched his teeth and stalled by straightening up the mess, forcing his rising temper under control. He stood his files again in their place, avoiding his colleague's eyes. There was still too much at stake. Even though Sherry now knew his secret, that videotape was still a threat. It would still kill her to see it—Doug shuddered, thinking about it—and although Pastor Steven was now in his camp, what if copies were indeed sent to other leaders within the congregation? He couldn't risk others seeing the depraved things he'd done, things he'd watched.

Doug crossed his arms and waited. He did not sit down.

"Have a seat, Doug."

"I think I'll stand, thanks."

His colleague slowly removed his feet from the desk, and his eyes narrowed as he stared up at Doug.

"I need you to do something else for us, Doug."

Doug gave him his best stony-eyed stare.

"Gil's people out in California will be bringing a tangential deal to the table today; an add-on to the original plan. It'll require them to invest more in fixed capital than we had anticipated—some updated satellite systems—and will delay our mutual revenue expectations by a few months. But it'll be more than worth it. The additional deal is a valuable commodity and must be approved. Do you understand me?"

"Yes, of course," Doug said. "You want to put a deal I already found wanting in even greater jeopardy by further delaying revenues."

"Don't worry. The blip will be minimal on the downside, and the upside is enormous."

Doug snorted. How many times had he heard *that* one?

"Don't mock me, Doug." His colleague rose to his feet and his eyes were darts. "I see no reason to mention the reason why I'm expecting your agreement. But it's there, nevertheless. It's always there."

"You don't need to remind me."

"Good. Then we understand each other. You should be expecting a call from one of Gil's people today. Because it's a satellite deal, it'll probably be Jill who calls you."

Doug stiffened, and the COO turned his head, leveling an intent stare. "What?"

"Nothing. I'm really busy today, and I don't need the headache."

"Well, you'll be avoiding a worse headache by cooperating, my friend." He walked out without a backward glance.

Doug wanted to spit in his direction. "I'm not your friend, you arrogant—"

A fragment of Scripture floated into his mind. *Pray for those who persecute you...*

Doug turned away from the door, muttering, "Forgive me Lord, but I'm having a hard time with that idea."

He tried to resume his work, but the Scripture kept bothering him. Finally, he sighed and rested his forehead on his desk.

Lord, forgive me. He may be crooked, but he's also a lost soul. He has far more to fear—for all eternity—than I do. I pray that You would reach him before it's too late. Turn his heart. And, Lord...protect me and my family from his plotting. Help me know what to do.

He stayed there for a moment, his head against the polished wood of his desk. When he finally looked up, his cares had not left, but he was at peace. It was in God's hands.

He reached for his phone and dialed an extension.

"Alice, I'm swamped this week, and I need to pass along a project to you. We may be adding a piece to the Silicon Valley deal, and I need you to shepherd it along. Just give me reports as you go, and I'll sign off at the end. I need you to call Silicon Valley today and introduce yourself to the head of their satellites program. Her name is Jill..."

Doug crossed the threshold, his stomach in a knot. The kids came charging up to knock him over, all talking at once about their day. Sherry was cutting vegetables over by the sink. She didn't look around.

He gave each of the kids a turn and then patted them on their bottoms, shooing them out of the room. He stood his briefcase by the door and took a tentative step toward his wife.

"Hey, hon." He held his arms out slightly.

"Hey." Sherry glanced over her shoulder and kept chopping. "Sorry I can't give you a hug, but my hands are all gross."

Doug nodded as if he understood. The night before, when they'd gone to Eric and Lisa's for their second discussion, she didn't want to smudge her wet nail polish. The night before that she'd had arms full of laundry. He allowed himself a much-needed glimmer of mirth at what the excuse would be tomorrow.

He stepped up beside her and gave her cheek a peck. She accepted the kiss, but her eyes stayed fastened on the vegetables.

"Did you have a good day?"

"It was fine." Chop. Chop. Chop.

"What did you all do?"

"I helped out at school, then we went to the park."

Doug stood silent beside her, waiting to see if she'd say anything else. Her face was blank. Chop. Chop. Chop.

"Uh—what're we having for dinner?"

"Stir-fry."

"Can I help?"

"I'd rather just do it myself."

He studied her profile, the wisps of glossy dark hair escaping a simple clasp at her neck. He longed to hold her and stroke her hair and say again how sorry he was for her pain. He longed for her even to cry on his shoulder. But she was so distant, so tense.

Yesterday, at their second meeting with Eric and Lisa, he had reached out to caress her bare arm. She had cringed from his touch.

That one incident, more than anything else, showed Doug how far they had to go, showed him the depth of the consequences of his sin. That night he had waited until she headed for the guest bedroom, and he had cried himself to sleep.

"I guess I'll go change, then?"

She gave him a polite smile. "Do whatever you'd like. Ten minutes till dinner."

Doug hesitated. "When are we going to—"

"I made a list, based on our talk with Eric and Lisa. You can look it over after dinner and we can make some final decisions once the kids are in bed."

☆ ☆ ☆

Lisa looked at Sherry over a cup of tea, listening to the raucous cries of the kids on the trampoline outside.

"So what did you all decide?"

Sherry stirred her teacup, not looking up. "Well, a few things I guess." She gave a sad smile. "Doug was so eager to agree to all of my conditions. He agreed that I can look through his belongings at any time, and he won't keep any locked cabinets. He'd already bought software for the computer so he can't easily access those sites, and if he does I'll know about it. For the next few months, he's promised to let me know where he is whenever he's not at the office or at home, and he'll answer his cell phone at all times. I'll make his hotel reservations and specify that he must have no access to the movie channels. It was all hard on his pride, but he agreed."

"Anything else?"

"Well, the accountability partners. I can ask them anything without going through him. He agreed to marriage counseling with Pastor Steven. I'd love to find a Christian support group for women, but we obviously can't ask around at church so I'll probably have to wait. There's a few other things…" Sherry sighed. "I know I should be happy and supportive, but I'm still just so…raw. I can't show him much love or affection. I can't stand to sleep in the same bed. I know he's worried that I'll leave."

"Will you?" Lisa's voice was calm. There was a long pause.

"No. No, of course not. How could I? He's doing everything he can to make things right. I feel betrayed and hurt, and I may have a hard time trusting him. But…despite all of that…I *know* him. I know his heart is good, even if his behavior is bad. And…I've made so many mistakes in my life, too. The Lord gently reminded me of that in my prayer time this morning."

She went to the window. Lisa was silent behind her. She watched Genna try to stand on the trampoline and fall, giggling, as the older kids bounced around her. She got up again, only to collapse in a heap. Time after time, never tiring of the game.

"I fell so many times, Lisa. Over and over again. Willful disobedience, pursuing momentary pleasure over what my conscience was telling me was right. How can I condemn my husband? I wasn't a Christian then, and he is, but still…temptation is temptation. Satan attacks in many guises, with many traps that are hard to resist. And we're sinful creatures. I know Doug has asked for and received God's forgiveness. And if God could change me when I was a wreck spiritually, how much more can He heal and change a committed believer—a believer who desperately *wants* to change? I guess I just have to believe that God can give us our marriage back."

"Have you told Doug this? Told him what you've just told me?"

Sherry shook her head.

"Why not?"

"Because...because I want to punish him." Sherry balled her hands into fists and turned back to her friend. She could feel the wetness on her cheeks. "He betrayed my trust, betrayed everything I thought we had together. I may have to let him off the hook, but I want him to suffer first. At least to suffer some tiny amount of the pain he's caused me!"

Lisa came to the window and hugged her. "You do what you think is best, and what you need to do. I may think that you're only hurting yourself, holding on to this pain so tightly, but it's only been a few days since you found out, and I don't know how I'd react if I found myself in your shoes. I will only say one thing. You must pray for Doug, even if you have to force it. He needs your prayers, even if he doesn't yet have your affection. That will help all the way around—it'll help you heal, and it'll cover him during a difficult time."

"I know. I have been. Even when I don't feel like it." She gave Lisa a wan smile. "I bet God had you challenge me to an hour of prayer every day, just so I'd be able to walk through this."

"Could be. I wonder, too, if it wouldn't help for you and Doug to share with our home group something about your struggles. Otherwise, you'll just have a wall up that everyone will sense, and you won't feel free to talk about the most important thing going on in your lives at the moment. Something for both of you to think and pray about."

"I don't know. For me, I think it would help. But Doug...well...I know he'd worry about how it made him look."

"Then perhaps he needs to stop worrying about his image so much and let the Lord protect that. He needs true, honest fellowship—you both need it—and the prayers of more than just two friends. It'd be nice to show folks that we're not all perfect little robots out there; that Christians have secret problems and hurts and needs just like anybody else. If you could bring yourself to be open, I think it would be a blessing not only to you but to the whole group."

Sherry hesitated, surprised that her primary concern was for Doug's feelings. She nodded. "I'll ask Doug what he thinks."

"You said that God could give you your marriage back. Well, I believe He'll do better than that. This is an awful time, but He wastes no lessons, and He takes what the enemy meant for evil and turns it to great good. I bet in a few years you'll both look back and thank God for all He did in your lives, for all the healing and intimacy. I believe you'll end up with a stronger marriage than before."

Sherry glanced out the window, watching Genna again rise and fall. "May it be so."

A strange look came over Lisa's face, and she grasped Sherry's hand. "Can we pray for a minute? Pray for you and Doug? I also feel this need to pray for the church right now."

Sherry followed Lisa back to the table and sat with bowed head, waiting for her to begin.

Lisa waited a moment. "Lord, I feel like You have a purpose here that's greater than just restoring Sherry and Doug's marriage. That You have something for the church. Father, I don't even know how to pray, but I ask that Your will would be done on earth as it is in heaven, and that everything You have purposed will come to pass. I ask, Lord, that You give Pastor Steven wisdom and strength to guide our church." She paused. "And now, Lord, about Sherry and Doug…"

THIRTY-FIVE

"O God, what do I do?"

Pastor Steven sat on a quiet bench in a distant garden, his head in his hands. A leafy green wall shielded him from a nearby paved pathway, where people occasionally strolled arm-in-arm, or bicycled by without a glance. In this little enclave, even the distant hum of the few cars did not intrude. This spot—his spot—was quiet.

And today, he needed it more than ever. He sat with his Bible in his lap, but his eyes stared unseeing. He wasn't struggling with God's words, but his own obedience.

He had told his secretary to reschedule all his appointments for that day, had not explained to his staff what was burning within him. Only his wife knew. His dear wife, his best friend. The one whom the Lord had given back to him despite his years of addictive sin. She was at home that day. Was fasting and praying for him, while he struggled—like Jesus—in a garden.

What would he do? Did he have the courage to follow his Lord? To be crucified with Christ, if that was what his King required? Today, the nails were not made of iron, but of spiteful words, of whispered slander, of public offense and back-stabbing.

Today, he would have to decide whether he would stand before the people and bare his soul, knowing that it might again be ripped to shreds.

He felt his soul was about to shatter under the weight of such obedience, such desperate pain. He grabbed his head, crying out aloud. "How can your people be so cruel, Lord?"

A brilliant light flashed before him, radiant and terrible, a consuming holy fire.

"Because they do not see the log in their eye."

Dazzled, Steven looked up...and fell prostrate on the grass. A great shining being was standing before him, his brilliance enfolding Steven like a cloak. His voice was deep and laced with the sadness of the Ageless One.

"They do not see their own sin, their own great and desperate need. They judge others because they do not first judge themselves. And they judge those outside the body of Christ, rather than challenging those who have already been redeemed.

They cannot unconditionally love the unlovable because they have not yet been broken. They have not yet seen and repented of their judgments, of their selfishness."

Steven warred between awe and terror, his mind groping to remember everything the great messenger said. He tried to open his mouth, to ask the only question that mattered.

"What does the Lord desire of me?"

"The Lord wants His church to be broken before Him. There are many secret hurts, secret sins, and the saints of God will never fully minister until those are revealed and healed. Until then, much ministry to this lost and hurting world will not look like that of the Lamb of God. The people of God must look like Jesus; must share His unconditional love with the world. Each precious saint must confront his or her own condition. Until then, they will be secretly judgmental of the very sheep they are trying to bring into the fold."

The messenger's eyes blazed. "But the Lamb of God sacrificed Himself to take away the sins of the world! That message must be shared and received! Your Body has been chosen by the Almighty One to bear this message to a lost lamb, a lamb on whom much depends. But they are not ready to receive this one. They must be broken, must be awakened!"

Steven had so many questions, but they were all stilled. So many thoughts, but they were put aside. He was insignificant, a vapor…and yet precious, and priceless beyond words.

"It is such an honor—" he found himself choking up, and fought to regain control. "Such an honor that the Lord would choose to speak to me."

With shock, he realized that the great figure was leaning down, resting a hand on his shoulder. "You, Steven, are greatly beloved of God, just like your namesake, a man full of His grace and power. You have walked through the fire and the valley, and have been chosen for this time. You must choose to sacrifice yourself and minister this message to your flock, and they in turn must choose to sacrifice themselves, and minister Christ's love to the lost lamb that is coming. Much depends on it."

Steven bowed his head, somehow sure of what he must say. He closed his eyes, and quieted his heart. "May it be unto me, as you have said."

The light disappeared, and he was again in the quiet and the stillness, surrounded by green.

The rain beat on the roof of the church as the congregation finished singing and remained standing, awaiting the pastor's familiar prayer.

Pastor Steven looked out on his flock, at the freshly scrubbed upturned faces, and breathed a quiet prayer as he reached the lectern and opened his notes.

"May the words of my mouth, and the meditations of all our hearts, be pleasing in thy sight O Lord, my rock and my redeemer." He couldn't remember ever meaning the words more.

He motioned for the people to take their seats. Someone remained standing off to the side, and Steven glanced over. It was his wife, arrayed in brilliant blue, on the front row. She was looking at him, waiting to catch his eye. She put her hand on her heart and mouthed the words, *I love you.*

He nearly lost it, felt the tears rising perilously close to the surface. Then his wife took her seat and gave him a saucy wink, as if to say "we're in this together."

"Good morning, everyone. Sorry about that little interruption there, but I just realized that my wife was making eyes at me."

There were many titters and outright laughs as people settled in for what was clearly an unusual start to a sermon.

Steven quieted his heart. It was before him now, he had the mandate of the Lord, and that was all he needed. The results were in God's hands.

"I have a special message to share with you today. One I believe the Lord has given me for just such a time as this. It may be difficult to hear and challenging at times, but please bear with me. And in case there are still any children in the room, a fair warning for all you parents: We will be talking about some adult matters."

A few people got up here and there, ushering their young children out. The other faces were quiet, intent, and even more curious.

"Please turn with me to our texts for today. First, Matthew chapter seven. Listen to the words of Jesus. '"Do not judge, or you too will be judged. For in the same way you judge others, you will be judged, and with the measure you use, it will be measured to you. Why do you look at the speck of sawdust in your brother's eye and pay no attention to the plank in your own eye? How can you say to your brother, 'Let me take the speck out of your eye,' when all the time there is a plank in your own eye? You hypocrite, first take the plank out of your own eye, and then you will see clearly to remove the speck from your brother's eye.'"'"

Steven looked up from his Bible. "Please keep a marker on this place. We'll come back to it. Next, let's look at Luke chapter eighteen, starting with verse nine. 'To some who were confident of their own righteousness and looked down on everybody else, Jesus told this parable: "Two men went up to the temple to pray, one a Pharisee and the other a tax collector. The Pharisee stood up and prayed about himself: 'God, I thank you that I am not like other men—robbers, evildoers, adulterers—or even like this tax collector. I fast twice a week and give a tenth of all I get.'

"'But the tax collector stood at a distance. He would not even look up to heaven, but beat his breast and said, "God, have mercy on me, a sinner."'"

Steven raised a hand for emphasis. "And then Jesus goes on to say something remarkable. Look at this. 'I tell you that this man, rather than the other, went home justified before God. For everyone who exalts himself will be humbled, and he who humbles himself will be exalted.'"

Steven laid aside his Bible and looked out at the congregation. "Many of us have heard that story, many times. And most of us think, 'Thank God I'm not like that Pharisee!' Well, I have news for each and every one of us. Even by thinking that, we *are* being like that Pharisee. And we're proving Jesus' point!

"We as Christians in our day often act like the religious leaders of Jesus' day. We don't mean to or intend to. But you know what? The Pharisees probably didn't mean to or intend to either. They thought they were doing what God required. So Jesus came along to challenge them, to show them that they were putting the law and all their many rules ahead of God's heart. His purpose wasn't to condemn but to correct. But many of them wouldn't listen."

Steven looked up, and he caught the congregation in a powerful gaze. "So this is my question for each one of us today: Are we willing to listen? I believe God has given me a special message for us as a church body. Of course, we must always test a message to see if it's consistent with the Word of God. But if it is, it will be up to each one of us whether we'll listen and accept the message, or close our minds and reject it."

There was a profound silence in the room, an intent waiting, punctuated only by the soft drumming of the Creator's rain on the roof. Steven was overwhelmed by the powerful, electric certainty that the Holy Spirit was there, that the Lord was anointing the words of his mouth.

"I have often missed the point of this story because I focused on the arrogant words of the Pharisee and assumed this parable was simply about the dangers of pride in one's self. After all, who prays like *that?*

"Well, I realized something this week: This story is not just about that sort of pride. It's about exactly what the Bible says it's about in the introduction! It's about one way pride is demonstrated, about what happens when we are confident of our own righteousness: *We look down on everybody else.*

"And this is where the hard challenge comes in. Today, in this church, we have to confront whether we are guilty of exactly that, and whether as a result, we drive away the very people we want to reach—the lost, the hurting, the little lambs that Jesus pleaded for. We make those who *know* they are sinners feel uncomfortable among us, who are confident of our own righteousness!"

He saw some faces awakening to shock at his challenging tone, and he relaxed a little, giving a disarming smile.

"Now you, like me, may think you'd never do that, but let me illustrate the point with a real-life example. I'm going to tell you a true story of a man I used to know. And I want you to be aware of your reactions as I go. What are you thinking in your heart of hearts as you hear this man's tale? Because what you're thinking as you hear the story is probably about the same thing you'd be thinking if you actually met him. And he would sense your reaction.

"So here's the story. This man professed to be a Christian from a young age. He got married, had kids, and eventually became the pastor of a large, prestigious church. He was sold-out for Christ, had a television program, wrote a couple of books, and ministered to thousands every week. He looked wonderful on the outside, and everyone loved and respected him. But on the inside he had a dirty secret. He was addicted to pornography."

In a flash, Steven saw a range of expressions on the faces before him. Distaste, condemnation, compassion…and flickers of guilt.

"This man was so into the filth of pornography that he began lying to his wife and his staff. He'd lie about his whereabouts when he was off buying his trash at porn shops and bookstores. Then he actually hid those disgusting magazines in his church office, just so he could look at them during the day and satisfy his secret cravings.

"Now let me ask you—what would you say about this man? Be honest. If you're like most of us, your feelings at this point are not kind. In fact, they're judgmental. 'How dare he?' you ask, with righteous anger. 'There's no way a man of God could behave in such a depraved way?' 'Is he even a *Christian?*' 'I would *never* do that!' 'He should be immediately removed as pastor.'

"And on that last one, I'd probably agree with you, for reasons I'll get to later. But let me push back a bit. You've heard about his *behavior,* now let me describe what was going on in his head and his heart. What if after telling you that story, I now explain that this pastor was anguished over his sin. He knew he was a sinner, and he desperately wanted to stop. He groaned for God's help and mercy."

He looked up and cocked an eyebrow. "It perhaps makes a little difference to your indignant thoughts, but not much. I bet that at least half of you are thinking, 'Who cares if he was anguished? He could stop if he really wanted to!'

"That's really the crux, isn't it? We judge someone who's sinning because we think, 'They could stop if they really wanted to.' And sometimes that's probably right. And sometimes it may not be. But it doesn't really matter, does it? When we ourselves don't struggle with that particular problem, it's easy to 'be confident of our own righteousness and look down on everybody else.'

"But should we? I say no, and for one much-overlooked reason. People often quote the passage where Jesus said, 'Do not judge,' but in the context it's clear that Jesus commanded us not to judge *hypocritically*. 'First take the plank out of your own eye, and then you will see clearly to remove the speck from your brother's eye.' What I'm arguing today is that for us sinful humans, it is very, very difficult to judge purely and not hypocritically. We have an awful time seeing that log in our own eye, much less removing it. And you know something? Once we go through the pain, self-examination, humility, and heartache of removing that log, suddenly we really don't feel like bashing the guy next door for his speck of sawdust.

"We often think it's our right—sometimes even our duty—to point out where others are sinning. Now, the Bible is very clear that there's a distinction between trying to correct Christians who are in sin, and trying to correct those in the world.

"In 1 Corinthians 5, Paul has some pretty strong words about this. 'I have written you in my letter not to associate with sexually immoral people—not at all meaning the people of this world who are immoral, or the greedy and swindlers, or idolaters. In that case you would have to leave this world. But now I am writing you that you must not associate with anyone who calls himself a brother, but is sexually immoral or greedy, an idolater or a slanderer, a drunkard or a swindler. With such a man do not even eat. What business is it of mine to judge those outside the church? Are you not to judge those inside? God will judge those outside. "Expel the wicked man from among you."'

"In other words, look first to the sin inside the body of Christ and deal with that. 'Okay,' you say, 'I can do that.'" Pastor Steven rubbed his hands together in mock glee. "'I've been waiting to sharpen my claws on that person who's addicted to pornography; let me at him!'

"Oh, but wait. Aren't you forgetting something? Do you have a log that needs to be dealt with first? Hmm…let's look at all the other things on this 1 Corinthians list besides sexual immorality. What's next? Greed."

"Uh-oh…" Steven's voice deepened portentously and despite themselves, the frozen congregation laughed.

"Well, let's skip greed. I know I worry about money a little too much, am a little too attached to my stuff. Let's just go on down the list. Surely nothing else in the list applies to me, and I can get on with skewering that poor pornography addict."

Steven ran his finger down the list. "Idolatry. *Doh!*" Steven slapped his hand to his head. "Do I lean on anything other than God to sustain me? Do I ever rely on my intellect, my money, my marriage, my work ethic instead of my sovereign Lord?

Okaaay, this exercise isn't working out the way we thought it would, is it? Let's just move on down that list.

"Slander. Do I ever gossip? Do I ever talk about someone behind his back? Do I make myself look good, but stir up dissent against others? Am I critical of my boss, my coworkers, or those in leadership, having never walked in their shoes?" Steven looked out over the congregation, wishing he could just for a moment be spiteful and call out a few names of those who had made his life miserable.

"I think you get the point. What Jesus is saying is that we have to be constantly aware of our own sinfulness and at least be trying to deal with it in humility before we go confront others about their sin. That's the solution for being 'confident of our own self-righteousness and looking down on everybody else.' And inside the church, there's a clear biblical pattern for discipline that's not designed to bash the sinner and make him or her feel awful—and make us feel self-righteous for pointing it out—but is designed to bring the sinner to repentance, to make that person whole again.

"Jesus came to this earth not to make us feel good, but to save us from our sins. That was the whole point. And unless we come to a real understanding of our own sin, we will *never* fully understand or accept what our Lord and Savior did for us. We will continue to believe—however secretly—that we can work our way into heaven. That He owes us a place in heaven, because we've been a pretty darned good person, thank you very much.

"But He owes us nothing. Sin is not just an immoral action—it is anything that separates us from God. And our very nature does that, day in, day out, every day of our lives. All we deserve, truly, is to be lost in the darkness for all eternity. We are more sinful than we ever dare realize. *But,* thank our Lord, that is not the end of the story. We're also more loved and forgiven than we ever dared hope! That's the Good News, the message we carry to the world. That through the blood of Jesus, in spite of ourselves, we have been redeemed. God loves us so much that all we have to do is accept that redemption for ourselves, to accept the trade that has already been made: Jesus' life for ours."

Steven stood straight and tall, his eyes flashing, feeling the surge of the Holy Spirit, the breathtaking love and power of the Almighty in that place. People were sitting forward in their seats, hardly breathing, captivated. It was electric. And it was time.

He turned a few pages in his notes, letting peace settle again upon the crowd.

"So now, let's return to that story I told you at the outset. How would you deal with the pastor who's living both in secret sin and in secret grief at his behavior? Put aside for the moment whether he should be pastoring the church while in that sin—

as Corinthians made clear, he shouldn't be. But think again, in your heart of hearts, how he should be dealt with *personally*, as a man.

"Suppose, for that purpose, he is not a pastor, but a fellow member of your congregation. A well-loved, respected man with a wife and kids. He secretly indulges in graphic Internet pornography by night, and comes to church on Sunday morning. What to do?

"I can see that some of you are still skeptical that such a man should be treated gently. So I have something to tell you before you make a judgment."

He drew himself up, cast a last glance at his wife, and cast himself on the mercy of the Lord.

"I was that man."

He waited while the words sank in, while the astonished gasps resounded around the congregation, while the gasps turned to frozen stillness, all eyes staring.

"Less than ten years ago, my friends, I had a dreadful secret: I struggled with impure thoughts, impure desires. I was in bondage to pornography. I fought it with every ounce of my strength, but time…and again…it conquered me."

He looked out at the dear, well-loved faces, and the tears began to come. He described how he hated himself, wanted to stop, wept before the Lord. But always in secret, and always unable to stop it on his own. He described how it nearly destroyed his marriage, how his wife uncovered his web of lies and deceit. And he described how, through the intervention of one divinely appointed friend—another pastor, who himself had had that struggle—he was brought slowly, slowly along the path to deliverance and healing.

Steven wiped his eyes with the back of his hand. "It is impossible to overstate the importance of compassion and healing for those caught in this sin—like many secret sins. The very fact that it's secret keeps it in a dark place, where Satan rules and God's light cannot shine. But I'm telling you this story today, and revealing years of secret shame, because I know—*I know*—that many in this congregation have this same struggle. It isn't discussed, but it's there.

"And now, I'm speaking to my brothers out there…and to their wives and those that love them. There is hope! There is healing! But you must confess your sin, one to another, and seek help and accountability. Yes, it's hard to set aside your pride. But there is no pride worth being held in bondage by Satan himself, tormented in the darkness. The pain will pass, and the freedom will be beyond belief. There may very well be consequences—there often are consequences of willful sin—but God will be with you every step of the way. And you will finally be free.

"I'm confessing this to you, my dear friends, to provide an example of one very important principle: Everyone has a story. The next time you feel inclined to judge someone, examine not only yourself and your logs, but your assumptions about them. Is that unbeliever on drugs? Who knows what they have gone through. Is that woman a constant, shameless gossip? Who knows what secret insecurities she's hiding. Is that driver on the highway rude and aggressive? Who knows what in his past has caused that rage? People usually don't just wake up one day and decide to become a jerk or a druggie or a gossip. There are reasons. And although those reasons do not allow us to excuse them, they force us to try to understand them.

"Jesus was able to minister His unconditional, nonjudgmental love to prostitutes because He loved them, and He knew that every one of them had a story. They didn't just wake up one day and decide to sell their bodies and flaunt God's law. There were reasons why they fell, perhaps even reasons that would make our toes curl should we hear them. We too can have true love for the unlovable if we—with the Lord's help—come to an awareness of our own sin, our own humility, and of the reasons for compassion to the lost and hurting among us."

Steven closed his Bible. It was done.

And just as suddenly, he was attacked by a massive wave of fear. What was he thinking, sharing something so personal—something sexual and depraved—from God's pulpit?

He tried to motion the worship director on to the last song, but he was frozen. They would kick him out. Another church, another family, lost. He forced himself to glance up at the congregation, the many faces, and his eyes swam with tears. This was crazy. He had to get himself under control.

And suddenly, someone stood. A couple, holding hands tightly, in the middle of the congregation. Sherry and Doug.

Everyone's heads swiveled around, and there were low murmurs.

Steven could feel his tears hot on his cheeks, stunned at the brave action, the brave salute from faithful friends.

And then another man stood. A single man, gripping the back of his chair. Then another couple, and a woman, and a divorced single mom. Then his wife stood.

Dozens were rising to their feet. Someone began to applaud, and soon half the congregation was on their feet, applauding.

Steven could hardly see through his tears. He gestured his wife up to the stage, and she bounded up like a twenty-year-old and hugged him close.

He kept an arm around his wife and motioned for silence, wiping away the wetness from his face. The whole congregation was standing, silent, still.

"Thank you." Steven looked across the stage and spoke in a choked voice to the music director. "I would like to change the last song, please. There's only one that seems appropriate right now."

And so in that place, the bride was awakened as the poignant strains of "Amazing Grace" floated to the heavens, every word heard and sung anew.

Amazing grace, how sweet the sound, that saved a wretch like me!
I once was lost, but now am found, was blind but now I see...

THIRTY-SIX

T he voices were warm and cheerful, the smiles—as far as she could tell—genuine. Linda Hanover stuck close by Angela Dugan's side as the younger woman maneuvered her way through the church lobby, introducing her as she went.

"Nice to meet you, Linda... Welcome... Good to have you with us today... Hope you enjoy the service..."

Linda could only smile and nod, hopelessly lost as to names and faces, uncomfortable in the unfamiliar environment. She was wearing the one nice dress she owned, although Angela had assured her that no one would care what she had on. She followed Angela to where her husband had saved them two seats. The two women sat down just as the small choir began to sing.

It was happening again. As the pastor preached, and as the choir sang its final song, Linda choked up and tried to wipe her eyes on her sleeve so no one would see. This love, this new life, was overpowering. How had she missed it all these years?

Her thoughts turned several hundred miles away, to Ronnie alone in the big city, and to who-knew-what temptations and struggles her beautiful daughter must face every day.

If only she would come to know You, Lord. Please, Lord...

And suddenly, without knowing why, her tears were no longer for herself.

The music was pumping and Ronnie's night was in full swing when Marco grabbed her on the fly. He had one of the other dancers by his side, her eyes glazed from an excess of cocaine.

"We've had another request for the girls to double up on stage. Extra five hundred dollars tonight for the takers. Tina's in. Want it?"

"No thanks. Not my thing."

"Fine."

Marco hurried over to another girl, who gave an eager nod. He gave some quick instruction to the two dancers, and they disappeared backstage.

Within moments, the stage went black, and the DJ announced the next act. Ronnie turned away as the two girls appeared onstage and every man in the audience began to hoot and cheer.

School would start in a few weeks, and she still needed some extra tuition money, but she would just have to work extra hard for it. A five-hundred-dollar windfall for the five-minute act wasn't worth it.

She took the opportunity for a short rest and changed into a different outfit. She paused in front of the mirror in the empty dressing room, and looked at the view. She had been working out almost every day, and it showed. She looked and felt fit.

Tiffany came breezing in and began touching up her makeup. The two girls gossiped for a moment, comparing notes. Ronnie was again narrowly beating Tiffany's take—the fifth night in a row.

As the girls went back on the floor, Ronnie saw Marco gesture Tiffany into his office. A few minutes later, Tiffany reappeared in a stunning silvery sheath dress beside a table of four men having some sort of party. The little group headed toward one of the private rooms. Ronnie growled in good-natured annoyance. Her friend was going to beat her take this evening after all.

The night wound down, and only a few dancers were left on the floor. The small private party had dispersed, except for one middle-aged man whose eyes followed Tiffany's every move around the room.

Ronnie watched her friend finish yet another table dance for him and shook her head. The man was short, fat, and had a comb-over, but he appeared to be a generous tipper.

"Ronnie!" Tiffany appeared breathlessly by her side. "I can't believe it! Did you see that? He gave me a thousand dollars!"

"Wow! Jackpot."

"And that's not all." Tiffany winked at her. "He wants me to go out with him."

"Really?" Ronnie peeked over her friend's shoulder and shuddered slightly. "Go for it, girl. Too bad he's not much to look at."

"Who cares? He's loaded. We're going to go get a middle-of-the-night breakfast somewhere right now. I have to kiss Marco for setting it up!"

"Marco? What do you mean?"

"Oh, he knew the guy or something. He convinced Wade to get the private room and now he's smitten."

"Wade? Great name, at least."

Tiffany turned her head to check on her customer. "I better go. This could be the big time, Ronnie. I don't think I'll be back home tonight."

"Be careful, okay? Call me if you have…you know…any problems."

"Ronnie, please. I hardly think I'll have a problem with *him.*" She made a face. "And we're probably going to get a hotel room since we can't go back to his place."

"Why not?"

"Well, technically, he's married."

"What!"

"See, I knew you'd do that! Don't freak out on me. He and his wife are separating. He just hasn't found another place to live yet."

Ronnie gave her a doubtful look. "I don't suppose you want to come back to the apartment? I could make myself scarce…"

"Better not to have him over. That's not how these things work."

"Okay. Be careful."

Tiffany gave her a secret little wave and turned to head back toward her admirer, her silver dress shimmering in the dim light.

"Well? How'd it go last night?"

"He's made of money." Tiffany was hurrying around the apartment, collecting her things for work. "Some big hotshot with Speed Shoes. We ate great food, stayed in a penthouse suite, and were basically catered to all day. He's got an incredible sports car, a house in West Palm Beach, and a ski chalet in Aspen. What a life!"

"Are you going to see him again?"

Tiffany paused and flashed her roommate a grin. "You underestimate me, dahling. He's coming to the club again tonight, and we'll be spending all next weekend together. Marco's giving me the weekend off."

"You're kidding!" Ronnie gave an incredulous laugh.

"Oh no, Marco's really supportive. He even gave Wade the key to his penthouse for last night—apparently he had rented it for the week but wasn't using it or something."

"I'm not talking about Marco, silly. I'm amazed at *you!* You're taking a big moneymaking weekend off. What's come over you?"

"*Wade's* come over me, Ronnie. He lives the life I want." She finished packing up her outfits for the evening and her face turned serious. "He's my ticket. He's totally smitten."

"But you hardly know him."

"I know him well enough to know what he'll do for me. He gave me another thousand bucks to buy some clothes for next weekend. Cool, huh?"

"I guess."

Tiffany's grin turned to exasperation. "Ronnie, don't take away my fun with this! Can't you just be happy for me? I feel like a princess who's just found a fat, bald, and incredibly rich Prince Charming."

"Sorry. I'm sorry I'm so darned practical. I'm glad you found a sugar daddy; I really am. But I don't want you to get your heart involved with some guy who's twenty years older—"

"Give me a break." Tiffany rolled her eyes. "No heart involvement, now or later. You know that. But new clothes, new jewelry, new places…maybe even a new car if I play it right. He wants a beautiful young thing on his arm, and I'm happy to oblige! Ta ta!"

She swept out the door, and Ronnie went slowly into her bedroom to finish gathering her things for work. What was it about Tiffany's new situation that bothered her so much? She was with a wealthy man who obviously liked her very much and showered her with money and gifts in return for her attention. What was wrong with that? Ronnie was climbing into her own car, when it hit her.

Her friend had just become a prostitute.

THIRTY-SEVEN

Linda Hanover picked at her dessert, embarrassed at all the attention. The Dugans—both generations—had taken her to a popular restaurant in a nearby town for her birthday. They had even arranged for the waiter to bring out a plate of rich chocolate cheesecake as a surprise, decorated with one lit candle.

The staff had gathered around the table, clapping and singing a raucous birthday song. Linda's cheeks had been red ever since. No one had ever done anything like this for her before. She'd hardly ever been out to eat before, at least to someplace nicer than fast food.

The waiter came back and handed Mr. Dugan the bill.

"Are you sure I can't help—"

"Not a chance." Mr. Dugan smiled. "You'll be starting that job at the clinic next week, and after that you can help all you want. Until then, it's on us."

"Thank you."

The waiter stopped back by to gave Mr. Dugan his change. "Here you go, sir." He looked at Linda and grinned at the half-eaten dessert in front of her. "So, has that cheesecake gotten the best of you?"

"I'm afraid so. I haven't had any chocolate this rich in…well…I don't know when."

"You'll just have to come back more often. Our cheesecake is famous far and wide. We've had dessert chefs stop by from all over. You done with that, ma'am?"

She pushed the plate toward him, and he began to clear the table.

"So did you talk to your daughter today?" Mr. Dugan asked.

Linda sat up straight. "I forgot to call her back! She called me before she left for work, but Angela was on the other line. I promised I'd call her right back, but I plumb forgot." She looked at her watch and sighed. "She'll be way too busy to take a call now. Dinner shift and all."

The waiter cleared Linda's cheesecake plate. "Your daughter work at a restaurant, too?"

"Yep, a big one, apparently. In Atlanta."

"Which one?"

"A place called The Challenger. I've never been there."

The young man hooted. "Not surprising, ma'am. I wouldn't want *my* mother to go there either! But I've been there a few times and it's a blast." He elbowed Mr. Dugan in the side. "The girls are dynamite, if you know what I mean."

He turned back to Linda, a teasing expression on his face. "So your daughter a dancer or one of the waitresses?"

Linda heard the words in slow motion, watched the widening eyes of those around her. "A waitress. She's a waitress."

"Ah. Well, good money in that, too, of course. All the girls who work there are drop-dead knockouts, not just the strippers. It's an upscale place. Good tips." He picked up his dish tray and set it on his shoulder. "Thank you, folks. Come back any time. We'll save some cheesecake for you." A grin crossed his face, and he was gone.

Linda jumped when Mrs. Dugan put a hand on her arm. "There's a nice path down by the river. We could walk for a bit."

The whole group trooped outside and headed down the street toward the river. A pedestrian walkway lit by old-fashioned lamps wound its way along the restaurants and shops that lined the river. Linda hardly noticed.

After several minutes of silence, Angela took her husband's arm, and sighed. She looked at Linda. "Well, it doesn't sound like Ronnie is a waitress, does it?"

Linda couldn't walk any farther. What was happening right this minute to her daughter…her baby? She felt a tear roll down her cheek, then another.

Mrs. Dugan took her arm and led her to a bench. The two women sat down, and the others stood nearby. "Did you suspect this at all before?"

"No…*nothing* like this. I can't believe it. I won't believe it. Maybe it's not true…maybe she is a waitress."

The words fell flat, sounding wrong even to her.

Linda closed her eyes. She could hardly blame Ronnie, especially after all the lost years where she had not been a proper mother to the girl. When she had let those things happen to her. She bowed her head, trying to lay her guilt at the Lord's feet as she'd been taught, to realize that she was forgiven and that her heavenly Father could make all things new…and could still change her daughter's heart.

The others laid hands on their friend and began to pray.

One by one the members of the S-Group slipped away from the clamor as the quarterly meeting broke up. At three-minute intervals each man headed toward a little-used hallway and a stairway landing, where he paused to ensure his departure hadn't been noticed in the general din. Then each man made his way up to a blacked-out office on the next floor.

They were delighted that those in the regular group not only missed their unobtrusive departures, but also appeared to be oblivious to the increased activity on the other floors of the building. Over one hundred people had walked up and down the three flights of stairs and past dozens of closed doors in the last few hours, without recognizing any significance in the new ranks of computers, control rooms, video screens, and small satellite dishes that sprouted on every floor.

The S-Group members were deep in discussion when Tyson finally arrived. He took his seat, gesturing to Waggoner to continue briefing the others on several areas of progress.

"The pieces are coming together. We've got at least half of the technical people lined up and have identified some likely sites. Mostly dams, some bridges, some other infrastructure. We're still working on a way to get at the levies around New Orleans and St. Louis. We're not sure of those yet."

One of the other members frowned and looked at Tyson. "But we only have half of the technical capacity we need. Where are we on the other half? We're a total no-go without every single piece of the puzzle in place."

"We still have plenty of time. We'll get there." Tyson gave a sly grin. "It's not a scientific process, after all. We're dealing with people's dirty little secrets. Some targets don't come through and we have to develop new ones."

"Are all of the pieces of the puzzle that *are* in place those who have been compromised? Or is anyone cooperating for money?"

"A little bit of both, frankly. In everyone we're dealing with, we've planted the false trail that this is all about white-collar money laundering or some such thing. So of course even those who've been compromised feel better when they are properly compensated."

"Will they be able to put the pieces together after the fact?"

"Of course. But we'll be long gone, and at the moment we're so well disguised behind layers of intermediaries it's unlikely they'll ever penetrate it. Unless someone's a turncoat. I'd hate to think that such a thing is remotely possible, but I suppose we must come up with a contingency plan, just in case."

"In my experience, it's far better to come up with a preemptive plan than a contingency plan," Waggoner said. "Let's find the best deterrent possible, and dish it out to anyone we're even remotely concerned about. Even if we pick an innocent person, the rest will think twice before breaking silence."

Tyson nodded. "Okay, let's think about when to do that, and how. Only one condition—no one gets killed. You can inflict whatever discipline you feel is neces-sary, but it must be quick to heal and no mortality risk. We do not need the authorities sniffing around."

Waggoner looked agreeable. "I've got some good men. They have some very effective techniques that leave no lasting scars."

"Done. I want you all to make a list of anyone you suspect. We must have total loyalty, and if we can't buy it, we must still enforce it."

"What about all the new analysts and technicians in this building?" one of the others said. "You know I'm concerned about the security aspects of having so many uninvolved people—"

"I know you're uncomfortable, but we've been through that." Tyson said. "The new staff members are doing—as they think—marketing analysis for a legitimate, stand-alone company. Sure, some of our staff down there know the drill, but they're the ones who are supposed to be keeping our secrets. They're the ones we have to make sure aren't jabbering to their clueless colleagues. Besides, all the secure areas are kept locked, and anyone who breaks the company's security rules is fired imme-diately. And even if someone did get curious and break the rules, there's no way they'd understand the larger significance of what they'd seen. Only our most trusted lieutenants know the full picture, and they're being well-compensated for their silence."

Tyson looked at each face in turn, then sat down and turned to Waggoner. "I did not mean to get off on a tangent. Please continue with your briefing."

Marco clicked his cell phone shut and strode out of his office, into the hallway. He caught one of the staff on the fly.

"Tell Sasha I need to see her right away."

Less than a minute later, Tiffany poked her head into his office. "Yeah, boss?"

"Come on in and close the door. I have another business proposition for you." Marco walked over to the sideboard and poured her a drink. "How are things going with Wade?"

"Wonderful." Tiffany grinned. "He's smitten, and he's very, very generous. I just got back from twenty-four hours on his yacht. We flew in from the Florida shore just a couple of hours ago."

"Well, you deserved the days off. I hope you've been enjoying them."

"Yeah…of course."

"Well, I have a favor to ask in return. One that should prove profitable for both of us."

"Shoot."

Marco set down his glass and walked to his window, looking out at the club. "You may not realize this, but the partners that own this club also have businesses in other industries. Sometimes, we like to use the club as a way to get business in those industries."

"Like...what *kind* of industries?"

"Oh, nothing like what you're thinking, probably. Real white-collar industries like technology, advertising, finance, you name it. This club generates cash, and that cash gets reinvested in a lot of different businesses. And like I said, from time to time we try to use our club here to generate business leads or clients in those areas."

"So what does this have to do with me?"

"We'd like your help making an important connection. Your friend Wade is a big shot at Speed Shoes and is responsible for choosing the advertising agency that will create their new Super Bowl commercials. They decided last year to ditch their old one, so the massive Speed Shoes account is up for grabs."

"He mentioned something about that. I wasn't paying much attention."

"Well, here's my proposition: I'd like you to *pay* attention. I need you to convince him to hire our advertising agency to create the commercials. Privately, of course, so that no one knows."

"But...why would he listen to me? I hardly know anything about business or—"

"Yes, but you know *him*. Intimately." Marco turned from the window and came to stand beside her. "I'm very confident that he'll agree. Especially if you show him a few carefully selected pictures that we have."

"What—"

Marco picked up a remote control from his desk and pointed it at the television monitor. The screen sprang to life with several still shots of Tiffany and Wade at the penthouse suite their first night together.

Tiffany gasped. "How did you—"

"Sasha, Sasha. Don't be alarmed. This has nothing to do with you. Wade is a longtime associate of ours, and he's frankly owed us some help for quite some time, but has been reluctant to do so. We had to get some leverage over him, and this seemed to be a perfect opportunity. And by the way, Sasha." Marco put down the remote and walked over beside her, standing very close. He softly ran a hand down her shoulder, her arm. "You looked good in those pictures. I don't think Wade will mind one bit."

Tiffany shivered away from Marco's touch, disguising her nerves by coughing. "You said this was a business proposition. What are you proposing, exactly?"

"That if you're our broker, so to speak, and convince Wade to hire our advertising agency, you'll get 10 percent of the cut."

Tiffany's eyes widened. "But that's—"

"A lot of money. It could easily be fifty grand. Or more. But remember, this has to be completely confidential. You can't tell anyone about this deal."

Tiffany thought for a moment and felt a grin creeping back onto her face. "Where do I sign up?" She glanced over at the television monitor. "And I don't think I'll need those pictures. I have other means of persuasion."

"So where are you going this time?"

Ronnie sat on Tiffany's bed, munching on a sandwich as she watched her best friend scurrying around the room. A small suitcase lay open on the bed beside her, and Tiffany had laid out a selection of clothes—new clothes, purchased with Wade's money.

Tiffany held up a pair of black Capri pants, muttering to herself. "Wade likes these, but not the khaki ones…where are those cute shoes?"

She got down on her knees and looked under her bed. Ronnie could hear her batting things away, fishing in various boxes.

A muffled voice came from under the bed. "Here they are!" Tiffany pushed herself back and sat up, handing Ronnie a shoebox. She brushed her hair back out of her eyes. "I *can't* go to the beach without those sling-backs."

"Never." Ronnie kept a straight face. "First rule in blackmail and seduction—wear the right shoes."

Tiffany made an annoyed sound and yanked the box back from her friend. "I wish I'd never told you. I knew you were never going to let me forget about that."

"I just think it's weird that Marco would resort to blackmail to get some random business deal approved. I can't believe you'd go for it."

"You're just jealous. You'd go for it in a second if you were in my shoes. Besides, Wade owes Marco a favor and hasn't been delivering; it's the least he can do. And if I can help my boss *and* make a small fortune in one fell swoop…well, why not?"

"But without using the blackmail pictures, how are you going to convince Wade to approve this deal? You don't know anything about advertising or commercials…or business!"

"Give me a little credit. I'm not a total idiot—"

"I'm not saying you are!"

"—and I may not be a slick Madison Avenue businesswoman, but Wade isn't interested in a Madison-avenue businesswoman. He's interested in me. I make him look good to his colleagues and friends, and I stroke his ego. He takes care of me very nicely, and I make him feel like the most virile male on the planet. He won't risk losing that, especially since I'm only asking him to pick one good New York advertising agency instead of another. It'll be an easy choice for him."

Ronnie stared at her friend. "I don't know whether to admire your insight or be angry at how easy it is for you to manipulate this guy."

"Ronnie…" Tiffany shook her head. "I've been manipulating this guy from day one. The difference now is that I know him well enough to know what he needs emotionally and how to give it to him. I make him feel powerful. That's what every man wants." She looked over her shoulder at her friend and winked. "You're already doing that exact same thing whenever you do a table dance at the club. You just didn't realize it."

Ronnie shook her head in reluctant admiration. Tiffany snapped her suitcase shut.

"Stick with me, kid. I'll teach you everything you need to know."

Tiffany stood on the top deck of the yacht, allowing the wind to whip through her hair. She wore a bikini and sipped a drink, oblivious to the party sounds all around her, oblivious to everything but the feel of the wind. And what she would do with an extra fifty grand.

She'd first proposed the idea to Wade a couple hours ago, before the guests arrived. At first, he'd been taken aback and had started to click into business mode, but Tiffany had deftly made sure that didn't happen.

A short time later, she brought it up again and subtly planted the message that this was a key to retaining her favor. Marco's ad agency colleagues would be in Atlanta in a few days—what a coincidence—and why didn't he just meet with them to see what he thought.

Wade had nodded sleepily—a meeting couldn't hurt—before drifting off, his head cradled in her lap.

Tyson slapped the cell phone shut. He excused himself from the meeting he'd been in and wound his way around computer monitors, satellite dishes, and out of the bustling floor area. In a few moments he was at his computer, tapping out a message to Proxy.

Target met with ad team today, agreed to proposal. Broker says target's company surprised with the choice, but not disagreeable. They welcome the "fresh approach" of our team.

Tyson reviewed the short message, chuckling as he read the end. *If they only knew.*

THIRTY-EIGHT

Tyson poured a drink in Marco's deserted office and knocked it back. He poured another one, then stood at the one-way window, restless, watching the early evening activity on the club floor. This was getting ridiculous.

He was looking at his watch for the third time when Marco strolled through the door.

"What kept you?" Tyson said. "I'm supposed to report to Proxy in twenty minutes!"

Marco raised his eyebrows and, without a word, walked over to the bar and began preparing himself a drink. Tyson took a breath and forced himself to lower his voice.

"You know that Proxy is anxious to get all the pieces in place and get moving. He's concerned that you, Marco, are not anxious enough."

Marco took his time settling into his chair, then swiveled to face his colleague. "And I know that you, Tyson, are lying through your teeth. We're right on schedule. I have delivered the most important piece of the puzzle thus far—and will deliver the rest as promised—and I doubt whether Proxy would be happy to know that you're trying to threaten me."

"Well, he'll never know, will he? What you think is irrelevant. Proxy talks to me and me alone, and I think you better learn that lesson fast."

He nodded toward the window, where he could see the new girl, Macy, table-dancing for a nearby patron. "You need to activate her, Marco. Her and the others. Sasha's good, but she's not enough. We have very little time, and we need to work fast before they become suspicious."

"Last year, Proxy agreed on a schedule, and I'm sticking to it. I won't rush it and risk it backfiring. These things take time."

"And I'm telling you, you're out of time." Tyson leaned down and locked eyes with the club manager. "Consider this your new schedule—begin the next phase immediately."

"But Proxy never—"

Tyson slapped his hand on the desk. "Forget Proxy! You take orders from me;

I take orders from Proxy. If I give you a direct command, you obey it as if it came from him."

Marco stared at him for a long moment, then rose to his feet and gave an exaggerated salute. "Yes, sir!" He dropped his hand and stared into Tyson's face. "And privately, sir, I think you're a fool."

Marco watched Tyson stalk out of the office. He was a sharp Ivy League hotshot and had proven that he knew his stuff, but he was getting too big for his britches. He was beginning to feel the power, and it was affecting his judgment.

It was foolish to push further so soon. Marco wasn't sure that Macy was ready, nor the other two girls he had in mind. He thought a moment, then dialed Tyson's cell phone number. It rang only once.

"What?"

Marco kept his voice calm. "Would you run my question about the schedule by Proxy, next time you contact him?"

Silence. "Fine. I'll let you know what he says."

Marco thanked him and hung up. He turned to his computer and tapped out an e-mail to each of the girls. Might as well get started.

"Did you get this?" Ronnie walked into the kitchen where Tiffany sat in the window nook, eating a late breakfast. She was waving a printout of an e-mail. "What's the deal with this party next weekend?"

Tiffany continued crunching her cereal and reading a magazine. "Oh, Marco rents these party boats from time to time, and takes key clients out. We work the parties as entertainment."

"You mean we have to dance somewhere other than the club? I'm not sure I like that idea."

Tiffany glanced up at her roommate, a small smile on her face. "Do you like the idea of a few extra thousand bucks for an easy day's work?"

"Who pays?"

"The guys, mostly. Sometimes Marco, too. It just depends. I'm not sure what the deal is with this one. I hadn't heard about it before."

"Who'll go from the club?"

"They usually pick four or five girls. It's a fun day, honest. You'll love it. It's more like fun than work."

"Except for the stripping."

"Lighten up, would you? Sheez, you'd think you didn't play to a crowd of men every night, the way you're acting."

"It's different onstage." Ronnie struggled to explain herself. "I'm putting on an act. I'm—you know—a different *person.*"

Tiffany stood up and walked to the sink, washing off her breakfast dishes. She gave Ronnie a compassionate glance. "I know. I felt the same way at first. But honest, you keep your stage persona there, too, you know."

She lifted her chin and assumed a pose. "You're Macy, the new hot dancer, whether or not you're in the club, going shopping with the other girls, or entertaining at a private party somewhere. It makes no difference that it's daytime and you're on a boat instead of on a stage. Just keep your mind on the money you'll be making and you'll be fine."

Ronnie started to ask another question when the phone rang. Tiffany reached for it, then handed it to her roommate.

"It's for you, *dahling.* I've got to get going. I'm meeting Wade for some cocktail party thing this afternoon."

"Hello?"

"Hi, hon."

"Mom! Hi! How are you?"

"I'm doing fine, sweetheart. I started that job at the clinic, and I feel like I'm getting back on my feet. I'm going to start paying rent soon."

"That's great, Mom—"

"But really, I was just checking in to see how you're doing. I get concerned when I don't hear from you."

"I know, Ma, I know. I think about you a lot, really, I do. I just…" She sighed and plopped down on the window seat. "I just get so busy. I'm sorry."

"I understand. I was the same way when I was your age. But tell me how you're doing, hon." There was a strange pause. "How's your job at the restaurant?"

"It's fine. I…uh…got promoted a while ago, which is why I'm making more money. I've even saved up enough for tuition. You knew I start classes this week, right? I'll start with summer school."

"I'm proud of you, honey. Are you nervous?"

"Well…" Ronnie gave a sheepish laugh. "Yeah, of course. A little, anyway. I hope I can handle the course load, working and going to school at the same time. But if I can—if I can take summer classes each year—I might even be able to graduate on time!"

"Are you sure you can handle that—working and school at the same time?"

"I can handle it, Mom. I'm not stupid, you know."

"I never said you were."

"Well, actually, you did, sort of."

"When! When did I do that?"

"You implied it plenty during high school, whenever I got a bad grade on a test or something. You'd say that it just went to show that I shouldn't get too big for my britches with any grand ideas for my future."

There was another long pause, and suddenly she heard her mother's voice go taut with emotion.

"I'm so sorry, Ronnie. I really messed you up, didn't I?" There were some sniffles. "Please forgive me. I think I was so resentful at being stuck in a dead-end life that I took it out on you. I'm so sorry."

Ronnie stood with the phone in her hand for a long minute, listening to her mother trying to regain control on the other end of the line.

"Mom...I love you. You know that, right?"

"I know, hon. Not that I've done anything to deserve it."

"I always knew you loved me. Even when..."

Her mother's quiet voice finished the sentence. "Even when I didn't protect you as a mother should?"

"Well..."

"It's okay, you can say it. I'm starting to come to terms with all I never did. Please forgive me."

"Well, you were trapped, too. I'm glad you're out of there. Please tell me you won't go back."

"I won't. I promise."

"Mom...what's happened to you? You sound...different."

"I feel different. I feel free."

"Well, you are. You're not under his control anymore."

"No, I mean spiritually free. I feel like I'm finally discovering who God intended me to be."

"You didn't join a cult or anything, did you?"

A quiet laugh. "No, don't worry. Nothing like that. I've...I've started going to church with the Dugans."

"Oh. Well, that's good, I guess."

"Very good. I hope you can come back for a visit sometime soon and come to church with us."

"Well, I work all weekend, you know."

"Just sometime, maybe. Maybe you can find a church there. Maybe one of your friends has a good church."

Ronnie tried not to laugh at that one. "I'll ask around. Well, I should go. I've got a lot of stuff to do today."

"Okay, sweetheart."

Ronnie hung up the phone and stared at it before shaking her head and walking out of the kitchen. What on earth had happened to her mom?

THIRTY-NINE

The Sunday night service was over, but the ministry time was just beginning. Ronnie's mother was down front, kneeling on the wide steps to the altar, pleading with God.

She was surrounded by people—mostly women, but a few men—who had heard the news and were standing in prayer with their new sister. Linda didn't care that her face was tear-stained and her makeup had run. There were no secrets anymore. No reason to worry about what people thought. The only thing that mattered was her daughter. And these new friends—these people who already seemed like lifelong family—knew it, too.

This was a battle now and they were an army, storming the gates of hell on behalf of a little lost lamb. Linda had no idea yet how to do spiritual warfare. But she knew that she would pray for her girl until Jesus brought her home.

The morning sun hadn't yet cleared the mists when Ronnie slipped out of the apartment, careful not to wake Tiffany.

She paused on the open landing of the stairs and looked out at the trees that lined the complex. They were lush and green, the closed buds dotted with moisture, the full bloom of summer ready to wake to a new day. For just a moment, Ronnie found herself wondering how the flowers knew to sleep at night, how a tree knew to spread its leaves toward the sun…how it could all just be an accident. There was something cosmic in the stillness around her, a sense that a deeper mystery would unfold at the slightest touch.

She took a deep breath to settle her jitters then padded down the stairs toward her car, her backpack slung over one shoulder, her sandals making little noise in the stillness.

She had agonized for an hour over what to wear to orientation day, terrified that the slightest mistake would draw attention to herself. She wanted to get in and out, to make no friendships and answer no hard questions. She would study hard at school and work hard at work, and the two worlds would never mix.

She had finally settled on the basic student uniform: jeans and a simple T-shirt. No one would notice her.

"Ronnie!"

Ronnie started and looked around the half-full auditorium. The admissions director, Mr. Woodward, was coming toward her with a smile. She stood from her aisle seat to meet him, clutching her registration packet.

"Welcome to Georgia State." He shook her hand. "I was so pleased when I saw that you had accepted our admission and would be starting so soon."

Ronnie noticed other students staring, curious at the exchange. Her cheeks flushed. "Thanks…thank you. I'm surprised you remembered me."

"Not at all. You seemed like a motivated person, and I know you'll do well here. And frankly, you seem like someone who can beat the odds, and we want to help and encourage that in any way we can. We believe people like that can change the world if only they get the breaks and the support they need. So I'd like to hear how things go for you here. Well, almost time to start. Please call me, Ronnie, if you need anything."

She found herself nodding at his back as he moved away, shaking a few more hands and sharing words of welcome with others he recognized. She took her seat again, curious as she watched him work the aisle. He looked like he truly cared about those he spoke to, making people feel at home.

Ronnie picked the final textbook off the shelf and rechecked her course list. That had to be everything. She hefted the tall stack of books in her arms. Time to find out the damage. She waited in the long checkout line, and held her breath as the cashier hit a few keys.

"That'll be two hundred and eighty-three dollars."

Ronnie winced. "I was afraid you were going to say something like that. Do I need to get all these books right away, or are there some that I can wait a few weeks?"

The cashier—a middle-aged woman with orangey hair—shrugged. "No idea, doll. You want 'em or not?"

Ronnie glanced at the line behind her, which wound among the bookshelves, at least fifteen people deep. The girl behind her looked at her watch.

"Um…"

"Look, we can't wait all day for you to decide. Either pay or come back when you know what you need."

Ronnie felt a tap on her shoulder. The girl behind her leaned forward, a small smile on her face as she gestured at one of Ronnie's thick textbooks.

"You have Barnes for Biology 101?"

"Yes."

"He spends the first part of class going over a high school refresher. He won't get to the textbook for at least two weeks. And I bet you won't need half of those little literature books until later in the summer. Just keep the main text and you'll be fine for a bit."

"Thanks." Ronnie gave a sigh of relief as she separated out the unnecessary purchases. "I feel totally clueless today."

"Everyone is the first week of school."

The cashier scowled and gave Ronnie the new total—one hundred dollars less than the original. Ronnie paid in cash and retreated with another word of thanks to the girl.

She stepped out onto the sidewalk and glanced at her watch. She would need to hustle to make it to work on time.

The next morning, Ronnie tried to stifle another yawn as she climbed the stairs heading for her second class. She saw a familiar face coming toward her and paused, glad for the excuse to rest.

"Hi, Mr. Woodward."

"Good morning, Ronnie." He peered at her in the green-tinted light that filtered through the old windows. "Goodness, you look tired."

"Yeah." Ronnie gave another huge yawn. "I had to work late last night and didn't get much sleep."

"I can see that. Too bad you have a nine o'clock class this morning."

"It's the only time they offer Biology 101 in the summer."

"Well, maybe after classes you can go home and take a rest."

No, after classes I need to go to work and exhaust myself all night.

Ronnie gave him a noncommittal smile. "Maybe. At least tomorrow's Saturday."

"Are you getting a sense of how you'll balance things, putting yourself through school and all?"

"Um…not yet. Soon, I hope."

"Well, I'm sure you'll figure it out. And remember to come see me if you need anything."

FORTY

D oug Turner grabbed his suit coat off the back of his chair and stepped out of his office. Mary was on the phone.

"I'll be back in forty-five minutes. I have to get something to eat."

Mary put her hand over the receiver, calling after him. "Don't forget the executive strategy meeting at three o'clock. New client."

Doug looked at his watch and sighed. "Make it thirty minutes, then."

He headed downstairs and out the door, making a beeline for a bustling little deli nearby. This pace was crazy. Almost two-thirty and he hadn't eaten yet. But what else was new? He was making a concerted effort these days to be home by seven—not seven-thirty or eight-thirty like before—but that meant he needed to get to work extra early, often leaving before anyone was up.

The kids, at least, appreciated his extra attentiveness, even if they didn't know the reason for it. Sherry probably did, too, but they still weren't at ease with each other. He ached for the day she would give him a spontaneous hug and snuggle into his arms like she used to early in their marriage, secure in his love for her, before the stresses of life had begun to pull them apart. There had been a few signs of their old playfulness returning, but too few—and they only made him yearn for the old ways all the more. With God's help, he held out hope. It was the hope that was keeping him sane.

That and the surprising support of their home group. It had been so hard to confess—in general terms—what he and Sherry were going through. But after that astonishing church service when they felt moved to stand up and support their pastor, it somehow made it easier. They had little left to lose. And they had unexpectedly gained so much. Their home group had become a haven for them, a place of desperate honesty, a place where everyone knew all their stuff and loved and supported them anyway. Doug had never seen anything like it, and he was quite sure the church hadn't either. Pastor Steven's sermon that day had started an earthquake, and it seemed the rumblings were getting stronger with time.

For the tenth time that day, he thanked God for surrounding him and his wife with such dedicated friends, and for helping him to stay pure. He'd had some mighty struggles, but the protections he and Sherry put in place had—to his surprise—really helped. With his Internet filtering software on all his computers—unbeknownst to his colleagues, he had even installed a copy at work—he could no longer access those awful sites. And since Sherry was now checking his credit card bill, he wouldn't be able to pay for them even if he could. Amazing the pressure it took off, knowing former failing points were no longer an option!

At times when he'd been tempted to get around the system—to sneak into a bookstore on his lunch hour to buy a dirty magazine, or to take a quick detour to a shop selling *X*-rated videos—he'd called Eric or Pastor Steven. Even though he had to force himself to make the calls, once made, they brought such freedom. Knowing that his brothers knew his weakness and loved and supported him anyway had empowered him to somehow resist the temptations even more.

He snapped open the cell phone as he stepped into the deli, noisy and crowded even at this hour. The voice mail answered and he left a quick message.

"Hi, sweetheart. Okay, I'm at the deli. It's…2:35, and I'll probably be here for twenty minutes. Then I have to run back for a meeting at 3:00. You can call me back, or since Mary is at her desk you can check with her if you'd like. I love you."

He hung up and clipped the phone back in its holster, thinking how mortifying it had been at first; reporting his whereabouts to his wife any time he left the office, allowing her to call and check with Mary to corroborate his whereabouts. It had been even more mortifying to bring Mary into his confidence and explain in vague terms why he needed her patience with Sherry's repeated calls. But now, weeks later, it was no longer humiliating; it was just the way it was, the way it needed to be to reassure his precious wife. God was dealing with his pride, too, he realized. And that couldn't be a bad thing. Once he gave up his pride it had somehow allowed Sherry to trust him just a little more, allowed her to make the repeated check-ins almost a game between them, her way of helping him without fear. And anything lighthearted was a boon these days.

Doug gave his order at the deli counter, then took his sandwich, chips, and soda to one of the small tables that lined the shop, said a quick prayer and thankfully dug in.

He had to admit his constant check-ins provided him very little leeway, which had helped in several moments of weakness. He was sure that, if he had wanted to, he could have figured out a way around the system, could have still found a way to sneak around.

But he didn't want to. He was being healed, was feeling freedom for the first time in his adult life. The last thing he wanted was to provide the enemy a new foothold. He knew if he even cracked the door the tiniest bit, that could be enough.

The phone at his belt vibrated—there was no way to hear a ring in here—and he opened it without looking at the readout.

"Sherry?"

There was a pause. "No, Doug. Sorry to disappoint you."

"Sorry, Jordan. I was expecting a call from my wife."

"Ah. Before the meeting at three, can you check your calendar and make sure you're available for a get-together next Saturday with our new client?"

"Saturday? I'm sorry, I need to keep that free—"

"I guess I wasn't clear, Doug. I need you to be there. I just needed to make sure you weren't planning to be out of town."

"Maybe I should go out of town." Doug sighed. "Saturday is family day, chief; you know that."

"Not this weekend. Just check and make sure you have it on your calendar. We'll need to confirm with the new client at the three o'clock meeting."

Before Doug could respond, the line went dead. He polished off his sandwich with no further enjoyment and hurried back to the office. Mary caught him at the door.

"Did Jordan find you?"

Despite himself, Doug made a face and Mary suppressed a giggle.

"Yes, he did. Something about a get-together next Saturday?"

"That's it."

"Do me a favor. I couldn't get ahold of Sherry. Would you keep trying her while I'm in the meeting and explain the situation? We weren't planning on being out of town, which seemed to be the only excuse Jordan would accept. I guess I'm hoping she has something scheduled that we just can't get out of. Buzz my cell phone to let me know. Just leave a text message."

The new client wrapped up his introduction and looked around the small conference table with a self-satisfied air. He pointed at several graphics on the conference screen behind him.

"So you see how the production triangle fits together—we provide the digitizing and production technology that allows a signal to be sent and received, our clients provide the content to be broadcast, and our partners provide the satellite space. Since you geniuses have the capability to link diverse systems, we need you to develop the protocols for linking the triangle—linking our hardware, their content, and the software necessary to actually complete a satellite broadcast."

Doug raised a finger. "So it sounds like your ultimate purpose is to be a one-stop shop for anyone looking to get content from point-to-point via satellite broadcast. Like what sort of content—television shows?"

"Like anything you would want or need to be broadcast by satellite, which these days is almost anything. It doesn't have to just be television signals. It can be anything from a television commercial to a sophisticated code that will remotely operate robotic hardware. It really doesn't matter what sort of signal it is."

Doug's phone vibrated at his waist, and as another person in the meeting asked a question, he took a surreptitious glance at the readout.

Wife says, "If you have to, you have to. I'll take the kids to White Water that day."

Doug sighed, though he could hardly blame Sherry for going ahead and scheduling the outing without him, given how unpredictable his work schedule was at times.

Twenty minutes later, Jordan and his new client stood and shook hands like the old friends they apparently were.

"I've been waiting a long time for the opportunity to do a deal with you all," Jordan said, "and this looks like a good fit. We'll send you a package in the next few days. In the meantime, we're all on for the yacht party Saturday, if you and your partners are still able to join us."

The client's face lit up. "Ah, Saturday. I've been looking forward to it. You took one of my partners to a party like this before, not long ago, and Wade hasn't stopped talking about it yet. Wade said—"

"Everyone got it on your calendars?" the COO asked, looking around the room.

Doug was watching the exuberance on the face of their new client. The man looked like a child who'd just been handed a bag of Halloween candy and couldn't wait to dive in.

Very odd, Doug thought. It was just a boat party. Probably a long, hot day of sitting on the deck of a cramped cruiser and pretending to enjoy the shallow company and conversation. He couldn't wait until it was over.

Tyson's e-mail chimed. Another note from Proxy.

He has agreed to come on the yacht. They must have plenty of cameras so nothing is missed. Have Marco pick the right girl. Even if target is uncooperative, the pictures will be enough.

We would like to keep this target operational, if at all possible. Your investigator indicated that he and wife are in marriage counseling. His secretary is

THE LIGHTS OF TENTH STREET 265

*also worried about him. Possibility exists that he told wife about his weakness.
Therefore, Marco must deliver good additional leverage, soon.*

This would be so easy. Their investigator had uncovered further evidence that this target was desperately concerned about losing his wife and would do anything to keep her. Even if Marco's girl failed, they would have plenty of pictures of the target lounging on the deck of a ship, surrounded by lovely young things wearing nothing much at all.

FORTY-ONE

Saturday dawned clear with a hint of rising warmth in the air. Ronnie Hanover checked an on-line weather site and learned it should get into the seventies. Yippee. At least her skin wouldn't turn blue.

Ronnie showered and shoved a bikini and a change of clothes into her carry bag. She stared at the stack of untouched textbooks on her floor. "Why did I agree to this? What was I thinking?"

There was a quick knock on the door, and Tiffany poked her head into the room. "Ready to go?"

"Ready as I'll ever be."

"Oh, stop grousing, girl! You sound like my mother. This'll be fun!" Tiffany bounced into the room and picked up Ronnie's carryall. "Good food, good drinks...and lots of cash for a short day's work."

"I still don't know why I agreed to it."

Ronnie allowed herself to be propelled out of the apartment and into Tiffany's yellow convertible. She tried to relax as they sped toward their destination—a large, private lake an hour from Atlanta. Tiffany bubbled on about the men that would be there, who they were, what they did—how much money they had.

Ronnie listened with half an ear. Maybe if she got sloshed it would be okay. And maybe she wouldn't mind a sugar daddy, like Tiffany's friend Wade. It would be better, in some ways, than the stage work—just one guy, rather than many. And she sure wouldn't mind the perks Tiffany enjoyed: all the new clothes she could want, some great jewelry, and enough cash that she was thinking of buying a house. A nice house.

Ronnie watched the trees speed by. But would it be worth it? What would she be giving up? She looked sideways at her friend. *Had* Tiffany given up anything by acceding to such a calculating relationship with Wade? Not really—she got what she wanted out of it, just like he did.

For just a moment, she let her mind replay the rush of power she felt on stage. She wouldn't mind having that in a relationship—having some guy wrapped around her little finger. It would be nice to be in control, to be the one in the driver's seat for a change. Already, that was one thing she'd gained from her time on stage: confidence. She was in control of her own destiny. She'd never be a victim again.

"You'd better hurry or you'll be late."

Sherry Turner tried to shoo Doug out the door, but he pulled a jar out of the fridge and calmly began smearing grape jelly on top of the peanut butter on three slices of bread.

"Not until I finish helping you get ready for White Water. The cooler's almost packed, so you should be able to avoid the highway robbery of the snack bars at the park."

He heard a squeal and glanced over his shoulder to where their two little banshees were chasing each other around the kitchen table, hardly able to endure the wait.

"But you'll miss your boat," Sherry said. "They'll set off without you."

"I guess I'm hoping that might happen and I can still go to the park with you guys."

Sherry snorted. "More likely, they'll wait for you, and Jordan will make your life miserable for holding everyone else up."

"Yeah." Doug finished wrapping the last sandwich. "Well, I guess I'm done anyway. I'll have my cell phone if you need me."

"Okay." Sherry hesitated, then gave Doug a hug, the second one that morning. "Have fun."

"I'll try. But I'd have a lot more fun being with you."

Doug gave her and the kids a quick kiss and left the house before Sherry could see the redness in his eyes. Those hugs this morning had been like water to his desperate thirst.

He drove away thanking God and praying for his family, for himself, for the Lord's continued protection and grace. He kept the car radio off. The only sound was the humming of the engine and his quiet prayers. It was an hour drive to the lake, and he knew that this morning—like so many others recently—he could fill it entirely with fellowship with his Lord.

A few minutes later, the minivan backed out of the driveway and headed toward the highway.

The giant figure following close behind could see the van practically rocking with the exuberant excitement of the two children. When the family reached their destination, Caliel watched as the kids went running through the payment booths and into the delights of the day. Sherry kept trying to keep Genna by the hand, but she was skipping and bouncing, and Sherry finally let her run ahead with Brandon. Caliel kept an eye on them—and on the watchful dark forces that loitered here and there—as he called his team together and conferred about their mandate.

Every face was grave. This would be a painful assignment, but the order had come from the Lord of Hosts. Caliel watched Genna run back to her mother, and tug on her hand, pulling her along, saying something about a new ride, a new feature of the water park. The timing was coming soon, too soon.

They would carry out their orders without question, trusting in the ultimate plan and purpose of the Almighty. The Heavenly Father loved this little family so much. Despite what this day might look like to them, His heart for them was always and only good. Caliel prayed that the family would not stumble because of it, and that they would at some point be allowed to understand the reason for this day.

Caliel and his team sent forth a simple prayer for guidance, and for the good purposes of the Father to prevail, and then broke ranks, heading to their assigned tasks. One angel hastened away to rendezvous with others of their unit. The timing had to be perfect.

Tiffany parked in the marina's lot and nodded at the men standing on the quay, talking.

"There you go, Ronnie! One of those has your name on it."

Ronnie peered through the windshield. "Oh, goodie."

Tiffany pushed her Gucci sunglasses up on her nose and grinned at her friend as they walked toward the group.

"Ready?"

The men caught sight of them and one of them stepped forward. Tiffany squealed and ran forward. She kissed him long and hard, and the man fairly smirked with pride when he looked up, keeping Tiffany close by his side.

"Wade, you remember Macy, don't you?" Tiffany said.

"Of course." He extended a hand, which Ronnie shook.

As some of the other dancers arrived, Wade made the introductions around to the other men.

How bizarre, Ronnie thought, to be politely shaking hands with someone you're going to undress in front of in a few minutes. She shook herself and put on a polite smile. "So, Wade, are these men your colleagues?"

"Partners. Not necessarily colleagues, but partners. Some work with me, but most belong to companies that work with us to produce our broadcast marketing materials—commercials, corporate films, that sort of thing. Several of these guys are key players in producing our next Super Bowl commercial."

"Ah."

Ronnie started to say something about the advertising contract Tiffany had cajoled him into, but caught her roommate's dagger glance and thought better of it.

A sports car pulled up, sending gravel flying, and Marco stepped out. He strode up and said hello, then gestured for everyone to get onboard.

"Is everyone here?"

One of the men said they were still waiting for a colleague. No one seemed to mind the delay. Ronnie watched as Marco huddled with the man who had spoken, curious that they seemed to know each other well. She'd never seen him in the club, that she could recall. Marco beckoned them onto the boat, and they disappeared down an interior passageway.

A well-dressed young man wearing tailored khakis and an expensive shirt appeared at Ronnie's elbow, and she allowed him to help her onto the boat. He looked ready to talk, but she gave him a sweet smile and asked if he knew where the restrooms were located. He pointed around a few corners.

She found the restroom—the "head," the man had called it—with little trouble. She was touching up her makeup and preparing to go join the party when she heard voices approaching down the little corridor outside. They stopped for a moment well shy of the door, but Ronnie could hear them as if they were standing in the same room.

"Well, he promised he'd be here, and he's not the type to break his word."

The second voice was Marco's. "I hope so. We have the perfect girl with us today. He's married and she's not the type to be a marriage breaker, so he'll probably have his guard down around her more than any of the other girls. That will be the easiest means. She's still new and untested—she's never done a party like this before—but we can't wait any longer. We'll see how she does."

What on earth were they talking about?

Ronnie thought about barging out into the hallway and asking, but thought better of it.

The men moved on down the hall. Ronnie waited a few minutes, then slipped out of the bathroom and found her way back to the party by another route.

Five minutes later, Marco found her. He took her arm, and for just a flash Ronnie felt a strange terror overtake her, a certainty that he knew she'd overheard him and that he would kill her as a result.

Ronnie forced herself to shake off that crazy thought, dampening her racing heart. What was wrong with her? Marco was *family!*

He pulled her aside, talking in quiet tones. A new man was coming on the boat today. Would she keep him company? His name was Doug and he was a big shot finance guy at one of Wade's partner companies. Marco had never met him, but heard that he was a bit reserved. Could Ronnie draw him out, make sure he had a good time? He probably wouldn't tip her anything, but Marco would cover that. Just take good care of him. And next weekend, he added, he had an even bigger party he'd like her to cover.

Ronnie agreed, nodding, surprised at her own disappointment. So no sugar daddy. At least this weekend.

She looked around the room. "Where is this Doug guy?"

"He should've been here by now. He probably just got stuck in traffic."

Marco left Ronnie watching the deck and made his way to a back room. He stepped into the small space and greeted its occupants, closing the door behind him.

"Are we ready?"

The two men turned and gave him a thumbs-up. They pointed at several monitors showing crystal-clear views of the main party room.

"We've got this room wired, and most of the other places they could go."

"Bedrooms?"

"Of course!" One of the men looked insulted. "What do you take us for, amateurs?"

Marco grinned and slapped him on the back. "Hardly. I'm just sorry that you have to spend this beautiful day cooped up in here, rather than out enjoying the show."

"Oh, we'll enjoy the show all right." The second man was talking. "But we expect you to sneak us some of that food you shipped on board. We can't give up *everything* you know."

"Deal." Marco made ready to depart. "Don't spare the film."

"Don't worry, chief. We'll get plenty of pictures of Mr. Doug Turner enjoying himself."

Marco's eyes gleamed. "Perfect."

"Mommy, can we go on that one? Please, please, *please?*"

Sherry took one look at the impossibly high water slide—more like a vertical wall, surrounded by the park's lush landscaping—and gave a strangled laugh.

"Goodness no, Genna! I don't want you to break your neck! I don't care if that older boy told Brandon he could handle it; it's too much for either of you. And look at it—I don't think you *really* want to do it."

Sherry squatted down beside Genna and gestured to the top of the tall tower where teenagers waited to plunge down the slide and into the splash pool far below. "See how high that platform is? You'd probably climb all the way to the top, and then change your mind anyway."

"But, Mom!"

Sherry held up a finger. "No whining or we'll have to leave. That's the rule for today. Okay?"

When her daughter nodded, she stood up and took Genna's hand. "We have all day to do as many rides as you want. And anyway, it's Brandon's turn to pick our next ride. Brandon, what's next? Anything but that water slide!" She looked around. "Brandon?"

Her six-year-old son was nowhere to be seen. Sherry turned a full circle, raising her voice. "Brandon!" She turned again, her voice mounting to a panicked shout. "Brandon!"

Genna's eyes were wide. "Mommy, what—"

"I can't find Brandon, honey. He was here just a moment ago. Brandon!"

She was swamped with a feeling of unreality, her eyes sweeping the morning crowds. She held fast to Genna's hand, turning another full circle, her voice tight. "O dear God, help me find him."

"But, Mommy—"

"Not now, honey!" Sherry spotted a security station and began pulling Genna toward it, even as her daughter resisted her efforts. "Genna, stop it! We have to get some nice policemen to help us find Brandon!"

"But, Mommy, he's going to fall!"

"What?"

Sherry swung around and followed the direction of her daughter's hand, pointing toward the steep landscaping around the vertical water slide. Her son was creeping upward where no one was intended to be, climbing over wet stones and plants.

"Brandon!" Sherry screamed, and dozens of heads turned her direction. She ran wildly forward. "Stop, Brandon, stop!"

Sherry reached the base of the landscaping, hardly noticing the ruckus behind her as other park-goers shouted and pointed, as park security made desperate attempts to tell the workers on the tower to stop the ride.

Sherry scrabbled to climb the steep stones, her eyes full of the small towheaded boy, who had just reached the edge of the slide, his little hands gripping the lip of the smooth orange material, his face intent.

Her son couldn't hear her desperate cries. The next teenager to go was sitting on the edge of the slide, crossing his arms over his chest as instructed. He lay back, and the tower worker pushed him off.

Caliel and his comrades slashed their way through the besetting forces, thrashing their way toward the precious child who had been tempted closer, ever closer to destruction. Their forewarning of the malicious plan had not lessened the pain of watching the plot unfold. But the Lord on high had allowed it to go only so far and no farther. His power blazed forth, and Caliel leaped toward the boy.

He reached Brandon as the teenager hurtled down the steep vertical drop, holding the two apart long enough to keep Brandon from climbing full onto the slide. Caliel's face was full of desperate pain as he watched the speeding form brush aside the half-teetering child, the small body flying through the air, landing with a crack on the stones, and then tumbling unconscious to the splash pool below.

"BRANDON!"

Sherry plunged headlong into the splash pool. She scrambled to her feet and caught Brandon up in her arms, crying his name. His eyes were closed, head lolling back, his left arm hanging at a dreadful angle.

Burly lifeguards and uniformed security alike leaped into the pool and cleared a path back out through the gaping crowd, working with amazing speed to lay Brandon on a shallow ledge and breathe life into his lungs.

Sherry could feel strangers holding her, hugging her, even heard a few voices praying aloud for her and her son.

"Brandon…" She was weeping now. "Baby…"

"It's okay." A uniformed woman had a blanket about Sherry's shoulders, holding her back, preventing her from interfering with the emergency team. "It'll be okay. It's okay."

Sherry wanted to flail at her, to scream that it wasn't okay, that her baby was unconscious or dead, that she would never be able to live with herself—

"He's breathing!" A shout went up from the emergency team. "Get a blanket here, stat!"

Sherry tore free of the uniformed lady and pushed forward, her eyes wild. Someone tried to hold her back, but she sensed someone else reaching out a hand.

"It's the mother... Let her through... The mother..."

Brandon was lying on a low ledge, retching and coughing. A shirtless lifeguard and a slender female EMT hovered over him, covering him with blankets, speaking soothing words. They stood as Sherry appeared, clearing the way.

"Careful..." She heard the words in a dim corner of her mind. "Careful...broken arm...he's okay but let him lie flat a minute..."

She reached her son and collapsed to her knees, wiping his mouth, stroking his hair, telling him how much she loved him, how she couldn't have lived with herself if anything happened to him.

His eyes opened, and a jagged wail came from his mouth. "Mommy...!" He tried to reach for her, and cried out in pain. "Mommy!"

She embraced him, crying also, careful of his broken arm. He buried his face in her shoulder, and she buried her face in his hair, rocking him, her voice choked. "Thank You, Jesus. Thank You, Jesus."

The gaze of the hovering figures swept the crowd. Caliel ensured that the strangers holding and hugging the terrified Genna were guided to Sherry's side.

Then his gaze turned stern and he gave swift orders for the pursuit and destruction of the enemy forces that had dared to come against the children of God. Just because the Lord, in His unfathomable wisdom, had allowed the evil ones to act on their constant malice for a short time, did not mean that they would not bear the consequences of their actions.

As the angels drew their swords, their faces blazing with righteous anger, Caliel turned back to the groups below, his gaze anxious. The call must be made, and soon, or it was all for naught.

Marco was leaving the control room when one of the men whistled for him to return. His subordinate was tapping on one computer monitor, showing the marina parking lot. A car had just pulled into the lot.

"Is this your guy?"

Marco looked close at the profile visible through the car window. "It's him." He stood up and a slick smile crossed his face. "Let the party begin."

Doug turned off the engine and sat in the car. The yacht was still sitting at quayside, and he could hear laughter and music.

With an effort, he opened the car door and stretched to his feet. He could hear women's laughter in the mix. How odd. He had assumed it would just be men since the new client didn't have any women executives on his team. Doug shrugged and reached to get a small satchel out of the car. Perhaps a couple of the men had brought their wives.

He made a quick search of the satchel—swimsuit, towel, and a change of clothes. His hand brushed his cell phone, and he looked at the display. No signal out here. He might as well leave it in the car.

The EMT finally stood aside, and allowed Sherry to gather Brandon up into a hug. He clung to her like a limpet, all first-grade pride swept away in the desire for his mother's comforting arms.

Caliel dropped through the crowd, standing close by Sherry's shoulder, speaking urgent words to her. She was so dazed, all her attention attuned to the limpet, that the words just bounced off. They didn't penetrate.

He heard the urgent message from heaven, and tried a different tactic, reaching out his hand toward the boy.

Sherry started as Brandon raised his head and looked at her, his left eye already beginning to swell.

"Daddy!" He wiped his nose on his arm. "Where's Daddy?"

"Daddy's away for the day, remember?" Even as Sherry tried to reassure her son, the thought registered. She had to catch him before he left on the boat.

"Where's my bag?" Her voice was urgent, startling the EMTs and security personnel. "I have to call my husband!"

The female EMT unclipped a phone from her belt. "I don't know where your bag is, but you can use this."

Sherry grabbed the phone and punched in Doug's number. It rang, and then a tinny voice came on. "The cellular customer you are trying to reach is unavailable. Please try again later."

Sherry closed her eyes in frustration. *Try again. Pray, and try again.*

"Lord, I don't know why you allowed this to happen, but please, please let me get Doug so he can come be with his baby."

She punched the numbers again.

☆ ☆ ☆

Doug tossed the cell phone on the car seat and closed the door. He started to turn away, then stopped short. Was that ringing he heard? He unlocked the door and grabbed the phone.

Huh. It had a signal now. But the call was from an unfamiliar number.

He hesitated—then pressed the answer button.

Thirty seconds later, he was jogging toward the yacht, the phone still pressed against his ear, his face white.

"Jordan! Jordan!" He reached the gangplank and hollered down toward the party sounds. "Hold on, sweetheart. I just need to tell them I'm leaving." He hollered again.

A young woman came around the corner, her eyes welcoming. She stopped just short of the gangplank.

"You must be Doug."

"What? Yes. Where's Jordan?"

"Jordan? I don't know who—"

A man came hustling down the hallway from the other direction. "You must be Doug Turner."

"Yes. Listen, I need to get a message to Jordan. Would you tell him I'm very sorry. My son has just had a terrible accident at the water park. He was knocked unconscious and broke his arm. I've got to go meet them at the hospital."

"Of course, I'll tell Jordan." He gestured down the corridor. "He's just on the aft deck. Would you like to come tell him yourself?"

"No, I'm sorry. Please just tell him that I have to leave now. I really apologize."

Ronnie followed Marco as he hustled down the hallway toward the party room. He made his way to the man he'd spoken to out on the quay and pulled him aside again. Suddenly, there was an eruption from that end of the room, and Ronnie realized it must be the man Doug had asked for—Jordan—cursing at the top of his lungs.

What sort of man would get angry that a child had just hurt himself and the father wanted to rush to be by his side? What sort of people were they?

FORTY-TWO

A few weeks later…

S o, what did you think?" Tiffany's eyes sparkled in the darkness of the club's almost-deserted parking lot.

Ronnie opened her car door and threw her bag in. "Oh, I think I'll probably keep seeing him."

"Probably! Okay, okay, you can play cool with me. I know better, my friend. I bet if he comes back tomorrow night, you leave with him again. At least if Marco has his way."

"I don't care what Marco says."

"Yeah, but you sure care about a guy who's prepared to shower you with *those.*"

Tiffany pointed at the sparkling earrings Ronnie wore, the perfect complement to her new dress. All courtesy of Glenn, an ultra-rich manufacturing tycoon who'd taken a serious interest in the last seven days. He had met Ronnie at another boat party the previous weekend, and had started coming to the club the next night. Ronnie had left with him the night after that, and had hardly slept at home since. She'd been hard-pressed to make it to her classes on time. She'd be glad when summer semester ended, and she could register for only afternoon classes in the fall.

"You coming home tonight?"

"Yes, finally. You?"

"Yes!" Tiffany giggled. "Together at last, huh?"

"I haven't even had time to do laundry."

"Me, neither. Worth it, though, isn't it? C'mon, you can say it. 'You were right, Tiff.' C'mon, I know you're thinking it."

Ronnie tried to suppress a smile. "You goof. Oh, okay. You were right."

"You're glad you got your sugar daddy."

"Yes, I'm glad I got my sugar daddy." Ronnie found herself blushing. "So leave me alone, okay? Don't rub it in!"

"He leave you some cash yesterday?"

"Yeah, said he didn't like me being burdened with such a high car payment. So he just wrote a check directly to the car company for three months' worth!"

"Whoo, baby! You owe him big time!"

"Don't I know it." A mischievous smile crossed Ronnie's face. "But I think he finds it an even trade."

Glenn kept an arm around Ronnie as they worked the elegant gathering at his corporate headquarters, smiling and shaking hands with a hundred business colleagues. At Glenn's direction, Ronnie had worn her latest purchase—a stunning black dress—and the diamond earrings he'd given her on their first night together. She looked the equal of any of the well-groomed corporate wives in the room. And quite a bit younger.

She noticed that several of the middle-aged "original wives," as she had taken to calling them, were just as proprietary about their husbands as Glenn was with her. She saw one woman take one look in her direction, and hastily usher her balding husband over to the punch table. She chuckled to herself. As if!

Ronnie smiled and nodded until she thought her cheeks would crack, but it was important for her to be here. Glenn's company was rolling out its latest gee-whiz electronics prototype—a television remote control device that recognized the owner's voice and responded to verbal commands. It was a coup for the company, and a big night for its president. She knew she was the slim, young trophy on his arm, and it surprised her that—far from bothering her—she ate it up. She wasn't as refined as Glenn's crowd, but she was sharp and she could hold her own.

"So what do you do for a living?" one of the corporate wives asked her.

"I'm studying to become a physical therapist."

"How fascinating!"

Glenn's cell phone gave a soft trill just as the woman launched into a story about when her "dear husband" had been in physical therapy.

"Excuse me for a moment, ladies. I need to take this call," Glenn said.

The corporate wife merely nodded and plowed on with her story, but Ronnie hardly heard a word. She had seen the display as clear as day for just a second, and was sure that it showed Marco's number.

What was Marco doing calling *him?* It wasn't like he knew Glenn ahead of time, like he had Wade. He hadn't set her up with Glenn, as he had done with Tiffany and Wade. It had all just been random circumstance. Hadn't it?

Ronnie searched her memory even as she tried to keep one ear open to the woman beside her.

No…Marco hadn't appeared to know Glenn. Glenn had been invited by another person attending that second boat party and was introduced to Marco and

Ronnie at the same time. Come to think of it—the man introducing them had been at the first boat party, too. A memory leaped to mind, and Ronnie straightened. He was the one that had been so furious when that guy had gone to tend to his stricken son!

"What's wrong, dear?" The corporate wife was looking at her, puzzled.

"Nothing. Just needed to stretch my back. All this standing, you know. But you were saying about your husband…"

"Right, dear. So he had only been in bed for two weeks, when the physical therapist…"

Ronnie watched out of the corner of her eye as Glenn spoke quietly into his phone. Every now and then, his gaze would rest on someone else in the room, his face hardening. Ronnie shivered, feeling like a curtain had been pulled back giving her a glimpse into a side of Glenn she'd never seen. Not that she knew him all that well to begin with.

A moment later, he was back at her side, smiling and nodding, preparing to pull Ronnie away and on to the next introduction.

"Who was that?" Ronnie kept her voice casual as they moved across the room.

"Who was who?" Glenn nodded at someone nearby. "Hi, Bob!" He lowered his voice. "What are you talking about?"

"The phone call. Must've been important to interrupt your big night."

"Oh, it was no problem. Just my sister checking in about something. I try to be available to my family."

Ronnie nodded, but filed that lie away for further reference. What on earth was going on?

Marco welcomed the men into his home, trying not to show his unease. Tyson made the introductions, but Marco knew they were all aliases. They looked like men named Omar, Abdulla, and Karim; but had names like Owen, Arthur, and Kevin.

"And of course, you know Glenn."

"Yes, of course." Marco shook Glenn's hand, then gestured the group to sit down. "I hope the product rollout went well last night?"

"Very well," Glenn said. "Made more wonderful, of course, by the presence of your lovely friend."

The other men in the room all chuckled. They had all seen Ronnie; either in person at the club or in the videos of her performances that had been passed from man to man—just one of the perks of the job. Glenn was one lucky man.

Only Marco didn't smile. "Yes, of course." He hesitated. "Although I'll say it again, Glenn...I don't like her being so close to the action. It's fine using the key girls to compromise someone. It's quite another thing to use them as a reward for loyal service. This girl is smarter than you think. I worry that she'll stumble onto—"

"Marco, Marco." Tyson slapped him on the back, hard. His face and tone were jovial, but his eyes carried a clear warning. "No need to worry so much. Besides, our friends here didn't come to talk about Glenn's love life."

More chuckles, and Marco backed off. They didn't want to hear it; fine. But he wasn't comfortable with the arrangement. At some point, it might force some hard decisions—decisions he would hate to make.

"So what was it like last night?" Maris was leaning on the bar, her tray empty as she waited for the influx of evening customers. She was smacking some gum—strictly against the rules—and pumping Ronnie for the dish on the prior night's event.

"It was...rich. You could practically see the money dripping off the ficus trees. The reception had the best food, the best drinks. And of course, no expense was spared in their big presentation of the prototype. It was all high-tech razzle-dazzle."

Maris scowled. "And while we have a recession on! Probably for some product that will only make a difference to a handful of rich folks, too."

"Not really. It's actually really cool. *I* want one."

"What is it again?"

"It's this—" Ronnie made squared-off movements with her hands. "It's this sort of box thing that you hook to your television set and program your voice into. Or they have these designer ones that sit on your coffee table and have pretty designs on them, so you can use them as an accent in the room. With this box, you never need to go looking for your remote control...it does it all by voice. You can just talk, and it recognizes your voice and does whatever you say. Really cool. They're ramping up production right now, and it should be out on shelves before Christmas. Everyone's going to want one! One of the big magazines apparently said it was going to be *the* hot thing this year."

"I guess I can see why." Maris gave a grudging shrug, then looked to where a small group had just come in. "Well, time to go to work. No more loafing!" She waved a finger at Ronnie. "Go on, now. You'll distract these men from my work."

Late that night, Ronnie snuggled against Glenn in the car as they headed back toward his condo. He had a house on a lake, but generally spent his weeknights at the condo near his corporate headquarters.

"Babe, do you mind if we stop by the office? I need to get some stuff out of the factory."

"That's fine." Ronnie tried to hide a mighty yawn.

"Thanks. Sorry. I know you have school tomorrow."

"That's okay." Ronnie tried to sound chipper. "I'm up for anything."

He rubbed his hand along her arm and leered sideways. "You always are."

Glenn pulled through the security gates and parked. There were a surprising number of cars for three in the morning. "Come on in."

"Can I?"

"Sure. Just don't tell anyone. It's strictly off-limits to outsiders. Security, you know." He made a face. "Everything is so security-paranoid these days. But I have a few ways around the system."

Glenn walked straight up to a security desk, while Ronnie hung back. He greeted the security guard with a whispered instruction. The guard looked over his shoulder, met Ronnie's eye, and whispered something back. Both men snickered.

Glenn came over and took her arm, leading her toward a security station labeled "guest entrance." "I have an understanding with some of the night guards. They ask no questions, let my personal guests pass without having to sign them in, and they not only get to keep their jobs but get generous bonuses at the end of the year. Works like a charm."

The gate in front of Ronnie buzzed, allowing her to pass through. She raised an eyebrow as the guard averted his gaze. "I can see that."

Glenn grabbed her hand and hustled down a long corridor until they were out of the guard's sight.

At the end of the corridor, they were greeted by a set of double doors, armed by a keypad. Glenn punched in a code, and the doors swung open without a noise.

Ronnie looked around and felt her lips parting in astonishment. They were in a massive room with a bare concrete floor and a ceiling that soared at least forty feet. Giant pieces of machinery were bolted into the floor on every side, dwarfing them. The room was dark, the equipment silent and still, but far to the right, beyond a massive wall, Ronnie could hear the muffled roar of machinery and see light blazing out from under several broad doors. The shadows of dozens of feet moved back and forth in the light beyond the wall.

"The night shift." Glenn took her arm. "Come on. I've got to pick something up."

He steered her away from the activity and toward one of the many windowed offices that looked out on the rest of the factory floor. Ronnie realized that the light was on and there were two men inside, deep in conversation.

Glenn halted in the shadowy hall. He dropped Ronnie's hand and glanced around.

"What's wrong?"

"Oh," his laugh sounded strained, "some of my managers appear to be working late. And technically I shouldn't have brought you here. I always tell *them* it's against the rules." He gave her an apologetic shrug.

"What, you want me to hide?" Ronnie was joking, but Glenn nodded.

"Would you?" He backtracked, trying the doors of several other offices. All had windows and all were dark and locked. Glenn produced a master key and opened a door for her. He pointed to a chair beside a small desk. "If you stay in here, stay seated, and keep the lights off, no one will notice you."

He closed the door, and Ronnie sank into the chair with a sigh. She kicked off her shoes, rubbed her aching feet, and thought how quickly the morning would come. Maybe she'd skip class.

Her stockinged foot brushed against something hard on the floor. She tried to push out of the way with her foot, but it was too heavy. Yawning, Ronnie looked closer. It looked like that prototype television remote control thing the company was manufacturing.

She reached down and hefted it to the desk, surprised to discover that one whole side of the device was missing. A back panel gaped open, revealing a mass of internal circuits and parts. Several wires trailed from the jumble, onto the desk.

She poked at them, hoping she wouldn't electrocute herself, and one moved, loose in her hand. She grimaced, thinking she'd broken something, but then realized that the wire was attached to a rectangular black part that was loose inside the larger jumble. It was heavy, smooth like a spare battery from a laptop computer, and had several wires running from it.

A massive yawn escaped her lips and she pushed the part back into the jumble then set the whole device aside, laying her head on her arms, trying to get comfortable. She thought she would be asleep in ten seconds flat, but the presence of the black box on the desk kept impinging on her brain. Finally, she sat up, exasperated at her own fastidiousness, and moved the heavy device to the floor again. Despite Glenn's tendency to think *he* was allowed to bend every rule to his own purpose, she had noticed that he didn't extend others the same leeway. Maybe it was better that he not think she'd been snooping.

She put the box back where it had started, and gratefully laid her head down again.

She was awakened by a hand on her shoulder, and jumped. Glenn was standing over her, his eyes gleaming in the darkness.

"You scared me!" Ronnie put a hand to her heart. "Don't *do* that."

"Sorry it took me so long, babe. The managers had a few questions."

"Doesn't anyone *sleep* in this company?"

"Nope. That's why we make so much money. Let's go." He rubbed her shoulder, bare in her summer dress, his fingers lingering.

As Glenn ushered her into the car, clearly eager to get home to his condo, she set her mind to completing the task ahead. At least now she was being properly compensated for what had always been taken from her, by persuasion or force, with no thought for her feelings. It was as good an arrangement as any.

FORTY-THREE

The hallways were crowded with students as Ronnie darted out of the class-room, a blue book test clutched in her hand. On the cover was a red-circled A- and the word "Congratulations!" Her finals were done, and she had a whole week before fall classes started.

One semester down...about one hundred more to go.

She ran down the stairs and hesitated for a moment on the landing to the admissions office wing, then pushed through the door. The admissions office secretary was gone from behind the desk, but the admissions director came out with an inquiring look, and his face broke into a grin.

"Ronnie, good to see you. You need more help with those financial aid people?"

"No. It turns out that because my mom's not divorced yet, Seth still needs to sign all the bank forms. And of course he absolutely refuses, which puts me right back where I started. So I'm stuck paying my own way for another semester. Hopefully, by spring semester it'll all be resolved and I can get one of those scholarships."

"I can't believe it's taking this long," Mr. Woodward said. "We've got to get the board to revisit those requirements and give us some flexibility for cases like yours."

Ronnie nodded, but she really didn't care that much anymore. She was rolling in cash, courtesy of both Glenn and the club. It would be nice to not have to work most school nights, though. Once she got her scholarship, she could probably cut back to just Friday and Saturday nights.

The familiar figures flashed across her brain. The scholarship would probably pay her full tuition plus some living expenses. Then two nights at the club—plus what Glenn continued to give her—would be more than enough to cover a basic lifestyle. She made a rueful face. Of course, her idea of "basic" had changed radically in the last six months, and she wasn't all that willing to give it up. Plus, she told herself, she needed to keep sending money to her mom.

"So, what can I do for you?" Mr. Woodward was staring at her, a curious look on his face.

Ronnie started, and brought herself back to the present. "Sorry, I was just thinking about the money stuff again." She felt suddenly shy. "Actually, it wasn't anything you could do for me...it's just that you've already done so much for me, and I wanted…I wanted to show you this."

She held out her test booklet, cover facing him.

"Aw, Ronnie, that's great." He gave her a hug, then released her quickly, stepping back. "That's just great. What's the final tally?"

"Two A minuses, one B plus."

"Good for you! Congratulations."

"Yeah, it looks like I'll be around to bother you for the next year, at least."

"Never a bother, Ronnie. Listen, I've been meaning to give you something for a few weeks now. Hold on a second."

He disappeared into his office. Ronnie was so used to men reappearing with expensive gifts in their hands that she was mildly disappointed to see him carrying a simple flyer. He handed it over.

"I thought you might be interested in this talk. Our church always does a back-to-school thing for students. They set up sort of a festival with displays on different topics—how to budget your time, what software might help you the most…" A fleeting grin crossed his face. "How to apply for financial aid.

"There's a lot more that's relevant to the church, too. Some resources for students who have a tough time finding their way spiritually, that sort of thing. Anyway, they kick off the night by serving a great dinner, and there's a pep talk for the whole group by one or two speakers who know the college scene." He shrugged. "I'm one of the speakers this year."

He gestured to the flyer. "Take a look; it's next weekend. My wife and I would love to have you join us, if you're interested."

Ronnie stared at the page, then stowed the paper in her pocket. "I probably can't get off work, but it sounds interesting. I'll ask. You never know."

"Really? You don't mind?" Ronnie stared at Marco, eyebrows raised.

"I think we can get someone to cover for you. You rarely take a night off, and I think it might be good for you. You need to go lighten up, do something fun for a change."

"What?" Ronnie tossed her head. "You don't think I'm having fun with Glenn?"

"You know what I mean. Something that's not work. I just want to make sure our top moneymaker doesn't crash under the stress of work *and* school. If this—" he gestured at the paper Ronnie held—"this church thing can help somehow, I'm all for it."

"Thanks, chief." Ronnie left the room and headed back toward the dressing room. He was just full of surprises.

☆ ☆ ☆

"Ronnie, this is my wife." Mr. Woodward made the introductions, hugging his wife to his side on the church sidewalk. "Jo, meet Ronnie, one of our Georgia State students."

Ronnie shook her hand. "Nice to meet you, Mrs. Woodward."

"Please!" The woman laughed. "Call me Jo. Mrs. Woodward sounds so *old*. Well, let's not stand out here in the heat. Come on in."

Mrs. Woodward held the front door open, and Ronnie ventured inside. She hadn't been in a church in years—not since one of her friends was killed in a drunk-driving accident.

She looked around the large foyer, surprised at the contemporary look of the place. Good Shepherd Church was large and airy and didn't look like...well, like a church.

Mr. Woodward pointed toward a set of doors off to the side. "The dinner is first, in our fellowship hall. The college fair is afterwards, so you can take as much time or as little time as you want." He looked at his watch. "I need to leave you all now to go coordinate with the host for the evening. Ronnie, you okay?"

Ronnie nodded, not at all sure that she was.

Mr. Woodward kissed his wife on the cheek and vanished up a nearby flight of stairs, just as a group of women came up to chat with them. Ronnie stuck close by her host's side as the introductions were made. She had the prickly feeling that people would be able to see right through her charade.

"Well, welcome, Ronnie." One of the women gave her a broad smile. "We're always glad to meet young students. If you don't have a church, we'd love to have you come worship with us."

Ronnie shifted, uncomfortable.

"I'm sure Ronnie appreciates the offer," Mrs. Woodward said. "Right now, though, she just wants to know how to get through the first week of fall classes!"

The women laughed and backed off. Ronnie relaxed a bit as Mrs. Woodward steered her into the large dining area and began looking for a seat at one of the half-full tables.

Ronnie glanced around at all the hustle and bustle...and froze. A man stood at the front of the hall, not twenty feet away, setting up a microphone on stage.

She recognized him. He always sat near the back of the club—sometimes with a group, but more often alone—looking slightly ashamed of himself.

He turned, microphone in his hand, and headed toward the doors, coming in their direction, muttering about a missing circuit. Ronnie felt detached from her feet.

Turn away! Run to the restroom! She couldn't make her feet work.

Jo tapped him on the arm as he passed. "Hey, Bud."

"Hey, Jo."

"Can I introduce you to a new friend of ours? Ronnie, this is Bud. He's one of our best production guys. A real whiz."

Bud shook her hand, distracted, then looked into her face. She saw the belated flash of recognition, the blank shock…the flicker of shame and anger.

Ronnie made her mouth work. "Nice to meet you, Bud."

He dropped her hand and took a step back, a strange look twisting his lips.

"I've got to get this mike working." He fled out the doors.

"Guess he was in a hurry," Mrs. Woodward said. "Sorry about that."

Ronnie's mouth was too dry to respond, so she merely nodded and allowed Mrs. Woodward to guide her to a seat. She sat down, stiff, hardly hearing a word of what was going on around her. What was she doing here? This wasn't her world! The people at her table, the others she had met, they were doctors and lawyers and teachers. She might make just as much money as some of them—more probably—but she was still on the wrong side of the tracks.

Out of the corner of her eye, she saw the man with the microphone reappear at a different door, gesturing another young man forward. He whispered something to the other guy, a rascally smile on his face, then pointed in her direction. From this distance all his temerity had gone, and he was busy spreading the word.

The other guy shook his hand as if he had been burned, and punched his buddy on the arm. An older woman came up and wagged a finger at the two friends, then was stopped short by whatever they told her. She glanced in Ronnie's direction and vanished from the doorway.

Ronnie tried not to look, not realizing until that moment how much she wanted to be accepted in this world. This, after all, was where she wanted to head; the whole reason she wanted to go to college in the first place. She could feel tears welling up and blinked them back.

Buck up, girl. Remember, life stinks.

How long before the rumor got back to the Woodwards that they had hosted a stripper at their table for the night? How long before her financial aid package was history, before Mr. Woodward started turning his back in the hallway instead of giving her one of his quick hugs? Her lip trembled. How long before the juicy fact that she was a stripper made it into some file that future employers would look at and blackball her before they ever met her?

She was smothering. She couldn't breathe. She had to leave. Now. Leave.

The older woman reappeared in the doorway and headed into the room, closely followed by two or three others. The woman pulled aside a man in a clerical collar for an intense chat.

The man glanced Ronnie's direction, then shook his head and said something to the determined older woman. She practically pointed toward the table where Mrs. Woodward sat, deep in conversation. Several heads near the whispered discussion began to turn, ears perked.

Ronnie hugged her purse to her side and stood, forcing the tears back. Mrs. Woodward broke off her discussion and looked up.

"Do you need something?"

Her own voice sounded strange in her ears. "Where are your rest rooms?"

"Just through those doors we came in, straight across the lobby."

"Thanks."

She walked out of the fellowship hall, her back rigid, feeling all the eyes on her. Once in the lobby, she headed straight for the exit.

Hold it together, hold it together, hold it together…

Her steps quickened and she slammed out the doors, pushing them open with a furious force, jogging down the sidewalk, the tears blurring her vision.

She was running now, heading for her car, the nice car she had bought by taking her clothes off for the man in that church. She was crying now, picturing Mr. Woodward's face when he learned.

She fumbled with her keys, opened the lock with shaking hands. She knew she had just lost a friend, the only person who had seemed to believe her capable of a better life. She collapsed into her front seat and slammed the door.

She caught a glimpse of Jo Woodward running out the front door, her eyes scanning the parking lot, her face worried, intense. Ronnie caught her breath on a sob and slammed the car into drive, her tires squealing as she sped away. She averted her blurry eyes from the rearview mirror, away from the woman who tried to run after her, calling, then stopped, her hands to her cheeks.

Ronnie made it two miles before she began to shake. She pulled into an abandoned parking lot, fell across the front seat, and sobbed.

FORTY-FOUR

The next few months passed in a blur. Ronnie kept her head down, going from school to work to Glenn's bed with numbing regularity. She was rolling in cash, but took no pleasure in it, was taking interesting classes, but found them lifeless. Her secret was out, and the reason she had wanted to go to school—to make something of herself, to maybe even be a physical therapist someday—seemed as distant as Mars.

She had seen Mr. Woodward a few times on campus since that dreadful night, but had always darted into an empty classroom or around a corner before he spotted her. She had ignored the few messages left in her school box or on her answering machine, asking her to come meet with him, to call his wife at home. She tore up the notes and pressed "delete" on the voice mail messages without listening to them. After a while, they stopped trying.

She threw herself into her work at the club, boxing into a little corner of her mind the table dancing, the lascivious looks, Glenn's increasing demands. And she did it well, enough so that she was the top moneymaker for three months running, much to Tiffany's disgust. Tiffany, of course, sensed her detachment and asked from time to time what was wrong. Ronnie always blew her off, making a joke of it, locking away her feelings about that night at the church.

What did those people know anyway? It wasn't like what she was doing was wrong—it was just unacceptable to the respectable crowd. The lily-white people at their church dinners were just uptight. And hypocritical, too. If she'd looked around the room, she might have recognized half a dozen other men. Why should she care what they thought?

She had nothing to be ashamed of.

As the months passed, she sensed a change in the atmosphere of the club, of Marco...even Glenn. She couldn't put her finger on it, but everyone was stressed, angry, tense, stretched like a bow string ready to snap. Thanksgiving brought no merriment, the first days of December no holiday cheer. Glenn had become abrupt, even rough with her at times. And Marco began snapping at everyone, ordering them around like a field marshal. There were more closed-door meetings, more visitors to Marco's back office, more demands on the girls to do the special parties, to act as messengers, to broker deals. They were all well compensated and no one complained. On the contrary, they jumped at the lucrative opportunities. Ronnie wondered if anyone else noticed that the same girls—herself, Tiffany, and two or three others—were always selected for the out of the ordinary jobs. Out of the ordinary, of course, except that one way or another they always involved taking their clothes off.

But no...she was the only one who was detached, who seemed to be observing it all from the outside. She wished she could snap back into one world or the other wholeheartedly, but she couldn't. She'd tasted the other world, but couldn't have it. So she lived in the club world, and tried to drown the secret longings.

Life stinks, remember?

"Macy!" Marco stuck his head out the door and hollered for her. Ronnie came running down the hallway. "Glenn is on the phone. He says he's been trying to get you for hours. He can't make it over here tonight and wants you to meet him at his condo when you're done. Here, can you talk to him? Make it fast. I'm expecting a call."

She forced herself to smile and took the phone from Marco's hand. "Hi, Glenn."

"I need to see you tonight. What time can you be here?"

She tried not to give an audible sigh, to keep her voice soothing. "Oh, baby, tonight is not a good night. I'm supposed to work late and—"

"Any night's a good night, if I say so. Be here by two o'clock."

"But the club doesn't even close by then, and I have that test tomorrow—"

"Two o'clock, Macy. And wear that little blue skirt I got you." He hung up the phone.

She set the receiver down, slowly, aware that Marco was watching her. He raised an eyebrow. "Everything okay?"

"He was ticked. He's been so stressed lately. What on earth is going *on* with everybody?"

"Yes, well, people just need a break sometimes." Marco bustled her out of the office. "Maybe you can convince him to go on a vacation. Take you to Cancún or somewhere."

Ronnie sighed and turned away as he closed the door behind her. She fingered the diamond-and-platinum bracelet that sparkled on her wrist, the latest gift, and set her will to the long work night ahead of her.

☆ ☆ ☆

"Where's the blue skirt?"

Ronnie stared at Glenn, her stomach churning. She had crept into his condo, using her key, hoping against hope that he might be asleep. But he was lounging on the wide couch in the living area, staring at the door, his eyes glassy and a tall-neck beer in his hand.

"Oh, honey, I'm sorry. You said you wanted me here by two o'clock, and I didn't have time to go home and get it."

He rose from the couch, his voice grating. "And you're late. I've been waiting for thirty minutes, Macy. And you know I don't like waiting. I'm not good at waiting. Come here."

"Glenn, you're drunk. I'm not sure—"

"I said—" he flung the beer away from him, smashing it on the floor behind him—"come *here!*"

She fled for the door. She gasped as she felt him grab her hair, pulling her back and down. Her knees hit the cold tiled floor, and she yelped in pain.

He bent over her, his fingers intertwined in her hair, pulling her head back, forcing her to look up at him.

He pulled her up again, her head still bent back, and steered her toward the couch. He pushed her roughly down. She sprawled on the soft material, panting, hyperventilating, as he removed his belt.

Her eyes wild, she knew what was coming. She'd seen what had happened to her mother when she resisted—and what had happened to her. From experience she knew it was better to put up with it, to close her mind to what was happening. It would be over soon enough.

Ronnie slipped out the door of the condo, shaking, trying not to limp from the pain. Glenn was sprawled on the sofa, snoring, his appetite sated. Until the next time.

Ronnie pressed her hand to a bruise she could already feel, tender on her cheek. There couldn't be a next time. She couldn't do this, couldn't allow him to do this to her. But how could she stop it? Who could she talk to?

The image of Mr. Woodward rose in her mind. She pushed it away. Yeah, right. Where had that come from? She must be hurt worse than she thought, if she thought *he* would help her.

She reached her car and slipped inside, cradling her purse. At least her wallet bulged with several new one-hundred-dollar bills. He'd thrown them at her afterward, reducing her to fresh tears while he went to get another beer. Good thing he'd paid her before passing out on the sofa.

She sat stock-still as the weight of her thought hit her. *Good thing he paid me.*

She put her head on the steering wheel, her eyes dry, staring at nothing. She really was a prostitute. No getting around it, no sugarcoating it. She winced as the steering wheel pressed the bruise on her cheek. She was probably just getting what she deserved.

She sat for five minutes, feeling pulped and worthless, before summoning the energy to drive away. Then she groaned, realizing that she needed a textbook for the test tomorrow, and she had left it in her locker. She would have to pull it together enough to stop by the club on the way home. Either that or just quit school entirely. She sighed and checked the clock on the dashboard. There were probably still a few people at the club, closing up. She would just have to avoid them.

Twenty minutes later, Ronnie parked in The Challenger's darkened back lot, the only car there. Only a few staff cars were left in the other lots, the night winding down to a close. She had fixed her mussed hair, but the bruises might be visible by now. She just wanted to get in and out without being noticed.

She slipped through the club's back door and heard distant thumps and clatters and dim voices talking about going to an all-night bar or complaining that they had to get up too early in the morning.

The hall was deserted, half the lights already off. She walked quickly toward the break room and, hearing no one, poked her head inside. Empty. She hurried to her locker and retrieved her book, then hurried back down the hallway. She paused for a long moment, listening; then, satisfied she was alone, yanked open the door to the back parking lot.

A wide-eyed face loomed up out of the darkness, and Ronnie shrieked and jumped sky-high. She staggered back, her hand on her heart.

"Maris! You scared me!"

Maris panted a moment. "What the heck are you doing here? You left hours ago."

"I had to come back to get something. What are you doing, coming in the back door like this?"

"They'd already locked the front door and I couldn't get anybody's attention. I forgot something, too; think I left it here when I was closing up." She yawned. "I'm bushed. I just want to get in and out without talking to anyone."

"Me, too."

Maris looked at her more closely. "What's going on?"

"What do you mean?"

Maris glanced up and down the hallway then pulled Ronnie into the ladies' bathroom, staring at her face in the fluorescent light. She pressed a finger to Ronnie's cheek, pausing when Ronnie winced.

"*That's* what I mean, girlfriend. What's going on. Who's hitting you?"

"No one."

Maris folded her arms across her chest and just stood there, barring the doorway.

"Okay, fine. Glenn, the guy I'm seeing. He was drunk tonight and got a little carried away."

"A little carried away," Maris repeated, shaking her head. "Don't do it, Ronnie."

Ronnie looked up, surprised as the use of her real name.

"Please, girl," Maris said. "I knew you before your fancy stage name. You're still Ronnie in my head. Always will be. Just like your friend Tiffany." She hesitated. "You want my advice, you should get out of it. Just leave. You can find another job somewhere else. Somewhere they won't trade you like a piece of meat for their deal of the day."

Ronnie sighed. "Look, I know you were disappointed when I started dancing."

"Hey." Maris held up her hands. "It's not my role to be disappointed or to cheer you on or to hold your hand. You gotta do what you gotta do. I'm just saying I can see the writing on the wall. I've seen it too many times. Better you leave now than get your spirit broken. You've got a different spirit than the other girls. Even Tiffany."

Maris nodded, her eyes direct. "Oh yeah, girl, don't think I don't notice these things. You're different. Always have been. But this stuff'll break you eventually." She started to say something then shrugged. "That's all. You're the one that's got to decide if you're going to respect yourself. You do with it what you want."

Ronnie stared at her. "Okay."

Maris nodded, then turned away. "Got to use the john. See you." She disappeared into one of the stalls.

Ronnie cracked the door, looking up and down the hallway. Still empty.

She stole the short distance back down the corridor, out the door, and to her car without being spotted. Well, except by Maris. As she drove home, she turned over in her mind what Maris had said. There was no way she could quit, obviously, but she could respect herself enough to tell Marco and ask for his help.

"*What?*"

Marco stared at Ronnie in disbelief, then in rising fury. He took two quick steps out from behind his desk and put his hand under her chin, turning her cheek to the side. The ugly bruise was well covered by makeup, but was still visible. Too visible to do stage work that night.

"I'm going to kill him. I'm going to *kill him.*" He turned and slammed his fist onto his desk with a force that made Ronnie jump.

"Sorry. Sorry, I didn't mean to startle you. I just—I don't *believe* that he did this to you!"

Marco paced the room, using every word in the book to describe Glenn, then abruptly turned back to her.

"Tell you what. You go home, take the night off. Put your feet up and recover for a couple of days, okay?"

Ronnie looked at him in surprise. He waved a hand and put on a scowl.

"Don't thank me. I'm just looking out for my own best interests." He paced some more. "You ditch Glenn. Do not see him again. This is just unacceptable." He slammed his fist into the desk again. *"Unacceptable!"*

Marco abruptly turned back to her. "Glenn doesn't know where you live, does he?"

"No. But he does know my phone number, and he could probably find the apartment that way if he tried hard enough." She shivered.

Marco muttered under his breath, then returned to his chair, his face calm and cold. "I will deal with this. You go home and relax. Don't worry; it'll be taken care of."

"What're you going to do?"

"Leave that to me."

"But…I don't want anything—you know—*bad* to happen to him. I just want him not to do that again."

"Don't worry. He won't."

Tyson stared at the darkening ocean as Marco's tirade blistered through the phone. Marco sometimes got too worked up about things, but this time Glenn really was the fool. Drawing this sort of attention at this stage of the game was inexcusable. Not to mention putting one of their best girls out of commission for days.

He reassured Marco that he would take care of matters and ended the call. His feet crunched on the soft sand as he headed back up to the house.

The others members of the S-Group looked up, curious, when he came in.

"We have a problem." He briefed them on the breakdown of discipline, the awkward situation. "Suggestions?"

"Wish we could just whack him and get it over with," one of the others said.

"I've been concerned about Glenn from day one. He's got the skills and the money motivation, but he's never taken the thing seriously enough."

Another member shook his head. "Can't eliminate him. He's too critical right now, and it's too soon. We're just ramping up all the pre-Christmas sales. Another month, maybe, but now?" He shrugged. "We just have to find a way to bring him back in line without raising outside suspicions."

Tyson folded his arms. "Marco's relieved that the girl won't be near Glenn anymore. He's been fretting she might learn too much. Paranoid."

The others didn't smile. "Yeah, maybe, maybe not," one said. "Let me just refer it to my boys, the two that did that other job for us. Our backslider will be in bed for two days, and on day number three he'll be back at his post like a good boy, ready to act his age again." He looked around. "Any objection?"

Seeing none, Tyson nodded. "Go ahead then. We can't afford to have Glenn go after the girl before we get to him. It's got to be done tonight."

He waited while the man went to make a call on his cell phone. "When he comes back, we need to move on to the next order of business." He gave the others a smooth smile. "We're ready for the first trial."

Ronnie heard the phone ringing, but didn't answer it. She was deep in the bath, bubbles up to her nose, meditative music wafting from the CD player.

She felt herself stiffening more with each ring, waiting for the call to go to voice mail and leave her in peace. What if it was Glenn? What if he'd found out where she lived? She forced herself to take a few deep breaths, remembering Marco's words.

It'll be taken care of…

How, she didn't want to know. She also didn't want to think how she would replace the income Glenn had brought her. She'd have to cut back a bit. Or maybe she could do more of these special jobs Marco kept proposing.

The phone stopped ringing as voice mail picked up. Later, snuggled in her robe, Ronnie listened to Marco's voice on the recorder and breathed a sigh of relief:

"Macy, thought you'd want to know that Glenn won't be coming back into the club. And he won't be looking to bother you again. He's been warned off, you might say. He'll probably not be walking too good for the next few days either, but he had it coming. Well, that's it. Just thought you'd want to know. I put you down on the schedule for Friday night. Give you two more days to recoup."

Ronnie put down the phone and crawled into bed. When was the last time she'd gone to sleep before midnight? At least she'd finally be chipper for her classes the next day.

FORTY-FIVE

N o."

Doug Turner crossed his arms, staring at the surprise, the latent fury on the face of his colleague.

"What do you mean, no?" the COO said.

"I mean no." Doug took a breath, settling his stomach. "I told you at the outset that I will do nothing illegal, blackmail or no. I'd rather face public humiliation than go to jail."

He gestured at the paper the COO held, a document certifying that they did not own stock in a company they had, in fact, partly acquired the previous year. "I'm not signing that."

The COO gave the small chuckle that always infuriated Doug. "It's just a small, closely held company that no one cares about. No one will ever find out—"

"Forget it. You can just forget the whole thing." Doug grabbed the telephone and punched in Jordan's number, watching the COO's eyes narrow.

Jordan's secretary answered. "Yes, Doug?"

"I need to see Jordan right away."

"I'm sorry, he's in a meeting—"

"No. I need to see him *right now.* Interrupt him. Now."

There was a pause. Doug could hear the secretary lay the receiver on her desk and knock on Jordan's door. He could hear Jordan's annoyed bark, the secretary's quiet explanations, the returning footsteps.

She picked up the phone. "He said he'll be in your office in two minutes."

"Thanks." Doug hung up and stared at the company's chief operating officer. "It's time we got this all out on the table, don't you think?"

The COO glared at him and didn't answer. Both men stood, waiting through the pause, facing each other across Doug's desk like gunfighters ready to draw.

Doug's thoughts turned to Sherry, to their conversation just last night about how to handle the blackmail that still hung over Doug's head. Their family was healing, and Doug could no longer accept succumbing to the COO's corruption. Late at night, snuggled in his arms, Sherry had kissed him and assured him that when he decided to take a stand, she would stand with him no matter what happened.

He had lain awake for hours, listening to his wife's quiet breathing, giving thanks for the return of their marriage and her unconditional support in the inevitable showdown. He just hadn't thought the showdown would happen so quickly.

Lord, Thy will be done…

Jordan barged in the door to Doug's office. He stopped in front of the desk and glowered at both men, letting loose a string of curses for good measure.

"I was right in the middle of a big meeting. Would you please tell me what's going on?"

Doug walked over to the door and closed it. "Jordan, for the last nine months, I have been blackmailed into approving deals and signing documents against my better judgment."

Jordan looked at his COO, who stared straight ahead.

Doug continued. "I have some personal problems that our colleague here somehow found out about, videotaped, and threatened to release to my wife, my church, and anyone else I cared about, unless I did his bidding. The first deal I was forced to approve was the Silicon Valley deal, and there have been a half-dozen since then. But I can't do it anymore. I need to know where you stand on this, if you had any part in it, and what you intend to do about it. If you knew about this, I will submit my resignation here and now."

Jordan held up his hands. "No! No, Doug, don't quit. I wondered why you kept changing your mind on things but I had no idea…" He turned to the COO, his voice rising. "What were you doing, plumbing the company for personal gain? Using us as your personal piggy bank?"

The COO continued to stare straight ahead, his neck rigid, looking like he was just inches away from lashing out and punching both of them.

"No, sir. I was just trying to make the company all it could be. Just trying to earn us all more money, chief."

"Oh, that's a bunch of—" Doug cut off his protestations at Jordan's quelling look.

Jordan stuck his face close to the COO's. "So you decided to destroy the morale of one of our best people, just to bump up our profit margin?"

Receiving no answer, Jordan turned back to Doug, the fury still vibrating. "And you—did you do anything illegal?"

"No, sir. That's what started this. He wanted me to, today."

Doug gestured at the page in the COO's hand, and Jordan snatched it away.

"What is this?"

"He wanted it to look like we don't own a piece of a company that is in fact a partial subsidiary. Wanted me to file it with the government. And that would instantly become securities fraud."

Jordan stared at the paper in his hand, then ripped it in two. He pointed to the door, speaking to his COO without looking at him.

"I need to finish my meeting, but I want to see you in my office in thirty minutes. Understood?"

"That's *it?*" Doug stepped forward. "He wants to commit securities fraud, and you're going to let him off with just a scolding?"

"Listen, I need to get to the bottom of this," Jordan said. "I don't know who to believe at this point. You'd better chill, too. But know that we will do whatever it takes to get to the bottom of this and we will take action, if necessary."

He looked at his watch and his lips pressed together in a taut line. "Meanwhile, we might be losing a very prominent client. And if we do, you both are in for it. Now if you'll excuse me…" He swept out the door without a backward glance.

The COO also turned and left without a word.

Doug shut the door behind them, then felt his legs go weak. He sat in his comfortable leather chair and picked up the phone.

"Come in."

Jordan held open the door to the office, gesturing his COO inside, his expression severe. He noticed Doug standing at the other end of the executive hallway, watching the transaction.

He shut the door behind him and faced his COO. The man took one look at him, and broke down laughing.

"Oh, Jordan, you are *good,* man. I don't know how you kept a straight face."

Jordan motioned for him to keep it down and took a seat behind his desk. "I thought you were going to punch me there for a second." He began to pull out a cigar, then reconsidered.

"So what're you going to tell our boy scout down there?" the COO asked. "We can't let him leave the company. He knows too much. He'd be an easy target for any Feds snooping around the money trail."

Jordan tried not to roll his eyes. Little did his COO know; it wasn't the money trail that Jordan was worried about. He settled back into his chair.

"Our tracks are well hidden; don't you worry."

"You always say that, chief, but you never say how." He held up a hand, fore-stalling Jordan's usual comeback. "Don't worry, I trust you. But I just want to be sure I'm going to be able to provide for me and my family in the style we've become accustomed to."

"I would've thought that you'd be amply reassured of that by now. Didn't you get another payment just…what…two days ago?"

"Three, boss, three. And it's already spent."

"What this time? A new boat? The summer house in Cancún?"

"Nope. A ski chalet in Banff. To go with all our new ski gear."

"Amazing. I've never seen anyone able to spend money as fast as you."

"It's a gift."

Enjoy it while you can, buddy.

Jordan sat forward. "So we need to figure out what to tell Doug. First, and I mean this seriously—scrap the tape. It appears to have served its purpose and any inadvertent use would backfire at this point."

"Too bad. It was a work of art."

"Second, I tell our man that I can't fire you because you're too crucial at this point in the big Speed Shoes deal, etcetera, etcetera. Also, I'll say that you claim the tape was made half on a lark, and you were never really serious about using it."

"Whooo, that'll burn his buns!"

"Probably." This upstart man was going to get on his nerves pretty soon, but he needed him. For now. "I'll tell Doug that I've been considering firing you anyway, but that I really can't consider it until after the Speed Shoes deal is done."

"Which could take months."

"Which could take months. But he doesn't need to know that. I'll tell him I'll see if you're being a good boy by then, and we'll go from there." He hesitated, and a ghost of a smile crossed his lips. "Plus, I'll tell him that you've agreed to apolo-gize."

"What? Give me a break!"

"It's the only way to even *remotely* persuade him that you've had a change of heart. That's the only thing I can think of that would help ensure he stays on board. That, and the fact that I'll give him a big raise for his trouble and loyalty."

"Fine." There was some grumbling, but he subsided. "So I really have to apolo-gize?"

"You really have to apologize. Make it sincere. And give him a copy of the CD and let him break it in two."

"I could have a copy."

"You could. But you'd better not." Jordan leveled a warning glance at his COO, and the room grew very still for a moment. "You understand me?"

"Yes, yes. Okay, I'll get rid of the copies, too."

Jordan held his gaze, waiting until the man shifted and looked away, uncomfortable.

He couldn't afford any wild cards. He needed Doug to trust him, needed him to stay. It was true that he couldn't afford to have him wandering loose, with all he knew. But it was more than that. The blasted board liked him and would ask all sorts of impossible questions if he left in a huff. There were still far too many original board members from his brother's tenure at the company, directors who were truly independent and could not be replaced without arousing suspicion. This would indeed be a bad time for Doug to leave; he couldn't let that happen.

He shook himself out of that train of thought and stood, tacitly dismissing his COO, his mind already turning to means and methods.

He buzzed his secretary, who came in as the COO was leaving.

"Yes, boss?"

"Please arrange a lunch meeting with Doug today. By twelve-thirty if possible. I need to be back for that two o'clock meeting."

"Sure thing. Anything else?"

"Make reservations at 103 West. Give the maître d' my name."

The secretary's eyes rose skyward at the mention of the exclusive restaurant, but she left the room without a word, closing the door behind her.

Jordan stretched, a catty smile crossing his face. It would work, and this chapter would be wrapped up. One way or another.

Doug stirred sugar into his coffee to stall for time. Jordan was sitting back in his chair, his little presentation over, watching him with worried eyes.

"I'll tell you what," Doug said. "You keep him away from me, and I'll go home and discuss the whole thing with my wife. I'm sure she'll be thrilled about the raise and the vacation, but that's not the only thing at stake here. We want to be sure that this company is operating in an ethical manner, and that I'm not inadvertently digging myself into a hole. Not to mention that I don't think I can ever work with him again."

"We can take care of that," Jordan said. "We'll just tap one of his subordinates to liaise with you whenever necessary. No problem." He lowered his voice in a conspiratorial manner. "It'll be good for his ego to be taken down a peg or two.

"Then, depending on how he seems after the Speed Shoes deal is wrapped up, we'll revisit the whole thing and see if he still needs to go. And I've told him that if he tries anything funny again—with you or with anything fraudulent—I'll fire him on the spot. As I told you, I'd been considering making a change anyway, as I wasn't 100 percent happy with his performance before. But it would be devastating to operate without him during one of our biggest deals of the year. Especially since, as you know, I'm pretty lousy at operational details."

Doug let his guard down enough to chuckle at that one, then tried one more tactic. "Jordan, don't you think the board needs to know about this?"

His boss gave a nervous laugh. "No, no! They're not operational folks either; they wouldn't realize how critical it is to have a long-term COO at this point in the game. This isn't the right time to bring this to their attention. I'll put it on the agenda at the next board meeting."

Jordan shook his head, his smile rueful. "You just keep being so gosh-darned honest, and we'll do fine. I apologize again that you were placed in such a rough spot for so long. Unfortunately, we can't reverse any of the deals you've approved—we're in them too deep now—but you come straight to me if you're being pressured to do anything against your better judgment again."

The two men sat in silence for a minute, sipping their coffees.

"All I can say, Jordan, is that I'm going to have to go home and talk to Sherry about it. And pray about it."

"Sure. But please let me know by tomorrow, if you can. Because if you are leaving, that'll require us to do some serious scrambling. And I don't even want to think about that unless I have to."

The two men stood, the conversation over by mutual consent, and headed out of the restaurant.

Back in the office, Doug walked down the executive hallway and noticed the COO in his office, waiting for him, a contrite look on his face. He braced himself to see what would happen during this "apology," and pushed open the door.

Doug stood beside Sherry, rinsing dishes, giving her the postmortem on the day. Sherry stopped rinsing as he repeated what the former blackmailer had said, and looked at him, incredulous, her voice rising.

"And you *believe* him? You think that jerk was sincere?"

"I didn't say that. I'm merely repeating the conversation."

She looked at his face, then put a sudsy hand to her cheek. "I did it again, didn't I? Darn it, why can't I ever learn?" She leaned forward and kissed him, trying awkwardly to hug him without getting soap on his clothes. "I'm sorry. Forgive me. I'm listening, really I am."

Doug smiled down at her. "I know you are. Thank you for being aware of how that sounded."

"It would be better for me to catch it *before* it left my mouth, but I'm learning." He returned her hug, glad to feel her arms around him.

"Go on." She stepped back and playfully tapped his nose, leaving sudsy bubbles on the tip. "You were saying?"

"Thank you *very* much." Doug wiped the soap off, smiling. "I was saying that he seemed embarrassed the whole time—like Brandon does when we catch him at something he knows is wrong. It was weird. I honestly don't know what to believe. I guess there's at least a possibility that he was being honest—that once he was caught, he realized how stupid his actions were and felt bad about it." He shook his head. "I just don't know."

"Well, what do you want to do?"

"I don't know. For some reason, I don't feel like God is telling me to leave. But that could just be because my eyes have been blinded by this huge raise Jordan's giving me!"

"Yeah, me, too. Let's pray about this after we put the kids to bed. Okay?"

"Deal." He stood behind her and gave her another hug, pressing her into his body. He rested his cheek against her hair, grateful to feel her pliant against him. "Thank you for standing with me in this."

She turned her head, and he could see a smile on her face. "No matter what, babe."

"No matter what."

FORTY-SIX

*C*ome thou fount of every blessing, tune my heart to sing Thy grace,
Streams of mercy never ceasing, call for songs of loudest praise.
Teach me some melodious sonnet, sung by flaming tongues above,
Praise the mount, I'm fixed upon it, mount of Thy redeeming love...

Doug Turner looked around him as the auditorium resounded with singing, a thousand voices lifted in praise. The words to the great old hymn were displayed on the large screen above the altar, every eye upturned, every voice lifting with a new-felt joy, a new vibrancy.

Doug closed his eyes and let the music wash over him, almost unable to sing from the fullness in his heart. He had no final answers at work—nothing but a sense to hang in there, to see it through. He had no final answers yet at home—although with every day that passed he knew God's healing. But here, he had the only Answer that mattered. The reality of God's redeeming love.

The music swelled into the last verse, the words meaning more now to this congregation, this body, than ever before. He felt the unabashed tears on his cheeks, and saw Sherry's lips trembling as she sang. Others around him were wiping their eyes. He pulled Sherry close, and husband and wife approached the Throne of Grace together.

Oh to grace how great a debtor, daily I'm constrained to be,
Let thy goodness like a fetter bind my wandering heart to Thee,
Prone to wander, Lord, I feel it, prone to leave the God I love.
Here's my heart, Oh take and seal it. Seal it for Thy courts above!

The music died away and the congregation remained standing, intent, as Pastor Steven came forward to close the service.

"...and if anyone would like someone to pray with you, we have a prayer team down front after the service."

Pastor Steven lifted his hands in benediction. "And now may the Lord bless you and keep you. May the Lord make His face to shine upon you and give you peace. Amen. Go in peace."

The congregation broke up as soft music began to play, a dozen people quietly making their way down the crowded aisle to the front.

Doug kept his arm around Sherry, his gaze thoughtful, remembering the recent times they had gone forward to receive prayer. The first time had been after Pastor Steven's courageous sermon months before—the first time that personal prayer was even offered after the service. That Sunday, the church staff hastily assembled a prayer team from people who already were skilled at praying for the needs of others and could keep a confidence—and they had been besieged. The congregation's emotions and needs had been blown wide open. Since then, dozens of laypeople had been recruited, trained in personal ministry and prayer.

Doug glanced at the front of the church where the nearest prayer team member was hugging a sobbing woman. One of these days, he thought, one day soon, he would be up there, healed and whole, ministering to others.

Lord, let it be so…

His thoughts were interrupted by a hearty slap on his back. Eric stood there, his eyes showing the faintest trace of red. "Hey, brother, what's up?"

"Looks like that hymn affected you the same way it affected me."

"Whew, it's those words. 'Prone to wander, Lord, I feel it, prone to leave the God I love…'" Eric choked a bit, his eyes watering with emotion. "It just kills me."

"Because it's so true. I know exactly what you mean."

Several others stopped by, shaking hands, giving hugs as the foursome stood half-in, half-out of the aisle. Sherry left Doug's side to intercept a forlorn-looking woman, placing a gentle hand on her arm.

"Hey there…how are things with your husband? I've been praying for him." She pulled her aside, glancing at Doug as if to say "I'll be a minute."

Doug watched as Sherry found an empty spot a few rows down, and the two women sat, talking intently.

There were others watching as well. Caliel surveyed the room, his face radiant. Here and there, dozens of people stood or sat in small groups, talking privately, praying for one another, even crying together, sharing one another's burdens.

Caliel rejoiced! The cloak of secrecy had been torn away, the cloak of darkness under which the enemy had been able to torment so many in solitude. Sure, there were still those who wanted none of the new honesty, the new transparency that had swept this body. But to most, it was like water to a parched soul.

There was still a ways to go before this body would be ready for the task entrusted to it. But—as in so many times and places before—Caliel had seen first-hand what happened when the King's hand moved and His children were willing to go beyond what was comfortable, to step into His plan. He had also seen enough of the waywardness of God's children to never take anything for granted. But here, in this place, Caliel marveled anew at the majesty of his Creator. His strength truly was made perfect in their weakness…as they submitted their weakness to Him.

The fast-food place was deluged with the after-church rush, the members of Eric and Lisa's small group pushing tables together to accommodate their number. The talk turned, as it had so often in the past few months, to the pastor's message and what God was saying to the church.

"I don't *want* to be just a Sunday Christian." One of the women slapped her hand on the table as she recalled their pastor's challenge. "I've been there, done that, bought the T-shirt. I don't want it anymore."

Sherry paused in helping Genna with her food. "What do you mean?"

"I don't *know.*" The woman sat back, frustrated. "I'm just feeling like my faith has to translate into something more meaningful, somehow. I want to be like—well, like this nurse friend of mine who went to work on a mercy ship that travels to the poorest places in the world as a floating hospital. They treat people who've never seen a doctor or a nurse in their lives, who can't pay, people who live with crippling pain or deformity that can be solved by a simple operation. My friend has nothing anymore—no possessions except a few clothes and a tiny little hammock on board this big old ship—but she writes me these letters just *bursting* with joy over seeing the little faces of children who could walk for the first time, the mothers or fathers who could hear or see or talk because someone cared enough to leave the comforts of their home and go reach out in Jesus' name."

Her eyes looked far into the distance. "Sometimes I wonder—I'm not tied down; I don't have a husband or kids yet. Why *shouldn't* I just leave my cushy job, my cushy house, and go make an eternal difference somewhere?"

"Why don't you?" Eric's voice was calm. "It sounds like this is pressing on you. Have you ever seriously thought about it?"

The woman crossed her arms. "I've tried. But I can't get past my selfishness. I like my cushy job. I like my cushy life."

Sherry chuckled. "At least you're honest. It's so hard to admit that we're just selfish. Selfish and insulated from what so many people go through every day." She looked sideways at her husband. "When Doug and I bought our house, we realized it was pretty expensive, and bigger than we needed, but we justified it. We said 'Well, now we have extra room we can use for ministry.'"

Several of the others in the group gave wry chuckles and nodded in agreement.

"Been there," one piped up.

Sherry shook her head in frustration. "But you know what? We haven't used it—not like that. Oh, we've had friends come and stay; that sort of thing. But we had originally said, 'Wouldn't it be great if a pregnant teenager could come live with us so she wouldn't feel she had to abort her baby?' Or, 'Wouldn't it be great if we could use the extra playroom downstairs to care for the kids of single moms who otherwise couldn't afford childcare while they worked?'

"But you know what? We've never done it! We've never housed a pregnant teenager or helped with high-risk kids. It would mean inconveniencing ourselves. When we know that ministry almost always means inconveniencing ourselves—at least until it becomes a way of life."

The previous woman gave a sad nod. "Part of me just doesn't want to think about it. I can go on as I am just fine if I ignore the needs all around me, thank you very much."

"Well, I know one small thing I can do about it," Sherry said. "Maybe you can join me. It's not the same thing as taking a needy person into your home, or some such thing, but it's a start. My friend Jo Woodward from college goes to Good Shepherd Church—you know, just a few miles down the road? Well, they're having an outreach on Friday night at a community center in one of the public housing projects. They're going to show a free movie for anyone who wants to come, and will have childcare for the kids, and games and popcorn. They do this every Friday night as a way to give the project families something to do and keep the kids off the streets. They always need volunteers. I was thinking it would be fun for our home group to join them from time to time." She looked over at Eric and Lisa. "I don't mean to put you on the spot, but what do you think?"

Eric's gaze was thoughtful. "I think it's a great idea. There's so much that's needed in those communities. So many of those kids have no fathers at home—"

"I know." Sherry felt excitement rising. "That's one of the things Good Shepherd encourages. They've actually seen these Friday night deals turn into special, ongoing relationships between some of the church members and the needy kids. They'll bring the kids to church with them, or take them out to the movies once in a while...just show them that someone cares for them. But even if you only go once, Jo said that just having godly men there makes such a difference. She says you should see all these fatherless kids just flock to the men that come in. They just want someone to roughhouse and kid with them like a dad should."

There was a long silence around the table. Several of the couples looked over to where the children of the home group members chattered contentedly away over their burgers and fries, happy, fed and secure in their parents' presence.

"Why don't we do it this Friday night?" Eric said.

Sherry beamed as the others agreed. "I was hoping you'd say that!"

The little boy ran up to give Doug one last hug as the volunteers finished cleaning the almost-deserted room. Doug scooped him up and threw him over his shoulder, laughing as the boy howled in mock protest. The others looked on as Doug set the boy down again, looked into his eyes, said a few words for his ears only, and sent him on his way.

The child ran out the door. His mother, moving slowly from an apparent injury, waved a listless good-bye and limped out without a glance.

The volunteers were left alone. All the lights were on, the movie screen had been put away, the linoleum swept clean of popcorn. Only the last few bags of trash were left to be hauled to the dumpster.

Doug and Eric hadn't been able to participate much in cleaning up, but no one minded. They had indeed been swarmed by children the moment they walked in. The little boy who had just left had hardly let Doug alone for a moment. Brandon had eyed the other child warily but had seemed tolerant of the preemption of his father. As long as it was temporary.

Doug walked over to Brandon and ruffled his hair. "Thanks for being such a good sport tonight. You were a big help. Did you have fun?"

Brandon nodded, then shrugged, then nodded again. "Jamal was nice. He doesn't have a mom or a dad, though. Says he lives with his grandma."

"A lot of these kids do. I've got to finish cleaning up and then we'll get going, okay?"

"Okay."

When Doug rejoined the others, he found that a heated discussion was in progress, the Trinity Chapel volunteers deep in debate while the Good Shepherd members looked on in some amusement.

"Well, why *don't* we do this at our church?" One of their home group members was looking at Eric. "Or something like it? I mean, goodness' sakes, we collect a lot of food, you know. But we just give it to other churches and hope it reaches people it should. Why don't we do any of the actual ministry ourselves?"

Before Eric could respond, Sherry jumped in. "Yes, and look at all those low-rent apartment complexes right along Tenth Street near the church. Just a mile away, you've got subdivisions filled with ritzy houses, but there at the gas station on the corner—at that little minimart—there are immigrants waiting every day for someone to come along and offer them a day labor job so they can feed their families. I'd think we could easily set up a system to bring some food or clothes to those folks who need it."

"And then we could invite them to church!" one of the other women chimed in. "After all, that's the whole point, isn't it? So many of these people need the hope of Jesus, but they don't know where to find it. It's just a matter of connecting the ministry outreach to the church."

"You know," Jo Woodward said, "our church has been talking about setting up a program to bus all these kids from this community center to church each Sunday. We'd give them breakfast on the bus—big incentive for the parents to let them come—and they'd go to Sunday school just like all the other kids. We've seen it work really well in other places, and we'll probably start it in the spring."

She stood with her hands on her hips, her face thoughtful. "I think you've got a great idea about turning your food pantry into a real outreach. I've been in those apartment complexes you're talking about, the ones where so many immigrants live. Our own family has had so many financial problems this last year that it's easy to feel sorry for ourselves—but one visit to those complexes puts it all in perspective. I think so many people are struggling to just put food on the table each day that they don't have the time or the inclination to seek out a church, to seek out reasons for hope. But if your church came to *them*, well, that's another story. I think it's a great idea."

"Yes, great idea," Lisa Elliott said, "if we can find someone to take the responsibility for it…and actually do the work."

"Well…why don't we do it?" Sherry raised her chin, as if expecting quelling looks, but got none. "Even if we just did it once, as a test, sort of, before the holidays. What could it hurt?"

Doug looked at his wife with affection. "It could just shatter our complacency, that's all."

The others laughed, but looked thoughtful. Sherry looked uncomfortable. "But then there *are* the inevitable tough problems, and I don't know that we know how to solve them. Like these women here tonight, for example. I can tell that a bunch of them are on drugs."

She paused and turned to the others in the group, her gaze rueful. "Don't ask me *how* I know that, I just know it." The others laughed as she continued. "How can we—or should we?—give handouts to people who are misusing the resources they already have?"

"That's a hard question," Jo said, "but I think we can get some people from our food pantry to help you decide your parameters. It's all about exercising compassion and wisdom at the same time. We've got some people who are really experienced—have done this for years—and know how to avoid the pitfalls. If you're really serious, I'll set you up with them."

Several people nodded.

"But in the end," Doug said, "it comes down to whether we'll be able to get the people in the congregation to do the work. It can't just be *us* or it won't work. It has to be something that people not only think is a good idea, but something they're willing to put shoe leather into. And…well…I'm just wondering whether we're up for it. At least right now."

"What do you mean?" Jo asked.

"I mean—Well, look, you've been to our church, right? We can be so…so judgmental. Whether they say it or not, a lot of church people will be judging the people that come to the food pantry, wondering if they're trying as hard as they can to find work, thinking that if they hadn't had three kids out of wedlock they wouldn't need our handouts. I think all those things myself. Are people who think like that really going to be able to minister to someone they're secretly judging? Because I can bet you that the people getting the ministry will be able to spot it a mile away."

"I think our church has matured more than you realize," Eric said, "more than may be apparent on the surface. The issue isn't whether the volunteers think that the single unmarried mom with three kids was irresponsible—in most cases, they'd be absolutely correct in thinking that. The issue is that we have to realize that we *all* have warts, that we *all* have logs in our eyes, as Pastor Steven said so eloquently that day. I have found that it really is impossible for me to hold in my head a realization of my own sin—say, that I'm being insensitive to my wife—and to be judgmental of someone else's sin at the same time. It just doesn't work."

He shrugged. "I think we should try it. I think it would be good not only for those we'd be helping, but also for our church. It's just the sort of thing that would help solidify the work that started when Pastor Steven stood up in the pulpit that day."

"This is just the sort of thing I've been praying for!" Pastor Steven was on his feet with excitement. Doug and Eric watched him pace back and forth in front of his desk. "We need something to galvanize the congregation, to get us outside ourselves, for pete's sake!

"So much has happened—there's been so much movement *within* the congregation, and that's great. But does it really matter if the movement just stops there?

No! We're supposed to be taking the Good News to those who need it, who have never heard it, who've rejected it or misunderstood it. This food pantry outreach is a great first step. And there are so many needs out there these days, so many *physical* needs as well as spiritual ones. The poor have just been decimated by this recession.

"Tell you what." He came to a full stop in front of his desk. "I'll need to run this by my leadership team, just so I don't make a unilateral decision. But assuming they'll give the green light, why don't you all get a team together and start planning the thing? We'll announce it to the congregation this Sunday." He puckered his lips, thinking, his gaze distant. "I don't know why, but I feel a real urgency to get this done—to get our ministry muscles back in shape. And get it done soon."

Caliel walked, unseen, through the crowd, watching and listening as the families streamed out of their apartments, curious about the mobile church stand that had been set up in the parking lot.

They all had received the flyer slipped under their doors, announcing in English and Spanish that Trinity Chapel would be setting up an area where residents could come for food, clothes, school supplies…and even haircuts and financial advice. So on this Saturday morning they came, staring at the beehive of activity that surrounded the truck the church was using as its base. Some sauntered by nonchalantly; others made a beeline for the stand, where a dozen smiling church members directed each person to the various ministry areas or translators, as needed.

Caliel smiled as he watched the action, both physical and spiritual. Shining angels who watch-cared over individual church members shared greetings with colleagues who shepherded the apartment residents. It was good to touch base, to mutually guide the process of sharing, of love, to feel the presence and the pleasure of the Lamb of God.

Caliel watched the Holy Spirit fill the Christians with love and power—both those who gave and those who received. The power of that love was almost palpable, transforming all it touched, changing what could have been a perfunctory handout into real ministry. Caliel saw many an earnest conversation, many a personal prayer. Even the language differences posed no barrier to ministry, as the Lord touched those who were prayed for, whether they had an interpreter at their side, whether they understood every word or not.

☆ ☆ ☆

"Gracias, gracias!" The young woman, beaming with delight, accepted the bag of groceries and placed several small items of clothing into the bag.

Sherry smiled at her. "De nada."

Two little boys clung to the woman's legs, unsure about all the fuss and bustle.

Sherry reached down and ruffled their hair, smiling as they peeked out from behind their mother's skirt.

"Dios te bendiga." *God bless you.*

Shy grins appeared on their faces. "Gracias," their little voices said in unison.

The woman looked at Sherry with watery eyes, then put down the groceries and reached to give her a hug. "Dios te bendiga."

Sherry watched them walk away and said a silent prayer. She saw Doug talk with another family, shaking their hands, pointing down the road in the direction of their church. That family, too, left with full arms and smiles on their faces. Doug appeared briefly by her side.

"They spoke pretty good English. They'll be coming on Sunday with some others from the complex."

Sherry stood on her tiptoes and kissed his cheek. "Great. Thank you."

Someone called for Doug—a family needed some financial advice—and Sherry again found herself alone, watching the milling people and the nearby apartment complex.

On the first floor, a door opened, and a new family ventured out. They hesitated when they saw the crowd, then came slowly forward. A man, his face dark and bearded, wearing the clothes of his native land, led a small group of women and children forward. The women wore headscarves and clutched the hands of their children.

Sherry noticed that several in the crowd turned to look. There was a subtle pulling aside, some sideways glances, some whispers as they passed. Sherry stepped forward, smiling, and extended her hand to the man at the head of the little group.

"Hi, I'm Sherry. I'm glad to see you all."

"Hello." The man's voice was heavily accented but clear. "I am Azim. Are you from the Trinity Church, to give away the food and clothes?"

"We are, Azim. Why don't you come and see if there's anything you need?"

He nodded, head held high, and gestured the women forward. With shy smiles toward Sherry, they began looking at the clothing, holding the pieces up to their children, turning little shoes over in their hands, their faces eager.

Within five minutes, the women had picked out things they needed, and Sherry took the little group over to the truck to get some groceries. As she filled up several bags, she smiled at one of the women.

"What is your name?"

"Aisha."

"That's a beautiful name. What country are you from?"

The woman's smile dimmed. She looked down. "We are from Saudi Arabia."

"I hear you have a beautiful country."

The woman looked up in surprise and nodded. "Yes. It is."

"Do you like America?"

"Yes." The eyes were downcast again. "We have good jobs here, good schools for the girls. It is where we want to be."

"Has it been difficult for you, with everything that has happened?"

"Yes." The word was quiet. "Yes, difficult."

"I'm so sorry." Sherry finished packing the bags and turned to face the woman. "I imagine it is…hard sometimes for people to know how to act, what to say. It's easy to fear what we don't understand."

Aisha nodded, looking at Sherry, her face forthright. "We are surprised that you would serve us, would serve those who are not of your faith. Azim, my brother, he thought you would turn us away."

"Oh no! Not at all. We're followers of Jesus—*Isa*, I believe you call him. And Isa tells us to love everyone, no matter what."

"In Islam, Isa is the healing prophet. We revere him."

"We believe Isa is more than that. We believe He is the healer because He is the Son of God."

Aisha shook her head. "We do not understand this. How can there be two gods? We believe in one God, Allah."

Sherry smiled. "We do believe in one God, the one who created heaven and earth. But Jesus and God the Father are one." She looked at the small line that was growing beyond them. "You know, this requires a longer discussion, but I'd like to continue it sometime. Perhaps next time we come back, I'll bring a book that'll help me share with you what we believe."

Aisha gave her a shy smile. "Perhaps." She took a bag of groceries and called another woman over to receive the second. "Thank you for helping us."

"You're welcome. God bless you. We'll see you again soon."

Sherry watched as the little family trailed away, again collecting sideways glances as they headed back toward the building, to shut themselves inside.

Lord, You died for all of us. Bring someone in their apartment complex—someone who knows You—to befriend them, to be kind to them. Help me to remember to pray for that family.

Caliel also watched as the Muslim family disappeared inside their building, watched the spiritual forces at work, and prayed that that encounter would someday bear fruit.

The ministry time drew to a close, the parking lot clearing of residents, the tables and racks now almost bare. The church members packed away the remaining items, talking a mile a minute, comparing notes, clearly on a ministry high.

Caliel exchanged glances with his team members, their eyes tender on those in their care. They all knew the time was short, and this was only one step. But for a moment, they allowed themselves to revel in the presence of the Lord, His pride in His children.

Something caught Caliel's attention, and he realized that it was Loriel, arriving at speed. His eyes were grave as he went to greet his commanding officer. The next steps would come soon enough.

FORTY-SEVEN

The old prewar building was a hive of activity. All regular external meetings had been moved or postponed, and all internal ones were short and to-the-point. The first test was going live in twenty-four hours, and there was a lot to do.

Tyson took the stairs in the building two at time, checking that all was running and ready. He checked in with the managers in each department, nearly out of breath from running from one to the other.

Most of the people in the building didn't know what they were preparing for. Nor would they. Even those with few scruples would balk at the intended results of their labors, if they were to ever discover them. But 95 percent still labored under the misdirection of the "white-collar crime" cover story, and were more than willing to line their own pockets in exchange. The other 5 percent were the top loyalists, people who—like Glenn—knew the score and had ideological or monetary incentives to persevere to the real end.

Only one major worry niggled at Tyson; the persistent feeling that they had a breach. A few things had happened that had made him wonder; small things, like the bust of the Florida drug-running tunnel. Every large organization had its tattlers, of course; no way around it. And, he reminded himself, most of their organization was straight organized crime—nothing fancy. A breach could never affect Proxy's main plot, could probably never even get close. The loyalist team was handpicked, and only they had the full story. He had to admit that some external players could probably piece a few things together if they happened to be in the right place at the right time. But even then, no way could they learn enough to compromise the primary plan. It was just impossible.

Tyson pulled to a stop in front of a door with a keypad, entered his code, and slipped inside. The people in the room hardly looked up, intent on the banks of equipment in front of them. The broadcasting studio was small, but more than adequate for their purposes. And they had some of the best encryption people in the world ensuring that they could cover their tracks. If anyone ever even thought to look for them.

Tyson flicked on a television set on the wall. He picked up a DVD lying to the side.

"Is this it?" he asked no one in particular. "Is this the final version?"

One or two of the busy heads nodded without looking up.

Tyson pulled up a chair and slipped the DVD into the television's built-in player. The screen sprang to life with an image of running feet and a jazzy musical background. The camera zoomed into a panorama of figures: a sports star jumping hurdles, a woman jogging along a misty morning river, kids playing a pickup game, a pro basketball star exploding into an impossible, slow-motion slam dunk.

He kept his eyes on the screen and spoke over his shoulder. "Is this the one-minute or the thirty-second version?"

Someone behind him answered in a distracted voice. "Thirty seconds, chief. Since that's the one we're using."

"Fine." He watched the entire commercial twice, then stood and stretched. "They did a great job. What's the cue?"

No one answered him, and he tapped one of his men on the shoulder.

"What? Oh, um...the slam dunk, chief."

Tyson's lips curved in a smile. "How appropriate."

"So did he show it to you?" Ronnie Hanover eyed Tiffany curiously as her friend changed into a conservative cocktail dress.

Tiffany was leaving early, heading out for another night with Wade, a night to celebrate the launching of what had become a series of commercials that would culminate with the Super Bowl ads in January.

"I'll see it tonight. They just finished the first one. The ad people will show it live at the party. They were going to have the company Christmas party anyway, so they're combining the two."

"Cool." Despite herself, Ronnie was jealous. Marco had asked if she wanted to accompany another executive to the same party, but she just wasn't ready for another sugar daddy. The bruises had barely healed. Maybe in another few days she'd do this special off-site party Marco kept mentioning.

"See ya."

Tiffany met Wade at the entrance to the hotel, where well-dressed guests were thronging into the ballroom. She gave him a long kiss. He'd been talking about getting her a new car, so she might as well play it up and see what happened.

She held her head high as Wade took her arm and guided her into the ball-room—even though no one could know it, she *had* brokered this deal. She half-knew many of the people in the room from previous events on Wade's arm. She smiled and worked the room, secure in herself and her abilities. She made Wade look good, and he rewarded her handsomely.

An hour later, Wade left her side and appeared on a small stage, under a giant screen.

"Ladies and gentleman, could I have your attention. Welcome to our holiday celebration and the launch of our new high-impact national advertising campaign. Speed Shoes is pleased to announce the first in a series..."

Tiffany clapped along with the others at the right spots, scanning the festive crowd, watching the polite expressions. Her gaze lingered on two men from the advertising agency standing alone at the back of the crowd. They were clapping as well, but seemed tense, keyed up. She recognized one as a man that Marco had tried to set Ronnie up with.

Wade was wrapping up his little speech, enjoying his time in the spotlight. "We'll be watching it live here in a moment, and the clock will begin to tick toward the most effective Super Bowl ad in the history of advertising."

He gestured for the lights to be lowered, and the screen above him sprang to life with a scene from a popular cop drama.

Tiffany watched the two men. They were whispering together and looking at their watches, seeming hardly interested in the upcoming commercial. Odd, since they created it. And why were they so stressed? They should be enjoying themselves and their success with a major, high-profile account.

One man turned his head and looked straight at her. Tiffany realized she'd been caught staring—staring at them instead of the screen. The man's expression tightened, and Tiffany gave him a coy grin and pointed at the screen as if to say "congratulations."

The man relaxed and, noticing her figure and long bare legs for the first time, made eyes at her. Tiffany returned the look, confident that Wade would let nothing come of it.

The screen flashed to black, and Tiffany looked up to watch the long-awaited results of her very profitable labors.

The world was black outside the windows of the security station, set into the clifflike concrete wall above the towering dam.

Inside, two guards sat in front of a bank of monitors that flickered between every conceivable interior and exterior view. Another two guards waited in a nearby break room for their next shift, watching a popular police drama beamed in via the satellite dish outside. Another two teams were outside in the cold keeping an eye out for anything amiss. In half an hour, each of the four teams would rotate to a different post.

No one was overly worried, but just that morning another special alert had been issued. The threat of terrorist activity was judged to be higher than usual. No specifics, of course, and the men were annoyed at having to work longer hours so close to Christmas. But these days, each industry, each company, had its own way of responding to heightened terrorist threats, and this was theirs.

One of the guards walked the path that circumnavigated the giant reservoir above the dam. Hundreds of millions of gallons of water sat silent and still, undisturbed under the stars. From his position on a gentle slope, the guard could look downward over the water and over the lip of the dam, to the dark river ravine below.

The river was managed, of course, as the dam engineers constantly let out the appropriate amount of water to keep it running smoothly—without flooding the cities and towns just a few miles downriver. This dam wasn't one of the largest, or the most productive, but it had faithfully served the residents of this area for the many years since that time, without incident.

The guard turned and looked upriver. In warmer weather, many of those residents came here to relax amid the natural beauty of the river and the upper lake. The recreational area ended at a concrete barrier across the lower lake, a half-mile upriver from the dam, but every now and then some bumbling tourist pulling an overpriced boat on a trailer managed to get himself lost and find a little-used back road into the restricted area. Because their dam wasn't particularly large or profitable, and was in a remote area used primarily for recreation, the massive perimeter was not fenced in. There was really no feasible way *to* fence so much land; unless what you were fencing was an army base or a missile silo or other such installation. The municipality that owned the dam relied on signs, monitoring, and sturdy fencing near the dam itself to discourage the back-roaders. But once or twice, a tourist had managed to miss all the warnings, and to put in at points on the lower lake where the firm bank made a perfect natural boat ramp down to the water.

The guard shook his head, tolerant of human stupidities. He'd been there for one such case, under a bright August sky, when the infuriated boat owners had been confronted by guards appearing out of nowhere on Jet Skis, to be told that they would have to pack up and leave forthwith. A Hawaiian-shirted man—half drunk, and in a party mood, had demanded to see a map that proved they were on restricted space before he would incur the trouble of loading up his boat. The guards had, with some amusement, shown him their official identification—along with the loaded weapons that were strapped securely at their sides. The blustering boat owner had rapidly decided that was all the road map he needed, and had departed at speed.

Chuckling at the memory, the guard scanned the dark water—and froze. He blinked, thinking the memory had come to life. No, there it was again: A motorboat, calmly drifting down from around a bend, was headed straight down the middle of the lake. Toward the dam.

The guard cursed and sprinted forward, grabbing his radio out of his belt.

"Code Red all teams! Code Red all teams! Unsecured boat heading toward home base, over!"

The radio crackled to life as he tried to keep pace along the shore. He pressed the transmit button again, trying to talk and run at the same time. "Appears unmanned! No one in the cockpit! Thirty seconds to home base, over!"

He heard his supervisor's calm voice over the radio. "Sending team to intercept. Can you tell if it's a threat?"

"Negative…home base…" The guard was panting now, unable to keep up with the boat. "No way…to know. But it feels wrong. Nighttime…unmanned… how'd it get here?"

He heard his supervisor ordering out a team to intercept the boat, but he knew they'd never reach it before it reached the dam. He began sprinting again, arriving at the dam and taking the downward steps two at a time, down toward the verge. His view was momentarily blocked by the high stairway walls, but he could hear the security boat's engine being revved.

Inside the security station, the break room was deserted, a spilled coffee cup betraying the haste of the guards' departure. The lonely television flickered with the final moments of an intense police scene, then went black, transitioning into the commercial break.

Perched high up along the outside of the dam, the small satellite dish received its signals, transmitting them to the television inside and any other receivers within range. One such receiver sat quietly nearby, gently rocking in the wake stirred up by the nearby security boat and the man who had come aboard in haste to hook up a towline.

☆ ☆ ☆

The guard emerged from the staircase to see three of his colleagues busy in and around the intruding boat, which now bumped gently up against the dam. He caught his breath—and was blinded by a roaring flash of light. From fifty feet away, he was thrown back onto the steps, shielding his face from the heat of the explosion.

He shouted out for his colleagues on the boat, trying to regain his equilibrium, to stand, to do something. He saw his supervisor run out onto the deck of the security station, also shielding his face from the flame, trying to see with his eyes what couldn't have been true on the monitor.

The two men locked eyes, and they turned and fixed their gaze on the top of the dam. A chunk looked like it had been bitten out by a ravenous giant. Cracks were forming, right down to the waterline, where two boats were burning down to empty hulks—hulks that would quickly sink or be washed over the dam. Along with millions of gallons of water.

The supervisor disappeared from the doorway, and on his radio the guard could hear the alert going out. "Breach in progress! Move away from the river! Alert the towns!" Within moments, over the crackle of the flame and the sound of the groaning dam, the old sirens could be heard far below.

In slow motion, he watched the cracks spread, illuminated by the flames in the darkness, the vision of hell. Then there was a great crumbling and a roar as a giant chunk gave way.

Tyson and the other members of the S-Group sat perched on their island wicker chairs, staring, intent, at a bank of television sets, each turned to a different cable channel. Different channels, same news.

Tyson watched the anxious reporters—some soaked or covered with mud—documenting the sudden tragedy that had befallen the river valley. The nighttime pictures were murky, lit only by the lights of cameras and emergency workers. But that was enough to see the houses torn apart, the cars flipped high on the ravine, the body bags, the shattered families. The darkness and cold added to the confusion, the horror. It was feared that hundreds, probably thousands, had been killed, one of the worst flooding tragedies of the past hundred years. Shaken reporters looked into the cameras and spoke of the impact of such a tragedy during the Christmas season.

The newscasts were full of speculation as to the cause of the breach, the theories spreading like wildfire. But no one would stick his neck out and say the *T* word. Not until they had more information.

Tyson sipped his glass of wine. It was all part of the necessary cycle of destruction and rebirth. He was just helping it along. And getting paid handsomely in exchange.

"Turn that up!" Tyson gestured toward the man nearest a particular television set, where a reporter stood, microphone in hand, shivering amid the carnage.

"Sources now tell us this was a deliberate explosion, a bomb aboard a small boat of some kind. Again, we're coming to you first with the news that this was no accident. This was a deliberate act of malice with—it appears—the intent to destroy thousands of innocent lives. We can only speculate who may be behind this attack and whether this horrific act will result in even greater loss. Again, let's take you to the precarious situation on the dam just a few miles upriver from where we stand."

A helicopter shot showed the beleaguered dam, the partial breach down the middle and across one side, the remaining mass of water pressing on the weakened structure. Sober-eyed commentators safe in their television studios interviewed engineers about the chances that the rest of the dam could go. It was astounding, the engineers said, that only that top rectangular piece had broken free so far...the pressure for a complete breach was enormous...authorities must swiftly let out more of the water in as controlled a manner as possible.

The members of the S-Group scowled. On a scale of ten, this was probably a four. But since this was just a warm-up, a test, the pressure was off. And regardless, their client was pleased.

There were yells and cheers in the dusty early-morning streets as the enemies of the Great Satan got word that another blow had been struck, another great loss inflicted. And during the infidels' celebrations of their heretical Christmas holiday season, at that. It could not be better.

Men gave each other impromptu presents, teens fired automatic weapons in the air, chanting national slogans, and children danced in the streets.

Mr. Mohammed watched from a third-floor window, his arms crossed, his tight lips now curving in a smile. Ah, the younger generation. Passionate, pliable, and steeped in the old teachings without question. The perfect tools that they needed now and for the foreseeable future; for as long as they fought this shadow war against the great enemy of Islam. As was their custom, their team would gather at prayers soon and give thanks to Allah for their success.

He ducked back inside his informal command center—a sparse two-room apartment—and continued the debriefing via secure cell phone with several of the operatives involved. Being infidels, caring only about money, they had not been willing to be martyrs for the cause. But it hadn't been necessary; the boat had been remotely guided from a pickup truck parked nearby.

The bomb could have just as easily been detonated by the same operatives, but that wasn't the point. The point was the test, and it had worked beautifully.

Mr. Mohammed turned and watched the scenes of devastation on CNN, the tragedy not two hours old. The test run had proven that the real event would be a great success, Allah willing.

He disconnected from the American operatives and punched in the number that would reach his backers. He stood at the window, watching the ongoing celebration in the streets. Just imagine what these streets would look like after Super Bowl Sunday.

Everyone clustered around the break room television set, eyes stretched with disbelief, watching the horrific scenes. Several of the girls were crying, their makeup running. Maris chain-smoked, tears in her hardened eyes, angrily jabbing out one cigarette only to light another within minutes. Ronnie sat next to her on the couch, unable, like the others, to look away from the devastation of this new kind of attack.

The room was crowded with so many staffers away from their posts, but it didn't matter. The club floor was practically deserted, most patrons having rushed home to turn on their own televisions once the news was announced. The only busy area was the bar, where Nick had a small set turned to CNN. He plied the shocked customers with drinks, which they paid for and drank like automatons, all attention focused on the news.

Within half an hour, Marco came in, his face somber. He announced that they would close up early that night; that everyone could go home. His voice was brusque and he never looked toward the television set. Instead, his eyes searched the crowd in the room and settled on Ronnie. He jerked his head toward the door.

"Can I talk to you a minute?"

Wiping her eyes, Ronnie picked her way through the haphazard cluster of sitting and standing staff members and followed Marco out into the hallway.

"I need to schedule this gig for you on Saturday night." He spoke with no further preamble. "The special Christmas party with some business partners at my place. We'll just have one dancer. You up for it? I'll pay you directly, no money to change hands there."

Ronnie tried to attend to what he was saying. How could he expect her to focus on business right now?

She sniffled a little, one eye still on the television set, glimpsed through the doorway. There was a heart-wrenching shot of a child crying in a policeman's arms.

"Oh, Marco, isn't it *awful?*" She sniffled some more. "How could anyone *do* something like that?"

Marco made an impatient movement with his hand. "Yes, awful. But I need to know the answer now, or I need to pick another girl. You in or out?"

Ronnie closed her eyes, trying to concentrate. "In, I guess."

"Will you be able to pull it together by then?" Marco's tone was cold.

Her eyes flew open again. "How can you be so…so *heartless?*" She could feel her ire rising and turned her back on the television screen. "Yeah, I'll be fine by the weekend, enough to earn my keep for the party. Sure, no problem, Marco, if that's all you care about!"

He scowled at her, irritated, and turned away, saying over his shoulder. "Fine, I'll put you on the schedule." He vanished into his office, and closed the door behind him.

Ronnie muttered a few choice words in his direction, then turned and headed back into the break room. School finals were in progress, and she had no idea how anyone was going to be able to concentrate on their tests tomorrow.

FORTY-EIGHT

Y ou still want to go to the game?" Sherry Turner was pacing around the living room, the television set on—as it had been almost continually since the dam attack—but muted. "You think it's safe?"

On the other end of the line, Jo Woodward sounded exasperated. "Who knows, these days? Who would've thought three days ago that some remote, peaceful river valley would be *unsafe?* But it's the same thing I thought after the 9/11 attacks—I hate the idea of letting the terrorists win."

"Yeah, I know. Doug will be home any minute, and I'll ask him what he thinks."

"How's the outreach going, by the way? The food pantry thing?"

"Hopping. All those immigrants that depend on day labor jobs have been just decimated these last few days. We've been collecting lots of extra food and have taken it over twice already this week."

"God's timing is amazing. What would those people have done if that hadn't already been in place?"

"I don't know. And it's been important from a spiritual standpoint, too. Like everyone else, they've been really shaken by this. Even before, so many new people from the complexes were coming to church that we were considering starting either a Spanish service or a simultaneous translation. After this, I think it'll be a must."

Sherry looked up as Doug came in the garage door, loosening his tie. He set his briefcase beside the door and came to give her a peck on the cheek. He mouthed the words *who is it?*

Sherry whispered, "Jo Woodward. About our plans for Saturday night. You still want to go?"

Doug slipped the knot on his tie, considering. Then he nodded. "If the kids were going, I might not be so quick. But I think we have to get on with normal life."

In Sherry's ear, Jo was saying, "We have to get on with life, you know?"

Sherry almost giggled. "Doug just came home and he said the same thing."

"Well, then, let's do it." There was sudden hesitation in the cheery voice. "If you're—you know—still up for it."

"Hey! None of that nonsense!" Sherry laughed outright. "We *want* to treat you to this game. We've been talking about it forever, and you agreed to let us, so no backing out now!"

Tyson slipped into his cluttered office and checked his e-mail for anything new from the client. One by one, the members of the S-Group arrived for the next planning meeting. When all were in place, Tyson stood and addressed the small group.

"The client is pleased. They are releasing to us the first bonus in the payment package—the first bonus for the first job delivered."

There were careful smiles and nods. "About time," a couple of people muttered.

"We've all been under a great deal of stress these last few weeks, and we think it's about time we combined business with pleasure. It's the holidays, after all. We'll meet Saturday at the house of one of our principals—Marco, who most of you know—and after the all-day strategy session, we'll have a little all-night bash. I'm told that as entertainment, we'll be joined by one of Marco's showcase girls, who have—all unwittingly—been of so much use to us.

"Just one caution: I don't know which girl Marco will be able to get for Saturday. Remember that some are more…amenable…to various attentions than others. These girls are thoroughbreds and each one needs to be handled differently. Some are more relaxed, some more jumpy."

One of the men looked irritated, his eyes hard. "What are you saying?"

"I'm saying that you should all remember how much we have invested in these girls before you act, okay? Remember the lesson we taught Glenn, just recently, for the breakdown in discipline."

One or two of the men nodded, but Tyson had an uncomfortable feeling they would do exactly what they wanted to do, whether he liked it or not.

Ronnie stepped back, uncomfortable. What was *with* these guys tonight? They weren't playing by the rules.

She gave another desperate glance around, looking for Marco. Again, he was nowhere to be found. Dozens of drinks had been knocked back, and she could tell that the men in this elite little group were used to getting their way.

Another man put his arm around her, his hands wandering, unwelcome. She again fended off the inappropriate touch, trying to act calm even as her heart began to pound.

"Uh—sorry, gentlemen. I'll just be a moment. I need some air."

She hurried out onto the deck, shivering in the chill air. The deck had a dizzying view of a plunging hill beyond, putting to rest any thoughts she had about climbing over the edge and down to the ground floor to try to find her boss.

She heard footsteps behind her and spun around, face to face with three of the men, their expressions leaving no doubt of their intentions. She opened her mouth to scream, but one clamped a hand over her lips, pressing her bare back against the wooden railing.

"Now, you be a good girl, you hear? You don't know who we are, but you'll do just what we say. We're paying your salary; that's who we are. That's all you need to know. And if you don't cooperate, we'll toss you over the edge. I don't care how much we have *invested* in you."

Ronnie closed her eyes, blocking out the strange words, the drunken and ruthless eyes. No choice. Again, no choice. She stopped struggling, stopped caring, and watched from afar, from behind the wall that had been built brick by brick since she was eight years old.

"Sorry, Macy. Sorry." Marco repeated the words over and over, his voice regretful but calm.

He waited through her shuddering tears as she clutched at him, shivering, fighting off shock. She was sitting in the front seat of his luxury car, his long overcoat covering the few clothes she had been wearing when it all started. He had to get back to the party for the bigwigs, but had snuck out to drop her at the subway. He would have someone bring her car to the club in the morning.

"I'm sorry I wasn't there." He gave her arm a final, awkward pat. "They had me busy downstairs." In the back of his mind, he wondered whether he had purposely been diverted away. They must have known that he would never consciously allow one of his girls to be abused, no matter what the orders were.

Ronnie gave a final few gulping sobs, trying to pull it together so she could get out of the car. Act normal, girl. Even when everything was crumbling, act normal. All she wanted was to get home and crawl in bed, never to come out. She climbed out of the car, stiff and shaky, and slammed the door behind her. Where was all the indignation, the fury that Marco had poured out on Glenn?

She wove her way into the station on shaky legs, bought a token, and climbed the stairs that led to the aboveground platform of the rail station. She had to stop halfway up, bracing herself against the concrete stairwell to stop her head from spinning. Once on the platform she shivered from cold as well as from shock, Marco's overcoat providing little defense against the wind.

The subway was alive with chatter about the play-offs, the Falcons having narrowly beaten the Eagles in the final minutes of the game.

Doug and Sherry stood near Jo and Vance Woodward, clutching the standing subway poles for balance as the train rocketed them toward home. The subway gradually emptied, and the two couples were able to find seats together.

Sherry sat snuggled in the crook of Doug's shoulder, content to watch, listen, and enjoy the security of her husband's arms again. In the last few months he had become a different man. In their early counseling sessions, Pastor Steven had warned them that every husband—just like every wife—responded differently, that some would need more time, more healing, more patience than others. No one could predict the path that each couple would need to walk.

One more time, Sherry breathed a prayer of thanksgiving that their path, while painful and dark at times, had been a path to restoration. Her husband was becoming more whole, more loving with every day. Somehow, being forced to confess and confront his problem so openly had freed him.

Doug told Sherry that he had to be on guard every day—that he always would have to be, that the temptation would always be there if he let himself open the door even a crack. She had grown used to asking him the tough questions and loving him through both the bad and good answers. But it was so worth it to see him living without the fear that regression was inevitable. He had been, really and truly, set free.

The train approached the last stop, and Doug took Sherry's hand as the foursome made their way to the doors. Jo and Vance filed off first, Doug and Sherry right behind them, pushing through the crowd waiting to board. Vance stopped suddenly, causing Doug to bump into his back.

"Jo, look!" Vance said.

Jo put a hand to her mouth. "Oh, my gosh. That's—"

"That's her!"

"Go, quick!"

Shivering, Ronnie waited to board the train. She felt dizzy and faint. She would not cry in public. *Would not cry.*

A gentle hand gripped her arm, and she jumped.

"Ronnie?"

Mr. and Mrs. Woodward stood there, their kind eyes darkened with worry.

"Ronnie, are you okay?"

Ronnie felt Mrs. Woodward's hand tighten on her arm. Then she heard Mr. Woodward's concerned voice. It sounded odd, as if it were coming through a rapidly deepening tunnel.

FORTY-NINE

Ronnie's head was pounding, her mouth dry. She lay still, letting other sensations arrive one by one.

She was lying on a bed. She could feel the weight of a thick, soft comforter, smell a gentle scent.

It was dark. No, her eyes were closed. She unstuck her heavy lids and opened her eyes.

The brilliant rays of midday shone on the floor by the bed.

Ronnie lay still for a minute, letting the questions rush in as her mind cleared. What was going on? Where was she?

Heavy floral curtains hung at a nearby window—expensive curtains. Her eyes wandered the unfamiliar bedroom. There were tasteful pictures on the wall, antique furniture, and an elegant lamp on the table by the bed. A glass of water stood there, beside a large leather-bound book with "Holy Bible" on the front.

Ronnie sat straight up, wincing at the pain in her head. She reached for the glass of water. She needed to wake up, to snap Alice out of Wonderland.

She sipped the water, welcoming the reality of the pounding against her brain. And memory rushed back. Marco's party…the attack…the shaky drive to the MARTA station. The Woodwards!

She vaguely remembered being revived from a faint, talking incoherently, being helped down the stairs and into the backseat of a van, where she must have passed out again.

Uncomfortable and embarrassed, she fingered the soft blanket on the bed. Suddenly, she gasped as a thought hit and she looked down at herself, taking in the unfamiliar nightshirt for the first time. She groaned and fell back against the pillows.

She heard steps coming near, and the doorknob turned. Mrs. Woodward walked in, saying something in a whisper to another woman.

They both stopped dead in their tracks when they saw her sit up. For a frozen moment, no one spoke, and then Mrs. Woodward smiled.

"Sorry, Ronnie. We left the room just a few minutes ago. We didn't want you to wake up alone."

Ronnie stared at them, uncertain what to say. Her gaze traveled to the woman standing by Mrs. Woodward.

"This is Sherry Turner," Mrs. Woodward said. "You're in her guest bedroom." She came forward and sat on the edge of the bed. "Ronnie, I want to tell you something before another minute passes, before you decide its time to get up and leave."

Ronnie's eyes flickered to Sherry Turner, wondering what she knew. What they both knew.

Mrs. Woodward didn't look nearly as uncomfortable as Ronnie felt. "You should know that all of us—my husband and I, and the Turners—know at least a little about your situation. For months now, Vance and I have felt just awful about that night at the church, about what happened. That's why we tried to contact you. You deserved better, and we are sorry."

Ronnie felt the color rising in her cheeks. She looked down and fingered the unfamiliar nightshirt.

"What...what happened last night?"

"I was thinking of asking you the same thing." Mrs. Woodward's voice carried a trace of dry humor. "I'm a nurse by training, and when you fainted on the platform, I did a quick evaluation. I...uh...it was pretty easy, really, to get an idea of what had happened to you.

"You probably don't remember it, but you were semidelirious and fought the idea of us taking you to a hospital. I thought it was better that we bring you to a home where you could get some personal care, anyway. It looked to me like you were experiencing neurogenic shock, and that you needed a safe place to rest, more than anything else." She smiled. "I worked in a hospital for a few years, and they are hardly restful places."

"How long have I been out?"

"A good twelve hours, I'd say." Mrs. Woodward looked at Sherry Turner for confirmation, and she nodded. "We ran into you around midnight, and it's nearly noon now. Noon on Sunday."

"Noon. I'm so sorry. I can't believe you put me up for the night. I should leave." She made a move to get out of bed.

Both women stopped her. Sherry pulled up a chair and sat beside the bed.

"Listen, Ronnie, you don't need to go anywhere if you don't want to. You look like—Well, you look like you had a pretty rough time last night, and both the Woodwards and us want to make sure you're in a safe place. You don't need to go anywhere if you don't want to."

Ronnie looked at their faces, confused. "But I've got to get out of your hair. What do you mean?"

☆ ☆ ☆

Sherry took a deep breath, trying to form the right words. This was where the rubber met the road. Ministering every now and then at a food pantry or apartment outreach—and mostly leaving the ministry at the door—was one thing. This was quite another. This was deciding whether they were going to inconvenience themselves for someone who clearly needed help—and a lot of help at that, probably—or whether they were going to shunt her off to a shelter or some ministry that dealt with "people like that."

The Woodwards had been willing to take her in, but they had a tiny little house and no extra room. Doug and Sherry, on the other hand, had those extra bedrooms…and that pesky original intention to use their large, beautiful house for ministry. Sherry smiled ruefully as she looked into Ronnie's perplexed eyes. How like the Lord to take them up on it.

Sherry laid a hand on Ronnie's arm. "I'm saying, Ronnie, that we'd like to help you. If you want a safe place to go, you're welcome to stay here for a while." For just an instant, she watched the girl's eyes widen with surprise, then the shutters came down with a clang.

"Why would I need a safe place? And I don't know you—how do I know you're any safer than anyone else? Why would you think I need your help?"

Sherry glanced over at Jo. "Well, Ronnie, it's pretty clear that you got done pretty badly last night. You were covered with scratches and…and there was blood on your underwear."

Ronnie dropped her face into her hands. How did they expect her to deal with this, with two near-strangers staring at her?

Mrs. Woodward's voice was gentle in her ear. "Ronnie, I need to ask if you want to report—"

"No!" Ronnie's head flew up. "No, no, no. I can't report anything, and it wouldn't matter anyway."

"What do you mean it wouldn't matter?" Mrs. Turner looked surprised. "The police can—"

"No." Ronnie's voice was louder now. "I said no, d'you hear me? It would just make things worse."

There was a long pause, and then Mrs. Woodward raised her hands. "Okay. Okay. I just thought we should ask."

"Well, you asked." Ronnie looked at the clock on the bedstand. "And I need to go. I need to…uh…be at work tonight."

"Are you sure you want to do that?" Mrs. Woodward said. "I mean…you're an adult, you can do what you want. But is that the best thing for you, Ronnie?"

"I have to make a living. Everyone has a job, and this is mine." She looked directly at Mrs. Woodward. "It's the only way I can live and go to school, since I can't get a scholarship."

"Yes, I know. Vance told me—"

"And besides, it's good money and it's fun. Can't ask for more than that."

She pushed the sheets back and swung her legs over the side of the bed. The two women stood, reluctantly.

"Thanks, and everything. Really. A lot of people would've just left me there on the platform to be picked up by the police." She shuddered at the thought. "So, thanks. But my roommate will probably be worried about me, and I have to get ready for work."

Mrs. Turner walked over to a chest of drawers and rummaged through it. She held out a pair of gray leggings and a plain black T-shirt.

"Here, these should fit you okay. Enough to get home in, anyway. We didn't wash the clothes you were wearing—just in case, um, you wanted to report anything. They're in a bag in the top drawer. And there's also a new pack of underwear there that you can open."

"Okay." Ronnie looked at the clothes in her hand. "I don't know what to say. Thank you."

"Ronnie, I don't know you well," Mrs. Woodward said, "but I'd like to get to know you. And we—" she gestured at Mrs. Turner—"both our families would like you to know that we're here for you if you ever want to talk, get away, or just want a home-cooked meal."

Mrs. Turner nodded. "I know you say it's not necessary, but the offer of a safe place is a standing offer, should you ever want it."

"Why are you doing this for me? What's in it for you?"

"Nothing." Mrs. Turner smiled. "Nothing except that we know you're a single woman trying to make it on your own in a big city, away from home, and you've had a hard row to hoe. I guess we just want to help."

"And," Mrs. Woodward jumped in, "because this is how we think perhaps, just perhaps, God can show you how much He loves you. We'd very much like to convince you of that."

"Thanks. Really, thanks."

She made ready to change, and Mrs. Turner pointed out the door to the bathroom for her to take a shower, if she wished.

"Come downstairs when you're done. I'll be glad to drive you home."

Ronnie just wanted to get home to her own familiar apartment, familiar clothes, familiar roommate. Tiffany would be crazy with worry by now. If she was home.

She changed and picked up her belongings—just the small bag of clothes, overcoat, and purse—and ventured downstairs. The two women were chatting in the kitchen. She cleared her throat.

"Mrs. Turner—"

The woman turned toward her and held up a hand. "One thing, just so you know: Please call me Sherry. Mrs. Turner sounds like my mother-in-law!"

"And please call me Jo," Mrs. Woodward said. "We're not that much older than you are, for pete's sake!"

They asked if she would like anything to eat, but she just wanted to escape. Sherry said she would drive her home, as Jo had a previous commitment.

Five minutes later, they were making their way along the back roads toward Ronnie's apartment. After a few minutes of silence, Sherry cleared her throat. "You work at The Challenger, don't you?"

Ronnie was unable to speak. It seemed so improper, here in this family minivan, with this religious woman who had taken her in.

"Don't worry, Ronnie. I'm not judging you."

"How'd you know? About the club, I mean."

"Um, I'm not sure how to say this but…my husband recognized you."

Ronnie shot a glance sideways. "He's a customer?"

"Not now, he isn't." There was a note of steel in the sweet voice. "But there was a time, not that long ago, where he had fallen into— Anyway, he'd gone to that strip club many times, and he said he recognized you as one of the waitresses."

"When was the last time he was at the club?"

"About six months ago."

"Oh. Yes, I was only a waitress then."

"He said he'd never seen you…otherwise."

"That's the truth." Ronnie shrugged. "In case you were wondering."

Sherry pulled up at a stoplight, turned her head, and gave Ronnie a long look. "Thank you for letting me know."

The light turned green, and Sherry pulled away in silence. Ronnie watched the trees flash by, the beautiful subdivisions, the luxury apartment complexes. Just like the Turners'—and just like hers. There wasn't that much difference between them.

"Uh, Sherry, do you mind if I ask you something?"

"Go ahead."

"Why on earth would you and the Woodwards invite me over again—invite me to get to know you? I'm just a girl from the wrong side of the tracks and I know it. And you know it, too. You saw me...you know what I am."

There was a long pause and then Sherry spoke in that peaceful way of hers. "Well, I'll give you an honest answer, if you don't mind."

"I hate baloney. Give it to me straight. You think you'll get points in heaven or something?"

"No." Sherry smiled briefly. "It's for two reasons. One is that Jesus tells us to take in those who are hurting or in need, just as if we were taking Him in."

"Oh."

"Have you ever read the Bible?"

"No...not really."

"Well, in the Bible, Jesus tells this story about the Good Samaritan—"

"The Good Samaritan!"

Ronnie stared at her, then looked out the window, hardly listening as Sherry recounted the story. The image of that old, folded note from her only visit to Sunday school rose in her mind.

"You have a gift. A gift of healing, of helping people. Just like in the story of the Good Samaritan, you care about other people and it shows."

"What's wrong?" Sherry's voice was concerned. "Ronnie?"

Ronnie kept her face turned toward the glass, feeling tears dangerously close to the surface. "I don't want your pity. What do you know of my life?"

"I know more than you think, Ronnie. I know it because...I lived it, too."

"What do you mean? How could you have lived my life?"

They pulled up at another light, and Sherry put the van in "park" and turned to face her. "I'm sure there are differences, but for several years I bet I lived a life very similar to yours in many ways."

"What do you mean—you were a *stripper?*"

"Not a stripper—nothing as obvious as that. But I was a lot like a high-priced call girl. I'd sleep with whatever man asked for it, whenever they asked for it, wherever they asked for it. Oh yes. Nothing so obvious as getting paid for sex, but pretty darned close. I'd keep two or three men on a string at a time. I loved the attention, the gifts, the jet-setting off for a weekend of shopping in Paris. I knew what I wanted, and had my ways of getting it."

☆ ☆ ☆

Sherry pulled away from the light. Was she right in sharing her most intimate secret with this woman? She continued to feel the nudge of the Lord, the nudge that said this conversation was not an accident, was serving a purpose.

Sherry allowed herself an ironic smile. Here, she'd been supporting Doug in the freedom that came with confessing one's most secret sin. About time she took some of her own advice.

Ronnie listened as Sherry told her story from the time she graduated from college as a bitter and unfulfilled twenty-one-year-old, through all her relationships, all her bed-hopping, her drug use to dull the pain. She listened as Sherry described what it was like to be called to a man's bed late at night, only to have to wake up early and surreptitiously leave in time for the day…just like her. What it was like to use the man, use the relationship rather than enjoy it…just like her. What it was like to feel like her dreams would never materialize, that this was all there was, that life stinks, so better to eat, drink, and be merry, right?

Ronnie's lips parted in shock as, one by one, Sherry described the elements of both of their lives. Only…what had changed? How could she get from where she was to where Sherry was now? She had to know.

In response to Ronnie's question, Sherry described the arrival at rock bottom one night, the television show, the preacher, the anguished call to her college room-mate, the prayer…Jesus…rebirth. Joy. Salvation.

Ronnie listened, her eyes and ears full. Even when they pulled up at her apart-ment complex and Sherry found a parking spot, Ronnie made no move to get out of the car, drawn, in spite of herself, to what this woman was saying.

But no—it could never work with her. Could it? Whatever Sherry had done, she had never been a stripper, never a prostitute. Besides, Ronnie admitted to her-self, she liked the money, the acclaim, the glitz and glamour. After being so poor so much of her life, she didn't want to give that up.

"I don't suppose," she said in a flippant voice, "that you could have Jesus and stripping, too?"

"Jesus befriended the prostitutes, you know. But once they met Him, they didn't want to stay that way. It's impossible to really meet Jesus and stay the way you are. God will change your heart, and you'll change your life."

"That's what I thought," Ronnie muttered under her breath. She looked up and stuck out a hand. "Well, thanks for the ride, Sherry. It was very illuminating."

Sherry returned the handshake. "If I might suggest…can we invite you over for dinner next week sometime, after the Christmas rush? Do you work most nights?"

"Mostly weekends now. I might work a few weeknights since I don't have classes over the holidays."

"Well, would you be up for that? Up for a home-cooked meal with us and the Woodwards? A nice family dinner—say, a week from Monday?"

"Uh—okay, I guess."

"Great. We'll look forward to having you. And remember, Ronnie…the other offer stands." She scribbled her name, address, and phone number on a piece of paper and handed it over.

Ronnie took it and escaped the minivan as quickly as she could.

FIFTY

Ronnie barged into the club half an hour early. She still felt ill, but she had to come. She would give Marco a piece of her mind and demand extra pay—a *lot* of extra pay—for the previous night's debacle. Reluctantly, she had brought her stage clothes with her. Although she might set a slower pace for herself that night, she didn't want to forgo work entirely. During this holiday season, Sunday night patrons were in a cheery mood and accustomed to throwing away a lot of cash.

She banged into the break room, the kitchen, the dancer's dressing room—no Marco. She tried his office door, but it was locked and there was no answer to her pounding. He wasn't on the floor or in one of the private rooms. The club was lazy and slow in the late afternoon, and the few staff on duty didn't know where to find him.

"I think he's at a meeting or something." One cook yawned, lazily kneading a batch of dough. "I guess it must be off-site. I'm sure he'll be back before dinner starts."

She turned away, frustrated, and stepped out into the deserted hallway. She heard a door closing and spun around in time to see Marco's office door close with a click.

She hurried down the hallway, gave the most perfunctory of knocks, and barged into the room, her voice raised.

"Marco, you are such a—"

The room was still darkened and the person in it wasn't Marco. Maris stood by the desk, hands on her hips, smacking some gum.

"Oh please, finish the sentence." Getting no response, she cocked an eyebrow. "Need something, honey?"

"Yeah…Marco." Ronnie made an exasperated noise. "I thought you were him."

"Sorry to disappoint ya." The gum smacked as Maris made her way around the desk and began fiddling with Marco's computer. She held a Palm Pilot in one hand. "I'm just entering something into his schedule for him."

"How'd you get in? He's here, then?"

"Nah. At a meeting or something. Should be back soon." Maris slipped her

Palm Pilot back into her apron. "You want me to tell him something? Or are you working tonight?"

Ronnie swayed from a wave of weariness and leaned against a bookshelf. "I'm supposed to be working. I just don't know if I can."

"Are you okay? You don't look so good."

"I don't feel so good."

Maris stood still and stared at her for a long minute. "It happened again, didn't it?"

Ronnie closed her eyes and nodded.

"When?"

"Last night."

"At Marco's private party?"

"Yeah."

Maris punched a last few buttons on the computer, came around the desk, and took Ronnie's arm. With surprising gentleness, she guided her out of the office, locking and closing the door behind her.

Ronnie allowed herself to be guided down the hallway and into the break room, where Maris eased her down onto one of the couches. Maris vanished out the door without a word, and less than a minute later returned with a glass of ice water and two unlabeled pills.

"Like aspirin." She handed them to Ronnie, who obediently swallowed the tablets. "They'll make you feel better. Here, put your feet up."

She got a stool to prop up Ronnie's legs, and then just stood there looking down at her, her expression uncharacteristically soft, concerned.

"Thanks." Ronnie sipped the water, her head clearing a bit. "Sorry. Again."

They heard banging out in the hallway, and both women looked toward the door. They heard Tiffany talking to someone outside, swearing like a sailor.

"Where is she? *Where is she?*"

Tiffany swept into the room, spied them, and ran to Ronnie's side. She fell onto the couch beside her roommate, and took her hand.

"I got your voice mail on my cell phone." She was breathless and there were tears in her eyes. "I'm so sorry I wasn't there for you when you needed me. I'm so sorry!"

She gave her roommate a hug, then pulled back and gazed into Ronnie's face. "Are you okay?" When Ronnie nodded, Tiffany blinked the tears from her eyes. "I'm going to kill him! I'm going to *kill* Marco for letting you go through that and then dumping you off to take the *train!* That—that—There are no words to describe him. I don't think any of us can ever trust him again!"

"So what else is new?" Maris said. She looked at her watch, then back at Ronnie. "I've got to start my shift. You going to be okay?"

"Yeah." Ronnie let go of Tiffany's hand and reached out for Maris's. "Seriously, thanks for your help."

"Yeah, well, what else am I gonna do? Just protecting our star performer." With an ironic nod at Tiffany, she corrected herself. "One of them anyway." She swept out of the room as quickly as Tiffany had swept in.

Tiffany watched her go. "She's nicer than I thought."

"Yeah, I think there's a heart down there under all that bluster." Ronnie sagged back against the couch. "I don't know if I should work tonight."

"I guess it depends on whether you can handle the pace. Can you slow it down a bit?"

"Guess I should. Won't make as much money, though."

Tiffany grinned. "Great idea. Do that."

Ronnie found herself laughing with genuine mirth at her friend and constant competitor. "You jerk. And here I thought you were all worried about me."

"I was worried about you. I still am. All these bad things keep happening to *you*. It makes me nervous. Did you get home okay last night?"

"Uh...actually, you're not going to believe this."

"What?"

"I ran into some...friends from school. They let me crash at their house."

"Well, thank goodness. I was just crazy with worry when I finally listened to your voice mail this morning. And then I couldn't reach you."

"Sorry." Ronnie maneuvered to the edge of the couch and forced herself to stand, creaking and stretching like an old lady. "If I'm going to dance tonight, I'd better do some warm-ups."

"Yeah, it looks like it. Well, I'm going to go get ready. You okay, for real?"

"Yeah. I'll come along in a bit. I'll wait here until Marco gets back. And then I'm going to give him a piece of my mind."

Marco clenched his teeth, trying with all his might not to fly across the room and punch Tyson in the face. He knew the self-satisfied, Ivy League snob would have him terminated in a second, and then—to preempt Proxy's anger over losing a star player—trump up a compelling reason why the action had to be taken. Disloyalty, perhaps, or double-dealing. Marco, of course, wouldn't be around to defend himself.

So he sat and seethed. Tyson had not only refused to admit that doing the girl was a serious mistake—he had laughed, blowing the episode off as a necessary diversion. After all, he told Marco, *you* recruited them to be used in whatever way we deemed fit.

Tyson had elbowed one of the other men, his eyes still glassy from a hangover, and made a crude joke about the valuable use of that particular girl.

That particular girl. As the conversation turned to the next topic on the agenda, Marco wondered why he was responding so violently to these attacks on Macy. After all, a month from now any of the girls might be history if they were in the wrong place at the wrong time. But he *liked* Macy. Even amid the small team of special girls he had raised up, she stuck out. She looked like the others, danced like the others, had served the same general purpose—but still, she was different. He admitted to himself that he had planned to keep his team—especially Macy—out of harm's way somehow on Super Bowl Sunday. Giving them just a little warning couldn't hurt, could it? By the next day, he'd be gone, and they'd be out of a job. But at least they'd be safe. Unlike Tyson, he didn't view them as disposable.

Disposable.

As he listened to Tyson coldly predict the massive human impact of the impending action, Marco's instincts suddenly told him that Tyson would never leave potential witnesses in place. One way or another, he somehow knew, his girls would be eliminated.

He tried not to care, tried to turn his attention back to the matter at hand, but the image of Macy's face—and Sasha's, and the other girls'—rose up in his mind. Somehow, he had to find a way to protect them.

"So how's the distribution going?"

Tyson looked over at Glenn as he asked the question. The man had been sullen ever since his disciplinary action—he had told Marco he blamed that stripper girl for getting him into trouble—but had proved unwilling to relinquish his part in the lucrative action. Tyson smiled to himself. Especially since Glenn *had* to know that bowing out of the deal meant a quick trip to the bottom of the Atlantic.

Glenn cleared his throat, not quite looking Tyson in the eye.

"The distribution is better than expected. As you know, the product has become *the* must-have item on everyone's Christmas lists. I'm sure you've seen the commercials. And despite the economic climate, sales have been brisk since our product requires no fancy adaptation; you just plug it in. We've already exceeded our Christmas sales projections, and we still have four more shopping days. After the holiday, of course, we'll be offering the promotion to convince any latecomers to buy the thing 'just in time for the Super Bowl.'"

"Any word yet on the market penetration or demographics?" one of the other men asked. "Our clients will be asking."

Glenn shuffled through some papers and found what he was looking for. "As of last week, more than 75 percent of all relevant retail outlets are carrying the product, and the rest plan to pick it up quickly. Apparently, the early adopters are those you'd expect—upper-middle-class singles and families with more disposable income, who value convenience and enjoy buying new toys. By Christmas, we expect almost 8 percent market penetration—by D-Day, a bit more."

"Good work!" The questioner sat back, surprised. "That's higher than expected—truly amazing."

"Well, it's a well-designed product that meets a real need." Glenn did not smile, stuffing his papers back into their folder. "But thank you."

The other man looked at Tyson. "Our client will be pleased that the targets are so overwhelmingly upper-middle-class. From their point of view, it couldn't be better."

Tyson allowed himself a self-satisfied smile. He had, of course, thought of that right up front, even if these yokels hadn't. "I know."

As the participants filed out of the meeting, Tyson pulled aside several of the S-Group. He spoke in a low voice and did not look across the room to where Glenn was collecting his folders and preparing to depart.

"So, gentlemen, once this after-Christmas promotion starts, it'll essentially run on its own, correct?"

"Yes." Several of the men nodded, then seemed to catch Tyson's drift. Their eyes gleamed.

Tyson leaned forward and dropped his voice even more. "Am I to assume then, that at that point our friend Glenn becomes no longer necessary?"

Waggoner waited as Glenn brushed past the little huddle, leaving the room without a backward glance. "That's accurate, chief."

"Make the plans, then," Tyson said. "He's too much of a wild card, too disgruntled to trust once he gets his money. We'll have to make plans for him—and any other potential witnesses—shortly after the holidays."

"Hey, honey! I'm home!" Doug pushed his way through the garage door, slamming it shut with his foot. He carried two large festive shopping bags into the kitchen and set them on the island.

Sherry turned from the stove, spatula in hand. "Hmm, what'd you get me?" She wiggled her fingers as if she were going to peek inside the bag.

Doug slapped her hand, eyes twinkling. "None of that! You'll find out in two days."

"Don't tempt me, then!" She put on a mock-pout and waved the messy spatula in his face. "Off with you! Skedaddle! Take your mysterious packages away!"

Doug hastened up the stairs, chuckling to himself, and managed to make it into their room without being accosted by two more sets of curious eyes. He closed the door behind him and dumped the goods on the bed.

A little nightshirt—a *very* little nightshirt—for Sherry. The latest electronic game gizmo for Brandon. A set of books for Genna…socks…perfume… He pawed through the bags and placed each item in its appropriate pile, ready for wrapping.

He pulled out the last item, a fairly heavy box that had taken up half the large bag. He'd gotten the last one on the shelf. Within minutes, three more people had come looking and had had to put their names on a waiting list. He would call this a "family gift" but knew it was really his present to himself. He liked the latest toys and gadgets, and had finally given into the barrage of commercials for the thing. It was a great idea, the perfect thing to have during the relaxed week between Christmas and New Year's. Lots of games on. And of course, the New Year's celebration itself.

He laid the box on the bedspread and clumped halfway down the stairs. He poked his head around the banister, calling for Sherry. She appeared around the corner wiping her hands on a dish towel.

"Hey, hon, did we ever set up that New Year's dinner?"

"Not yet. I suppose you want *me* to do that?"

Doug gave her his best little-boy grin. "Would you?"

"You're impossible! Okay, fine, I'll call the Woodwards tonight."

"That'd be great. Keep it small."

Sherry flicked her dish towel at him, cracking it through the slats on the stairs. She smiled at Doug's mock yelp and waved her hand. "Go back to your present wrapping! I'll make the call right now."

"I love you, you know."

"Yeah, yeah, yeah." Smiling, Sherry vanished around the corner, and Doug heard her pick up the phone.

He walked back up the stairs, unable to contain the grin on his face. They hadn't been this playful in years. It was so fun again to be married! Doug sent up an earnest prayer of thanks. Then he hastened down the hallway to find some wrapping paper before the little hooligans who shared the house found their presents.

FIFTY-ONE

Marco banged through the kitchen doors, muttering to himself. The cooks eyed each other but didn't say anything. The waitresses took one look at his face and decided against a cheery holiday greeting.

He barked out questions about the evening's preparations, hardly waiting for the answers. A couple of times he asked the same question over again. After a few minutes of prowling around, he left the kitchen and headed toward his office.

Tyson looked up, irritated, when Marco came in, but he took a look at his face and didn't say anything.

"Let's get down to business." Marco sat behind his desk. "I'm already late this evening, and I've got a lot to do. As do you, I'm sure."

"Agreed." Tyson popped open a briefcase and handed over a single sheet of paper. "Here's the final list. We're hoping for an even wider distribution of the product, and Proxy wants your girls to help grease the wheels."

"I don't recognize all these names." Marco drummed his fingers on the desk. "Who's this?" He pointed. "And this?"

"They are two high-up officers at the only large chain that's been slow in stocking our product. No one knows why they chose to miss Christmas sales, but we need to get them on board. We could conceivably increase our market penetration to over 8 percent if this chain stocked the product for a few weeks before D-Day. And both men will be in town for a week after Christmas for some meetings. They'll be steered toward the club. A perfect opportunity for your key girls to make something happen. I know several of the girls are gone, but some are still around, right?"

"Just two."

"Hmph. Christmas. No one wants to work. Well, maybe you can mobilize the others once they get back. In the meantime, get started on this. It's worth a double bonus to you if the girls succeed."

Marco didn't smile. "I'll work on it. But it's hard to accomplish anything substantive this time of year."

"What better time for some of these corporate bigwigs to be in an expansive, generous mood?" Tyson narrowed his eyes. "You know Proxy doesn't appreciate excuses."

"I'll try to make something happen," Marco said. "But in the meantime, answer me a straight question. What do you plan to do with the girls? I notice their schedules are blank well before the big day."

"You know better than to ask me that, Marco. That's my jurisdiction, not yours."

Marco went cold. Everything about the girls was his jurisdiction. But everything about the larger plan—including what witnesses and evidence to eliminate—was in Tyson's. As he had suspected, the girls would never make it to Superbowl Sunday.

"Is there a problem?" Tyson seemed to be staring through him, reading his thoughts.

"No problem. I've just got a lot to do. Especially adding these deals to my plate."

"I'm quite sure you can handle it."

"I'm quite sure I can. In the meantime, I need to ask a favor relating to the Speed Shoes deal. The girl that set it up for us has been very pleased with her bonus."

"As she should be."

"She'd like—discreetly—to get a copy of the ad campaign if at all possible. To get a copy of the commercials, sort of like a memento since she brokered the deal. She can't ask Wade, obviously—he'd wonder why she cared. So she asked me if there was any way I could get her one."

Tyson shrugged and opened his briefcase again. "Sure. Actually, I have a CD copy right here. There's only three files on the CD—one for each ad in the series— and if you just click on a file, the commercial will run. I'm pretty sure this is the final version."

Marco took the CD from him. It was in a paper slipcover with DEMO written across the front. "Anything else?"

"That's it. Just find a way to get these final distribution deals approved."

Once Tyson had left, Marco popped the CD into his computer. As promised, three files showed in the window. He clicked on the first one, and watched the ad that had been unveiled—and used so well—that fateful night a few weeks ago. The second ad—scheduled to be shown just after midnight on New Year's Eve—ramped up the volume a bit, whetting appetites for the final commercial to be shown on Super Bowl Sunday.

With interest, Marco clicked on the third file…and cocked his head in surprise.

Instead of running a third video clip, an error message popped up. "Unknown format. Specify."

He clicked on it again. Same problem. His eyes narrowed. Could it be...?

He went to the door and jerked it open and hollered at a passing waitress.

"Get Maris in here!"

The waitress scurried off, and less than a minute later, Maris came strolling through the door.

"What's eating you, boss?"

Marco gave her a look, and made an exasperated sound. "I have a file here I can't open. You're the only one in the place that's not a total computer moron. Any ideas?"

"Gee, thanks for the compliment."

Maris started forward, but Marco put out an arm, blocking the computer. "Just tell me how to open it."

She put her hands on her hips. "Well, I'm not going to be able to figure out how to open it unless I can *see* the thing! Good grief, Marco, I'm not going to eat it!"

She pushed past him and he relented.

She frowned at the screen and began fiddling with the keyboard.

"It looks like it's some sort of audio file, but your computer won't open it. Maybe it's an MP3—"

"Like I know what that means."

"Just hang in there, boss. It'll just take a second." Maris's fingers flew over the keyboard so fast he couldn't keep up. "I'm going to download an MP3 player onto your computer here, to see..."

Several minutes and a half-dozen curses later, she straightened.

"Aha! There!" The file opened, and she peered closely at the screen as strange sounds emanated from the speakers. "Ach—it's just computer babble."

She waved a hand, annoyed. "It doesn't make any sense. I probably corrupted the file in trying to open it. Sorry, chief, I tried."

"No problem." Marco gestured toward the door and hustled her out. "Thanks anyway."

He shut the door behind her and returned to his desk, eyes gleaming as he listened to the magic coming over his speakers. That was computer code! It had to be *the* code developed over at Tyson's fortresslike building, the code that would be embedded in and transmitted with the television commercial on some impossible-to-hear frequency. One thing was sure—Tyson would never have knowingly given him a copy of the thing.

Marco leaned back in his chair and put his feet up. He should call Tyson on his cell phone and tell him what he'd found. He should…but he wasn't going to. Maybe this could give him some leverage over his condescending superior, some additional protection. Maybe he could use this to gain some additional protection not just for himself, but for his girls. He'd have to think about that.

Marco copied the file onto his hard drive and changed the name. Then he took the CD out of the computer, put it back in its slipcover, and set it in a drawer.

Until he figured out how to use it, he'd just act like the little disc didn't exist.

"See you after Christmas!" Tiffany gave a blithe wave and blew a few kisses. "I'll come back and make you all jealous with my tan!"

A chorus of grumbles from the other dancers followed her out the door. A four-day jaunt to the Virgin Islands was a nice Christmas present from her sugar daddy. She'd be back and ready for work—lithe and sun-bronzed—by Saturday night. Several other dancers were gone on similar warm-weather excursions. The rest of the dancers sat at a scattering of tables, counting out their money, trying to figure out what to do with the evening. There had been so few customers, Marco had decided to close early this Christmas Eve.

Ronnie counted out the DJ's take, her mind turning to her empty apartment. It would be a lonely Christmas without Tiffany around. At least on the other days, she'd fill the time with work. With so many other dancers gone she could make a boatload of money without even trying. She thought about her mother's plea to come home tomorrow, and almost wavered. Most of her colleagues had no home they cared to go to on Christmas day. At least she had her mom. But no—she had explained to her mother that the "restaurant" needed her to work; it was one of their busiest seasons.

She pushed away a nagging guilt at having been away from home for so long. At least she sent back lots of money to help her mom set up her new apartment and pay off her last medical debts. She'd even helped her buy a better car.

Ronnie heard the new lightness in her mother's voice whenever she called, the conversations now sprinkled with religious talk. Whatever had happened to her mother, though, seemed like a good thing. It wasn't creepy-religious, just…just *nice*. Sort of like the Turners and the Woodwards. Just nice and wholesome.

The Turners and the Woodwards might, for whatever reason, still want to befriend her even though they knew she was a stripper. But that knowledge would kill her mother. Especially now. Best to avoid her altogether.

Ronnie left the club and headed out of the driveway, feeling rudderless. She didn't want to go back to her apartment—they hadn't even put a tree up. What was the point, when it was just her?

She drove down Tenth Street, looking at the decorations, the festive lights that festooned every building, every restaurant, every shop. Lights of all colors blinked and sparkled as couples walked arm in arm along the busy sidewalk. Even the low-income apartment complexes where all the immigrants lived were draped with decorations, people bustling in and out on their last-minute Christmas errands. Ronnie watched it all from behind her car windows, feeling empty.

Some pretty white lights draped on elegant trees caught her eye. She saw the banner out front and, on an impulse, pulled into the busy parking lot.

There were hundreds of cars in the lot, their occupants emerging and streaming into a massive church building. A sign proclaimed "Vespers. Christmas Eve. 8:00 and 9:00."

Ronnie got out of her car feeling for a moment that she was in a foreign land. It looked like there were hundreds of people there. She slowly followed the others streaming in. She could get lost in this crowd.

She slipped into the back, took a program, and found a seat. Despite what seemed like thousands of people in the room, the sanctuary was hushed, pensive, only a soft murmur of conversation rising over the gentle chords of an organ being played somewhere up front.

Two dozen people in robes took their places in a loft behind the altar. The whole congregation quieted as the choir director raised his hands, and the choir began to sing.

Ronnie sat, transfixed by the music. She didn't understand the Latin lyrics, but it felt sweet...reverent...holy. Had she ever heard anything so beautiful? She closed her eyes and let the sound wash over her, caught up in a pure, unfamiliar feeling. Almost as if she were being wrapped in strong arms, loving arms. Her skin prickled and she felt she could have sat and listened all night. It was as if there was something *there*...something she could almost touch if she just knew how.

The priest came forward and read the Christmas story. She had heard it before somewhere, heard about the baby born in a stable, about the angels singing, about the shepherds traveling to greet him. She wondered if the angels' voices had sounded like the music she had just heard.

Peace on earth...goodwill to men...

She could almost believe in peace on earth. Here, this night, she could almost believe.

The service ended with more lovely music, the congregation standing as chimes were played, then filing out quietly and heading to their cars. There was little chatter. Everyone seemed as subdued, as pensive, as she.

She didn't want to leave. She was reluctantly heading to her car when she heard a voice at her side.

"I thought that was you."

She turned quickly. Marco was standing there, bundled up against the cold.

"Marco, what are you doing here?"

"Oh, I don't know. I didn't have anywhere else to go, so I figured I'd stop in. It's Christmas, after all."

"Yeah. Me, too." She looked at him, curious. He seemed subdued, quiet. "You okay?"

"Yeah. Just thinking."

"About what?"

"Nothing. Just—" He gave up with a shrug. "Well…nothing."

Ronnie gave him a small smile. "I think I know how you feel." A strand of music played again in her mind, and she stilled, trying to recapture the feeling. "That was beautiful."

Marco nodded, and started to turn away. "Merry Christmas, Ronnie."

Ronnie smiled at the use of her real name. "Merry Christmas, Marco."

The two of them parted, went to their cars, and drove away, neither with any particular place to go.

A large figure broke away from his troop as ordered, and followed Marco out of the church parking lot. He settled beside him in the car, speaking to him, trying to get through.

Others had tried before, with little success. But this night, the Spirit was moving. The Lamb of God knew those who were not as hardened as they might seem. He was, after all, the One who had looked into the eyes of those on His left and His right as they hung together, gasping for breath, and had known their hearts. He had welcomed a dying criminal into the Kingdom.

And this man, also, did not have much time. So the One who did not desire that any should perish was reaching out to him…again…and again. He would continue to do so until his time ran out.

The mighty angel watched his charge with somber eyes. The words did not seem to be getting through. But the music might. Gently, he began to sing, recreating the melody that had resounded through the church that holy night. The Latin words became the lyrics of heaven, the Word of God to a lost and hurting soul.

☆ ☆ ☆

Marco passed through the security gates and pulled into his hilltop home. He wandered through the house, looking at the trappings of his life, wondering what it was all for.

He went to the bar and poured himself a drink. He wasn't used to such melancholy thoughts. What it was all for, he knew, was money. And lots of it. That had always been enough.

He stared around the empty place, wishing he had convinced one of his women to come over for the night. It wasn't too late to just pick up the phone. There were many who would come at his beck and call.

He went out onto the deck, the spectacular night view laid out before him. Holiday lights shone throughout the neighborhood, many of the wealthy residents having gone all out. His next-door neighbor had employed five people for a day to lay out an elaborate lighting scheme on their hedges and trees.

Marco had been too busy plotting how to blow his next-door neighbor up to worry about Christmas decorations.

He rested his arms on the railing and twirled the ice in his glass. What was he doing? How could he have come this far? A snatch of the choir's song played again in his mind, and he closed his eyes, trying to recapture the feeling he had had sitting alone in that congregation. Almost as if he wasn't alone. He remembered the look in Ronnie's eyes—the look that said she, too, had felt it.

And then another memory flickered in his mind. The memory of her screams…then her silence, her acquiescence to three brutal men. Here on this deck. Right here, where he was standing.

He pushed himself away from the railing and went back into the house. He took another swig of his drink, his eyes hard, cold, staring inward. He had done a terrible job of protecting her up until now. But he would find a way to protect her when it mattered.

"I'm worried about Marco."

Tyson had finished showing Proxy around the secure building, the first time Proxy had been able to tour his high-tech domain with no one else around. It was Christmas Day, but neither Tyson nor Proxy had any use for the holiday. They'd get the best Christmas present imaginable in just a few weeks, if all went well.

The two men were sitting in Tyson's office comparing notes. It had been a long time since they'd been able to sit down for a face-to-face discussion.

"What do you mean, worried?" Proxy sipped a spring water Tyson had brought him, watching Tyson search for words.

"Well—Look, let's be frank. You know Marco rubs me the wrong way. You know it, I know it, Marco probably knows it. But let's set that aside for the moment. That's not my motivation here. There's a problem with Marco. He's...he seems to be wavering somehow. I can't put my finger on it. If I didn't know better, I'd say he was worried about the girls."

"How so?"

"It's almost like he doesn't want anything to happen to them. He was asking questions about our intended disposition of the girls. I didn't tell him, of course— he might inadvertently give something away—but I just got a bad feeling."

"What do you suggest we do about it?"

"Well, in all honesty, I think we might have to consider plans for removing him. Permanently, I mean."

Proxy sat silent for a minute, then leaned back in his swivel chair, staring at the high-up warehouse ceiling.

"Marco has been a loyal player, a key player."

"I know that."

"And most of what we've accomplished would've been impossible without the work he's put in. There's no sign that this 'wavering' you mentioned is any more serious than a sentimental attachment to his team. It hasn't kept him from doing his job, and doing it well. He has been thoroughly loyal from day one."

Tyson gave an internal snort, careful not to let Proxy hear him. Proxy was growing soft, blinded by Marco's so-called "loyalty." The only thing Marco was loyal to was himself and his expected payout.

"I can hardly bump off a key operative because of a hunch, with nothing else behind it. Can I?"

"I suppose not."

"I was already concerned that eliminating five girls at once would cause more problems than it solved. The more we start removing people right and left, the more attention is going to be attracted, and the more chance that someone will stumble across something before the big day. We can't afford that to happen, can we?"

"I suppose not."

"You *suppose* not?"

Proxy was no longer idly looking at the ceiling. He was staring directly at Tyson, his eyes ice-cold.

"I mean yes, you're correct. Of course we can't afford anyone to come even *close* to the real plot. That's why, I might add, we've planted many false trails for people to follow. And of course we've planned a last-minute group accident for the girls, so that no one is suspicious…and if they *are* suspicious, by the time anyone investigates it'll be too late. You don't need to worry about that, chief. We've got this well in hand."

Proxy continued his cold observation. "Except for Marco, you're saying."

"I'm saying we should watch him. Carefully."

Tyson tried to keep his face impassive. For all Proxy's money and vaunted experience, he was an old-fashioned strategist. He didn't understand the ground-level realities of the current situation. That was why he'd hired Tyson, wasn't it? He should trust his right-hand man to know what was best, and let him do it.

Proxy nodded and moved on to the next subject.

Tyson began to seethe. Just as with his Fortune 500 CEOs, Tyson was again subject to the decisions of an inferior strategist. He'd had the corner office, the staff members hopping at his every word…but it was all in vain without the final say, the final power to make decisions. Proxy had assured Tyson that he was hiring him to run the show. And now Proxy couldn't even let him make a decision about whether to eliminate a possible security risk.

Tyson answered Proxy's questions and engaged in deliberations over their next steps, even as his brain began running on a parallel track. If he got one more sense, one more piece of evidence that Marco was a concern, he would take matters into his own hands. As the old saying went, it was easier to act first and ask forgiveness later. Not that he would need forgiveness. Proxy was astute enough to recognize Tyson's contribution when it mattered.

FIFTY-TWO

D id I hear that a *stripper* stayed in your home last week?"
Sherry Turner tried not to laugh at the shocked look on Melanie's face,
her voice carefully lowered as she glanced around the crowded church
lobby. When Sherry nodded, the older woman put a delicate hand to her chest as
if she would faint at any moment.

"But, dear, don't you think that's dangerous? And right before *Christmas!* What
about the children?"

"I think it's the best thing possible for the children. Just like with the food
pantry outreach. It's giving Brandon and Genna a chance to see that their family
doesn't just say all the right words about what Jesus would do—that we actually *do*
what Jesus would do. And isn't Christmas the best time for there to be room at the
inn?"

Melanie looked torn between discomfort at airing such a distasteful subject in
public and a desire to go tell her confidants this juicy piece of gossip. But Sherry
no longer cared so much what people thought. Just as it had been liberating to discover that all the perfect Christian soldiers around her had just as many hurts
behind their flawless smiles, it had been empowering to be a part of getting the
church's "ministry muscles back in shape," as Pastor Steven had put it. The past six
months had seen a veritable earthquake inside Trinity Chapel.

Not everyone had been comfortable with the changes. Sherry tried to be
patient with Melanie, a woman who clung stubbornly to the old ways, uncomfortable with the influx of unchurched people who didn't know how to dress or
act, didn't know the unwritten rules of what Christians should look like, should
talk like. Melanie desperately wanted to keep their church looking perfect and
clean, attractive to the average suburban churchgoer, regardless of the spiritual consequences for all those slowly dying in secret. To be fair, she had supported the food
pantry outreach, but her comfort level went only so far. Poor people—okay. Span-
ish-speaking immigrants—maybe. But *strippers?* Heaven forbid!

It wasn't just strippers and prostitutes who needed healing, Sherry thought, eye-
ing Melanie's strained face.

"I'm sure you were well intentioned, dear," Melanie said, "but I can't say that

I approve of you taking this person into your *home*. Especially after…well…the *troubles* your poor husband has had. Doesn't it seem, dear, that you should not have put him in that position?"

Sherry tried to keep her voice even, as anger seeped around the edges. "Melanie, *you* are probably well intentioned, but you don't know the whole story. Of course I thought of the impact on Doug. Of *course* I did! We talked about it, and he agreed it was something we needed to do *and* something he could handle. Doug was going to run it by some trusted friends this morning, just in case."

"Yes, but *dear*—"

"Hello, ladies."

Sherry turned to see Pastor Steven's smiling face, his arm around his wife.

"Sorry to interrupt—"

"No problem," Sherry said. "We are done here."

"Oh? Well, in that case could you tell Doug that I'd like to speak with him before he leaves? I think it was wonderful that you took in that young lady last week, but since he said she was probably coming over for dinner soon—and just in case she does take you up on your longer-term offer—I have a couple of thoughts to share."

"Thank you, Pastor." Sherry couldn't help taking some satisfaction in watching Melanie's mouth gape open. "I appreciate your encouragement. I'll go find Doug right away."

She smiled at the pastor, gave Melanie as friendly a nod as she could manage, and went in search of her husband.

She climbed the stairs to the sprawling children's area, her irritation with Melanie continuing to rub her like sandpaper. Finally, she stopped in the middle of a hallway. *Lord, forgive me for judging Melanie. I was like that, too, after all.* She hesitated, then plowed ahead. *Help me to love her as You do.*

Doug waited to tell Sherry about his talk with Pastor Steven until late that night, when they put the kids in their beds and fell gratefully into their own.

"Pastor Steven said that if we ever take someone like Ronnie into our home, that we need to be aware of a few things."

When he paused, Sherry started to open her mouth, then snapped it closed. Doug rolled toward her and kissed her nose.

"Thank you for not interrupting. You've really gotten better."

"I'm trying."

"He said," Doug continued with a small grin in her direction, "that we do need to be careful to watch out for her response to me."

"Her response to *you!*" Sherry started to sit up, then fell back against the pillows. "I would've thought the biggest concern was the other way around."

"He cautioned me about that, too. He said that it could indeed be a stumbling block depending on how I handled it, and said I'd have to be very sure that this was God's will, especially since my healing has been so recent. But that wasn't really the main thing I learned. Years ago, Pastor Steven apparently did some work ministering to people in the…you know, the sex industry. He said these girls have been so emotionally messed up, so used by men—and sometimes abused, like Ronnie was—that when a Christian couple reaches out to them, the husband is probably the first kind, safe man she's ever met."

"Ahhhh." Sherry gave a sigh of understanding.

"And so of course, inevitably, she'll gravitate toward him. Apparently, these women sometimes have powerful spiritual forces at work in their lives—not surprising, I suppose—that work to suck men into their trap."

"You make them sound like black widow spiders."

"Not unlike that, actually. Lots of these girls are accustomed to luring men in—and once they're out of the strip club environment, it may be totally unconscious—and then, of course, that begins to destroy them. Pastor Steven said he's seen husbands who ended up having a one-night stand with this sexy girl they'd taken into their home." Doug saw alarm spring to his wife's face. "Of course, he said those were mostly men who'd never confronted their own issues and were secret pornography users or whatever."

"Still, I'm not sure I like the sounds of this," Sherry said. "After all you've gone through—" Melanie's snide comment came to mind, and she slapped the bedsheets with both hands. "Darn it, maybe the woman was *right!*"

"Huh?"

"Oh, Melanie practically accused me of sabotaging your healing by taking in a stripper."

"And I bet that just burned your beans."

"You could say that. But maybe she was right."

"I don't know. In the end, it comes down to what God wants us to do. We can make ourselves crazy with trying to figure out the pros and cons, so in the end we just need to pray for the Lord's leading. It'll be a moot point if Ronnie has no interest in changing her life. But if the Lord *wants* us to take her—or someone like her—into our home for a time, I just have to trust that He'll give us wisdom and protect us from the traps. And if we're not supposed to take her in at all, as long as we're praying about it I have to assume that He's able to warn us against it."

"I guess."

"Well, like I said, it might be a moot point. I'm even wondering if she's really coming to dinner tomorrow."

Two seconds after the doorbell rang, Sherry was there, yanking the door open. "Ronnie! Welcome back."

Ronnie stood awkwardly just inside the door, then she shrugged. "Well, I couldn't think of any excuse to cancel, if you want to know the truth."

Sherry steered Ronnie into the living room, where the Woodwards waited. "I like your honesty, girl." She looked on as Vance and Jo gave Ronnie warm hugs, then gestured her to a seat. "Well, sit down, sit down. Do you want some hot chocolate?"

Sherry watched Ronnie settle into a chair and begin talking with the Woodwards, then she moved into the kitchen to check on Doug—busy at the stove—and bring out the drinks. She breathed a prayer of thanks that the girl had indeed come and for the powerful peace that had settled over their home. She and Doug and the Woodwards had gathered an hour early to ask the Lord's blessing and presence over this night, asking that no dark forces would prevail, asking that the Lord's will be accomplished, that Ronnie would be touched by the Spirit. Somehow, Sherry could feel the results.

The room was packed with angels, radiant with the light of the Lord, the excitement and anticipation palpable as they waited for their orders. This was unquestionably the Lord's territory, and the few demons that had been allowed in—for the moment, attached to Ronnie by legal right—were unable to do anything but cower in the presence of blazing holiness.

Caliel eyed the miserable demonic crew, counting the moments until they gave up and fled the scene. They hung on for longer than he expected, warring between their desires and their pain, but the end result was inevitable. With intense satisfaction he watched the dreadful creatures loose their holds on the young woman and retreat at speed.

Instantly, the heavenly host erected an impenetrable wall around the home—and around Ronnie—ensuring that the events of this critical night would be protected.

Caliel gathered his troops and handed out their assignments. As the members of the heavenly host sped to their tasks, their thoughts turned toward the hand of the King. This time, this night, all heaven seemed to be poised, waiting.

Caliel prayed for the Lord's will to be done. So many things hinged on this night, and on the few nights to come. He knew they would need more strength, more power, more understanding. He prayed, fervently, for the success of his team.

A cadre of great beings traveled at speed southwards, to a small town. The group split up, one heading to where a middle-aged woman sat alone at a kitchen table, eating dinner and reading a newsmagazine. Some unpacked boxes still adorned one side of the room, but her furniture was in place, pictures were on the wall, and it was finally beginning to look like home.

The angel dropped into the kitchen, his voice soft but urgent. The woman didn't stir, all her attention on a feature story about the dam breach. The great messenger put a hand on her shoulder and spoke again…and again.

Linda Hanover looked up from her magazine. What was that? She turned in her chair. It was almost as if she had heard a voice calling her name. Her eyes scanned the small apartment. Nothing there, obviously. How odd.

She started to turn back to her dinner when she heard a crash across the room. She started from her chair to see a cluster of books sprawled on the floor, pages splayed. She'd suspected that stack wasn't stable when she stopped unpacking to go fix dinner. Hopefully, none of the books were torn in the tumble.

She knelt to gather the tomes into a neat stack. The top book leaped out at her, and she ran her hands over the cover. It was a historical novel Mrs. Dugan had given her, about a young frontier prostitute and a man who reached out to her in the love of Christ.

Her thoughts—as they always did—turned to her daughter, and then to the Lord. She gasped, clutching the book to her chest, her head spinning from the power of the sensation.

Pray. She had to pray. What was going on? Trembling, she said a quick prayer for her daughter, set the book on the floor, and started to go for the phone to call the Dugans.

No, child. PRAY.

She fell back to her knees, her face to the carpet, words spilling from her lips.

"Dear Lord, what is going *on?* Lord, take care of my daughter. Lord, help me understand how to pray. God, save my baby!"

For what seemed like hours she clutched at the floor, tears staining her face, in deeper intercession than she had yet known, groaning with this weight of prayer. She felt so small, so inadequate.

A pounding on the door roused her.

Linda levered herself to her feet and yanked open the door. The Dugans—parents and children—stood in the hallway, eyes wide.

"What's going on?" Angela stepped inside the apartment, followed by her husband and in-laws. "We were having a family dinner and felt this urgency to come over here. Are you okay?"

"It's Ronnie. I don't know what's wrong, but it's Ronnie." Crying, Linda blurted out all that she had felt in prayer—the danger, the need for salvation, for protection.

The Dugans guided her back to the sitting area. At Linda's shaky direction, Angela dialed Ronnie's phone number, then the number for the club, trying to find her. No luck.

As the Dugans talked and prayed with Linda, Angela's attention kept being drawn to the phone. Finally, she rose to make some additional calls.

Most people were home, and said they would pray immediately. So many had joined Linda in her weekly trips to the altar, grieving and pleading with the Lord for her daughter, that they somehow felt like Ronnie was their girl, too.

A number of people—somehow sensing the same urgency—asked for directions, and within half an hour, the apartment was crowded. As the night marched on, the group sang, prayed, and read Scripture as the Lord led. The night grew late, but no one was inclined to leave. They were unsure exactly of what was going on but absolutely sure that this was where they needed to be.

FIFTY-THREE

Tyson stood in the high-tech command center, munching a stale sandwich and watching over the shoulder of a young underling who was finalizing the second Speed Shoes ad. It would also carry an embedded signal, but this one would do nothing but test, check for hitches, and confirm their capabilities for the real blow. It was a shame to let such an opportunity pass by—nearly as many people would be watching the ball drop on New Year's Eve as would watch the Super Bowl—but it was just too risky. No use giving the authorities any chance to suspect something before the big day.

From time to time the underling would growl at some perceived mistake, barking out orders to the other underling working alongside. "Check the source code in the Hex Editor...

No, make sure it's an MP3, not a WAV file."

Tyson had no idea what they were talking about. He was just glad he had such people working for him.

The underling finished his task and swiveled in his chair, accepting kudos from the high-level managers in the room as his rightful due.

"Who wants CD copies of the final version?"

Everyone nodded, and Tyson watched as the kid popped a CD into his computer and downloaded the video clip, then downloaded a second file onto the same CD.

"Wait—what're you doing?"

"Downloading the files, boss." The underling looked up, puzzled. "You wanted copies, right?"

"What *files?*" Tyson gripped the kid's arm, hard. "I thought it was just the video file. For the advertisement."

"But I always put the code file in there, too, you know, so you have it on the same CD if you need it. This one's the final version...an MP3 file, just like last time. You won't hear much more than machine noise, but if you want you can play it using—"

Tyson tightened his grip. "You did this last time? You put the code onto the CD you made for me last time?"

"Yeah, sure, chief. That one was the MP3 file that piggybacked on the first commercial, the one in mid-December—"

Tyson dropped his arm and made for the door, unaware of the looks of consternation that followed him out.

He punched in a cell-phone number, one he had memorized but never used. Until now. He waited, impatient through several rings, then he heard the familiar voice on the other end of the line, sounding distracted, busy.

"Jordan here."

"I'm sorry, I must have the wrong number. I was calling for Mr. Proximus."

The attention of the other party sharpened abruptly. "You do have the wrong number."

"Sorry." Tyson hung up and looked at his watch. The rendezvous would happen in twenty minutes. He would need to hurry.

"I've got to run to a meeting." Jordan hurried out his office door, shrugging on a coat.

His secretary looked up, surprised. "But I thought you had this big deadline you wanted me to—"

"Shelve it." Jordan pulled on some gloves. "Go home and have dinner with your family. This meeting just came up. We can finish the rest tomorrow."

"Sure thing, chief!" She began closing out her computer, then frowned at something on the screen and turned back his direction. "What do you want me to do about—"

The hallway was empty. She hurried to put on her coat, grateful to have her night back. Thank goodness something else had come up.

"What is it?" Jordan looked around the empty hotel suite, his eyes not really seeing the luxurious trappings and trimmings. He was nervous meeting outside the building, without proper security precautions. He was almost sure he hadn't been followed, but without the usual procedures he remained wary.

"Marco has the code." Tyson explained as briefly as he could. "I don't know if he even knows it, but he has it."

"He didn't call you to tell you there was an unfamiliar file on the CD?"

"No. So either he never saw it, or saw it and didn't know what it was."

"Or he saw it, knew what it was, and decided to keep it to himself. The code is insecure. I can't believe this! Three weeks out, and the code is not secured."

"I know. I accept full responsibility. I had no idea the programmers had put anything on that CD other than the commercials."

"You should've checked." Jordan's voice was cold but matter-of-fact. "But that's water under the bridge. What's our going-forward plan?"

Tyson outlined what he had arranged by cell phone on the way over. "It's ready to go as soon as you give the word."

"Do it, then." Jordan stood perfectly still, thinking. "And let me know immediately if there are any further developments. We'll need to know immediately if the code has somehow spread farther."

Tyson stared at Proxy's angry face and decided not to mention that the code might be in the hands of not one but two people—one of them the woman who had arranged the Speed Shoes deal to begin with. He would keep that problem to himself and order his men to take care of it on the side.

Proxy was pacing the suite now. "If the code has gone beyond Marco's hands, we may have to move everything up."

"Can we even do that?"

"New Year's Eve is tomorrow. We might be able to, but it'll be tight. Otherwise, we'll have to think about scrapping the whole plan."

"Over just one internal slip-up? But—"

"Over just one internal slip-up." Proxy bit out the words. "And I don't have to tell you that our client won't be pleased. But they would rather abort the plan than risk premature disclosure. After all, we can take the next month or two to investigate whether there has, in fact, been anything that would compromise the plan. And if not, we can always do it *next* year."

"I can see how they wouldn't be happy waiting a year."

"No—not when the post–Super Bowl plans are ready. But none of it will matter if the primary event doesn't come off. The client will not be pleased."

Tyson straightened. "Well, chief, I personally think we're okay. Just a few days ago you yourself pointed out how loyal Marco has been. I'm sure we'll have containment once we remove the existing risk. I'll give your go-ahead, and I'll let you know if there's any reason for further suspicion."

Proxy nodded sharply. "Agreed. Get it done. Quickly. And it must look like an accident." He stepped to the door. "Call me on the cell phone, as before. It's not ideal, but we have no other choice. We cannot allow any further mistakes." He gave Tyson one last meaningful look, and swept out.

Tyson made the calls from the privacy of the hotel suite, then traveled unhurriedly down to the main entrance and picked up his car from their loyal valet.

The boy smiled at the extra large tip. "Have a good night, sir."

☆ ☆ ☆

"Thanks for dinner, Mr. Turner—um, Doug. That was great. I didn't know men could cook so well."

There were some chuckles around the table, and Ronnie looked around, discomfited. Had she just made another faux pas? "Well...I didn't."

"Glad to surprise you, then," Doug said. "I enjoy cooking, though I don't get to do it that much. Sherry usually tries to have dinner ready by the time I get home so I can eat with the kids."

Sherry stood and began to pick up the dirty dishes. "Did your stepfather never cook, then? I know you said he wasn't a particularly domestic sort..."

Ronnie gave a grunt. "He only set foot in the kitchen to get his beer out of the fridge. Cooking was woman's work. I sort of thought every guy felt that way."

"Some guys, maybe." Vance Woodward stood and began helping Sherry clear the table. "Not all, by any means."

"You all are really strange, you know that?" Ronnie said. "Doug cooking dinner, Vance cleaning up. It's just...odd."

"Odd to you, maybe, but pretty normal to lots of people," Doug said. "It's just a matter of helping and serving wherever you see the need. There's this passage in the Bible that says we're supposed to treat others as we would want to be treated."

"That's the Golden Rule." Ronnie gave him a funny look. "That's from the Bible?"

"Yep. It's the way we try to live. Jesus said we should love God with all our heart, soul, mind, and strength, and love our neighbor as ourselves. Helping cook—or clean up after dinner—is just a small example of treating someone else the way we'd like to be treated."

Ronnie sat still for a minute, then jumped to her feet and picked up a few plates. These people were really religious—and kind of corny—but she suddenly felt lighthearted for the first time in months. She could feel a silly grin breaking out on her face as she ferried dishes into the kitchen and began slotting them into the dishwasher.

"Then this is the least I can do as thanks for a great meal."

Marco sat at his desk, staring out his window at the club floor. He turned a pen over and over in his hands, not even noticing that it was uncapped, the blue ink streaking a line across his hand with each turn.

What was he doing? He watched the stage as Sasha did her thing, her eyes smoldering at the men around her. She was playing them, masterfully. Just like he had played her and all the others. He pictured all of them—Sasha, Ronnie, the others—destroyed in some accident, some innocent-seeming tragedy.

Oh well, the police would say, what a shame. And they would close the books on another senseless accident, another death, without looking too closely. After all, they were only strippers…only prostitutes. Their lives were cheap.

Marco heard the knocking on his office door, the questions from his staff, but he couldn't rouse himself to respond. He continued to stare out the window, the blue pen twirling in his fingers, leaving streak…after streak…

He looked down, detached, at the ink staining his hands. It should be red, he thought.

"Marco!" Tiffany pounded on the door. "You in there? You have a question from the private party in room two!"

She made an exasperated noise and collared Maris on the fly.

"Whaddaya want?" Maris was busily writing on an order pad. "I ain't got all night. What?"

"Do you know what's wrong with Marco?"

"Whaddaya mean, dearie?" She checked her watch and noted a time on the order slip. "He sick?"

"I don't know. I think he's in the office, but he won't answer the door. It's locked. Private room two has a question for him." Tiffany was fairly dancing with impatience. "And I'm supposed to be meeting Wade in a few minutes. I've got to finish with them and get going."

Maris glanced up and tore the order slip off her pad. "Hang on a second. Stay right there." She vanished into the kitchen, her voice raised as she hollered the order.

Within seconds she was back at Tiffany's side.

"Private room two, you say? Okay, I'll get him and send him along. Go on back to your money men."

Maris knocked on the door and tried the knob. "Marco! Marco, you in there?"

She pressed her ear against the door and heard only some muttering.

She looked up and down the staff hallway, then reached into her cocktail apron and pulled out a thin metal shaft. She inserted it into the lock. Two clicks right, one left, and the doorknob turned.

"Marco?"

He was sitting in his chair, his back to her.

She advanced toward him, leaving the door open a crack. "Boss, you okay?"

He slowly turned to face her, and Maris gasped at the mess he'd made of his hands, his shirt. Covered with blue ink.

"Boss?"

Marco looked at her dully. "Hey."

"What's wrong with you?"

"I can't do it anymore."

She could feel a faint prickle of hope. The first crack in the dam. She went to his side, searching for the right words, every fiber aware that she had to get this right.

"What do you mean?"

"I'm in over my head." He waved a lethargic hand. "You wouldn't understand."

She took a deep breath. "Yes, I would." She crouched by his chair, fixing him with her eyes until he returned her gaze. "There's another way, boss. A way you can get out of this mess you've gotten into."

She reached into a concealed pocket sewn inside her apron and pulled out a business card. She handed it to him and watched his eyes widen with shock. He opened his mouth to say something, when they both heard a noise at the door.

Maris crossed the room in two great strides and opened the door all the way. Tiffany was standing there, a strange look on her face.

"He's okay," Maris said. "I was just sending him along. You need something?"

"Uh—I forgot to tell Marco that I had to knock off early and meet Wade tonight. He's at a bar with some of the ad agency people."

"I'll tell him. And he'll be over to your private party in a minute."

"Okay." Tiffany found the door being closed in her face. How odd. She replayed the overheard conversation in her mind.

I'm in over my head. You wouldn't understand.

"Yes, I would. There's another way, boss. A way you can get out of this mess you've gotten into."

She finished her set with the private party and was leaving just as Marco arrived. He seemed distracted, but otherwise okay.

"You all right, Marco?" she said.

He nodded and pushed past her, his brusque demeanor resurfacing. "Maris told me you need to leave. I guess it's okay. We've got enough girls on the floor."

"Gotta keep Wade happy, right, chief?"

Marco merely nodded and vanished inside the private room.

Tiffany changed and hurried to meet her man. At the bar, Wade and his two advertising agency colleagues rose to greet her. As usual, she gave him a passionate kiss, and as usual he seemed to appreciate it.

He held her chair and she slipped into the seat, giving his colleagues a big wink. She could play them, too, after all. He asked about work, and the small group listened as she amused them with a description of the night—leaving out the details of her dancing for other men, of course.

"The oddest thing happened just as I was leaving, though."

"How's that?" Wade was distracted, signaling for the waiter to bring another round of drinks. "What sort of thing?"

"I think Marco's having a nervous breakdown or something." She relayed how odd Marco had acted all night, how he finally went into his office and locked the door. She repeated the snippet of conversation she'd overheard.

"And then I could see Maris handing him some kind of business card. Isn't that weird?"

Wade shrugged and Tiffany brushed it off. "Anyway...whatever."

She blinked her eyes at him and asked about his day. She hardly noticed that his two colleagues were sitting rigid in their chairs, talking in low voices to each other as Wade caught her up on the doings of the day.

After a minute, one of them put a hand to his belt. "I'm being paged." He checked the cell phone, which looked dark and silent to Tiffany. "Hold on, I'll be back."

He left the table, weaving his way through the crowd and out the front door. Tiffany could see him through the window, talking on the cell phone, his body language stiff with urgency.

He returned and gave them a polite smile. "I'm afraid we're going to have to leave you for the evening. Something has just come up."

"Sorry you can't stay." Wade stood and shook their hands. "I'll give you a call tomorrow."

"Great." The first man looked at his partner, jerked his head, and the two of them vanished out the door.

Across town, Tyson clicked the cell phone shut and swore, tempted to throw the thing across the room. Then he shut his eyes, willing himself to calmness, to clarity.

He punched in another cell number. When the voice on the other end answered, he barked out one word.

"Status!"

"Just finished the car. We're in the next lot over. Waiting for your signal."

"Give me five minutes, max."

He hung up and dialed another number, activating a second team. They would be there in less than half an hour.

Finally, he made the third call, waiting, impatient, through three rings until it was answered.

He put on his best hectic voice. "Marco...?"

Marco put down the phone with a growl and looked at his watch. Why did they have to call an emergency meeting just when his night was heating up? His little nervous breakdown had put him behind. Not to mention the new idea rattling around in his head, breaking his concentration on the job.

He hadn't made a decision, hadn't revealed anything, hadn't promised anything. But it suddenly sounded good.

He pulled on his jacket and went in search of Maris.

"I have to go to a quick meeting off-site. They promise it'll only be twenty minutes—well, thirty counting the drive. Can you hold down the fort for half an hour?"

"No problem, chief. Seriously, it's not that crazy tonight. " She hesitated, lowering her voice. "This anything you want to tell me about?"

"Who knows?"

Marco hurried to his luxury sports car, pulling out onto Tenth Street and then taking the ramp onto the highway. He looked at the clock and floored the accelerator.

Two men followed a few car-lengths behind him. One fiddled with some equipment sitting on his lap, pointing an antennae toward the flying car in front of them.

Suddenly, the sports car swerved, tires squealing, only to veer back into its proper lane a moment later. The two men glanced at each other and grinned, backing off just slightly. This was going to be fun.

Marco gripped the wheel hard. *What was that?* The wheel had seemed to lurch left of its own accord, the car veering dangerously close to the median wall before he'd pulled it back. His mind raced. He'd had the car tuned up and inspected just a month or two ago. Surely they would have found problems in the steering or tracking systems—

"Aaaaah!" The steering wheel lurched again. Marco hauled with all his might and pulled the car back under control.

He wiped some sweat out of his eyes. This was crazy. He eyed the wide, welcoming shoulder on the highway and pressed on the brakes.

Nothing happened. The car continued to race at more than seventy-five miles an hour. Marco stomped on the brakes. Nothing. If anything, his speed was increasing. He pumped the brakes, stood on them, pleaded with them. The speedometer inched upwards. Eighty miles per hour…eighty-five…ninety…

Marco swerved to miss slower traffic, his mind racing, concentrating on not hitting anything. If the steering wheel veered just one time at this speed…

Suddenly, he grew still, cold, the utter certainty of his fate staring him in the face. This was planned. He was disposable.

The lights on the highway grew thicker as he fought to keep control, flashing past other travelers as if they were standing still. He was heading toward the most populous area of downtown; no way could he hold it for long.

The speedometer inched past one hundred miles per hour, and his thoughts grew somehow slow, somehow perfectly clear. He could see it all unfolding before him—the approaching stretch of highway congested with holiday travelers, the mass of red taillights indicating a traffic jam in progress; an impenetrable wall for a speeding bullet.

He had only seconds to decide. Only seconds.

Where was that music coming from? The music of that night, of Christmas Eve, was playing clear as a bell.

Was that the music the angels sang? Singing of a baby born in a manger. Born, the priest had said, as good news of great joy to all people…a savior…Christ the Lord. Born to die on a cross…crucified…suffering…for us.

Who are You, Jesus? He had never asked that question before, never prayed before. But he sensed it was the right question. The light was growing brighter. But not the red lights of the cars in front of him. Another light. Awesomely close.

I am the One who created you, who loves you, who has called to you for long years. Come to Me.

But, Lord, I'm not worthy. You are so clean. And I'm so dirty.

How could he approach the purity of that light, that loveliness? He began to sob, his heart breaking with longing. He had no words to express the fullness of his feeling, only the cry of his heart. *You know what I am, what I've done.* The tears blurred his eyes. *O God, what have I done?*

He watched as the light grew warm, tender. He sensed a hand reaching out to touch his brow, to wipe the dirt away. His heart broke at the touch of that hand.

*Jesus, I'm not worthy. I'm only getting what I deserve. But if there's any way…
take me.*

Today, My child, you will be with Me in paradise…

The squealing of tires shocked him back into reality, the sense of other cars close,
too close, innocent people before him and beside him, red taillights looming in the
darkness.

Lord, help me…

He sensed the wheel turning on its own, one last time, pointing the car directly
into the highway wall at one hundred miles per hour. Then the darkness was gone,
vanished into the whitest of light in the blink of an eye.

Dazed, Marco looked down at himself. He was clothed in purest white, unfamiliar tears streaming down his face.

Marco looked up to see an ageless figure coming toward him, tender hands outstretched, eyes dancing with delight. Delight…for him. Eyes overflowing, he ran
forward, stumbling, falling to his knees in the embrace of his unexpected Savior,
basking in a love he'd never suspected, never known. Basking in the reality of the
terrible price this One had paid, that he might be here, all undeserved.

FIFTY-FOUR

Cars were bunched in chaotic clusters around the accident, stopped where their occupants had swerved to avoid the disaster in progress or the traffic jam in front. People emerged from their cars, screaming in shock at the explosion, the fire, their own narrow escapes. Several hardy souls tried to venture toward the sports car, only to be driven back by the searing heat.

Two men watched with satisfaction as the flames began to subside, emergency vehicles arriving at the scene, lights whirling, sirens blaring.

The two men got back in their car and headed down the clogged shoulder toward a nearby exit. It had been fun, but they had the rest of their assignment to complete.

The man in the passenger seat pulled out a map and an address, working out the quickest way to the girl's apartment complex. He stared at a picture of the target and whistled, his eyes gleaming. He showed the picture to the driver, who glanced at it and made an obscene comment. Too bad they were under such urgent timing constraints or they would have been tempted to take their time.

Tiffany kissed Wade good-night in the parking lot, acting disappointed that they couldn't be together that night.

"Sorry, Sasha, but I've got a really early meeting tomorrow."

"I can't believe they asked you to work on New Year's Eve. Slave drivers."

"It's because it's New Year's Eve that we have such an early meeting. Everyone wants to knock off early." He pressed her into him. "Hmm. You could almost convince me to change my mind."

"Oh, baby. No, you go home." She pushed herself away. "I should be going anyway. I'll see you tomorrow night."

Wade reached for her and accepted another kiss before she shooed him away.

"Go on, now."

Tiffany watched him drive away. *Phew.* The man was a machine. She was glad for a night to herself. Not that it wasn't worth it, she thought, climbing into her brand-new little BMW.

She pointed the car toward home and turned on the state-of-the-art stereo, bouncing along to the radio, enjoying the cheery holiday season, not a care in the world.

"Check her computer!" The large man wearing a black leather jacket stood square in the middle of the frilly apartment. He scowled as his colleague went to turn on the girl's computer. "Hurry it up! The others should be getting to the club any minute."

"Well, get a move on, then! Check their CDs!"

The leather-jacketed man pulled boxed CDs off a rack by the stereo, opening each one to see if any had the word DEMO across the front of the disc. Nothing. He pulled books off of shelves, tore through neatly stacked files, ripped pictures off of walls, looking in every conceivable nook a disc could be hidden in.

Tiffany saw the neon lights of The Challenger in the distance. On impulse, she slowed and took the exit, then slipped in the rear door of the club and saw Maris hovering near Marco's office.

"Hey, Maris. He in?"

"He had to run to a meeting. Should be back soon."

"Do you know if he made out payroll yet?"

"Don't think so, dearie."

Tiffany shrugged and started to turn away. "Oh well, I'll try to come by tomorr—"

"Maris! Maris!"

Both women turned to see the young front-desk hostess running toward them, her face ashen. "The police are on the phone! Something—something about Marco!"

Maris was at the hallway phone in three strides. "Which line?"

"Line—" the girl was out of breath, struggling to remember. "Line two."

Maris punched the button. "Hello? Yes, I'm standing in for Marco—" Her eyes widened with shock as she listened.

The young hostess pulled on Tiffany's sleeve. "They said—they said there'd been a fatal accident!"

A crowd was beginning to gather in the hallway around the phone, the word spreading like wildfire.

Maris was still on the phone, scribbling notes on her order pad, the pen shaking in her hands. "Yes, sir, I'm still here. Yes, sir. How soon will they be here? I understand."

She put down the phone and looked at the growing crowd. "The police say—" she took a breath, trying to hold it together, "the police said there was a terrible accident on the highway tonight…and Marco was killed."

Cries of shock…grief…consternation. Several of the dancers began sobbing. Tiffany felt herself starting to lose it, clutching the girl beside her.

Maris raised her voice. "The police will be here within thirty minutes. They say no one is to leave."

"Why?" Nick was standing at the back of the crowd, a martini tumbler still in one hand. "Why the police?"

"I don't know. But no one leave, will you?" Maris looked at Nick and one of the bouncers, talking fast. "Would you go ask the DJ to make an announcement? And would you keep any patrons from leaving? It shouldn't take long."

She looked around at the others. "Everyone go back to your posts, if you can, or stay in the break room."

The crowd began to break up. Maris caught Tiffany's eye and pulled her aside, her face tight, her manner hurried. "Can you go tell the other staff—the cooks, the other dancers, the waitresses—what's happened? Make sure no one leaves?"

Tiffany could only nod her head, tears streaming down her cheeks. She set off for the kitchen, pulling out her cell phone with shaking hands, starting to gasp with great sobs. She had to find Ronnie. Ronnie had to come.

The second man emerged from Tiffany's bedroom, having thoroughly searched both the computer for the file and the room for the disc. He shook his head, and both men made quick work of the second bedroom. Nothing. It wasn't here.

And now they had a second girl to worry about.

The first searcher made a quick call on his cell phone and received authorization to abandon the search there and head to the club; their colleagues might already be there. They had to beat the cops there and find the girls at all costs. Neither must be allowed to escape.

Ronnie waved good-night to the Turners and Woodwards standing in the doorway and headed home. How strange but how nice that these two respectable couples would care about her. And how much pain she could have spared herself by returning the Woodwards' calls months ago.

The offer of a "safe haven" had again been made and again politely declined, just as she had also steered away from the delicate subject of her job. Her hosts had seemed to accept the redirection, even though Sherry had said—only half-jokingly—that she was a persistent sort and wouldn't keep letting Ronnie off the hook that easily.

Ronnie was surprised that she didn't mind the questions, didn't mind the obvious desire of these people to draw her away from her life at the club, to educate her about their faith. They were naive but sincere. In her life, she was used to the opposite.

She pulled onto the highway, ambivalent about taking the night off. Tiffany had probably made a boatload of money without her there to siphon off the best tips. Maybe she should go in, after all. It was only nine-thirty or so, plenty of time to still rake in some cash.

As she drove through the security gates of the apartment complex, her cell phone rang. She held it awkwardly against her shoulder as she pulled into a parking space.

"Hello?"

"Ronnie! Ronnie, O God, Ronnie!"

"Tiff! What's wrong?"

"Marco's dead! The police just called the club. Some kind of accident! Oh, Ronnie, can you come here? You've got to come!"

Ronnie felt herself backing out of the parking space and retracing her path out of the complex, hardly aware of what she was doing.

"Are you sure?" Ronnie pressed a shaking hand to her mouth, feeling the floodgates pressing against her eyes. "Please tell me you're not sure! Are the police *sure* it was Marco? What was he doing away from the club?"

"Maris said he had to run to a last-minute meeting." Tiffany was crying now, her voice distorted. "Please come, Ronnie. I've got to make a couple more calls."

"I'm coming."

Ronnie hung up the phone, feeling great tears leaking down her cheeks. She remembered Marco's face, just a few nights ago in that church parking lot, the unaccustomed vulnerability, the few moments of softness. Then the gates had come down again with a clang. But she had seen him as he really was, inside, beyond the bluster and the cold business dealings. Behind the hardened man who hadn't protected her, had abandoned her on the train platform that night. She grieved for him, for the man he was and the man he never got to be.

Is that where I'm headed? Ronnie felt the question rise up in her spirit. *To where I can suppress who I really am, become scarred by what I've chosen to do? Is that the end result?*

She sped toward the club, wiping tears from her eyes, her mind in turmoil.

☆ ☆ ☆

A shining team went with her, surrounding her, their faces fierce, their orders clear.

The saints were still praying, her mother and friends still on their knees for the young woman, though they did not know why.

Loriel led the way, his thoughts racing with the plan now in motion. The timing was going to be tight, and it would all depend on the next few minutes.

He looked down at the girl in the car, leaking fresh tears every few minutes, her hands clenched on the steering wheel. A shining being was in the car with her, speaking to her, trying to get through to her softened heart.

Loriel laid his plea before the throne of grace. This little one would be the key; the saints would be the key. But her life would be in mortal danger, might—in the end—be required of her. The night could end in great triumph or tragedy...or both. The Spirit had not revealed what was to come; only what the battle would be. The heart-searching by this little lost lamb, the intervention of the saints of God, might in the end save a nation, but they could not—in themselves—save a soul.

The Lord desperately desired her love, her submission...her surrender. But in the end, it would be her choice. With these wayward children, Loriel had seen even those with soft hearts be unwilling to lay down their will before the Way, the Truth, and the Life, unwilling to accept their need for forgiveness, unwilling to give up their independence. He had wept as they had chosen to descend, with pride intact, into eternal darkness.

Loriel desperately prayed that in all the coming battle, in all the conflict for so many lives, that the conflict for this one beloved soul would not be lost.

A thought struck him and he straightened, giving thanks for the inspiration as he called over another cadre of angels. They listened a moment then sped away, flying low, attracting no attention, heading back the way the little lamb had just come.

"So what did you think?"

Doug and Vance were in the kitchen loading the dishwasher.

"It's hard to know," Doug said. "She seems like a nice girl—very normal. You'd never know she was a stripper."

"Yeah." Vance gave a barking laugh. "That absolutely floored me. But it explained—partly anyway—why I had such a burden to pray for her, to reach out to her at school. It was the Lord, trying to get through."

The two men continued their task in silence. Doug found himself moving more and more slowly as they neared the final dishes. There seemed to be a weight on him, a growing concern, an urgent call forming in his mind.

Vance, too, stopped slotting plates into the dishwasher. It was almost as if he was listening to something.

The urgency blossomed and grew in Doug's mind until it was like a shout. He looked over at his friend. Vance, his eyes wide, stared back at him.

The men closed the dishwasher and headed into the living room.

They were met at the doorway by their wives, the same urgency in their eyes.

"What's going on?" Sherry finally blurted out.

Doug took her hand and led her back into the living room. Vance and Jo followed, and the four saints fell to their knees on the soft carpet. And suddenly, the words began pouring out…prayers for Ronnie. Prayers for protection, for salvation, for God's purposes to be accomplished. All four were gripped by something they did not understand, beseeching—for the second time that night—the throne of grace on behalf of one little lost lamb.

It was growing late…they had to get the kids to bed…they had things to do. But suddenly nothing was more urgent than hearing the voice of their Lord and praying with His heart.

FIFTY-FIVE

Maris let herself into the locked office, almost shaking with haste, and ran to Marco's computer. She pulled out her Palm Pilot and laid it on the desk by the computer, her fingers flying across the keyboard.

Three words from the police phone call resounded in her head—words she hadn't shared with her coworkers.

"...under suspicious circumstances..."

All her training told her this could mean only one thing—someone had taken him out. And why now, after all this time? She recalled Tiffany's face looming in the doorway, Tiffany who had overheard something she couldn't possibly have understood. But you didn't have to understand something to repeat it to the wrong ears...and Tiffany had been leaving to go meet Wade and who knew who else. Happy-go-lucky Tiffany, clueless Tiffany, must have said something...and someone *had* understood it.

And that meant they would be coming here. Looking for her.

Within seconds, she found the file she had discreetly copied to Marco's hard drive while helping him with the CD. All her instincts were telling her this little audio file was now critical, was worth discovery, was worth any effort to get it out of here, to get it to safety. She set up her Palm Pilot and beamed the file via wireless connection straight to her hand-held device, watching the download proceed with fevered eyes.

It was taking too long! This file was too large for her hand-held device to e-mail out. She would have to get the Palm Pilot itself out of the club and find a better e-mail connection or, better yet, bring the Palm Pilot straight in.

Maris looked at her watch, practically sick with haste. Three minutes. Too long...too long! They might be here any minute—might be here already.

She heard the soft beep and checked the face of the device: "Wireless download complete." She yanked the Palm Pilot off the desk and hurried for the door. She did not notice that the screen of the computer bore the same message.

☆ ☆ ☆

Ronnie came running into the club. She found Tiffany in the dancers' room, and the two friends hugged and cried for a few minutes.

"Where is everyone else?" Ronnie looked around at the sparsely populated room.

"In the break room, probably. Maris said the police asked everyone to wait."

Ronnie looked in the mirror and grimaced at her reddened, mascara-streaked eyes. She dumped her car keys on the makeup table. "I look awful. I'm going to go splash cold water on my face."

Tiffany gave her a dull nod. "It's not like any of us are looking too great right now."

Maris took a few breaths to settle her pounding heart, then stepped out into the hallway.

Almost immediately she was accosted by staffers. Where had she been? What did the police say? Would they still be paid tomorrow?

She tried to reassure everyone, answering their questions, urging them to wait in the break room until the cops arrived. Her brain was screaming at her to bolt for the back door. But there were so many people with questions, she couldn't move five steps without being accosted.

The young hostess tugged on her arm and told her two men were out front looking for her. They were talking to Brian, the bouncer. She thought maybe they were the police?

"Are they wearing uniforms?"

"No, just—you know—clothes."

"Tell them I'll be right there." She set off down the hallway toward the break room. Just shy of the door, she jerked to a halt, listening.

"Where is Maris, the waitress?"

The voice was unfamiliar. She heard one or two people say they hadn't seen her. Maybe she was in Marco's office?

"Go check." A different voice issued a curt order.

She heard heavy steps heading toward the break room door, and she set off down the back hallway, timing the paces in her head. She'd never make it to the exit...never make it.

She heard the heavy footsteps rounding the corner just as she pulled even with the ladies' room. She hurled herself against the door, ducking inside, and heard the man pounding on Marco's office door, just down the hall.

Trapped! She should call in, should at least tell her team what was going on. But her cell phone and other gear were in her locker in the break room, as inaccessible as the moon.

The pounding turned to kicking, and she listened to Nick's familiar voice approach the man, his tone alarmed.

"What are you doing?"

"Stay out of it."

"Hey, listen, you—"

The man's voice changed slightly. "I'm conducting an official investigation, and time is critical. I need to find the waitress, Maris."

"I'm sorry...I think she was in the office a minute ago."

There was a heavy thud, and the crack of a door giving way.

"Hey!" Nick sounded angry.

"Like I said—official business. Stay out of it!"

Maris started to pull open the bathroom door, every muscle tensed to spring down the hallway toward the exit.

Suddenly, someone pushed on the bathroom door from the outside, and she gasped, jerking back, her hand raised to deliver a blow.

Ronnie shrank back against the wall, her reddened eyes wide. "Hey!"

Maris shouldered past Ronnie and peered out as the door began to swing shut.

Good. The hallway was clear, the man—or men—still in Marco's office. Poised to move, she turned her head toward the back exit.

There was a sudden noise, and the heavy exit door was wrenched open from the outside.

Maris jerked back into the bathroom, letting the door silently swing shut.

"Maris?" Ronnie's voice quavered. "What's wrong? What's going on?"

Maris held up a sharp hand for silence, straining to listen through the closed door.

There was a male voice, talking so low that she couldn't capture all the words.

"...still be in the building...car's still here..."

A second voice was a bit louder.

"The PC was compromised. Someone had just downloaded something—and not to a disk. To a hand-held device of some kind. That bartender says she owns a Palm Pilot. She must have the file."

The first voice swore. "Find her. Search every inch. No one gets in or out."

"They say the cops are on the way."

"Better hurry, then." The voices began moving away, and Maris could hear them calling someone to stand guard over the back door. "And one other thing…" the voices were growing faint "…those other girls…"

Ronnie realized that Maris was staring at her long and hard. She looked back, puzzled, then Maris pulled her away from the door and into the large handicap stall at the back of the bathroom.

Ronnie tried to resist, her voice rising with alarm. "What's going *on?*"

"*Shhhh!*" Maris closed them into the large stall, locking the latch behind them. "For pete's sake, I thought you were smarter than that!"

"Fine! Would you please tell me what's going on?"

"If I told you, it would take all night. They'll be in here any minute."

"*Who* will?"

"Just listen!" Maris hissed. "I can't explain. But I need you to do something for me. Will you do it?"

Ronnie looked in her eyes and glimpsed something she'd never seen before. Something…fierce. Determined. Something beyond the snappy Bronx waitress she'd always known.

She took a breath. "Okay."

Maris pulled a Palm Pilot out of her apron and handed to Ronnie. "I need you to hold this for me for a little while, to hide it on your person." She brought out a pen, tore off a scrap of her order pad, and scribbled a series of numbers on it. "If anything happens to me, call this phone number. Give them this code, and you'll be connected to the right people. You'll need to get them this Palm Pilot immediately, if I can't. I just downloaded a critical file."

Maris showed her the long series of numbers, then tucked the torn slip of paper inside the Palm Pilot's leather sheath. Ronnie looked at the hand-held device as if it would bite her, her brain still ringing with the words, *"if anything happens to me…"* She looked back up at Maris.

"Who would I be calling, exactly?"

"The local branch of the FBI."

"The FBI!"

"I don't have time to explain. I need to get you out of here before they search the bathroom."

"Who is *they?* What're they looking for?"

"'They' are some very bad people, Ronnie. And they want what you're holding in your hand. They won't suspect you; they'll just think you were using the bathroom. But if you think they're suspicious of you—run. Don't look back. Get out of here immediately, and call this number."

She gripped both of Ronnie's arms and looked her straight in the eyes. "Ronnie, I wouldn't ask this under other circumstances. I don't want to involve you. But there's much more at stake here than you can possibly imagine—an issue of national security. Tens of thousands of lives could be at stake. Ronnie, this Palm Pilot—this file—*must* make it to the FBI."

"But what about you? What will they do to you?"

"Don't worry about me. I've got to get you out of here."

Suddenly, both girls heard voices outside the door, loud voices, heavy steps.

Maris whirled and hissed at Ronnie. "Climb up on the toilet and hide that Palm Pilot! Do it! *Do it!*"

Ronnie clambered onto the toilet seat as Maris whipped out of the stall, hurrying for the door.

With fumbling fingers, Ronnie untucked her shirt and slipped the Palm Pilot in the back waistband of her jeans. Then she crouched so her head wouldn't be visible over the top of the stall.

She heard Maris open the door, heard the sounds of discovery, heard men rushing in, someone being pushed up against a wall.

"What are you big lugs doing?"

Not ten feet away, Ronnie listened, shaking, as the men explained in graphic terms just what they were doing, what they were looking for. She heard Maris being bashed up against the wall, heard her choking with pain. Ronnie covered her mouth to keep from crying out.

"I don't know what you're talking about!" Maris again, weakly protesting. "I do have a Palm Pilot, but I left it behind the bar. It's down on one of the shelves where we stash our things."

"Show us." More pushing and scuffling noises, and they were out the door, voices raised, calling someone for assistance.

Down the hall, a stern-faced man wearing a black leather jacket watched as Maris was hustled out of the bathroom and past him. He whistled for the man at the back door to follow them.

The second man hurried over. "I thought you told me to block the exit."

"I'll watch it. The cops'll be here any second. Go help them search the bar."

He watched as the second man hurried toward the bar, and a small smile softened his face. As soon as the second man was out of sight, he looked upwards as if listening and nodded. Then he vanished.

☆ ☆ ☆

Out at the bar, a hard-faced man in a black leather jacket sneered as Maris was hauled out to the bar, oblivious to the dumbfounded looks from the patrons and staff. He began barking out orders. Where was the Palm Pilot? Search the bar!

Another man came running out to the bar from the staff area, then slowed, confusion on his face as he spied the leather-jacketed man.

"What are you doing away from the back exit?" The leather-jacketed man barked.

"Uh—I thought you— Someone else was watching it."

Leather-jacket nodded and lowered his voice, glancing around at the chaos all around him. "See if you can get someone on the staff to point out those two girls— Sasha and her roommate. If you find them, bring them here. Quietly. We'll need to find a way to get them out of here before the cops arrive."

Ronnie crouched on the toilet seat. She had to move. Mouth dry, she clambered down and hurried for the door, feeling the awkward weight of the Palm Pilot against her back. She felt like throwing up. She couldn't do this.

She listened at the door as Maris had done, and heard nothing. Shaking, she cracked open the door a trace. Nothing. She straightened and emerged from the bathroom as if puzzled about what had just gone on. There was no one in the hallway—and no one guarding the back door! She raced toward the dancers' room. Had it only been five minutes since she left Tiffany?

She banged through the door. "Tiffany!"

Tiffany turned at her cry, jumping halfway out of her seat. She put a hand to her chest. "Where've you been?" She gestured into the room. "This officer was just taking our names and statements. I'm next."

Ronnie looked at the man at the side of the room, talking to one of the dancers. He was not wearing a uniform, was only half-listening to the girl, his attention instead on this new girl who had burst into the room. His eyes were alert...hard.

"Good," Ronnie forced herself to act nonchalantly. "I hope we can help."

She stood close beside Tiffany, using her friend to block her movements, and grabbed her car keys from the makeup table.

Then she squeezed Tiffany's arm, trying to catch her eye. Her friend flinched and looked up to complain.

Ronnie's eyes bore into her friend's. *Please don't say anything!* With slightly raised voice, she said. "I've got to use the rest room. Didn't you say you had to go?"

"Uh—sure." She looked around vaguely. "We'll be right back."

The man across the room stiffened and opened his mouth to say something. Before he could, Ronnie had tugged her friend out the door, her heart pounding.

The back exit was still clear! She kept a vice grip on Tiffany's arm and started pulling her toward the door.

"Ronnie! What—?"

"Just run, Tiff! I'll explain later! Run!"

The two girls raced for the exit, banging through just as one of the dancers emerged from the dressing room, pointing, her face puzzled.

"But that's Sasha right there…"

Ronnie raced toward her car, feeling the Palm Pilot beginning to slip. With a sudden jolt, it jarred loose from her waistband. She grabbed for it and caught the end of the leather slipcover. The device slipped out and banged against the pavement. She scooped it up, fumbling with the case, with the keys, aware that there were shouts on the other side of the door, people running…coming.

She jabbed the car key into the lock, losing her grip on the leather case but throwing the Palm Pilot inside as she and Tiffany fell into their seats. She turned the key in the ignition, revved the engine, and backed out of her parking spot. Tiffany looked back, alarmed.

"Those guys want you to stop." She jerked and screamed. "Ronnie, duck!"

Ronnie heard two sharp noises, heard the glass of her back window shatter. She didn't flinch, somehow detached. She slammed the car into drive and stomped on the gas pedal.

Another man came running around the corner from the front of the club, holding out his arms, his face fierce to stop her. She set her jaw and pressed on the accelerator as Tiffany screamed, throwing an arm over her face.

The man leaped out of the way at the last second.

"You almost ran him over!" Tiffany was shouting at her. "What is *wrong* with you! That was a cop!"

Ronnie's tires squealed out of the lot. She made a hard left turn onto Tenth Street and darted onto the highway access ramp. If she could get just a one-minute head start, they'd never catch up. She could see three police cars—no lights flashing—heading down Tenth Street toward the club. Then the highway rounded a bend and the area was lost to sight.

"What is *wrong* with you? Stop this car!" Tiffany was pounding on her, her voice high with fright. The wind whistled through the shattered back window.

Ronnie raced onward, looking in the rearview mirror. Nothing. She reached an exit for another major highway and took it, speeding around the cloverleaf, sure she had lost them. Or maybe the arrival of the police had prevented them from following. Relief came in conflicted waves. She had lost them…but Maris…what about Maris?

Beside her, Tiffany's eyes were wide. "I can't believe you tried to run over a cop."

"He wasn't a cop. They were just pretending."

"What do you mean? They were there to take statements about Marco!"

"No, that's not what they were there for. Real police wouldn't have shot at us like that. They were looking for something. That's what Maris said."

"Maris? But she's the one who said the police would come. I don't understand."

Ronnie glanced sideways. "I think Maris was some sort of spy."

"A what?"

As briefly as she could, Ronnie recounted the intense moments in the bathroom, the transfer of the Palm Pilot, the way Maris had put herself in harm's way so the men wouldn't know Ronnie was there.

Tiffany's lips parted in astonishment as Ronnie described her nervous escape from the bathroom, the realization that the man in the dancers' dressing room was not a cop, was *also* looking for someone.

"And did you realize, Tiffany, that as we ran through the back door, someone pointed *you* out to that man? He was looking for *you.* "

"Me?"

"I don't know why. Do you?"

"No!" Tiffany began to shiver. "What do we do? If they can find us at the club, they can find us at home."

Both girls grew cold. They were fighting something huge…that they didn't understand.

Finally, Tiffany cleared her throat. "If you have Maris's Palm Pilot with the number for the FBI…don't you think we should call? We'd at least be safe there."

"Can you find it? I just threw it in. It should be down by your feet."

Tiffany groped around in the darkness. "Here. Okay, where's the number?"

"It should be inside the slipcover."

"There's no slipcover."

"Oh no. I dropped the case. And I don't know the number."

Tiffany was silent, then spoke slowly. "For Maris's sake, I hope they don't find it."

The leather-jacketed man picked himself up off the ground, cursing at the pain where he had hit the ground and rolled away from the speeding car.

He bellowed orders. Get someone after those girls! Get that waitress out here!

Several men ran to their cars and raced out of the driveway.

Another man dragged Maris from the club, her arm twisted behind her back. They were followed by a sizeable contingent of the staff, clearly stunned at the brutal treatment.

Her lips were pressed together in a tight line. The man who held her was talking in her ear, his voice low and cruel.

"And if you try to ask your friends for help, we'll be forced to kill every one of them right now, see? We've got a nice little gallery of hostages over there…they just don't know it. So don't say nothing." He opened the door of a nearby car and pushed her in.

The leather-jacketed man started to go around to the driver's side, when Nick ran up with two of the club's bouncers.

"Hey, those aren't police cars! I can't let you take her without some identification."

"This is all the identification you need," the leather-jacketed man made an obscene gesture, then wrenched open the driver's side door.

Nick barked at the bouncers and they moved forward. The other man turned from where he had shoved Maris into the backseat, and pulled out a gun. He leveled it at them.

"Or maybe *this* is all the identification you need."

The three men wavered, their faces taut with tension and anger. The leather-jacketed man shouted at his comrade as he swung into the driver's seat.

"No shooting—let's go!"

The man holding the gun jumped in beside Maris and slammed the door. He pressed the gun against her head and sneered toward the horrified crowd. The car made a left turn onto Tenth Street just as police cars began streaming into the parking lot.

FIFTY-SIX

S o where do we go?" Tiffany clutched the Palm Pilot as if it could give her the answers they needed. Her voice rose, high and anxious. "If we go home, they'll find us! Where do we go!"

Ronnie's thoughts were strangely clear. There was one place they could go…a place no one would ever think to look…a place they could get advice…could be safe.

She turned off the highway and began winding down a series of back roads, explaining briefly to Tiffany where they were headed. Tiffany looked at her as if she were crazy. She began to shake, crying silently in her seat.

"I can't handle this… They're going to kill us… O God…Marco…Maris…"

Ronnie, too, could feel the pressure building, the floodgates held back only by a severe force of will. She couldn't lose it. Not yet. Not yet. She spotted a familiar street and turned into a subdivision, large houses rising on every side, the windows dark, the garages closed. Only a few late-night lights here and there betrayed any activity behind all the shuttered doors.

She looked at the dashboard clock. Eleven-thirty. All these people went to bed so *early*. She crawled by the imposing homes, trying to determine the right one in the dark, beginning to think she was crazy.

Proxy stared at Tyson, his eyes crackling with fury as he spouted invectives. How could Tyson's men have failed to find the Palm Pilot? How could he have let the girls get away? How could he not have known they had a mole in the place?

Tyson matched his look, not giving an inch. Inside, he was rattled as he listened to the tirade, watched the eyes grow wild. This, then, was the real substance of the man; the severe brutality behind the cool business façade.

His whole team was, of course, made up of hard men, ruthless in their goals. But there was something different behind Proxy's look. Between the cracks in his cold manner there was something unnatural, something…unhinged.

Tyson and the others saw the upcoming human devastation as a simple matter of personal gain and ideological ambition—both goals that, in their cold-hearted calculus, were worth the cost. But now, Tyson stared into a mind that was not cold. This mind was anticipating enjoyment, drawing pleasure from others' pain.

He realized, with a jolt, that Proxy probably would have done it for nothing.

"How long until they get here?"

Tyson looked at his watch. "Ten minutes."

Proxy's eyes gleamed. "Have them bring her up. We'll get the information we need."

"We should get going, I guess." Vance Woodward gave Doug Turner a hug and thanked him for dinner. "The kids were all sacked out downstairs in the playroom, last I checked. Couldn't keep their eyes open any longer."

"Yeah." Doug stretched, feeling a wave of fatigue. "It's past our bedtime too. But I just—I just felt like we couldn't *not* pray."

"I wonder what that was all about?" Sherry said. "It all seemed so…strange. I hope Ronnie's okay."

Into the concerned silence came a sudden knock on the door.

Sherry went into the foyer. She peered through the side windows, gave a cry of surprise, and threw the door open.

The others hurried over and halted at the sight of two young women hovering on the doorstep, their faces white with fear.

Twenty minutes later, with the girls clutching mugs of hot chocolate and wrapped in warm blankets, the two couples listened, open-mouthed, to the end of the story.

By now, Ronnie was shaking, crying as she told of their narrow escape. Tiffany sat beside her, red-eyed but silent.

"You said…you said I could come here if I needed a safe place." Ronnie finished in a rush. "I didn't know where else to go. They could find us anywhere else."

Doug went to a front window and peered out around the shade. "There's nobody out there, that I can see."

Ronnie shook her head. "They couldn't have followed me. I changed highways too quickly. And there was no one behind me on the back roads. I would've seen their headlights in the dark."

"Okay." Doug walked back over and glanced at Sherry. Then he smiled down at the two girls. "I'm glad you came. This is the right place for you right now. We've obviously got a lot to talk about, but we can do most of that in the morning."

All of Ronnie's adrenaline was ebbing away. "What—what should we do about

Maris? Those police cars were almost there when we left, so maybe she was okay. But—" She lifted her hands—"I don't know what to think."

Doug glanced at the others. "We should try to get ahold of the FBI, at least. See what they say."

Ronnie sagged back against the couch, her brain dull. Shouldn't she be doing more? She was beyond thinking clearly. Another consideration pressed on her brain, and she asked Sherry and Doug if she could use their phone.

"I think I should call my mom, let her know where I am."

Doug pointed toward the kitchen phone, his voice cautious. "I wouldn't call anyone else, though. Do you have a cell phone?" He pursed his lips when she nodded. "I would ignore all calls until we get a handle on things; we don't want anyone to have a chance of tracing you somehow."

Ronnie put the call through, but it rang only once and went straight to voice mail. Her mom must be on the other line. Odd, after midnight. She hesitated, then left a brief message, playing down the drama of the night but hearing the exhaustion in her own voice. She left the Turner's name and phone number, then rang off. "I'll try calling you tomorrow, if I can."

When she returned to the living room and collapsed on the sofa, Vance and Doug were standing by the door, debating how best to contact the FBI. Vance and Jo had their coats on, a sleeping Blake on Vance's shoulder.

Vance's brow was furrowed. "We don't have the phone number, or that code that Maris gave her."

"I'll look up the main number in the phone book. Unless I just go down there."

"With all the security these days, you wouldn't get very far. Call first, and see what they say. And let me know what I can do." Vance looked over Doug's shoulder and smiled at Ronnie. "Unless something breaks, we'll see you tomorrow, okay?"

She gave him a weak smile. "Okay. Thanks for everything."

As Sherry and Doug said their good-byes to the Woodwards, Ronnie closed her eyes, feeling the tide of exhaustion rising, images and impressions flashing across her overwhelmed mind. Marco's face, in the parking lot on Christmas Eve…the sound of Tiffany's voice, breaking the dreadful news…the urgency in Maris's eyes…the rush of angry men…terror…hiding in a bathroom stall…the frantic flight from the club…

She felt movement nearby and opened her eyes again. Sherry was standing beside the sofa, looking down at the two girls. "While Doug tries to get through, let's get you settled in for the night. Neither of you are in much shape to go anywhere. He can always bring the Palm Pilot down there by himself, if necessary."

☆ ☆ ☆

The after-hours phone rang in the middle of a clamor. A multiple shooting had taken place downtown during a long-planned bust of a large drug ring, and several FBI agents were down. People ran through the darkened hallways, talking on cell phones, hurrying to jump in their cars and head to the hospital or liaise with the local police. Two of the kingpins had gotten away, and an APB was already out. Heads would roll if they weren't apprehended.

The phone rang again. A late-night rep snatched it up.

"FBI!"

A tired voice came through the phone. "I'm not sure who to speak with. I have something that should be of interest to the FBI."

Someone yelled down the hallway, and the late-night rep listened for a second before turning back to the phone.

"I'm sorry, sir. We're in the middle of something here. Did you say you have a tip of some kind?"

"I guess that's what you'd call it—"

"Let me transfer you to our Tips and Public Leads department, okay, sir?"

"Okay—"

The rep punched a few buttons and the call was gone, freeing him to run down the hall and hear the latest report.

Doug knocked on the guest room door, hearing Sherry's voice rise behind it.

"Come on in, sweetheart."

He opened the door and smiled at the three women clad in pajamas, all sitting on the queen-size bed, all sagging with fatigue.

"Well, I called. Someone in their Tips department took a message and said they'd get back to us. He said it probably wouldn't be until tomorrow." He let out a frustrated sigh. "I kept telling them that it seemed urgent—I told them about the Palm Pilot and what Maris had said—but frankly I think the person was little more than an answering service with no authority or understanding beyond just taking a message. They seemed pretty busy with something else. They weren't keen on me coming down there tonight."

"Maybe they'll call us back before the morning."

"Maybe. If they don't, I'll try again first thing." He looked at Ronnie. "You agree?"

Ronnie nodded. She lifted her hands in a gesture of futility. "I don't know if that's enough, but what else can we do? I just can't think straight anymore."

Doug looked at his watch. "I'll call them again in half an hour, just in case. But I'm afraid the answer may not be much different. You might as well go to sleep. I'll wake you up if anything changes."

Sherry smiled and got off the bed. She gestured the girls to get under the covers and, just as she would with Brandon and Genna, tucked them in. She grinned down at the two heads, peeping tiredly out from under the blankets.

"I would kiss you good-night, too, but that's probably going a bit far."

The two girls giggled, the words growing distant in their ears. Ronnie sobered and looked up at her hosts.

"Thank you. I don't know...I don't know what we would've done without you."

Doug put his arm around Sherry. "God wanted you here. Both of you. We'll talk more in the morning." He reached to turn out the light. "Good-night."

"Good-night."

The light went off, and two scared young women were asleep almost before the door had closed, shutting them in to the gentle darkness.

Across town, teams of dark distorted figures gathered, drawn by an activity that never ceased to rejuvenate them. They hovered like vultures around the big warehouselike building, growing more energized by the minute. One giant creature, his face contorted with foul delight, held firm control. The men gathered around the broken woman below him were trying to get information. He, however, was just enjoying the show.

Tyson watched the brutal spectacle, sickened and stimulated despite himself. Proxy's eyes gleamed at the woman's screams, his face contorted with pleasure equal to her pain. She had held out for a long time—more time than Tyson would have given her. But in the end, she had told them. Of course, she had told them.

And still, the screams rang in his ears. Proxy would not stop. There was nothing more she could say; nothing more she could give them. Except for the gratification of her suffering.

And so she suffered, begging, in her coherent moments, for mercy. For it to be over quickly. Begging God to take her life; pouring out long-lost religious sentiments that seemed to drive Proxy to a frenzy, making it worse.

"Shut up!" He lashed out with fervor. "You hear me? Shut up!"

The woman, bloodied and battered, seemed to gather a final force of will. She stared up at Proxy and quoted the old words that Tyson had heard somewhere before.

"Yea, though I walk through the valley of the shadow of death, I will fear no evil…for thou art with me." She faltered, then seemed to remember more. "Thy rod and Thy staff…they comfort me."

Proxy clamped his hands over his ears. "Shut up, shut up, shut up!"

"Thou preparest a table before me in the presence of my enemies…"

Proxy turned from the chair where she was tied and screamed at Tyson. His eyes were opaque, his pupils dilated.

"Get the video camera!"

"Thou anointest my head with oil, my cup runneth…"

Proxy snatched the video camera from Tyson, adjusted the focus, and handed it back.

"Keep it running."

Suddenly, the wild look was gone from his eyes, the flint-hearted businessman back in place. His voice was deadly calm. "As we know, snuff films fetch a great price."

Proxy snapped at one of Tyson's henchmen standing off to the side. The man came forward and handed his master a gun. Proxy cocked it and pointed it at the woman who had nowhere to go.

Maris looked directly into the video camera lens, her voice weak. "Surely goodness and mercy shall follow me all the days of my life…"

There was a ringing crash, and she gasped and slumped in her seat.

Tyson lowered the camera as the voice, small and receding, resounded in his head.

"…and I shall dwell in the house of the Lord forever."

Proxy gestured for Tyson to switch the camera off, then called one of the henchmen over.

"Get that tape to our regular channels." He wiped down the gun and returned it. "I don't know that there's been a film of a real live FBI agent in the pipeline before. Should fetch a good price."

He took Tyson's arm and steered him out of the room and up the stairs to Tyson's office.

"We're going to have to shift all plans to New Year's Eve." He looked at his watch. "That's tonight...twenty-two hours away." He stared at Tyson, daring him to disagree.

Tyson nodded. "It'll be tight, but there's no other choice. We do not know where the Palm Pilot is, don't know where the girls are. We can't risk it."

"Do you think she was telling the truth, that she just asked that stripper to hide it? That the girl had no instructions what to do with it?"

"I don't know." Tyson stared at a portfolio on his desk that showed pictures of all of Marco's girls. He focused on the picture labeled "Ronnie Hanover/Macy," and his eyes narrowed. "You were pretty thorough. I can't imagine that the woman could've held anything back."

"Yes." The word came out like a hiss, the eyes gleaming with a hint of their previous unearthly malice. "Yes. There was nothing held back. But still, we cannot take the risk. Those girls were chosen for their quick-wittedness. Let's call in the principals." He waved a hand. "Call! Wake them up! Wake everybody up! I will call our client and inform him of the change."

"He may not be pleased."

"He'll be pleased enough. Enough to stick to our original agreement."

"We'll be working right up until the last minute," Tyson said. "How do we leave the country?"

"We'll head to the jet a few minutes before midnight. We should be on the runway by the time everything happens, already cleared for takeoff. Presuming none of the operators have our little gadget in the traffic control tower—" he flashed Tyson a wicked smile— "we should be wheels up before anyone knows what's happened."

"It's going to be tight."

"Then get going." Proxy paused and poked a finger at Tyson's chest. "And assign as many people as you have to, *to find that girl.* Get a team posted downtown to watch the FBI building, just in case she knows more than we think. Go search every apartment of every coworker. Go find her family, her friends, her lovers. I don't care how you take her out—just do it."

Tyson turned the portfolio of pictures so Proxy could see it. "Are you sure you don't want us to bring her in instead, chief? After all, we need to find out what she knows—what she's done...don't we?"

Those unearthly eyes again, as he stared at the lovely girl. "Ahh. Yes. We do."

FIFTY-SEVEN

"Good morning." Ronnie stood in the kitchen doorway, blinking sleepy eyes.

Sherry looked up from her paper. "Good morning, Ronnie." She got up and gave the girl a hug. "Can I get you something for breakfast?"

"Uh…well, if you're sure."

"Well, you know, we normally tell houseguests they can sleep here, but *no food!*" She smiled as Ronnie blushed, and gently guided her to a chair at the kitchen table. "How about some pancakes? I was just making some for the kids."

"Okay. Thanks."

"Is Tiffany still asleep?"

"No, she'll be down in a minute." Ronnie looked around. "What's that noise?"

"Oh, that's the PBS morning cartoons being played at high volume." She stuck her head through the door to the living room. "Turn that down! And come say hello to Miss Hanover."

Two children still in pajamas shuffled into sight, looking shy. Sherry made the introductions, and Ronnie smiled at the kids.

"Hi there. What were you watching?"

"Barney!" The little girl clapped her hands.

"It was her turn to pick," her brother explained in disgust. "I wanted to watch Power Cars."

Genna ran over to Ronnie. "Want to come see?"

Ronnie raised an eyebrow at Sherry. "Go ahead, if you can stand it. The pancakes will be ready in five minutes."

Genna tugged on her arm, and Ronnie got up and followed along. She listened through two Barney songs as Genna sang along. During a break in the show, Brandon said, "TV turn to Power Cars."

The commercial disappeared and cartoon race cars began zooming across the screen.

Genna wailed and ran for her mother as Ronnie moved toward the television to investigate. Sure enough—the Turners had one of Glenn's voice-activated remotes.

She ran her hands across the smooth black surface. She had been so upset with

Glenn that she had thrown out the one he'd given her, smashing it in the Dumpster of their apartment complex. Tiffany had protested, but Ronnie said they had enough money they could buy one if they really wanted one.

Sherry appeared in the doorway to mediate the conflict, and Ronnie slipped away to go get Tiffany.

Sherry separated the two kids and—to loud wails—turned off the television. She went to check on the pancakes and found Doug in the kitchen, dressed for work.

"Hi, sweetheart." He gave her a kiss and settled at the breakfast table, swiping her newspaper.

"What did they say?"

Doug made a face. "Just like last night, I couldn't get through to anyone with decision-making authority. They were still in the middle of that other crisis. I think they're more open for business in about an hour. I'll call again from the office."

"You're going to work, after all?"

"Yeah, got a few things to cover before we knock off for New Year's Eve." He looked around and lowered his voice. "What do you want to do about our little get-together with the Woodwards?"

"Well, I think we should just go ahead as planned, and include Ronnie and Tiffany. It won't be the same—"

"But it's the right thing to do."

Sherry smiled at her husband. "But it's the right thing to do." She walked over and kissed the top of his head. "I love your heart."

"I don't know. I'm still pretty selfish inside. I was looking forward to a fun, relaxing evening with good friends."

"Yeah, me, too. But it's possible the girls will be with us for quite a while. We need to make them feel at home." She lowered her voice, glancing to ensure their children couldn't overhear. "Do you think it's safe, though?"

"We already talked about that—last night; don't you remember?"

"I was dead tired last night, dear heart! I just remember you saying something about trusting God to protect us and then I must have dropped off."

"Dropped off! *Jumped* off is more like it. Snoring within ten seconds."

She flapped a spatula at him. "Watch it, you!"

He went to the stove and wrapped his arms around his wife. He pulled her against him. "Mmm. I'm so thankful I have you back."

"Me, too, sweetheart." She made no move to escape. "So what *did* you say last night?"

"I simply said," he kissed the top of her hair, "that I think we're doing what the Lord wants us to do. We're welcoming strangers in His name. I have to think that this is why we were all so pressed to pray last night. I might feel differently if I had any kind of a check from the Lord, but I don't."

"I don't either." Sherry's voice came out slowly. "I feel like...somehow...we're in the right place at just the right time for these girls. And if God has steered them here, well...I guess it's His job to protect us. I guess I shouldn't worry so much about it. It's high time we started doing the stuff instead of just talking about it. I do think, though, that it's prudent to be cautious and keep some firm rules. You were right to tell the girls not to make or accept any phone calls last night, just in case someone was trying to track them."

Ronnie heard murmuring in the kitchen as she and Tiffany walked back in. Doug was standing close behind his wife at the stove, his arms around her as the two carried on a soft conversation.

They broke off when they heard footsteps, smiling, welcoming Tiffany, shooing them into some chairs, laying out fruit, pancakes and syrup. Ronnie allowed herself to be served, her heart aching at the image of Doug and Sherry snuggling at the stove.

Was this something she'd ever have? This happy home life—the husband, the two kids, the pretty house with a secure job and the respect of the community? No, she didn't belong here. This wasn't her world.

She stared out the pass-through from the kitchen, watching the morning sun stream through a bay window onto the neutral-colored sofas. Her world wasn't one of gentle lights and morning sun; it was one of darkness, of hard neon, of pounding music and sights that would shock respectable people.

She hardly listened as Sherry and Doug asked Tiffany questions about herself, putting the pieces together, questioning another girl from the wrong side of town.

Why did they care? Was this all pretense? Why would perfect strangers take in two scared strippers—two *prostitutes*—give them a bed, breakfast, and what looked like friendship, no strings attached? It didn't add up. Their nice religious sentiments made no sense to Ronnie. What were they getting from it?

She watched as Tiffany warmed to the couple—she had derisively called the house "yuppieville" last night when she and Ronnie were changing—and began answering their questions, telling these perfect strangers more than anyone at the club knew about her. And all because they seemed to actually care.

"Now, ladies." Doug broke her reverie, his voice turning serious. "We need to figure out what to do about everything that happened last night. I have some ideas, if you want to hear them."

Both girls nodded.

"The FBI opens for regular business in less than an hour. I'm going to call them from the office, and see if we can make better headway. But in the meantime, Ronnie, I'm wondering if we can attack this on two fronts. If we could figure out what Maris put on that Palm Pilot that was so all-fired important, we might be able to get more attention from the FBI."

"You'd think," Tiffany broke in, her voice angry, "that it would be enough to explain that we suspect Maris was an agent and she said to bring the Palm Pilot in immediately."

"You would." Doug sighed. "But I've actually known a few policemen and even an FBI agent before, and they can be both incredibly busy and incredibly cynical. They see hoaxes and juvenile plays for attention all the time. Those things take just as much time as the real leads. And we don't even know if Maris was her real name, so it may not be in their system at all. I think it usually takes them some time to sift through things and figure out whether something is worth following up on or not."

"And Maris thought it was urgent. A matter of national security, she said." Ronnie frowned. "Of course, I don't know what 'urgent' really means. She didn't give me any kind of deadline. So maybe a few extra hours is okay." She brightened a bit. "And after all, maybe the police came to the rescue last night, and she's already down there."

Doug looked at her with kind eyes. "Maybe. But that makes it even more imperative that we not wait. We should probably push as much as we can; do everything we can from our end. So I'll call them *again* in an hour, but I also think we should investigate the Palm Pilot. They aren't listening to us now, but if we can show them something specific, they might." He turned to Ronnie. "I tried it last night, and it's password protected, encoded somehow. I couldn't get further than the first screen. But we've got some great tech people at work that might be able to make some headway. My boss is also a genius with that sort of thing. If he has time, I'd like to run it by him and see if he can get into the Palm Pilot so we can see what's on there."

"Okay." Ronnie grimaced. "As long as we don't lose the thing, or no one swipes it!"

Doug laughed. "Don't worry. We have a high-security building. It'll be safe there."

☆ ☆ ☆

Jordan's secretary ignored her phone line, ignored the internal office intercom, ignored pretty much everything except her scowling boss and his incessant commands. He was in a foul mood, his usual energetic demeanor nowhere to be seen.

She typed as fast as she could on the keyboard, trying to keep up with the growing "to do" list. Jordan had emerged from his tightly shut office a moment ago, barked another order, and disappeared back inside. He had instructed her that he didn't want to be interrupted unless it was a true emergency—and maybe not even then.

So she ignored all attempts to get her attention, kept her head down, and worked as fast as she could.

Doug finally stopped trying to buzz her and walked down the long hallway to Jordan's office. He stopped in front of the secretary, smiling down at her. Everyone else but this lady was relaxed today. It was New Year's Eve for goodness' sake! She needed to lighten up.

"What do you want?"

"Jordan pushing you today?"

"Yes. What do you want?"

Okaaay…be that way!

"I need to ask Jordan a question, if he has a second."

"He doesn't. He ordered me not to disturb him for any reason today."

"I understand. But I think this is pretty important. I need his help with something."

"What is it?" The secretary lifted her eyes for a fraction of a second, continuing to type, making it plain that Doug was a pain in the neck.

Doug held out the Palm Pilot. "I'm wondering if he can help me break the encryption and get into this device. There's an important file on it that we need access to."

"I don't think that would count as an emergency. Ask someone else."

"Okay, fine! But if they can't help, I'm coming back. It's an urgent matter."

The secretary just kept typing. Doug made an exasperated noise and went back down the hall.

"Mary?" He stopped by his assistant's desk. "Who else, other than Jordan, is really good at encryption stuff?"

"Well, there's a couple of guys down on three—" Her eyes brightened. "And that new kid—the intern down there—he was able to decrypt our computers when the new security software went haywire."

"Good! Thanks!" Doug hurried down to the third floor and went looking for the resident boy genius. He was a college kid—sophomore at Georgia Tech—but seemed to know more about information technology than half the tech staff.

He found the kid in his cubicle, playing a computer game.

"Hard at work, are you?"

The intern jerked to his feet, stunned to see the chief financial officer staring at him.

"Uh—uh—sorry, sir!"

"No problem. I was just thinking we needed to lighten up today since it's a holiday."

"Uh, yes, sir!"

"At ease, boy." Doug chuckled, looking at the young man with his military buzz cut. The kid reminded him of himself at that age. Doug held out the Palm Pilot. "I have a sensitive problem I'm wondering if you can help me with. There's something on this device that we need to see, but we can't get in. And once we get in, I don't know if we'll be able to see the file. It would be the last file that was downloaded, if you can figure that out."

"How many layers of encryption?"

"I don't know. But it's pretty urgent. Can you work on it and bring it right up when you're done?"

"Yes, sir!" The kid took the Palm Pilot out of his hand. "Give me an hour or two and I'll see what's what."

"Thanks. And don't pass it around, please. If you can't get in, come tell me directly."

The intern nodded, already fiddling with the device and mumbling to himself.

Doug took the elevator back up to his office. Might as well try the FBI again; he'd waited long enough for a call back.

This time he got a more willing listener—someone with the title of "Special Agent"—but no more movement. The man seemed interested in his third-hand account of a possible undercover agent working in a strip club, but Doug could hear the skepticism in his voice when he relayed Maris's comment about national security. Doug finished his story and sighed.

"Listen, I know you probably think this is a hoax, but I'm just passing along what the woman said."

"Yes, sir—what the woman told the stripper, you mean. You didn't actually hear her yourself."

"Of course. But—"

"And where is this possible agent, now?"

"We don't know. But Ronnie said she thought her life was in danger."

"Uh, *huh.*" There was a pause, and Doug could practically hear the sigh over the telephone. "Tell you what. I see in the record that you've called four times now. I can tell you think this is important, sir—"

"I do."

"—and we always appreciate the tips provided by the general public."

Doug tried to keep the wry sound out of his voice. "I'm sure you do."

"So let me fast-track this and ask around. But it's too preliminary for you to come in for a meeting."

"You don't even want me to bring the Palm Pilot?"

"Well, sir, you're always welcome to bring in any item you think might be of interest. But that's your choice. I can't promise that someone will get to it right away."

Doug kept his mouth shut. He'd rather keep control of the device and see if he could crack it. Then maybe he'd have something concrete to get their attention.

The man was still talking. "If you still had that numeric code you said the strippers dropped, focusing this search wouldn't be a problem. But the FBI is a large organization, and I don't know who might've been dealing with this matter—if indeed someone was. It could've been an op run out of Washington, or even a completely different field office, for all I know."

"I understand, sir."

"We have your numbers, Mr. Turner—work, cell and home. Be assured, we'll get back to you if something comes up."

"Okay."

Doug put down the phone, looked at the clock and grimaced. He had three or four business-related things that had to be done today—financial things that had to be cleared before midnight at the end of the year—but all this other stuff kept getting in the way.

He promised himself he'd return to the mystery as soon as the tech-wizard intern showed up with the Palm Pilot, and closed his door. Maybe he could get some of these other things cleared off his desk in the meantime.

Behind his own closed door, Jordan was almost continually on the secure cell phone he'd gotten just for this purpose. He called Tyson for the third time that hour.

"I forgot to ask—any sign of the girl?"

"No." Tyson sounded frustrated. "We've made some progress, but haven't turned anything up yet. There is one bouncer, Brian, who Marco had drafted early on. Since he's loyal to us—he doesn't know the full story, obviously—he agreed to join the search. They've visited all the coworkers, but no one has seen the girls. And they tried calling their cell phones, but no dice. One of the dancers said Sasha left her purse and cell phone behind at the club. But the police confiscated it. And Ronnie's evidently not answering hers."

"She's smart."

"That's why she was in the group, after all."

Jordan swore. "Family? Any luck?"

"Not yet. None of the other dancers know much about where they were from. The only thing they do know is that the girls were best friends growing up. So, we find one, we find the other."

"All I want is that Palm Pilot!" Jordan slammed his fist on the desk. "The client was not pleased that the code had been compromised. If we get the thing, we should be able to tell whether anyone has looked at it or whether all this worry is for nothing."

"We're moving ahead with the preparations for tonight, though, Chief. You can reassure the client that, barring any last-minute problems, it should come off as planned."

"No problems with the ad time?"

"No, that was purchased months ago. We've added a few secondary networks, of course. And there were a few that wanted to run the commercial too late. But we paid big enough premiums that none of them minded bumping whichever other ads were slated for that time slot."

"What's our expected impact? Any numbers yet?"

"Not as big a splash as Super Bowl Sunday, of course. Probably about a million hits."

Jordan picked up a pen. "Give me the breakdown."

"With almost 8 percent market penetration of over one-hundred million households, that's at least eight million devices."

Jordan was scribbling, smiling. "Right. Go on."

"From our research, it appears that at least half of those households are in the Eastern time zone."

"Excellent."

"So assume—we're being rough, here—that about four million devices are in that time zone, and maybe 25 percent of those will be watching the ball drop live on New Year's Eve."

"Hence, one million hits."

"Well, we might actually get more, as presumably there will be more than one person watching in each household. In some households, there'll be parties of dozens of people."

"All sitting in front of their nice little television sets, one minute after midnight when the networks cut to their commercial breaks."

The satisfaction was clear in Tyson's voice. "So we might get two million or more."

"Two million." Jordan rolled his tongue around the words. "Ten times more than Hiroshima and Nagasaki together."

"And in such a simple way, too. No nukes to hide, no protected materials to steal, no massive money layouts. The victims even pay for the instrument of their destruction. Even if it's not Super Bowl Sunday, the clients are still getting their money's worth, boss."

"I can't wait to tell them."

FIFTY-EIGHT

Doug heard a tentative knock on his office door. "Come on in!"
The tech-wizard poked his head around the door. "Uh—sir?"
"Come in. Any progress?"

"Well, sir," the kid said, laying the Palm Pilot on Doug's desk. "Good news and bad news. The good news is that I got into the device—"

"Great! Good work!"

"Uh, thanks. But the bad news is that I can't get into the file."

"You found it?" Doug's face was eager.

"Yeah—well, you said it was the last file in, right? Easy enough. It's an audio file of some kind, but it was encrypted when it was downloaded. And *that* encryption is something I've never seen before. I don't know how to crack it."

"Well—thanks." Doug looked down at the face of the Palm Pilot, now lit up as if ready to bare its secrets. "Which file is it, by the way?"

"Let me show you. This is one sophisticated device, by the way. All the bells and whistles, and more. Fascinating." He looked up, curious. "Where'd you get it?"

"Long story."

The kid used a stylus to navigate a few steps. "Here you go—this file, right here."

Doug looked at it, reading aloud. "'Speedcode.mp3.' What does that mean?"

"No idea. Except it's an audio file in MP3 format. But like I said—can't open it."

"Can I download it?"

"Yeah, you might be able to." A grin crossed his face. "Well, *I* might be able to. I can try a few tricks to get around the system. You want me to try?"

"Please. But on my computer only."

The intern nodded. "I'll be back in a jiffy. Let me get a hard-link cable."

In minutes he was back, fiddling with the Palm Pilot and Doug's computer, linking one to the other, working his magic on the keyboard. Doug stood and watched quietly.

"Okay…did it." The kid looked up. "I put it in this document folder, see? You still can't open it, but at least you have it on your hard drive."

"Great. Thanks." Doug peered at the screen. "Anyone else at the company you think might be able to break into the file?"

"Well…I probably shouldn't say this, but there's no one in my department that could do it better than me."

"I see." Doug could feel his lips twitching.

"But—say. You know who might be able to manage it is Jordan. He rocks."

"Really? I guess it makes sense. He's been doing computer security stuff since before you were born."

"Yeah. But, I mean, I talked to him once in the cafeteria. I was fiddling with a laptop, trying to get something to work, and he walked right over and showed me how. He said I was the company's rising star, and he had his eye on me. What a gas!"

"Well, I'd agree with him there." Doug clapped him on the shoulder. "Please keep this between us. I'll call you if I need anything more."

When the intern left, Doug stood staring at his computer. Then he copied the file onto a disk and headed down the hall. Might as well make one more try.

He approached the secretary carefully. "Sorry, I'm back."

She gave him a slight smile. "Sorry I was rude earlier."

"Hard to be polite in the middle of a stampede, isn't it?"

"You can say that again. But Jordan has cheered up a bit in the last half hour. He's no less busy, though. You still need help?"

"I do." Doug showed her the disk. "We did break into the Palm Pilot and retrieved the file we need, but that's where we got stuck."

The secretary took the disk from him. "And you want…?"

"Jordan's probably the only person in the company who can break the encryption and get into that file—if anyone can, that is. We urgently need to see the contents. Actually, *hear* the contents, as it's apparently an audio file." Doug considered explaining, and then decided it would raise too many questions. "Please just ask him, if you can."

"I'll try." She laid the disk in an inbox on her desk. "I'll buzz you if he can take a minute."

"Thanks."

Doug headed back to his office, briefly stopping by Mary's desk. She, too, was unusually stressed, her temper a bit frayed by all the last-minute work she had laid on Doug's desk for review that he hadn't gotten to yet.

"Mary, I promise I'll get to all those files in the next hour."

"Okay." She looked like she was forcing a smile, her normally sweet nature set on edge. "I'd really like to get out of here before it gets too late."

"Sorry." Doug gave her a contrite smile. "Tell you what, keep everyone away for an hour. I'll turn off my cell phone, and punch out all this stuff." He thought. "Unless it's Jordan, they can all wait one hour."

She smiled in relief. "Deal."

An hour later, the secretary looked up as Jordan emerged from his office, tension jangling in his body like an electric wire. He picked up the few things from his inbox.

"What's this?" He held up the disk.

"Doug dropped it off. He said there's some encrypted file on there that they need to see, and he was wondering if you could break into it."

Jordan dropped the disk back into the inbox. "I don't have time for that today."

"I know…I told Doug. But he said it was urgent. He's come by twice."

Jordan seemed hardly to be listening. "Too bad. Can't do it."

"I told him." She shrugged. "He tried first with this Palm Pilot that he couldn't get into, but then he must've gotten someone—"

"The what? What Palm Pilot?"

The secretary looked up, surprised. "I don't know…just some encrypted Palm Pilot he wanted to get into. He must've gotten someone else to help because he was back an hour ago with that disk, saying he'd gotten into the device but couldn't open the file. He was wondering if you could."

Jordan picked up the disk, his eyes narrowed. "What sort of file?" His voice was slow, almost disbelieving.

"I don't know, boss. Some type of audio file—"

Jordan darted back into the office and slammed the door. She made a rude noise under her breath and turned back to her work. That man could be so exasperating at times!

The phone rang at Mary's desk. She answered, her voice rushed. "Doug Turner's office."

She listened for a moment, then picked up a pen. "I'm sorry, sir, but he's asked me to hold all calls." She winced and held the phone away from her ear. "Well, sir, he's got some big deadlines today, that's why he has his cell phone turned off. But I'll get him the message and—"

She sighed in exasperation as the caller interrupted her again.

"Okay, FBI, I understand." As she scribbled the message, another line rang on the phone. "Sir, I promise I'll get him this as soon as I can…okay…okay." The man finally hung up and she punched in the next call, moving on to the next emergency.

Jordan hurried to his computer and slotted the disk in, muttering under his breath as he waited for the computer to bring up Windows Explorer, an internal debate raging.

It couldn't be anything…could it? How on earth could it have any connection to what they were looking for?

Windows Explorer popped up, and he clicked on the A: drive to check the file name. His mouth dropped open. He looked at the file name and blinked his eyes. Speedcode.mp3.

His eyes went wild with fury, with haste. How had one of his *own people* come into possession of the code? He dialed a number with shaking fingers, got Tyson, and left him speechless.

They conferred in quiet, urgent sentences, Tyson dispatching his henchmen even as they talked.

Jordan buzzed his secretary, keeping his voice pleasant, level. "Could you buzz Mary and tell her that I'd like to see Doug down here?"

"Will do, Chief."

Caliel listened to the call come over Mary's intercom, listened to her ask Doug down to Jordan's office.

Lots of others were listening, too. The building looked as if light and dark, good and evil were split down the middle.

A shining cadre of great beings flanked Doug's office. His whole end of the hallway was bathed in crystal light, luminescent with the fierce presence of stern-faced warriors.

Beyond Mary's desk, the office grew dark, shadowy. Great dark beings hissed at the shining interlopers. The whole rest of the hallway was nearly black in shadow, only a thin no-man's-land separating deepest dark from shining white.

And they all listened as Mary told Doug of Jordan's summons.

As Doug emerged from the office, Caliel swept a giant hand over the contents of Mary's desk. She brushed her elbow over the stack of messages, and they fell to the floor. Doug passed her desk and had taken two steps down the hall when Mary saw the message slip.

"Doug!"

Doug turned, irritated. He had way too much to do—he couldn't keep jumping from task to task.

Mary held out a slip of paper, and Doug retraced his steps to take it.

"I figured I should tell you…this guy from the FBI called. He wouldn't say what about, just asked you to call him immediately. He seemed to think it was critical."

Doug wavered, then hurried back into his office. Over his shoulder he called back to Mary.

"If Jordan calls, tell him I'm on the phone and I'll be right there."

The dark creatures hissed and spat at the angels, now completely prevented from seeing or hearing what was delaying Doug. Even their unearthly sight could not penetrate the zone of painful light. Their eyes were red with fury. So close—so close! Well, they were still so close. Several of them sped off to take a look and came back with the report. Tyson's men were only a few minutes away. They would make quick work of this measly person who insisted on throwing a wrench in the works. They whispered the news among themselves, their eyes gleaming with expectation.

Caliel issued orders, and his frontline warriors advanced, faces fierce, pressing the zone of light just a little farther down the hallway…a little farther. The dark armies made threats, but none of them seemed inclined to be the first to take on one of the warriors. They backed away slowly…slowly.

Caliel eyed the space…just a little more…a little more.

"Halt!"

That should be enough. He called forward several watch-care warriors, briefed them, then assigned others to various posts. He watched as they sped off.

The heavenly host was infected with a firm exigency from above, each angel keenly aware of how much hung on every move, every step in the battle from this point forward.

Doug listened with alarm to the voice on the other end of the phone.

"Mr. Turner, I don't have time to explain. You must get that Palm Pilot down to the FBI immediately! And bring those girls!"

"But they're at home—"

"Don't waste time going and getting them. Just tell them to get down here!"

"What's going on?"

"I can't explain over the phone. Leave your office immediately and turn on your cell phone. I'll call you back in two minutes and give you directions as you go. Just head toward downtown!" He spewed out a phone number. "If something happens, call me back at this direct number! Get going!"

Doug scribbled the number as the phone clicked off in his ear. He grabbed the Palm Pilot, his cell phone and coat, then took several precious seconds to fiddle with his computer. He raced out the door, stuffing things in his pockets.

Mary looked up as he raced by. "What—?"

"I can't explain! I'll try to call you from my cell phone in a few minutes."

"Okay—" her words were lost behind him as he headed for the elevators, midway down the hallway from his office.

The angels' cordon was holding. The dark forces stirred, muttering, but they couldn't see! They couldn't see Doug leave his office, couldn't see him putting things in his pockets...heading out of the building. Several brilliant warriors escorted him down the elevator and to the parking lot, covering him as he raced out of the security gates and pulled onto the highway.

The dark forces still milled around the executive hallway, not quite looking at the blazing, impenetrable zone of light, impatient for Doug to emerge and head into their trap.

Doug's cell phone rang in his pocket, and he fished it out, driving with one hand.

"Yes!"

"Directions!" The special agent gave him simple, short directions. "Pass those along to the girls, then call me back."

"They're coming from a different direction. We should be there about the same time—maybe fifteen minutes?"

"Great." The line went dead.

Doug made the call and stunned Sherry. "I don't know what's going on," he finished, "but Ronnie and Tiffany need to get down here right away."

"Okay." He could hear Sherry calling them in the background, hear their answering queries.

"Give them my cell phone number so we can coordinate where to meet and I can give them more information as we go."

"Ronnie's cell battery is almost out. So many people from the club were trying to call her that she finally turned it off."

"Lord," Doug said, "extend the life of that battery. And protect those girls!"

"I'll get them on the way."

Doug hesitated. "I'm wondering if you and the kids should join us, too."

There was a long pause. "Are you worried about something? Vance and Jo are arriving here any minute to help make dinner."

"I don't know. I'm probably overreacting. You go ahead and stay there. I'll call you, though, if I hear anything to change my mind!"

"Deal." They could both hear the sound of someone beeping in on Doug's phone. "You get that. I'll get the girls on the road."

"Okay." Doug pressed a button. "Hello?"

"Did you get them?"

Doug recognized the special agent's voice. "They're on their way."

"Great. Okay, here's what you do when you reach the building." He described the logistics, the visitor parking across the street, the door to use, and the number to dial when they arrived. "But don't wait for the girls to arrive before you yourself come on in. We should look at that Palm Pilot right away. We'll be waiting for you just inside the gates, at the security area."

"Okay."

Doug could hear the man talking to someone in the background, his voice hurried. He came back on the line. "We have a lot of things to arrange here. Call me back if you need anything."

"Okay." And again, the line went dead in his hand.

Ronnie and Tiffany pulled on their coats, their faces anxious. Sherry handed them a slip of paper with Doug's cell number and explained everything Doug had said.

Sherry started to open the door, then paused and pushed it shut. "No, wait. I have to pray for you before you go." She put one hand on Ronnie's shoulder and the other on Tiffany's. "Lord, we need Your help. There's something going on that we don't understand and these girls are caught up in it. Protect them. Set your mightiest angels about them, protecting and shepherding them to where they need to go, that their feet would not be dashed against a stone. May Your will be done today! Amen."

She looked up and wrenched open the door, brisk and back in business. "Amen and amen! Get going. Ask Doug to call to let me know that everything's okay."

☆ ☆ ☆

Ronnie finished taking directions—reading them off for Tiffany to write down as Doug gave them to her—and clicked the phone shut. She eyed the battery indicator on her phone, nervous.

"He said to call as we pulled into the parking lot directly across the street, to see if he was still there. I hope we don't run out of battery."

"I hope we don't run out of luck." Tiffany finished writing and put the pen down. "This is all just too weird."

"Yeah. I hope—I hope Maris is okay. I'm afraid for her."

"I am, too. But we don't know…maybe the police showed up early enough to kick the bad guys out. Maybe they even arrested them. Who knows?"

Ronnie drove for another mile in silence, her mind turning. "I can't believe the Turners just took us in like that."

Tiffany shrugged. "Why? You said they were friends."

"Not really! I only met them a little over a week ago. The other couple—the Woodwards—I knew Mr. Woodward for several months, from school. But I'd only been over to the Turners once—last night!—for dinner."

"Huh. Weird."

Ronnie glanced sideways, irritated. "But don't you see what a big deal that is? They're this yuppie suburban couple that doesn't mind two strangers—exotic dancers no less—showing up on their doorstep at midnight. Isn't that amazing to you?"

"I guess."

"Oh, you're always trying to be so cool, you won't even admit it."

Tiffany rolled her eyes. "Well, what do you want me to say? That they're nice? Okay—they're nice. A little churchy-weird, but nice."

"Forget it. Keep your eye on the directions. Just forget it."

"Whatever. Hey listen, can I use your cell phone to call Wade? I was supposed to meet him at five o'clock, and that's only a couple hours away. I need to let him know I may be late."

"May be late! May be *late?* Tiff, you're not seeing him at all! Not tonight and not until we figure out what the heck is going on!"

"Why? It's not like he's one of our coworkers. Who's going to trace me to him?"

"Oh, just the half of our coworkers who knew you were his lover. Are you forgetting the gunshots, Tiff? Those men were trying to kill us! Think, girlfriend. We can't go back to normal until we figure out what's what."

"At least let me call Wade and break the date."

"No way. We have, like, no battery left. I'm not letting you waste it."

Tiffany crossed her arms, petulant. "You're acting like my mom."

"And you're acting like Sherry's six-year-old kid!"

Tiffany threw the directions at Ronnie. "Find your own way there, then!"

Ronnie grabbed the paper. "Fine! I will!"

Several hundred miles away, Linda Hanover wearily unlocked her apartment door and turned on all the lights, pushing back the gathering dusk. Why did every conceivable emergency come through the door right at quitting time?

She had, of course, told the other administrative people to leave early, saying she'd cover for them. Linda allowed herself a melancholy smile. She, after all, didn't have family at home waiting for her. Didn't have any delightful New Year's Eve plans to skip off to. Maybe she could go to a movie or something. She didn't mind going to movies alone.

She picked up the phone and accessed her voice mail. The time stamp on the very first message—announced in the usual robotic voice—startled her.

"Left today, 12:24 A.M."

Linda frowned. Why hadn't she heard the phone? Ah—there had been so many people around, praying until long after midnight, with people on and off the phone the whole time. Some phone calls had surely been missed amid the fuss.

The message began to play, and Linda listened to the account of the previous night with wide eyes, lips parting in astonishment as she scribbled down notes. No *wonder* they'd been spurred to pray! She had tried and tried to reach Ronnie on her cell phone, but it had remained firmly off, unanswered.

The phone rang near her hand and she snatched it up, but it was just Angela, inviting her over for a small party if she had no other plans. Linda told her friend of the harrowing events of the night before, leaving her, too, speechless. She eventually put down the phone, trying to decide what to do.

Biting her lip in uncertainty, she picked the phone back up. Her call was tentative, but the answer was welcoming. She smiled and went into the bathroom to get ready, at last firmly decided on how she would spend her New Year's Eve.

Jordan buzzed his secretary again. "Where's Doug?" The two men had arrived in his office, waiting and ready.

"Last time I checked, Mary said he was on the phone."

Jordan went to the office door, motioning the men to wait. "I'll go get him. Just give me two minutes and we'll have this all taken care of."

Jordan passed Mary's desk and pounded on Doug's door.

"Why didn't he come when I asked him to?" he barked at her, then jerked open the door.

With intense satisfaction, Caliel watched Jordan and his dark companions run back down the hallway, curses pouring from their lips. Caliel gave his remaining troop the prearranged signals, and they vanished, heading to the next beachhead.

Caliel knew, as he sped away from the thronging dark forces, that he hadn't left them for good. He could hear the other heavenly warriors around him praying as intensely as he. The main front in this war was still ahead of them.

FIFTY-NINE

With an eerie calm on his face, Jordan made two phone calls. One to his right-hand man, mobilizing his army. The other to his client.

A massive dark figure superimposed himself on his host as the man finished his second call to a small room in a distant land. A different sort of army would soon be mobilized, the strength of their hatred strengthening and rejuvenating his forces....taking the other side by surprise.

They would win. He could feel it.

He panted with the strength of his growing anticipation, his mouth dry, thirsting for it. He could feel the consummation so close ahead...so close. It was like a shout in the core of his being, a drug he'd been craving for years.

The last such fragrance of death and destruction had been too contaminated, the shock and grief of millions bringing much-needed energy, though tainted by the addition of unexpected prayer to the great Enemy.

It had been so perfect! The attack so carefully planned, so coordinated, the jihadists so malleable to their devious suggestions, convinced that as their speeding aircraft found their targets, they would be in heaven. He barked with pleasure, remembering their subsequent shock and despair.

But then came the prayers! He winced back from even the memory of the blazing Presence that had descended on the nation—on the world—as millions who had never prayed before dropped to their knees.

He didn't understand it. How could they have looked at the devastation unfolding over and over on their television screens and *prayed?* He paced the room, deciding, as always, that it must have been too paltry, the visual shock of the destruction giving way to the reality of only several thousand lives lost. This time...this time there would be no one untouched, no one who wasn't caught up in the chaos. Millions would die...the systems would fail...the nation would be in chaos...and they would turn from their God.

The great dark being, like the man below him, shook, trembled, crazed with anticipation. It was only hours now...only hours.

☆ ☆ ☆

Mr. Mohammed put down the phone and rose from his bed. He slipped out into a long, dark hallway, pulling on a cloak against the chill. He knocked on doors, sharp raps awakening the people within.

One by one, men joined him, some carrying their weapons slung about with rounds of ammunition. As always, they were alert and ready to move.

"We are not moving tonight," Mr. Mohammed told them, his eyes burning with urgency. "But we must seek Allah, petition his favor. The plan is precarious, resting on the edge of a knife. Allah will see it done."

His men murmured agreement, moving toward the space they had designated as their prayer room. Mr. Mohammed moved down the hallway and started to knock on a few more doors. Then he stopped.

No. These last ones were not pure of heart. They were of double mind about the plan, had searched the words of the Prophet and had several times brought questions about their course. They had not understood the brutal necessity and purity of taking the sword to the infidel until they capitulated or were overrun. They were influenced by the traitors in their land, the imams who sold themselves to the infidels, who spouted lies about protecting the innocent and the young, about promoting peace. The traitors even dared to say that it was the true believers—those fighting the infidel—who were betraying Islam!

He had memorized the words of the Prophet from cover to cover. And where there were contradictions, he was sure he knew the will of his god. Only with full submission to Allah would the world be at peace. And if that submission had to be forced—so be it.

No, these young ones could not be trusted to pray with pure hearts. He would let them sleep.

A great, shining being kept a wary eye on the proceedings. Watched as the men knelt on their prayer mats, with chanted prayers on their lips and destruction in their hearts. These lost children thought they were serving the one true God, the creator of heaven and earth, thought they were doing His will.

They did not know how deceived they were.

Mary sighed at the mountain of work Doug had left undone. And he hadn't even called back in. She decided to take a fifteen-minute break and go down to the cafe-

THE LIGHTS OF TENTH STREET 409

teria. She was going to need some strong coffee to see her through the rest of *this* day.

When she returned, the remaining assistants had gathered around the desk of Jordan's secretary, talking in low, perplexed voices.

"What's going on?" Mary asked. "Can't any of us get out of here on New Year's Eve?"

"I'm leaving soon," Jordan's secretary said. "I'm not sticking around just in *case* he comes back. We can finish all his projects the day after tomorrow for all I care."

"Jordan left already?"

"In a hurry." The secretary rolled his eyes. "He's been so weird lately. I have no idea what he's doing. The COO just came by with a question, and he was clueless, too. And look at this." She glanced around to make sure none of the few remaining executives were in sight, then led the little group into Jordan's office.

"See?"

In an oversized ashtray on the desk, burnt and almost unrecognizable, lay a computer disk.

"That's the disk that Doug brought down just an hour or two ago."

"That *is* weird," Mary said.

"And then he ran out without telling me where he was going or when he'd be back." She made an exasperated noise and led the group back out of Jordan's office, closing and locking the door behind her. "So I'm not waiting around."

The gathering broke up as the secretary turned off her computer and tucked her files away. Mary made a beeline down the hall, her mind whirring with awful suspicions. She walked faster and faster, bursting into Doug's office and staring at his desk.

His computer was missing.

She ran to her own desk and called Doug's cell phone. It went straight to voice mail, as it sometimes did when another person was calling in at precisely the same time. She left a message about the burned disk, the missing computer.

"Call me back, would you? This is all too strange."

"I think this is it." Ronnie turned into the covered parking lot and pressed the redial button on her cell phone. Doug answered almost at once.

"I'm in the parking lot."

"Me, too. I just found a space. We can go in together."

Within seconds, the occupants of the two cars had spotted each other. Doug waited while Ronnie parked. He pulled the Palm Pilot out of his coat pocket to give to Ronnie. She should be the one to carry it in.

☆ ☆ ☆

About forty feet down the street, two men in a nondescript car were jerked to attention by the buzz of a radio. It gave three prearranged beeps, then a male voice announced that the merchandise had been shoplifted and all units should be on high alert. If the merchandise was found, it should be brought back to headquarters immediately.

The driver of the car looked at the clock. They had been sitting in that spot down from the FBI building for about twenty minutes—on the verge of too long. He stared down the road toward the covered lot, impatient, waiting for their relief unit to turn in, then sat bolt upright.

His partner jumped in his seat. "What?"

"There." The driver jabbed his finger forward. "See those girls…is that them?"

His partner took one look, then scrambled out of the car. The driver turned the ignition key and pulled out of his spot, moving slowly. He whistled to himself in anticipation as he crept forward.

"That's our entrance, right there." Doug pointed at one of several gates with various FBI signage. Through the heavily barred gate, he could see two agents waiting for them, deep in conversation. He checked to be sure no traffic was speeding down the street, and stepped off the curb. "Let's go."

Ronnie heard running footsteps and turned her head. A man was advancing fast, his eyes intent, fixed on her. She gasped and pushed Tiffany ahead of her into the street, trying to run.

The man clamped his hand over her mouth and dragged her backwards, wrenching the Palm Pilot out of her hand. As he raised a truncheon to hit her head, she had a confused impression of Doug hurling his elbow at the side of the man's face.

Her captor dropped her, stumbling, and she screamed. In the middle of the street, a car had pulled up, and another man was wrestling with her roommate, a back door open and ready to receive her. Tiffany was scratching and biting, fighting like a cat, but losing the battle. Ronnie tried to run to her, only to be pushed forward with a mighty shove, propelled toward the melee and the waiting car. Shouts rang out from the gated complex across the street.

Doug was crumpled on the sidewalk, the truncheon by his side. Panting with terror, she watched as the second man dealt Tiffany a sweeping blow across the face, stunning her, pushing her in the car. As Ronnie was dragged around the car, she saw men running from the FBI building...uniformed men...running from the gates, shouting at the attackers to stop, drawing weapons.

The man holding Ronnie turned her toward the advancing guns. He opened the other back door of the car and pulled her in after him, squeezing her neck until she felt herself reeling.

Caliel had his sword out, advancing with the other members of the heavenly host, slashing through the armies of darkness drawn by their henchmen's call. Their blazing swords flashed with the urgency of those who wielded them, desperate to reach those in their care, desperate to overcome the unexpected strength of this onslaught. There was more at work here than they had realized—more dark prayers strengthening the arms of their foe.

He watched Doug move weakly, lifting his head from the sidewalk, his lips moving in prayer. Beset by an unbreakable army, Caliel cried out to the Lord of Hosts. It all came down to this!

A piercing bolt of purest light seared a path through the armies of darkness. The dark foes screamed, hands to their eyes, momentarily blinded.

Shouting his gratitude, Caliel dove for the car.

"Go! Go!" The man had his hand clamped around Ronnie's neck as she gasped in pain and terror, tears blurring her vision. He shouted at the driver. "They're coming! *Go!*"

Ronnie could hear the squealing of tires, but felt no forward movement. The driver's violent curses penetrated her fog. "It's not moving!"

"What do you mean it's not moving!"

Suddenly, she felt no pain, no terror, could hear no shouting or curses. The man still had his hand on her neck, but she felt no pressure. Everything seemed to be moving in slow motion except for her. The FBI men had drawn nearer to her side of the car, but their words seemed frozen on their lips. She turned her head the other way, saw her roommate slumped on the seat beside her, and knew—somehow, she knew—that was the direction she had to go.

Without thinking, without wondering how she was doing it, she slipped out from her attacker's vise grip and moved across the seat, reaching over Tiffany's unconscious body and gripping the door handle. She watched as the locked door opened under her hands and swung wide open at the barest push.

She stepped from the car, reaching back and lifting Tiffany out, weightless as a feather. She closed her eyes, swamped with the oddest feeling.

It almost felt like that day long ago when her dad had come up behind her as she tried to carry a heavy suitcase out of her room. She was saying good-bye, saying she could do it on her own, sniffling, tears streaking her face. Her dad had stood behind her, placing his hands over hers, holding both her and the impossible weight of the suitcase in his strong arms.

Ronnie held Tiffany's weightless body, feeling strong loving arms about her, tears again streaking her face.

Daddy...!

In a rush, time snapped into place and shots rang out, sending Ronnie to her knees, screaming again, holding her roommate. Doug crawled over and lay across the two girls, pinning them down. More shots! People surrounding the car, shouting!

Ronnie tried to tell Doug it wasn't necessary for him to protect her, tried to look into his eyes and tell him that everything would be all right. But he was glassy eyed and distant, heavy. She felt something warm and damp seep into her shirt, and her breath caught in her chest.

Running steps, helping hands, pulling Doug up and then laying him down, calling for a medic.

"...pressure to that wound!"

He flapped a hand feebly, trying to tell her something. She lifted herself up and scrambled over to him, tears flowing freely now, staring down in shock at the pain on his face...the man who had sacrificed himself for her. Such sacrifice...for her.

"Doug!" She saw the red wetness in the middle of his coat. "Why, Doug? Why?"

Another set of running steps, a man staring down at her. "Are you Ronnie? Is this Tiffany?"

She nodded, torn, as many hands lifted her up and bore her away. She looked back amid the crush. "Doug! Tiff!"

"We'll take care of them, ma'am. We need to hustle."

She tried to protest, despair threatening to swamp her, but the many men around her were like a rolling brick wall, unhearing, inexorable.

Just as they propelled her through the gates, a voice shouted after them. The man who led the pack stopped and looked back to see a female agent run up with something in her hand.

"The male victim said this device was in the car." She held out the Palm Pilot, its screen shattered. "He managed to gasp that out before..." she glanced at Ronnie. "Well, before he went unconscious."

"He's dead, isn't he?" Ronnie screamed. "He's dead!"

"I don't know if he's dead. He's losing a lot of blood, and he's unconscious. That's all I know."

Ronnie allowed herself to be tugged into the safety of the building, around corners and through several offices, great sobs racking her body.

Caliel dealt a swift, furious blow to the demon responsible and watched him vanish into blackness. Caliel knelt beside the man of God, his face as anguished as that of the humans feverishly at work about his still form.

He looked up. "O Ancient of Days, spare this man. Spare his family sorrow upon sorrow."

The answer came back to him, and he placed his great hands on the small chest, bowing his head. All around him, his troops, weary and battle-scarred, rank upon rank, went to their knees.

And Jesus stood among them. A thrill ran through the ranks as it had every time they watched, every time they saw the hand of the Healer at work.

"It is not yet your time, little one." The Lamb of God took the man by His hand, his voice solemn but deep with the breath of joy. "Awake. For you have much yet to do."

The man's eyes opened, and he looked with wonder at the shining figures all around him...at the One figure that mattered.

"Jesus," he whispered. "My Jesus."

The Lord smiled, caressed the dirt-streaked brow, and vanished.

SIXTY

Doug sat up, and the medic leaning over him shrieked and put her hand to her heart.

"O Jesus, O Jesus." The woman was panting, her eyes wild. "O dear God."

"You prayed, didn't you?" Doug said.

"I did—I always do. But I didn't think—O dear, sweet Jesus." She put her hands to her mouth, tears leaping to her eyes. "I've never seen—I mean—I lost your pulse!" She gulped several times, almost hyperventilating.

"Thank you." Doug stood up, drawing cries of astonishment from the many people in the area. He looked down at her. "Tell these people what happened, what the Lord has done. I've got to get inside. I was told—" his eyes twinkled— "that I have much to do."

He left the woman stammering to explain what happened to dozens of people with stretched faces, willing to suspend disbelief in what they had seen with their own eyes. Doug advanced through the gate and came to the security area, where he explained who he was. While they made the calls, he looked down at his blood-saturated coat, fingering the neat hole, feeling his own firm skin beneath. In a few hours he would probably be really freaked out by all this. But right now he knew, somehow, that their work was urgent, that time was drawing short.

He heard a short beep in his breast pocket and realized with surprise that his cell phone was still there, undamaged, and that someone must have left him a message. He was listening to Mary's voice mail about Jordan's odd behavior when he heard the sound of running steps.

The man who had taken Ronnie away burst through the turnstiles and just stood, staring at him in shock. He swore. Then swore again.

Doug smiled, turned off his phone, and shook the man's hand. "I think there's something better to say at this point. I'll explain as we go."

Ronnie sobbed in the arms of an uncomfortable-looking woman, a complete stranger. The female agent patted the young dancer on the back, saying "There,

there" like a broken record. Her boss had left, running back toward the entrance, leaving them alone.

Ronnie shuddered. She had gone to the Turners for help, and now Doug was dead, killed protecting her. And after such a miraculous, unearthly escape! How could she face Sherry...the kids...those sweet kids? Fresh weeping, hopeless tears. It was all so senseless.

She heard quiet footsteps, heard a man's voice soft, telling someone nearby that he'd like to speak with her alone for a few minutes. She felt someone crouching beside her chair.

"Ronnie."

Something in the voice was on the verge of laughing. She jerked her head upright, then screamed in shock and delight, jumping up and hugging Doug with all her might. Almost as suddenly, she pushed him away, terrified.

"Oh, I'm sorry! I must have hurt you!"

"No." Doug had a strange look on his face. "No, you didn't. God healed me, Ronnie. I can hardly believe it myself. But people were praying, and Jesus came and healed me."

Ronnie took another step backwards. "But your coat—the blood. There's the hole right there! How could you be standing here? Take your coat off! I want to see!"

Doug removed his coat and laid it on a nearby chair. Then he unbuttoned his shirt, his own hands stained with the blood that spread across its front. He held it open so Ronnie could see the smooth skin, unbroken.

Shaking, she reached out a hand to touch where the bullet must have gone in. Nothing. She felt herself growing faint and looked up at his face.

Doug smiled, and shrugged. "Someone else, long ago, wanted this sort of physical proof about Jesus himself, Ronnie. It's okay. But soon—very soon—you and I need to have a serious talk. God is doing a lot to get your attention. He has chosen you to be in the middle of something very important, but I know what He wants the most is you."

Ronnie felt disconnected from reality. She could only nod as people began streaming into the room.

"Yoo-hoo!" After the shortest of knocks, Jo poked her head into the house and looked around.

"I'm in the kitchen!" Sherry's distant voice carried through the sweeping front hall. "Come on in!"

Sherry accepted a kiss on the cheek from Vance, and thanked Jo for the bouquet of flowers she'd brought.

"Go put them in that vase, would you?" She gestured with her elbow, about the only part of her that wasn't covered with flour.

"What are you making? It smells great." Jo looked over, curious, as she held the vase under the kitchen faucet.

"Oh—well, I had a little time since Doug's still down at the FBI. So I figured I should make a fun New Year's Eve cake."

"Yum." Vance tried to dip his finger in the icing bowl and got his hand slapped. "Hey!"

Jo laughed. "So Doug's still down there. How's it going, do you know?"

"He called me before they went into a big meeting of some kind—he sounded really odd. Said he had something amazing to tell me, but didn't have time to elaborate before he had to go. He was turning off his cell phone for an hour or two, he said."

"So we don't know when he'll be back?" Vance said.

"Nope. He did ask us to pray for them; said there were some weird things going on, and it seemed urgent. The FBI was taking the whole thing ultraseriously."

Vance looked at the clock. "I wonder if he'll even be back before midnight."

Sherry gave her guests an apologetic smile. "Me, too. I'm sorry."

"Please don't worry about that," Jo said. "We're just glad we could be here."

Vance gave an emphatic nod. "I'd want to be here anyway, just so you're not alone."

"Thanks." Sherry hugged both friends in turn.

"And while we're thinking of it," Vance added, "let's pray for a minute."

Standing in the kitchen, amid the scattered pots and pans, flour and spices, the little group again approached the throne of grace.

Jordan's Mercedes sped down the street, piercing the late-afternoon rays like a black bullet, his face calm and deliberate. The two men followed him in a different car, ready to be sent off or pressed into service at a moment's notice.

Jordan's manner was deadly calm, but inside a voice was rising, raging that the plan was coming apart, that something had to be done.

He screeched around a few corners, then pressed redial on his cell phone.

"I'm almost there. We'll know in a minute."

On the other end of the line, Jordan could hear Tyson shouting for someone in the background to hustle. He came back on the line. "Let me know what you find.

And I just got the final word, Chief. Unless—well, unless something goes wrong, we're set for tonight. The networks' schedules are final; the ad is locked in place for one minute after midnight; the code is ready for broadcast. Just six more hours."

Jordan nodded as he watched two frantic pedestrians leap out of his way. "Six more hours. The supplications will carry us through. Nothing will go wrong. We'll see to that."

The supplications will carry us through?

What did that mean? What was up with this guy? Tyson rolled his eyes, glad Proxy couldn't see him.

"Uh...sure, Chief. He's got no reason to suspect you. Call me back once you know."

Jordan clicked off his phone and pulled into the subdivision, into the appropriate driveway. He watched in his rearview mirror as the other car found an empty spot on the crowded street with a direct view to the front door.

He got out and motioned for the men to stay put for the moment, then walked calmly up the path and rang the doorbell.

A young boy answered the door.

"Hello, Brandon. Is your daddy home?"

Tyson had barely hung up the phone when it buzzed again. One of his lieutenants.

He listened in growing fury to the news. The replacement shift had arrived at the FBI, only to find the street in chaos, the sound of gunfire ringing through the early evening. The men had run down the sidewalk, getting as close to the action as they could, mingling with a growing crowd. Their colleagues' car, recently riddled with bullets, was in the middle of the street, agents swarming everywhere. It looked like a man was down on the other side of the car, being worked over by paramedics. They couldn't get a good view; didn't know who it was.

Tyson clenched his eyes shut as if he could make the nightmare disappear.

"Could it have been one of our men?"

"Unclear. They thought our guys might have been inside the car, but couldn't tell if they were alive or dead."

"And no sign of the girls?"

"Not that they could see."

"So we don't know how our men were found out, or what they saw before all this happened?"

"No, sir." The lieutenant had a note of satisfaction in his voice. "But I do have one piece of good news for you."

"And what is that?"

"They got close enough to see a woman agent retrieve that device you were looking for—like a Palm Pilot—from the car and run it inside."

"And why is that good news?"

"Because it was shattered, completely destroyed. Bullet must've hit it—or our guys broke it on purpose when the gig was up. The replacement team left the scene to call in the news when they saw that."

"Tell them to get back there and keep watch."

"Already done."

Tyson hung up and his eyes narrowed as he considered the ramifications, a cold excitement again beginning to build in his core. The FBI might have the girls—probably had the girls—but they didn't have the file. What damage could the whores really do spilling their guts for hours?

He started smiling, glee breaking out on his face for the first time in twenty-four hours. This was a gift from the gods! It was perfect! The girls would have quite a story to tell. The meticulous men and women of the FBI would take their statements and keep them there, talking, questioning them, for hours…and hours.

And they only needed six.

It was going to work!

Tyson pulled up his e-mail account and typed out an urgent prearranged message to the members of the S-Group. They would all be wrapping up their affairs, finalizing their financial arrangements, making ready to head to the airport…and would wing off into the darkness as the corrupted land exploded into chaos.

The room was filling up fast with people—hardened FBI agents sprouting notebooks, laptop computers, and tape recorders.

Their leader—the man who had pulled Ronnie from the street—identified himself as Special-Agent-In-Charge Paul Jackson. He swept his arm around the packed conference room, introducing the group merely as "my team," then took a seat at the end of the long table.

Doug and Ronnie sat in comfortable chairs immediately to his right, with the others standing or sitting around the conference table in no apparent order. Agent-in-Charge Jackson pointed toward the empty chair beside Ronnie and said that, with luck, her friend Tiffany would be joining them soon.

He was explaining that the young lady was fine, she just had a slight concussion, when the door opened behind them and Tiffany was ushered in, looking slightly sheepish.

She sat down beside Ronnie, who gave her a relieved hug.

"Now." All eyes in the room turned to Agent Jackson as he stood. "As an update, we've heard from our colleagues on the police force that they took statements from all the club employees, but that our agent was not among them. She was apparently removed by force only moments before law enforcement officials arrived. There has been no further contact with her." His deep voice was heavy with regret. "And then we received a string of phone calls from Mr. Turner here, trying to call in some information that we eventually figured out—once we'd put all the pieces together—was extremely relevant. So now we very much need to hear what our guests have to tell us. I'd like to ask Ronnie Hanover to start."

The room suddenly became very quiet as Agent Jackson invited her to tell of the events of the last twenty-four hours, how she came to be in the possession of the Palm Pilot, and anything else of import she could think of.

Ronnie's voice sounded small in her ears as she relayed the story, trying not to tear up as she told how Maris had drawn off the men, allowing Ronnie to escape.

Doug picked up the story, explaining how, with no immediate response from the FBI, he had taken the Palm Pilot into work to see if his boss could decrypt it. He described the young whiz kid breaking into the device and finding the encrypted file Maris had downloaded. Described how he'd given his boss, Jordan, a copy of the file on disk. Described, with slow puzzlement, the message Mary had left about Jordan burning the disk, and how someone had broken into his office and taken his computer.

After a long moment, Agent Jackson pulled something out of a box at his side and laid it on the table. Ronnie strained forward and saw Maris's Palm Pilot, shattered beyond repair.

"Can...can you fix it?" Ronnie stammered.

"I'm afraid not." Agent Jackson's voice was grim. "Unless you can provide us with any new information, we may be back at square one. So we need to get into some more detailed questions."

"Excuse me. Can I cut in?" Doug's voice broke the depressed silence.

"Certainly."

He got up and went over to his bloody coat, still lying across a chair by the door. "I disobeyed whichever FBI agent I spoke with, when he told me to leave my office immediately."

A man across the room spoke up, surprised. "That was me."

"Well, sorry. But I'm glad I didn't do what you told me." He fished in the pocket of his coat and pulled out a disk. "I took an extra minute and made a copy of the encrypted file."

The room exploded in astonishment as Doug brought the disk over to Agent Jackson, who began to laugh, shaking his head.

"You might make a believer out of me yet, Mr. Turner!" He tossed the disk down the table to one of the notebook-wielding agents. "Get someone working on that right away. If it's a Bureau encryption, you'll need to check the relevant ops file for the code."

"Yes, sir." The young man darted out the door, disk in hand.

Agent Jackson turned to another woman, sitting halfway down the table. "And get someone looking into the background of Mr. Turner's boss—" he flashed a glance at Doug—"what's his name?"

Doug gave the agent Jordan's full name and what little he knew of his personal information. Once the woman had also hurried out the door, Doug turned back to Agent Jackson, his voice slow.

"But—how could Jordan be involved in this? He's just a businessman. I don't understand."

"I don't know, Mr. Turner, but it seems clear that he must be, somehow." He raised an eyebrow as if curious. "That surprises you?"

Doug felt as if his world were turning upside down and rearranging itself while he watched, dumbfounded. "But...what you're saying...is that there's a connection between my boss and these girls sitting here."

"Looks like it."

SIXTY-ONE

S pecial Agent-In-Charge Paul Jackson again stood at the front of the room, his voice commanding attention as he asked for silence. He pushed back a panel in the wall, revealing a large video screen, then lifted a remote control and pushed a few buttons.

The lights in the conference room dimmed just slightly, and an image appeared on the screen.

Ronnie and Tiffany both gasped. It was a picture of Maris—an official FBI picture, with profile information posted beside it.

Agent Jackson's manner was hurried. He gestured to a senior-looking man at the table. "For our visitors, and for those in this room who aren't already up to speed, I'd like to introduce Agent McKendrick from the New York Bureau office. He'll take it from here."

Agent McKendrick took Agent Jackson's place at the front of the room. He looked directly at the three visitors, his face severe.

"For reasons I will explain shortly, I'm about to discuss some matters rarely shared outside the Bureau. This information must not be repeated outside of this room, to anyone. Is that clear?"

The three nodded, and he continued. "I believe that if you have this information, you can help us put the pieces of the puzzle together more quickly. As you may know, the New York office of the FBI has one of the most experienced teams in combating everything from organized crime to counterterrorism.

"The woman you know as Maris is actually Larissa Madrid, a fourteen-year veteran of the Bureau. For several years, the Bureau has been following the operations of a large, well-organized national crime ring that appeared to be based not out of the usual cities, such as New York or Chicago, but out of the Atlanta metropolitan area. Agent Madrid—I'll call her Maris for your sake—moved to Atlanta to apply for a job at The Challenger, which was one of the establishments we had identified as playing a leading role in the crime ring."

Another picture appeared on the screen. Marco, caught on camera in the staff hallway, unaware the photograph was being taken.

"Maris spent most of her time monitoring this man and his contacts with the

421

larger ring. Marco, the manager of the club, was believed to be one of the top operatives, having ascended in trust and power after his predecessor was bumped off.

"Maris was fairly new on the job when Marco's predecessor blabbered to the club one night about a secret drug-running tunnel off the coast of Florida. She passed the information along to us, we conveyed it to the local authorities, and the tunnel was raided. Marco's predecessor was bumped off shortly thereafter, and we learned a valuable lesson about the quick-trigger tactics of this particular crime ring. We also began to suspect that there was something else going on."

He gestured to the screen as another photograph appeared. Another official FBI picture. The agent gave Ronnie and Tiffany a few moments to look at the picture, then asked. "Have you ever seen this person before?"

Ronnie shook her head, but Tiffany frowned. "It's been a long time—"

"Yes, it would've been over a year." The agent looked interested. "Go on."

"I *think* I remember Maris talking to someone I took for a common street punk, outside the club a couple times. The first time I was worried for her safety, but she waved me off and said it was okay. I think this was the guy she was talking to. But he sure didn't look like an FBI agent."

"No, he was one of our best undercover operatives. He went by the moniker of Snoop and infiltrated the crime ring, acting as an informant. We gave him bits of information to pass along so he'd be more and more trusted by the higher-ups. And it worked. He eventually learned some big changes were coming; there were some major reshufflings going on. He learned that the leader of the entire national ring—a man known only as Proxy, who somehow directed the operations from afar—that Proxy was ready to do something very different. The higher-ups were clearly preparing for *something*. Snoop understood it to be a new business line, but felt it would be vastly different from one of the usual criminal sidelines of drugs or prostitution."

Agent McKendrick turned back to the screen, not seeing the uncomfortable expressions that crossed the young dancers' faces. He sighed. "Unfortunately, Snoop was trying to get more involved in the operations side of the ring, and he got caught in a botched op. Our communications with local police broke down, and since they didn't get the message that we had an undercover agent trying to gain high-level trust, they conducted an unexpected raid. Snoop insisted on going back to business afterward, believing that the value of his information would keep him safe. Unfortunately, we never heard from him again. He was eliminated before he could learn and pass along the details of just what it was that the leadership was branching into. But Maris spent the next year on heightened alert because of his murder, and she gathered a great deal of good information.

"Over the course of the year, she became convinced that the people involved were not normal criminal masterminds. In fact, based on conversations she over-heard, and people who met with Marco at the club—and elsewhere, when she managed to tail them—she became convinced that there was planning going on for a number of breaches of homeland security. Of most concern, she believed they were arranging some sort of massive terrorist attack inside the United States."

"You mean—are you saying that Marco was a *terrorist?*" Ronnie said.

"A terrorist, a helper of terrorists; I don't know what you'd call it. But certainly, he appeared to be one of the top operatives of the group, and the group was plan-ning something. We just don't know *what.*"

"Well, can't you get someone else to infiltrate the team again?" Tiffany asked. "I guess the club would be too risky, but what about like what this Snoop person did?"

"It's too late for that. We believe there may already be an attack planned and set in motion. We don't have much time to stop it. That's frankly why we're hoping that the information you brought with you—and what you carry in your heads—might be the key to unlocking the puzzle."

"Why the urgency?" Doug asked. "I mean, I feel it, too—but if you don't know what the plan is, why do you think it's so urgent?"

"Because, Mr. Turner, Marco appears to have been taken out. We don't know why—whether he knew too much, whether he was viewed as disloyal for some rea-son, we don't know. But he was killed. In our experience, when a top-level operative is killed unexpectedly, it's usually a signal that something major is about to happen, and happen quickly.

"Although it's not quite the same, an infamous example of this was the assassi-nation of Ahmed Shah Massoud, the opposition leader of the Northern Alliance in Afghanistan just two days before the 9/11 attacks. The terrorist masterminds knew that the U.S. would respond militarily in Afghanistan and that Massoud was the one man able to unify the opposition troops and lead the country if the terrorist network was driven out. So he had to be taken out before the 9/11 attacks could proceed. When he was assassinated, our colleagues at the CIA knew that something must be coming, but they didn't learn what, in time.

"So in this case, we can only move ahead with all speed and try to ascertain whatever we can about what may be coming, in the hopes that we can do some-thing to stop it."

Doug felt light-headed. No wonder the Lord had moved heaven and earth to get them all together in this room right now. He prayed that they would be able to put the pieces of the puzzle together in time.

☆ ☆ ☆

"No, Jordan, I'm sorry." Sherry stared at Doug's boss, puzzled. "He's not here. He had to go to an urgent meeting downtown."

Sherry had offered Jordan a drink, had offered him a seat, but the man just stood in the middle of the foyer, a strange look in his eyes. Jo and Vance watched the exchange from the kitchen doorway.

"What meeting?" Jordan asked. "His phone is turned off. Where is he?"

Sherry started to open her mouth and felt almost as if she was being physically restrained. She smiled at Jordan and gave him an apologetic shrug.

"I wish I could tell you, but it's a confidential matter. A personal thing...nothing related to work."

She heard the chirp of Jordan's cell phone at his belt, and Jordan checked the display.

"I'll be right back."

He walked out the still-open front door and down the path until he was out of earshot.

Sherry heard Vance come up behind her, his brows raised to the ceiling. "That was strange."

"Yes." Sherry shivered. "He's not usually this...odd."

Tyson was sending last-minute e-mails, checking in with his various lieutenants as he talked to Proxy. He relayed the welcome news about the shattered Palm Pilot, sure Proxy would be as relieved as he. Instead, he was met with stony silence.

"He had the file on his computer, you know. I checked." Proxy's voice was cold. "He could have made a copy."

Tyson swore. "I didn't know that, no. But what are the chances that he actually did make a copy? And even so, what are the chances that the Bureau can figure out anything critical in just a few hours? The Palm Pilot—and all the information Maris had stored there—are gone."

"We can't risk it." Proxy's voice went distant again. "We must ensure that nothing goes wrong."

He explained what he had in mind, and Tyson allowed himself a cold smile. The man might be odd at times, but he was a strategic genius.

"Good," Tyson said. "Of course, it won't work unless you can get in touch with Doug."

"He's got to check his messages or answer his cell phone eventually. After all, he's a good family man. And his family will be wondering about him."

Doug watched as Agent McKendrick sat down beside Ronnie and Tiffany, a sheaf of papers at his side.

"It's hard to know where to start digging, especially if time is short. So let's start with the reports Maris filed over the past year. I'll walk you through what she found and what she surmised, and see if you can provide more details that will crack open an area for further inquiry."

He picked up the first piece of paper, but before he could open his mouth, the door burst open behind him and the young agent hurried back in with the disk.

Agent-in-Charge Jackson gestured the young man over.

"Sir, we cracked the file. It's a basic audio file containing machine noise of some kind. We haven't had time to analyze it, so we don't have a guess as to its purpose."

"Play it for us, would you...in case it means anything to any of us or our guests."

The young man slipped the disk into his laptop and fiddled with the settings. After a few moments, a faint sound emanated from the laptop's speakers. Machine noise, as he had said.

One of the men across the room spoke up. "Three years ago I worked at headquarters—the decoding department. There's something...familiar about that, but I can't put my finger on it."

Agent Jackson barked at him. "Well, get out there and help them." He turned to the young man. "Get a team of people together and get every brain working on what this could possibly be. Come back once you have some reasonable ideas, even if you're not sure what the final answer is. We'll run it by everyone in the room and see if it breaks something loose. Understand?"

"Yes, sir!"

The young man and the decoding expert hurried out, just as a female agent stuck her head back in, waving a file at Agent Jackson.

"Speak!" he growled at her. "Time is ticking. What'd you find?"

The woman rapidly described what she had found in Jordan's file. In the military as a young man, served in intelligence with several technical specialties, including decryption, satellite development, and strategic security. Posted in Iran (before the fall of the Shah), then Japan, then the Pentagon before leaving the service. He was an early adopter of computer technology, understanding computers and programming before most people knew what computers were. After the service, he worked in the security industry, regarded as not only a great technician but a strategic thinker and good businessman. Upright citizen, serving on many corporate and civic boards. Not a blemish, except for an odd note from his Iran days that he had taken too much time off, earning a reprimand for disappearing for weeks at a time to enjoy the countryside (he had said).

The woman flipped a page and kept reading. In recent years, Jordan started an information-technology company with his brother: the company—she nodded in Doug's direction—where Mr. Turner now worked. After the death of his brother last year, Jordan took full control of the enterprise, and it appeared to be prospering, making a number of aggressive but apparently profitable acquisitions, partnerships, and other deals.

The woman set the file down on the table beside Doug.

Agent McKendrick sighed. "So nothing obvious."

"Not right now, sir."

Doug pulled the thin file toward him and looked at the picture stapled to the top. It was a digital photo from the company's official website, Jordan smiling in his authoritative way and looking anything but a menace to society. There was just no way that Jordan was involved in this.

"What's that?" Ronnie asked.

He lifted the file so she could see the photo. "That's my boss."

Her eyes widened. "But…that's the mean guy from the boat party!"

"What?"

She drew Tiffany's attention to the picture. "Remember that first boat party I did, when I was supposed to hook up with some finance big-shot? I told you about that guy on the boat who was furious when the man left because his son got hurt? This is that guy."

Doug closed his eyes, disbelieving, then opened them again and looked at the girl beside him. "You were supposed to hook up with a finance big-shot that day?"

"Yeah, they told me just to keep him company, but I overheard Marco talking about him, and I think they wanted to compromise him somehow. But then his son got hurt and he left before I'd hardly met him."

"That was me."

"*What?*" Ronnie sat straight up in her chair, drawing curious stares from the others around the table. Agent McKendrick and the female agent broke off their conversation and looked toward them.

"That was me." Doug tapped the photo, his mind whirring. "And what you're saying is that my boss and your boss were trying to use you to compromise me that day. But Brandon broke his arm, and I never went on the boat."

At Agent McKendrick's curious look, Doug briefly relayed what they had just discovered. The female agent said she'd continue to dig into Jordan's background, and left the room.

"Well." Agent McKendrick turned to the rest of the room. "Since we don't have anything on that end yet, let's go through Maris's reports and see if we break something loose. Quickly."

Ronnie was getting tired, her voice raw from hours of talking, her mind blank from trying to remember the smallest details of her club life over the past year. It was after ten o'clock, and she desperately needed a cup of coffee. Beside her, Tiffany looked equally worn.

Agents McKendrick and Jackson had gone through the weekly—sometimes daily—reports Maris filed electronically, describing her findings, her theories. From the frustrated expressions on their faces, Ronnie knew they were still just dancing around the edges, hitting on nothing.

"Sorry to ruin your New Year's Eve like this," Agent Jackson said to the three visitors. "Let's at least take a coffee break, get you some food, and we'll continue in fifteen minutes. Okay?"

"I need to call my wife." Doug spoke up for the first time in two hours. "She's going to be worried."

Agents Jackson and McKendrick looked at each other, hesitating.

"Come on, I won't tell her anything. It's almost ten-thirty and I'm missing our own New Year's party."

Agent McKendrick waved his permission. Doug turned on his cell phone as the agent turned away and began talking to someone about bringing food in.

Before Doug could dial, the phone rang in his hand. He didn't recognize the number.

"Hello?"

"Hello, Doug. You're at the FBI, aren't you?"

Doug looked around the bustling room, beginning to feel a strange knot in his stomach. "Yes."

"I want you to leave the room—wherever you are—and go to the men's room. Somewhere you can be alone. Somewhere we can talk." The voice was eerily calm. "Go now, Doug."

Doug left the room and walked down a hallway until he found a single-person bathroom. He went in and locked the door behind him.

"Okay, Jordan, what gives?"

SHAUNTI FELDHAHN

"You gave them the disk, didn't you?"

Malice came clearly through the phone line. Doug caught his breath, answering without thought. "Yes."

"I thought so." There was an odd noise, like a wry chuckle. "Isn't it ironic that it's our resident boy scout who wants to throw a wrench in the works? Our religious nut who wants to tear down a divinely crafted plan? Yes, how ironic."

"Jordan—what are you talking about?"

"Well, you know what? You're not going to win. You and your new friends downtown. I'll see to that. You know where I am, Doug? You know where? Just take a guess."

"I don't know. Where?"

There was a moment of silence on the phone, some rough movement. Then a small, shaky voice came clearly through the other end of the line.

"Daddy?"

"Genna! Genna, baby, are you okay?"

The phone was taken away, and Jordan was back on the line. "Now, Doug, listen to me. Are you listening?"

Doug could barely force out an affirmation. *O God, O God…* Doug couldn't find any other words to pray.

"Here's what we're going to do, Doug. You're going to go back into your nice meeting with the FBI, and you will see to it that they are misdirected in every way, that you take some nice long coffee breaks, that you answer their questions with long, rambling answers. I want you to waste a lot of time, Doug. Do you hear me?"

"Yes." Again, he forced the word out.

"By now, if the Feds are clever, they will have figured out that the audio file on that disk is meant for broadcast. They won't know what it's for or how it will be broadcast, and of course I'm not going to tell you that." Again, the deathly chuckle. "You didn't expect I would, did you, Doug?"

"No."

"But *I* know what it's for, and I can't afford for someone to stumble onto it and stop the broadcast. A broadcast, Doug, that will take place in precisely eighty-eight minutes."

Doug looked at his watch. Midnight. That would be midnight. His brain was slow to process the facts, his entire being focused on his family, on the terror in the voice of his baby girl.

"My family…"

"Your family, Doug, your sweet family, is at this moment tied up in your living room along with your friends, listening to me talk to you. Are you listening, Doug?"

"Yes."

"I have several guns trained on them, Doug, several hired men who will have no compunction about putting a bullet through the head of your sweet little girl. In fact, we'll start with her, if you don't cooperate."

"O God! Jordan, no! What do you want, Jordan? I'll do anything! Please…please let my family go. I'll come take their place. Take me!"

Another chuckle. "Now, isn't that just like our nice boy scout? Unfortunately, if you were to leave the FBI at high speed, questions would be asked and someone would follow. No, Doug. You stay there, obtuse and obstructionist as you possibly can, foiling all questions for the next—oh—eighty-five minutes or so. See, Doug, I have a way of knowing whether the broadcast is going to happen. I have a way of knowing whether it's being loaded, whether it's about to run. I'll be able to tell, Doug, looking at my nice little computer screen, whether you've been a good boy and led the FBI astray. Because if not, at one minute after midnight, a bullet goes into your daughter. Then your son. Then your friends. Are you listening, Doug?"

Doug couldn't even respond, his brain frozen.

"Then, of course, your wife. Of course—" again, the hideous chuckle—"I might tell our boys to take their time with her."

Doug felt as if he was going to throw up, to collapse. He wanted to fling the phone against the wall, shattering the voice on the other end.

"Are we clear, Doug? If I do not see what I need to see and hear what I need to hear at midnight—if I find that someone has tampered with our broadcast—I make the call. What's your decision, Doug?" The voice was suddenly hard. In the background, he heard the cocking of a gun, heard some stifled screams. "I have the gun pressed against your baby girl's head, Doug. What's your decision?"

"I'll do it!" Doug shouted into the phone, begging, crying. "I'll do it! Don't hurt them, please! Please!"

"And what will you do?"

"I'll draw them off!" He was weeping now, the image of little Genna with a gun to her head more than he could bear. "Please, Jordan, listen to me! I'll distract the FBI, waste their time. Just don't hurt them, please!"

"And if you should foolishly decide to tell the FBI, hoping they'll mount a rescue mission—as, of course, the macho men of the FBI like to do—we'll see you coming. Our boys are good at such things. And your family will be dead before your little commandos can reach the back door." He paused for effect. "So keep your bargain, boy scout. Your family's counting on you."

Click.

Doug leaned against the wall, shaking, retching with sobs, his hand pressed against his mouth. How on earth was he supposed to go back into that meeting, pretend everything was normal, when he felt that he couldn't even take a breath without throwing up?

He took several deep breaths. He walked over to the sink and splashed water on his face, then dried himself with a towel. He looked in the mirror, despairing. No way could he hide these red eyes.

He didn't even know how to pray. *O God…help, Lord!*

There came, then, a moment of supreme clarity, the certainty of what he must do. He felt the steadying hands of the Master on his shoulders, comforting him, holding him, giving him courage.

He went down on his knees on the cold tile floor and wept into his hands.

"Lord, I have to tell them, don't I? I have to tell them. There's so much more than my family at stake. I have to trust my family into Your hands, in order to save many, many more."

The image of Genna…Brandon…Sherry floated in his mind's eye, and his words came out as sobs. "But, Lord—how can You ask that? They'll kill them."

They'll kill them anyway.

Doug put his face in his hands, recognizing another truth with supreme clarity. "Lord, my family—my friends—have all accepted Jesus. If—if they die, they will go to be with you." He began to sob again. "I entrust them into your hands. O God, take care of my family. Protect them, heavenly Father, as I do what I know is Your will, this night."

Caliel reached out to strengthen the man of God as he rose from the floor, wiped his eyes, and made his shaky way down the hall to the conference room.

As Doug entered the room and prepared to make the irrevocable stand, Caliel's face was sober. For he did not know the outcome of this night, did not know what would come of the decisions of dark-hearted men. The Lord, in His unfathomable wisdom, had allowed individuals the free will they seemed to desire above all else. And the heavenly host had seen—time and again—the consequences of that free will. Consequences that, in the fallen world, often caused the Creator and His creation immeasurable pain.

The Lord had even given the ultimate sacrifice to show His love, to draw His children back to Himself. All they had to do—*all they had to do*—was grasp this sacrifice, this salvation, and it was theirs. But so many—so many—still insisted on going their own way. And so, many times, the gracious Father let them have their way—even knowing of the great damage that would come to the ones He loved.

Caliel lifted his prayers again to the Throne, feeling both the infinite goodness and justice of the Lord of Hosts. Only when the last trumpet blew would there be no more consequences of the sinful path chosen by the children of Adam and Eve. On that day, every knee would bow and every tongue would confess that Jesus was Lord. But until that day, some consequences of sin would not be overruled.

All around him, the heavenly host was poised, tense, waiting…for the word from the Throne.

SIXTY-TWO

Doug stepped back into the conference room, unable to feel his feet on the floor. At one side, the decoding expert was deep in conversation with the lead agents.

"...and since some of the code was inaudible, I think we're dealing with a frequency intended for broadcast of some kind. At a guess, it's intended to trigger a remote receiver. We haven't had time to dig into it, but the audio appears to have a pattern to it, sort of like what we used in Afghanistan to detonate bombs via satellite. At least—" he threw up his hands— "that's what we surmise at the moment. But it does seem like a broadcast signal."

"I can confirm that." Doug closed his eyes, willing himself to continue. He could feel everyone in the room turning to look at him. "It's intended for broadcast. At midnight tonight."

Doug felt Agent McKendrick guiding him back into his former seat. Dimly, out of the corner of his eye, he could see Ronnie and Tiffany staring at him.

"Doug...Doug!" Agent McKendrick finally got his attention. "How do you know that?"

Doug sent up a frantic prayer for peace, then looked the agent in the eye and recounted the entire phone call.

Within five minutes, the room was a hive of furious activity. Agent Jackson barked out orders, calling in a special SWAT team, giving hurried instructions, getting directions and descriptions about Doug's house and subdivision...and reassuring the anxious husband and father that every care would be taken.

Again and again, Doug pushed back pure terror and prayed, releasing the care of his family to the Lord's hands. Prayers coursed through his mind even as he answered questions, drew maps and diagrams, and watched a team of hardened men, led by Agent Jackson, run out the door. Every reflex screamed at Doug to go with them. But he knew—somehow, he knew—that he had to stay, that he had to see this through.

"How can you be so calm?" Ronnie had tears streaming down her cheeks, and

Tiffany looked drawn and worried. "How come you're not stomping around, screaming or something? How come you're not demanding to go with them?"

Doug turned his head, feeling the weight of his decision pressing in on him, making it difficult to breathe.

"I believe," he managed to croak out, "that this is what God told me to do. And if so—" he closed his eyes— "I have to trust my family to Him."

Ronnie pressed a shaking hand to her mouth, a new awareness creeping into her tear-stained eyes. Beside her, Tiffany pressed her lips together in a thin line of disagreement, and shook her head.

"Everyone!" Agent McKendrick, the remaining senior officer in the room, raised his hands for silence. "If what Doug learned is correct—and it's possible, of course, that he was deliberately misled—then we have a little more than one hour in which to avert some sort of attack. God help us."

Agent McKendrick looked to the side and spoke to one of the agents.

"Go make sure that we've informed Washington, and that they have informed the president. Make sure that the specialists at headquarters drop everything and dig into Jordan's background to see if they can come up with *anything* that would provide a clue."

The agent made a move toward the door.

"Wait!" Agent McKendrick thought another moment. "Snoop helped us track one of the principals—a man named Tyson Keene—to a private jet at the airport. Check the file, get the information, and see if we can put a hold on air traffic out of Atlanta. And get an APB out on all the principals!"

The agent nodded and hurried out.

"Now." The senior agent looked at the three visitors. "The stakes just got raised. We're talking about some sort of broadcast, most likely via satellite. Does that ring any bells for any of you?"

"Yes," Doug said. He described the deals he'd been blackmailed into approving, deals that had to do—among other things—with linking satellites and broadcast technology.

"So do you have any idea what these partnerships were to be used for?" Agent McKendrick asked.

Doug shook his head. "Dozens of things, I would've thought. I mean, looking back at it now, I think Jordan was setting up an infrastructure that would allow him a wide range of possibilities, not just one particular satellite broadcast. He had everything from telecommunications to defense contractors woven into the deal.

You could use satellite signals to broadcast anything. I feel like the answer is just so close, but I don't see it!"

One of the other agents jumped in with a question. "Was there any deal that you approved that specifically had to do with conventional broadcasting? I mean straightforward stuff, like television or radio?"

"No...well, sort of. But it was tangential, and wasn't just one broadcast. We set up the technical specs for a new advertising agency that was creating a series of high-profile television commercials."

"Television commercials." Ronnie had been hardly listening, not understanding the technical discussion. But now she broke in, looking sideways at Tiffany. "Television commercials?"

Tiffany sat up straight. "Which ones?"

The room was suddenly electric. Agent McKendrick seemed to hardly breathe as Doug racked his memory.

"Uh...it was months ago, and for us it was only a small deal. Oh, it was for Speed Shoes...for the series of advertisements that would culminate at the Super Bowl."

"That's it!" Tiffany almost shot out of her seat. "That's got to be it!" She turned to Agent McKendrick and explained about Marco asking her to broker a deal, to seduce Wade into agreeing to use their advertising agency to create the Speed Shoes commercials.

Agent McKendrick thought a second, then looked up at his team. "Reactions?"

A tall agent standing in the corner spoke up. "That audio file Mr. Turner brought in could be either simulcast beside or embedded in the audio of a television commercial. Easily. But then—" he looked slowly horrified. "But then, it could trigger a receiver anywhere in the country, anything within audio distance of an active television set!"

A young woman across the table was busy on her laptop, speaking to Tiffany and typing at the same time. "You said that the commercials were made in a series, right?"

"Yes."

"Didn't Maris's report say something about one of the dancers going to a gala for the grand opening of one of those commercials?"

Agent McKendrick started to dig back through his papers, but Tiffany spoke up. "Yeah, that was me."

The female agent was looking at something on her screen, scrolling downward through a list. "What date was that, do you know? If you can possibly remember, I'd like to cross-reference—"

"I couldn't ever forget." Tiffany shuddered. "It was the same night that the dam exploded and killed all those people."

Every head in the room lifted. Everyone stared at each other.

"The same night the dam exploded..." The female agent's eyes were wide as she tapped her keyboard. "Hold on—wait." She looked at Agent McKendrick. "The file says the incendiary device on the boat had a remote receiver attached. The origin of the signal was never discovered."

"What time was it?" Agent McKendrick stood, pacing, his voice rising. "What time was the explosion?"

"Says here, 9:32 P.M. Eastern time."

"Call headquarters right away—get them to call the networks and find out what time the commercial played that night!"

The young woman hurried out the door and was back in minutes, holding a cell phone. "Nine-thirty-two, boss. That's it. There's a signal embedded in those commercials!" She held out the cell phone. "Headquarters wants to talk to you."

Agent McKendrick snatched the phone, glaring at his watch, giving orders to someone on the other end. "Find out when the next Speed Shoes commercial is due to air."

He waited, tapping his foot, then his eyes widened as the answer came back. "One minute after midnight."

Ronnie watched, tense, as Agent McKendrick demanded to speak to someone much higher up in the chain of command. With clipped sentences, he relayed the substance of what they had learned, what they expected, what needed to be done.

"We need to find a way to get *every single* network and station carrying that commercial to *shut down,* and shut down right away. Just pull the plug on the whole broadcasting industry. We can't risk letting that signal get through, even once we pull the commercial. The signal might have been intended to be sent *alongside* the commercial, rather than embedded within it. And if that's the case, the signal could still be transmitted on top of blank air. The only way to be sure of safety is if there's nothing being broadcast!"

He listened to the other end of the phone line, sputtering with haste. "We've only got thirty minutes, man! I don't care if the television networks lose millions; we've got to make them understand!"

More listening, lips pressed together. "We'll do our best, sir, but there's no guarantee we'll be able to find out. We need to make the networks understand the risk even if we don't know exactly what the signal will detonate."

He waited through another long sentence, and shook his head. "We'll try, sir." He hung up and looked around the room. "They'll see what they can do, but they believe it'll be almost impossible to pull the plug in time. It'll take time—too much time—to reach and convince all the decision makers. And it's technically difficult to shut everything down with any speed. I need a better solution, team. We have thirty minutes. Anyone?"

The decoding expert had slipped back into the room. He slightly raised his hand. "We could create a dummy signal to overlay the other one, a signal that would counteract the original message."

Someone else shook their head. "Too much time—"

"But it would only take two minutes to create a mirror signal—"

"But it would take them too long to e-mail it out to all the stations and have them upload it in the right place. We need something that'll pull the plug on all broadcasting."

The female agent had been drumming her fingers on the keyboard, her expression grim. Suddenly, she sat up.

"The old Emergency Broadcasting System—what are they calling it now?"

Agent McKendrick lifted his head, his eyes sharp. "The Emergency Alert System."

"Isn't that designed to transmit emergency messages to the public without the broadcasting industry doing a thing?"

Agent McKendrick lifted his phone. "I don't know. We need to ask FEMA—"

"No, she's correct!" someone else said. "That's our solution! If we get a presidential order to initiate an alert, a bunch of television networks are required to broadcast the alerts. Actually, I think it's all automated—we send the signal out, it trips a secret code in the broadcaster's digital equipment, and the emergency alert is broadcast. It all happens within seconds."

"We've rarely used that system, and I don't think we've ever used it nationally," McKendrick said. "That may cause panic, but we don't have any other choice. What should the alert say?"

"The alert could even be blank if we wanted. The key is that it will *replace* whatever other signals would've been broadcast, and without alerting the perpetrators until that moment. Using the system might solve the panic problem, too, by the way. You could call it a test of the Emergency Alert System, although people would probably see through that pretty quickly." He frowned. "There may only be one problem: I remember there being a bit of a flap over the fact that the new digital equipment was required to have a storage capacity of only two minutes. So we'd have to trip the system right after midnight and hope that's the only time window the perpetrators can broadcast their signal."

"Maybe we should use the EAS broadcast not just to counteract any other signals," the female agent said, "but to warn people that there's an attack planned and instruct them to turn off their television sets immediately."

Agent McKendrick dialed his cell phone again, but shook his head as he waited for an answer. "You know people. They'd either panic or keep the television sets turned on just to see what's happening. And since we still don't know what the attack *is*, we can't just create general national panic." He straightened, listening to the cell phone. "Hello, sir, I think we have a better solution for you."

Ronnie listened with a feeling of unreality as he rapidly outlined the team's suggestion, fielding fast questions and objections. She felt a germ of terror begin to grow in her gut.

"At this point, I think we have to acknowledge that nothing is foolproof. And the EAS system is ready to go. Nothing else is going to accomplish the same level of penetration in time."

When he hung up, McKendrick gestured to another agent. "Call Paul Jackson and make sure he knows that the EAS will go on at exactly midnight. If they're going to extricate the hostages, it has to happen before then."

He leaned on the table, his countenance heavy. "And we still need to figure out what the signal will trigger. I hope to God this whole thing works."

Beside her, Ronnie could see Doug sitting quietly, head bowed, his lips moving in silent prayer. She wondered if God really did hear the prayers of one lone man…and whether God would hear the prayers of one scared stripper.

Fifteen minutes to midnight.

Sherry Turner shifted a little, wincing as the plastic cords cut into her wrists, and looked at the clock for the hundredth time.

Fifteen minutes until—what? Release? She knew better than that. She traded glances with Vance and Jo, white-faced and sober across the room, and saw the same knowledge in their eyes.

The madman who had suddenly emerged from Doug's trusted boss, the unearthly hate-filled being who had swept through their home like a scythe, would never just let them go. She could still feel the anticipation, the lust that had quivered in the air with his presence. Not sexual lust, despite what he had said to Doug, but lust for destruction, for carnage. There had been an evil glee in his face that did not abate when Doug promised to draw off the FBI.

They would kill them anyway.

Sherry looked at her two children, sitting brave and quiet on the sofa beside her. Every time she looked at them—their sweet little faces, not fully comprehending, not fully grasping the situation—her heart felt as if it would shatter all over again. There had been moments of terror among the children, but few tears. Sherry had willed herself to not cry, to not let herself be anything but loving and strong for her kids.

Across the room, tied securely in chairs pulled away from the dining room table, Vance and Jo continually watched their son, gauging his reactions, trying to comfort him as best they could.

Sherry's eyes flickered to the foyer, where one of Jordan's henchmen sat stony faced, his eyes trained on the two families, a heavy-looking pistol across his lap.

At the window beside him, the other henchman stood still as a statue at the front window, watching the yard, scanning the street. Sherry had no illusions that they would not carry out their threat of quick kills at the first sign of the FBI.

Earlier, one of the men had disappeared outside for a few minutes, and had come back telling his partner that the house was fully equipped with motion-detector lights. And, as Jordan had so clearly said, the hostages would be dead before the commandos reached the door.

If they were even coming. Sherry knew what her husband had promised—Jordan had told them of Doug's capitulation, his eyes afire with glee—though she wasn't sure she fully believed it.

The henchman in the chair got up and conferred with the man at the windows.

Sherry watched as Vance quietly tested his bonds. Each time their captors had drifted out of his sight, he had tried a new angle, with no success. His arms were securely tied behind the chair at his back. She watched, wincing at the inevitable little sounds, as he tried to stand, the clunky chair rising with him, fastened to his every move. He too grimaced, and sat back down, carefully lowering the back legs of the chair to the floor.

"Mommy?"

Sherry's head snapped around at the soft whisper. Brandon was leaning toward her.

She glanced at the two men, still huddled by the window, half-in and half-out of sight. Perhaps it was safe. And if they were all going to eternity in a few minutes, she welcomed a quiet conversation with her son. She could feel the tears pressing on the backs of her eyes. After all, she didn't know exactly what heaven would look like, didn't know whether or in what form the parent-child relationship would last. So she looked at the beloved little face, memorizing every line, and whispered back, trying to smile, to be brave.

"Yes, baby?"

"Are you scared?"

She tried not to choke. "I am, baby, I am a little. But I know that God is looking after us. And no matter what happens, He's with us." She tried to smile. "You know that, don't you?"

Brandon nodded, his eyes big. "But, Mommy, I don't think you need to be scared of those bad people." He turned his head and looked toward their large fireplace, his voice dropping to a conspiratorial whisper. "The big man in the corner doesn't seem scared."

"What big man in the corner?"

"The big man over there by the fireplace. He's been watching us for a while. And he looks pretty brave, Mommy."

Sherry couldn't help staring. She choked back tears. "Well, you just tell the big man in the corner thank you for watching over us, okay?"

Brandon smiled, and leaned back against the sofa, darting an impish grin toward the blank corner.

Sherry turned her face away and dropped her head so her children would not see her tears, continuing her almost constant petitions to her heavenly Father.

O Lord God, please do send your heavenly warriors to fight on our behalf. And give your earthly warriors strength and wisdom. Please, Lord, spare us...

Agent Paul Jackson stepped from his car and closed the door lightly, without sound. All around him, others emerged from cars and vans into the dark shadow of a residential cul-de-sac. The street lights had already been cut and the teams were ready to go.

Several men had gone ahead to scout the lay of the land, and they conferred in quiet voices, doing a last minute briefing, letting everyone know the score. Each member of the team was told precisely where to go, and their leaders could communicate any last-minute changes through their earpieces if necessary.

They set out, lithe and quick despite the bulkiness of their gear, and headed into the trees at the end of the cul-de-sac, making for the neighborhood next door.

"But the Super Bowl was originally intended to be the climax of the series, right?" Agent McKendrick paced the front of the room. "So I would think that would mean an explosion in the Super Bowl stadium, to kill a hundred thousand people at once. But if they're doing it tonight, instead, that makes no sense."

"No, Chief," the decoding expert said. "The *commercial's* the key, not the event. What do the Super Bowl and New Year's Eve have in common? There are millions of people watching TV at the same time! They want as many people as possible watching that commercial."

"Right, right. The TV set becomes the venue for broadcasting that audio signal. But if they're going for the maximum viewership, then that must mean they're targeting anyone with a TV. But *how?* How can they possibly harm someone via a signal into their own home?"

"It would only work if each house also owned something that the signal would set off. And that means they have to have been making and selling that thing—whatever it is—for months and months. Like maybe they've created innocuous-looking smoke detectors that have a little receiver inside that would be triggered to release poisonous gas or explode a bomb or something."

Another person in the room—a newly arrived bomb expert—shook his head. "No, it would have to be something *in* the room with the TV set, to be certain of receiving a signal. You don't get a lot of smoke detectors in the family room itself."

"So what's *in* the family's TV room?" Agent McKendrick stopped pacing. "I think we're on to something, but what's the thing that gets triggered? It would presumably be related to television in some way."

"How about the remote control?" the decoding expert said. "Everyone has one."

"No, if it had explosives packed inside, it'd be too heavy." The bomb expert put a hand to his head, thinking hard. "It would have to be something that someone would expect to be somewhat heavy, and would have enough room both for the explosives and for whatever its ostensible purpose is."

Ronnie felt a memory pushing at the back of her brain and tried to push aside her fear long enough to concentrate and retrieve it. What was—

She gasped and sat up so sharply that everyone swiveled toward her.

Her voice was hoarse. "The…uh…that new kind of voice-activated remote control…that black box thing." She fumbled to describe it with her hands. "My…uh…one of my regulars ran a company that sold those."

"Could that be it?" Agent McKendrick looked at the bomb expert.

"It could. It really could. It's the right size, and it would be placed near or on a TV. If there's a shape charge inside, it would blow out the TV and use its flying fragments as the bomb. Most people aren't killed by the bomb blast itself, you know; they're killed by the shrapnel. That could really be it!"

"We've only got twelve minutes to midnight! Do we have one of those devices in use in this building?" Agent McKendrick looked around at all the negative responses and swore to himself. "How can we confirm this?"

"Wait!" Someone jumped up. "Hold on! I've got one in my car!"

The man ran out the door and returned, breathless, lugging a box, interrupting

Agent McKendrick, who was reporting in to his superiors in Washington.

"It's never been opened. We were going to return it to the store today." He started to rip the heavy cardboard open, and three others reached out to help him.

He pulled out the black box, ripped off the interior packaging, and laid the box on the table. The bomb expert pushed him aside and stood the device on its end, his eyes intent. He pulled a tiny screwdriver out of a small belt pouch and unscrewed the cover. He looked at the mass of wires, then pushed a few aside and tensely turned a heavy black piece over and detached it.

His face white, he gasped out "X ray!" and ran out the door. A sizeable chunk of the agents followed. Through the open door, Ronnie could see them running down a long hallway and rounding a corner toward the security station.

Within a minute, they came running back. The bomb expert tried to gasp out the news to McKendrick, but the senior agent handed him the cell phone and said, "Speak!"

"It's a—it's an antipersonnel fragmentation device—a shape charge. Packed plastic explosives, probably C4, surrounded by ball bearings. It'll blow out whatever TV set it's attached to, and kill or injure everyone in the blast radius. There's enough actual explosive to damage the house structure, if the TV is set against a load-bearing wall."

Agent McKendrick snatched back the phone. "Did you get all that!...Yes, sir! There have got to be hundreds of thousands of those devices out there!...I changed my mind. We *have* to use the EAS message to tell people to unplug those remotes and turn off their TVs!"

He looked at his watch, then clamped his hand over the cell phone mouthpiece and spoke to the others in the room.

"They're doing that now—thank God for modern technology." Something jarred his attention back to the phone. "Yes, sir!" He sagged in relief and found his way to a chair. "It's done. The EAS message will broadcast in five minutes, starting immediately after midnight."

The room was suddenly alive, the sounds of piercing relief and congratulations filling the air. Backs were slapped, hugs and handshakes exchanged.

Ronnie looked sideways at Doug, who was still sitting—as he had been for the last hour—with head bowed. She touched his arm, and he lifted his head, turning his tear-streaked face toward her.

"We only have five minutes. Five minutes for my family—" His voice broke and he could not go on.

☆ ☆ ☆

"Let's go." Agent McKendrick stowed his cell phone at his belt and pulled on a jacket. He held a radio in his hand, its red power light seeming to burn with urgency.

Doug looked up in confusion. "Go where?"

"Let's get you home."

He pulled Doug up from the chair, and the three visitors and several agents began hurrying around corners, heading for—Doug discovered—the FBI garage. They piled into an unmarked van and sped north on the highway, watching as the dashboard clock clicked over toward midnight.

SIXTY-THREE

The great being was no longer shining. He was cloaked from sight by the Spirit of God. He soared, all his efforts focused on tracking with his charge, hurrying the little car's progress, making sure the timing would be just right.

There were other angels everywhere, and these *were* shining, blazing with holy fire, attracting all attention. These were the colleagues who were fighting the battles, their shouts and exertions and cheers ringing out as they clashed with their foe, drawing them off, fighting a real fight but leading them ever-so-subtly away from the target.

The great angel pierced the clamor quietly, unseen, shepherding the little car, turning left, turning right, now stopping, now starting. Every uncertainty cost precious moments and it was his task to smooth the way. To smooth the way, and to conceal.

"So are there any blind spots?" Agent Jackson conferred with two team leaders, balancing a hand-drawn diagram on a rock between them, shading his special light so it couldn't be seen from five paces.

"No, sir." One of the team leaders pushed his night-vision equipment atop his head and pointed at several spots on the diagram. "Perhaps here...or possibly here. But we scouted the entire house and saw wide-range motion-sensor lights covering pretty much every area."

"Can we take them out without alerting the men inside?"

"No, sir. We're just going to have to run for it across the no-man's-land."

"That will mean that the hostage takers will get to their captives before we get to the doors."

The three men looked at each other. Finally one of the team leaders spoke up.

"I guess we're just going to have to run really fast, sir."

Agent Jackson stuffed the diagram into one of several cavernous pockets. He looked at his watch. "We have four minutes before the EAS broadcast. To your places. We're a go on my mark."

☆ ☆ ☆

"Gulfstream 232, sorry for the delay." The voice came crisp over the pilot's head-piece. "You got three minutes to midnight, you sure you don't want to wait on the New Year's celebrations?"

"Negative, tower. On a schedule. What's the holdup?"

"Unknown. We've got a temporary hold on air traffic out of Atlanta Hartsfield."

"Just Hartsfield?" The pilot looked behind him and snapped his fingers to get the passengers' attention. Jordan was at his side in an instant.

The pilot kept his voice even, speaking as much for Jordan's benefit as the tower's. "There's just a hold on air traffic out of *this* airport?"

Jordan wheeled and hurried to a table in the main cabin where a laptop waited. He pecked furiously at the keys, transferring his attention between the laptop and the nearby television that was broadcasting "New Years' Rockin' Eve" to all the interested eyes on the plane.

The voice of the tower was still clear in the pilot's ear. "Unknown, Gulf 232. Could be other area airports as well."

"Waiting for permission to roll, tower."

"Understood, Gulf 232. We'll try to get you out of here quickly."

The silence in the speeding van was broken only by the sound of Ronnie's stifled tears.

Why she was crying and not Doug, she didn't know. He sat directly behind her, his eyes red and weary. But the expression on his face was one she had never seen before. It was a look of complete surrender to the God that he clearly believed was worthy of such utter abandonment. It made no sense…and it broke her heart. She turned her head away, unable to stop her weeping.

Beside her, she felt Tiffany move closer and put an arm around her shoulders.

"It'll be okay." Her friend's voice was soothing. "We're not going to be blown to bits tonight. We'll be okay."

Ronnie kept her head turned away and whispered, "That's not why I'm crying."

"What is it, then?"

"It's Doug's family, Tiff! I just can't bear—" She broke off, unable to continue.

Tiffany snuck a quick glance over her shoulder. "I don't understand him. He looks so…detached about the whole thing."

"How can you say that? Can't you see what he's going through?"

"Not really. He should've gone with those SWAT team guys right from the beginning. I don't understand why he waited."

"He said he felt like he had something he had to contribute, like he was *supposed* to stay."

Tiffany removed her arm from Ronnie's shoulders, her voice sad and quiet in the darkness. "I guess I just don't buy it. I think he's just deluded. And it may mean he never sees his family again."

Up front, they heard the radio crackle. Agent McKendrick picked it up. "Yes!"

"We just got the signal. They're in position."

"Keep us informed."

The radio clicked off. Ronnie turned and watched Doug continue to stare straight ahead, that look—that look on his face. Her lips started trembling and she bowed her head, fresh tears coming fast, trying to think how this should be done.

"God." She whispered in her mind. "God, if You're up there. Please—please do something. Help them save Doug's wife...and kids...and the Woodwards. Please, God." More tears. "Don't let them die."

Sherry watched the two men confer again, prepare to switch places again, watched Vance again test his bonds as soon as they were out of sight and quietly try to stand, lifting up the chair...again, with no success in getting free. His expression had grown intense, concentrated, almost fierce. She knew that he would not let them be shot without somehow trying to fight, even with a chair tied to his back.

Jo looked across and caught her eye, her face taut with strain, her lips moving in constant prayer.

Sherry's eyes swiveled from her friends to the clock above the mantel-piece.

One minute.

Jordan stared at the laptop screen, his eyes taking on its eerie glow, swearing and muttering in an unearthly growl. He almost couldn't breathe, couldn't function, his being filled with a great and throbbing pain that would know only one release.

"It looks fine, but then why are they keeping us here? Why!"

He reached for his cell phone, hissing to himself, ignoring the strained looks between Tyson and the others. He clicked open his cell phone, then patted his pockets, looking for the number. It wasn't worth waiting until later; he needed blood, something to lessen the weight of these interminable minutes. After they were done, he would watch the little signal load on the laptop, would watch the news unfold—the inevitable carnage—in all its shocking, gratifying detail.

☆ ☆ ☆

The angel pulled up and hovered, shielding his charge from watchful eyes...including the mechanical eyes that surrounded the house.

He could not see his colleagues, but he knew they were there, surrounding the house, similarly shielded from the unearthly, hate-filled eyes inside. Off in the distance he could hear the sounds of the great battle being fought, but here—here it was dark, quiet, tense.

He watched as silent shapes began converging on the house from two sides, dark shadows flitting between trees and behind parked cars. Only moments...only moments...

And in an instant, he could feel the hand of the Master at work, moving all pieces smoothly into position. The angel felt a surge of holy power, of great trust, knowing that He had it all under His perfect control.

He shepherded his charge the last few feet, noting with satisfaction that the motion lights did not come on as she checked her little notepad one last time and lifted her hand to knock on the dark front door.

"Yes, sir."

Sherry watched in horror as the man at the window received a phone call, listened briefly, and pulled a gun from his belt.

"Yes, sir."

He walked away from the window and tapped his seated colleague on the shoulder, gesturing to the phone and then to the hostages. His voice was hard, unemotional.

"We'll take care of it right now and meet the others back at the building."

The seated henchman stood, stretching, lifting the heavy pistol from his lap.

"So it's a go, then?"

"Yes." The first man strode past the Woodwards and planted himself in the middle of the room, raising the gun toward the sofa.

Sherry tried to shout, tried to stand, but suddenly the firmest pressure she had ever felt held her fast in place, frozen, without words.

The man pointed the gun straight at Genna.

Knock, knock!

For a fraction of a second, concentration was broken. The shot rang out, shattering a distant window. And suddenly Vance was there—shouting and charging, rearing up in his bonds and swinging his body and the chair like a battering ram at the man's back.

The gun went flying, and the man turned to grapple with Vance, enraged and in pain, his henchman coming to his aid.

And suddenly the doors shattered. Bright lights—blinding lights—and men with guns came streaming through every door.

Sherry and the others screamed, cowering as the shots rang out, the two men falling, cursing, turning their guns on their attackers, Vance tangled in the middle of the melee, still tied in his chair.

And then, silence. A silence broken only by the terrified gasps of children and the sharp orders of hard-faced men in black, not yet ready to let down their guard.

"Search the house!"

"Any other gunmen here, ma'am?"

"Get a paramedic!"

Men surrounded them, cut their bonds, handed her terrified children into her arms. Jo cried out in relief as her husband was extricated from the pile, apparently unharmed, and rushed to embrace her and their son. There were two men on the floor: one broken and still; one being roughly hauled away.

And there was an unfamiliar woman cowering at the shattered front door, her hands slowly dropping from their protective position over her ears, a pocketbook askew on the doorstep. Her mouth opened and closed, unable to form any words.

Sherry stared at the source of the perfectly timed knock on the door. Holding her children close, she took a tremulous step forward, her voice disbelieving.

"Linda Hanover?"

Doug could hardly sit still as the van screeched to a halt amidst bright lights, throngs of spectators and emergency sirens piercing the night.

He had the door open before the van stopped moving, Agent McKendrick shouting after him to wait.

He didn't wait. He ran up the busy lawn, pushing past the men in black, hearing McKendrick close behind shouting in a hoarse voice to let him through.

The door to his house was shattered, broken off its hinges, but he hardly noticed. The sound and chaos faded away; there were no more senses but sight, and all he could see was what was inside.

A young woman—a beautiful woman—was kneeling on the carpet, arms around two small children, stroking their hair, comforting them, turning their faces away from the chaos in the living room.

O God… He could hardly believe it, rushing forward. *O God…thank You, thank You!*

There were embraces then, embraces like he'd never known before and never wanted to end. Kisses and tears and small hands desperately clasping him, and the sweet beloved scent of his wife, pressed against him, his cheek resting on her hair. He knelt and held them all and breathed it in, unable to comprehend how he had been given back what he had so recently given up, wondering if he could ever love his heavenly Father more than he did at this moment.

Across the room, he dimly saw the Woodwards huddling, rocking and crying with each other, wiping their tears away. And to one side, a shaken woman, a stranger, her face anxious, watching the door. She caught his eye and smiled a little, but seemed to sense that he had no focus for anything but the world in his arms and turned back to the door.

Ronnie allowed a tall agent to lead her up the path toward the front door, her stomach twisting amid all the noise and confusion.

She hovered on the threshold, hardly able to believe the evidence. It was impossible…and yet, there it was. The shaking, weeping, joyful results of all of Doug's prayers.

She put a shaking hand to her mouth, sudden tears blurring her vision.

It is real, isn't it? You're really there! It's not just a story, not a fairy tale. Her mind grasped for the words her heart was crying out. *O God…I want…I want…*

"Ronnie?"

She turned, unable to see from the tears. But that voice—

"Ronnie!"

She felt the arms go around her and gasped, suddenly clasping, grasping, sobbing in her mother's arms.

She was beyond asking how on earth her mother was here, beyond wondering at the tender change in this woman. She let her mother hold her like she'd always longed to be held as a little girl, allowed herself to weep unashamedly from love, from grief, from the unexplainable feeling that overwhelmed her.

The darkness receded, the dark corners of her soul clearing and lightening with the knowledge of what had to happen soon…very soon…

Caliel shot into the sky, his face alight! He blazed into the heavens, surrounded by rank upon rank of the heavenly host, their voices raised in such praise and thanksgiving that it seemed the very ends of the earth would echo.

And why not? The Ancient of Days had held out His scepter and death had been averted! In love and mercy and desperate care He had again—again!—moved heaven and earth to see His people set free, to save His little ones from the wiles of the enemy and the consequences of willful sin.

Caliel looked southward, watching with satisfaction as an airport scene unfolded almost as an afterthought. He watched as a raging beast was taken into custody, his lustful force unspent, unsatisfied, reduced to insignificance—at least for now—by the blazing holiness of the One who had orchestrated every step.

There had been not one lost! Not a one! Would the Lord's fickle children grasp what had been done for them this night? Would the talk shows proclaim the miracle...or the great detective work? Would they listen to Doug's stories or would his earnest calls toward Jesus fall on deaf ears? Would the news clips with their twenty-second sound bites broadcast his faith?

Every fiber of Caliel's being rejoiced with honor and love and adoration, joining the heavenly chorus that ascended to the Throne. He stood side by side with Loriel, his comrades, feeling—with intense thrill—the Almighty's pleasure in the work that they, too, had done.

He sensed the Father's tender gaze as He looked upon a beloved child. A little lamb taking shaky newborn steps, tottering, running into the fold. A beloved little lamb who was no longer...no longer lost.

SIXTY-FOUR

Ronnie held her breath and felt the water close over her head, felt her body immersed in it, felt the weightlessness, the peace, the silence. And then she was up, the cheering and clapping ringing in her ears, the water of new life streaming from her hair, her face…coming up clean.

The lights of the church shone through her water-dropped eyes like stars, their halos sparkling with myriad colors. But no—those were people. People she knew, standing, cheering up at her, clapping, their figures blurry with the water and her tears. Her mom…Doug and Sherry…Jo and Vance…shining like stars. Tiffany, smiling politely, clapped beside them, not understanding—not yet—the piercing love of the Savior.

She looked to the heavens and felt those loving arms again wrapped around her, those arms that would never abandon nor forsake her. She looked to the heavens, to her Abba Father, a smile in her eyes and one word filling her mind. Filling her, for the first time, with great joy.

"Daddy."

The publisher and author would love to hear your comments about this book. *Please contact us at:* www.multnomah.net/shauntifeldhahn

DISCUSSION GUIDE

1. What did you think of Ronnie? How did you view her at the beginning, middle, and end of the story? If you had met Ronnie halfway through the story, when she was already an exotic dancer, would you have viewed her differently?

2. How should Christians interact with someone living a sinful, even depraved, lifestyle? If that person is willfully sinning, does it matter how they got there? Does it make a difference whether the person in question is a believer or a nonbeliever?

3. What did you think of Doug? Did you view him differently once you saw that he was ashamed of his sin and felt unable to stop? Do you believe that people can be addicted to sex, the same way that people can be addicted to alcohol, drugs, or gambling, or is it just willful sin?

4. What did you think of Sherry? How did you view the way she interacted with Doug *before* she knew of his problem? Although a person bears the responsibility for his or her own behavior, are there things the person's spouse can do to either exacerbate or improve that behavior?

5. Consider the spiritual element of the story. Do you believe that there is a spiritual reality beyond what we can see, with angels and demons interacting behind the scenes?

6. Is there a spiritual analogy to the terrorists' use of Ronnie and Doug as pawns in their dark plot? What spiritual parallels do you see in how the enemy of our souls might operate, and how we might react?

7. How might you adopt the message of unconditional, nonjudgmental love to how you live your own life, and how you and your church interact with those outside the church?

8. For married readers: how might the marriage-related messages of the story help you in your own marriage?

THE STORY BEHIND THE STORY

Because of the importance and sensitivity of the issues raised in this book, I believe it is important to explain the story behind the story, to provide encouragement and resources for those who want to do further investigation.

Before I began this book, I had never given much thought to the sex industry, believing—as many of us do—that it was not touching me or my community personally. It just didn't seem to intersect my suburban, comfortable life in any way. What I didn't realize was that this industry impacts all of us in both subtle and pervasive ways, whether we are aware of it or not.

Further, although I knew that Jesus befriended prostitutes and others ostracized by society, I could never (to my shame) imagine myself doing the same. Now, after a year of research and writing, I count a number of former strippers as dear friends. And I realize that even in the depths of their entrapment in that life, they were normal people caught in an abnormal situation. That is not to excuse sin, but when we recognize that everyone has a story, it is much easier to look on them and love them as a *person,* rather than focusing solely on their behavior.

Several of the ministry leaders I interviewed put it like this: We must look at whatever root is behind the bad fruit on the tree. Aboveground, we see only the fruit—someone's visible behaviors. But hidden belowground is the root of that behavior—what that person believes about themselves, God, and others, rooted in events or relationships from his or her life. As these ministry leaders suggested, when we try to reach out and love the unlovable, we have to be willing to look beyond the often-distasteful fruit. When we concentrate on *behavior,* setting rules and saying "don't do this," we're simply pruning. But pruning only works to make something good come back stronger. Instead, we must see the *person* and address the roots that are behind his or her behavior.

I have come to realize that many of us need to come face-to-face with some issues we may have simply never confronted before, especially so that we may pray for and love those who are hurting—just as Jesus would.

How the Story Started

The Lights of Tenth Street arose from hearing the Christian testimony of a former stripper and prostitute, the first time I had ever (to my knowledge) met someone from that sort of lifestyle. She had grown up in a small, depressed town, was sexually assaulted as a teenager, and was lured into the strip club life thinking it would be a glamorous way to make lots of money. Instead it was depraved and an awful, dead-end trap. After she had spent years in that life, a Christian woman in her neighborhood knocked on her door, inviting her to her church's Christmas banquet. And when she took her up on it, to her immense surprise, she found nothing but love and acceptance in that church, even though she didn't know how to dress or act. The Christian woman ended up taking this jaded, world-weary young stripper into her home to live with her and just loved her into the Kingdom. That former stripper now has a wonderful ministry to other strippers and prostitutes.

When I heard that story, I somehow knew that the Lord was nudging me to write a book that would feature just such a girl, to show the incredible transforming power of unconditional, nonjudgmental love. But that wasn't all. As the months passed, I realized that the flip side of this sort of story—the consumer's side—leaves in its wake many devastated men (and, increasingly, even women) who have been ensnared by pornography. So there had to be two character plotlines—one to follow the young stripper, the other to follow the Christian couple who will eventually reach out to her…but to do so, the husband has to confront and be delivered of his own secret addiction. (And then, of course, in the post-9/11 world, the stakes for the rescue of the young woman were raised so that the battle for her soul also became a much larger battle.) As the book's title implies, I set these two plotlines on opposite ends of the same fictional street. Two different worlds; two very different kinds of lights.

Although there are many elements in the story, I want to use this chapter primarily to provide information and resources on the pornography issue. When I started the book, the issue wasn't even on my radar screen. And it just kept getting bigger and bigger. I was truly shocked to realize the depth of this problem in our culture, including among devoted Christian men.

Opening the Eyes of Women

I think it is safe to say that what shocked me as a woman would be no surprise to any man on the planet. And I bet that many of my female readers are in the same boat. I knew, of course, that men and women are different. But as I tried to get inside my male character's head, my eyes were dramatically opened to just *how* different!

It has become one of my main prayers that the Lord will use this book to open the eyes of women, that we might understand the cultural and personal battle all around us…including one that almost certainly affects the men and boys that we love.

TAKING THOUGHTS CAPTIVE

Women readers of *The Lights of Tenth Street* see inside a male character's head and come to understand, I hope, how every hour of every day a man has to "take thoughts captive"—thoughts and images that rise up, unbidden. It took a while for me to understand that men are just wired that way and that the emergence of the initial thought itself isn't sin, because the man literally can't help it. The key is how the man chooses to handle that thought—to "take it captive out of obedience to Christ" and push it away, or to let it play on the screen of his mind. Like all temptations, the temptation itself isn't sin; it's what we do with it that matters.

What I grew to understand was that, for men, temptation saturates our current culture. Several decades ago, men had to go looking for images that would titillate or arouse them. Now, those images slap them in the face with every commercial on television, every stroll down the street. And once something has been triggered in the mind's eye, the struggle can be wearying. As one of my male friends said, "a five-second glimpse might lead to five hours—or five days—of tearing that image down again and again and again." Most women don't realize how incredibly difficult it is to be a pure man in today's culture.

Again, that is not to excuse falling into sin; it is simply to face the reality so that we may know how to support our husbands, sons, and friends.

Men Don't Get It Either

It also surprised me to discover that men don't realize how truly different men and women are. So they may see a woman's lack of comprehension as a lack of support. I believe that husbands and wives will be able to offer each other so much more encouragement once they realize how wide the gulf is and how great is the need to bridge it.

With my husband's permission, let me give you just one example. After months of writing, I had interviewed many, many men about what goes on inside their heads when faced with certain situations. Jeff and I were riding in the car one day, rehashing some of what I'd learned. Jeff finally confessed that he didn't understand why this was such a surprise to me.

Jeff: "But you knew men are visual, right?"

Me: "Well, yes, of course. But since most women aren't, I just didn't get it. I just don't experience things the same way you do."

Jeff: "See, I'm not sure I really believe that."

Me: "Well, it's true!"

Jeff: "Maybe we just use different language to describe it. For example, think of a movie star that you find physically attractive—Tom Cruise, say. After we've seen one of his movies, how many times will that attractive image rise up in your mind the next day?"

Me: "Never."

Jeff: "I must not be explaining myself correctly. I mean, how many times will a thought of what he looked like with his shirt off just sort of pop up in your head?"

Me: "Never."

Jeff: "Never—as in *never?*"

Me: "Zero times. It just doesn't happen."

Jeff: (After a long pause) "Wow."

That little exchange did more to teach both of us how each of us are wired—and *not* wired—than almost anything else. And that understanding has already helped me (I hope) to be more supportive and protective of my husband in today's culture.

(I acknowledge that I am painting the differences between men and women with a broad brush. There are women who are also very visual, or who are themselves entrapped by pornography. Although I'm discussing this primarily from the man's side of things, it is my hope that ensnared women would also find help and healing through the resources listed below.)

How Our Culture Has Changed

Living in today's culture, it almost seems as if it's always been this way. But when we look at history, we can track a dramatic increase in the sexualization of our culture…and be forewarned about where we are going.

Dr. Jerry Kirk at the National Coalition for the Protection of Children and Families gave me this fascinating—and disturbing—perspective:

- 1940s—The Kinsey Report was released, setting perceptions—and expectations—about the nation's sexual behavior for decades to come. Although a third of Kinsey's subjects were convicts, his revolutionary declaration that 'people are promiscuous' soon found its way into the mainstream.

- 1950s—Hugh Hefner, via *Playboy*, popularizes the behavior Kinsey said was normal.

- 1960s—Following in *Playboy*'s lucrative footsteps, pornography explodes across America through 300 other soft-porn magazines, mainstreaming the message of sex outside of marriage for the first time.

- 1970s—In addition to the *Roe vs. Wade* decision legalizing abortion and promoting the idea of consequence-free sex, the 1970s also saw the advent of dial-a-porn phone lines that enabled a whole new group of users to engage in pornography without having to go out and buy a magazine.
- 1980s—With the advent of the VCR and cable TV, movie porn exploded, creating another exponential leap in the volume of people who would never have gone to a porn movie house, would never have dialed a porn line, but could now easily acquire and view pornography.
- 1990s to the present—Satellite television and, most of all, the Internet mainstreamed the pornography monster, ensnaring users of all ages and backgrounds.

As Dr. Kirk notes in his comprehensive white paper, *What Pornography Is Doing to Your Family and the Family of God,* "When we were growing up, most of us had the freedom *not* to see pornography. Our children and grandchildren have lost that freedom." What was only a multimillion dollar business in the 1960s has become a fifty-five *billion* dollar business worldwide. And it continues to grow every year. Almost every new media technology is driven by pornography, simply because its use is a near-guarantee of profit. In the early 1990s, Carnegie-Mellon studied the early functioning of business on the Internet and found that the only business making money was pornography. Today, pornography continues to be the most profitable on-line business sector.

But Is It Really That Bad?

One of the objections I have heard as I've pursued this subject is the question of whether pornography is really that harmful. After all, people say, "It's just a private thing," or "I can handle it," or "There's nothing really bad about the soft-core stuff."

About a year ago, an adult bookstore opened its doors in a fairly affluent area of our community (courtesy of a judge who had ruled that our county's ban on such establishments was too restrictive). Its parking lot was immediately filled, day and night, by a steady stream of clientele. I joined in a number of organized rallies and prayer walks around the property, and one day I ran into several staff members and frequent customers at the fast-food place across the street.

Curious, I asked them what they thought of our opposition to their business. One of the staff members shrugged and said, "It's a free country. You've got a right to do your thing—we've got a right to do our thing."

One of the porn-shop customers said he didn't really understand what all the fuss was about. "After all," he said, "what me and my wife choose to do in private is up to us, right? It's not like its hurting anyone."

I said that unfortunately pornography *does* hurt people—quite frequently. That those of us who were walking around outside with signs opposing the porn shop were doing it not just because we were concerned about the community, but because we were concerned about the impact of the use of pornography on families like his. I told him I thought he and his wife were playing with fire, and that although he could of course do whatever he wanted, that he was at risk of getting burned. And that perhaps his wife might be negatively affected by his need to use pictures of other women. The man shook his head and argued that it was silly to think that pornography could have any effect on him or his marriage. "It's just fantasy. I know it's not real. My wife knows that. How could it affect us?"

I've heard that argument many times since then, from people who sincerely believe (or are trying to convince themselves) that putting the content of pornography in their brain will have no real impact on them. Psychotherapist Dr. Victor Cline, an expert in this area, addresses this fallacy in his excellent report, *Pornography's Effects on Adults and Children.*

> There is a belief strongly held by some Americans that pornography (or obscenity), while it may be vulgar and tasteless, is still essentially harmless and has no real effect on the viewer.
>
> However, for someone to suggest that pornography cannot have an effect on you (including a harmful one) is to deny the whole notion of education, generally, or to suggest that people are not affected by what they read and see. If you believe that a pornographic book or film cannot affect you, then you must also say that Karl Marx's *Das Kapital,* the Bible, the Koran, or advertising have no effect on their readers or viewers. But of course, books and other media do have an effect on their consumers.

After a year of research, I could provide reams of statistics, tons of data on just how insidious and damaging pornography can be to individuals, families, and communities. I could talk about the public health threats and increase in community crime that spring up around the opening of porn shops or strip clubs, about the broken marriages that inevitably follow a certain percentage of new pornography users, about the massive percentage of our youth that are being bombarded with pornography and act out as a result. But all that data is available from the ministries and resources listed below, and I do not have space to develop it here. I simply want to ask the skeptics to take an honest look. You will find, if you are honest with yourself, that there *are* negative effects both at a personal and a community level, and we should be willing to address them.

The Role of the Church

It is tempting to focus on all that is wrong and expend our energies opposing it. But the Body of Christ must come to grips with two key truths: First, because we are supposed to be salt and light, we bear some responsibility for the decay and darkness we see around us. If we were truly lighting the darkness as Jesus asked, much that we are opposing would have no foothold. Second, therefore, we must resist the temptation to simply oppose, gripe, and attack. We must be for something, not just against something. The Church must light the right path—a path that celebrates and supports healthy families, strong marriages, and individuals tied to the community in which they live.

We can and often should oppose the opening of an adult bookstore or club in our community, but we must recognize that such places will exist in one form or another as long as the demand is there. The church should be working to dry up demand, should be reaching out to those who are hurting and ensnared by both sides of the sex industry. We should be fighting for spiritual and emotional health, should be encouraging our people not to bring certain things into our homes, should be educating them how to be wise and cautious to the impact the media can have on them. And once we have a loving impact on our community, then we will have much more credibility when we say that we don't want more strip clubs or porn houses here, because it is not good for this community we all care about.

We Can Win!

And the good news is: When we do that, we can win. Consider this passage from Dr. Kirk's white paper:

> Child psychologist Dr. Jim Dobson was right when he said "this is a winnable war…. Ordinary people are winning victories across America, and you can too. In Cincinnati [where the National Coalition is based] we have no "adult" bookstores, no X-rated theaters and no X-rated videos. Eight of the nine counties around Cincinnati have been cleaned up, and Citizens for Community Values, headed by Phil Burress, is working on the ninth…. Twenty thousand people have joined in the effort….
>
> From Oklahoma City, only two persons came to Cincinnati for training, returned home and started building a team. In six years, they closed down 150 sex establishments in Oklahoma County. What do you think happened to the rape rate? It went down 27% in those six years, while during the same time, it went up 19% across the state. That's a swing of almost 50%!

Friends, with the power of the Lord behind us, we can transform our cities and communities. But we need to look like Jesus, need to recognize the logs in our own eyes, and need to reach out in love to those we oppose. For although many of them are operating in willful sin, many are certainly also lost and hurting, ensnared in a life they would not have chosen, being used as pawns by an enemy who cares only to steal, kill, and destroy. As we do our part, they can and will be transformed by the love of Christ.

A Vision for the Church

In his talks, Christian care activist Tony Campolo often shares a story that resonates deeply with me because it so exemplifies what I personally want to reflect of the surpassing love of Jesus—and shows me how far I have to go. With his permission, allow me to share the story.

Several years ago, Dr. Campolo was in Hawaii on business. At 3:00 A.M., jetlagged and unable to sleep, he wandered out of his hotel and went for a walk, ending up in a dicey area of town. Since Dr. Campolo has spent years ministering in such areas in his native Philadelphia, he felt right at home. He went into a local all-night diner, sat at the counter, and ordered a cup of coffee and a donut.

Soon, eight or nine young women came in, clearly prostitutes taking a break from their work. The girls took seats on the stools all around Dr. Campolo, and began carrying on a loud, crude conversation. Dr. Campolo was about to leave when he heard one of them mention that the next day was her birthday. In the jaded manner of those who have seen and experienced far too much, too young, she added that it was too bad she'd never had a birthday party, and probably never would. The girls finished up their break, and Dr. Campolo watched as they left the coffee shop and went back to the street.

He turned to the diner's owner. "Do those girls come in every night?"

"Every night. Same time—right after 3:00."

"I overheard that one girl say that her birthday was tomorrow, and that she's never had a birthday party. How about if we throw her one? Do you think any of the others in here would want to participate?"

The owner lit up. "Her name is Agnes. I bet so!" He started going around to all the regulars, telling them of the plan. The owner insisted on making the cake. Dr. Campolo was in charge of the decorations.

The next morning at 2:30, Dr. Campolo came back into the diner with all the decorations. There was a great buzz of excitement as all the late-night, world-weary regulars waited for the young prostitute to come in on her break.

When she opened the door, the place erupted in giant shouts of "Surprise!" and "Happy Birthday!" as people pointed to the birthday cake with her name on it.

Upon walking into her very first birthday party, Agnes was so flabbergasted she was speechless. The beaming owner of the diner ended up blowing out the birthday candles for her. But before they could cut the cake, the young woman asked if she could have it for a while, instead of eating it. She wanted to show it to her mother. She grabbed the cake and darted out the door.

Amid the resulting laughter and conversation, Dr. Campolo thanked the good-natured owner of the diner for his help. Then he asked, "Can we pray for Agnes?" and bowed his head. He prayed for Agnes, her friends, and all the other girls working the streets.

When he looked up, the face of the good-natured owner had turned suspicious, defensive.

"Hey, what are you, a preacher or something?"

"Well, yes I am, actually."

His voice was hard. "What kind of church do you belong to?"

Dr. Campolo's reply was gentle. "The kind of church that throws birthday parties for prostitutes."

The owner stuck his finger at Dr. Campolo's chest. "There ain't no such church. Because if there was, *I'd be a part of it.*"

Dr. Campolo left that diner praying that the Body of Christ would catch the vision for how we might reach out to those Jesus spent so much time with when He was walking the earth. Having spent a year researching and writing this book, meeting so many different types of people along the way, I feel the same way.

Dear Lord, may we be the type of Church that throws birthday parties for prostitutes.

RESOURCES FOR READERS

In recent years, a number of excellent ministries and resources have arisen to help people who are struggling with sexual temptation, or have been affected by the behavior of others. These resources are also important for churches, organizations, and individuals who want to know how to minister to those with this need, want to influence policy in this area, or who simply want to learn more.

Suggested starting point

The National Coalition for the Protection of Children and Families, headed by Dr. Jerry Kirk, was an invaluable resource as I was researching and writing this book. Because the National Coalition is a ministry and policy leader in this field, with connections to all the relevant resources and ministries in the country, I recommend them as a starting point; they can offer both direct help and refer people on to other resources as needed. Specifically:

- *Help-line.* The National Coalition has a help-line (1-800-583-2964), staffed by a licensed therapist during the week (as of this writing, they are trying to raise the funds to add more hours). This line is available to anyone needing personal or family assistance or simply seeking further information.
- *Referrals.* The ministry has more than 700 referral points across the country; someone seeking help can be referred to a licensed, experienced Christian therapist in their area.
- *Internet filters.* They have evaluated 60 of the top Internet filters, and have established a website, www.filterreview.com, that walks people through what their needs are, and recommends a number of filters or blockers to choose from.
- *Materials and links.* The National Coalition has put together dozens of different types of materials for ministries, schools, adults, youth, etc. They also link to many of the top ministries in this arena. You can find resources that meet your needs by calling or going to their website, www.nationalcoalition.org.

Because of the National Coalition's benefit as a central clearinghouse, as well as their ministry heart and established integrity, I recommend them if you are moved to make a financial donation to this arena of ministry. Their address is 800 Compton Road, Suite 9224, Cincinnati, OH 45231.

Other Ministries and Organizations:
There are many other excellent ministries out there as well. This is by no means a comprehensive list, and I encourage interested readers to take some time and find the ministries with the focus that meets their needs.

- *Pure Desire Ministry.* Ted Roberts's ministry, founded by a man who has overcome his own struggles and now ministers to thousands of individuals every year through his book and through seminars across the country. Hosted by Easthill Church in Gresham, Oregon, this ministry also provides links to local partner churches around the country. www.puredesire.org, (503) 661-4444.
- *Focus on the Family.* Pure Intimacy is an online ministry of Focus on the Family, providing practical resources for individuals who want to overcome the grip of online pornography and affairs. www.pureintimacy.org. Focus also offers a pastoral care line, 1-877-233-4455, for pastors and their families. The main Focus help-line of 800-A-FAMILY can refer others seeking help in this arena.
- *Promise Keepers.* This landmark men's ministry has many resources and links to other relevant ministries and helpful articles. Go to their portal for this arena at www.promisekeepers.org/resc/resc120.htm or call 1-800-888-7595. In particular, please note their unique accountability software service, Eye Promise. Eye Promise allows users who want to stay pure to pick accountability partners, who are then able to see all sites the user visits. Customer service 1-800-456-7594.
- *Citizens for Community Values.* CCV is a grassroots organization with chapters in cities around the country, working to clean up communities, influence policy, and rescue those trapped in and by the sex industry. www.ccv.org, (513) 733-5775.
- *Obscenity Reporting.* This is an online resource for educating the public and reporting possible violations of obscenity laws. Reports made by the public about online (or other) violations are referred to the Justice Department in Washington, for investigation. www.obscenitycrimes.org.
- *Pure Life Ministries.* This ministry offers extensive materials, counseling, live-in aid for those in need of intervention, and off-site help for those

who are unable to attend the live-in program. The website has a special resources section for wives. www.purelifeministries.org, 1-800-635-1866.

Recommended Reading

Again, this is by no means an exhaustive list. You can find other resources that may meet your specific needs or interests via the ministries listed above.

- *Beneath the Surface: Steering Clear of the Dangers That Could Leave You Shipwrecked*, Bob Reccord, Broadman & Holman, February 2002. Synopsis: In this little book, Dr. Reccord compares King David's failure in sexual temptation with Joseph's victory, warning readers not to be complacent about their own vulnerability and drawing lessons for today's culture.
- *Every Man's Battle: Winning the War on Sexual Temptation One Victory at a Time*, Stephen Arterburn, Waterbrook Press, July 2000. Synopsis: While temptation is impossible to avoid, it is possible to rise above it. Presents testimonies of success, and a plan men (and their wives) can follow to freedom.
- *Pure Desire*, Ted Roberts, Regal, 1999. Synopsis: A comprehensive look from an author who overcame his own struggles, this book helps in the identification of addictions and outlines steps to set oneself or others free.
- *The Purity Principle: God's Guardrails on Life's Dangerous Roads*, Randy Alcorn, Multnomah Publishers, July 2003. Synopsis: God has placed warning signs and built guardrails to keep us from plunging off the cliff. This book covers training our children in sexual purity, protecting purity in dating (at any age), and maintaining purity in marriage.
- *Real Solutions for Overcoming Internet Addictions*, Steve Watters, Vine Books, July 2001. Synopsis: Examines Internet compulsions, including pornography, and provides advice from professionals, outlining steps people can take to beat their addiction.

ACKNOWLEDGMENTS

I could not have completed (probably could not have started!) this book without the professional and personal input of many people, and without the aid of the resources cited below.

CITATIONS

Scriptures and their paraphrases were drawn from the following translations: New International Version, New Living Translation, New King James Version, Revised Standard Version, Contemporary English Version.

"Hark the Herald Angels Sing." Words by Charles Wesley, 1707–1788; alt. by George Whitefield and others.

"Amazing Grace." Words by John Newton, 1779; last stanza by unknown author, 1829.

"Come Thou Fount of Every Blessing." Words by Robert Robinson, 1735–1790.

Information on satellite technology drawn from Charles W. Bostian, "Communications Satellite," World Book Online Americas Edition via AOL, http://www.aolsvc.worldbook.aol.com/wbol/wbPage/na/ar/co/126820, March 19, 2002.

Words to the pastor's benediction "And now may the Lord bless you and keep you, may the Lord make His face to shine upon you and give you peace" originates from Numbers 6:24–26.

The phrase "If any woman is going to get her feelings hurt, it's not going to be my wife" originates with basketball star David Robinson.

The suggestion to look at the root and not the fruit comes from Gene McConnell, founder of Authentic Relationships, International, in a November 19, 2001, interview, as well as from Jim and Chris Sharp of Abba House, Atlanta, in several 2001 interviews.

Jerry Kirk's white paper: *What Pornography Is Doing to Your Family*, and the Family of God, 9/95; is available through the National Coalition.

Dr. Victor Cline's report, *Pornography's Effects on Adults and Children*, copyright 2001, is published by Morality in Media, www.moralityinmedia.org.

The story about the birthday party for Agnes the prostitute is drawn from Dr. Tony Campolo's talks (it is also shared in his book *Let Me Tell You a Story*), and is used by permission.

RESEARCH ASSISTANCE

First, I would like to thank the women who courageously shared their stories and became my friends. To protect their privacy, I will not mention their names, but you know who you are. Special thanks to one friend in particular, who was always willing to meet for lunch on a moment's notice and answer dozens of very personal questions. Your life in Christ is an inspiration!

Many thanks to the dozen or more men, particularly my husband's colleagues and friends from church, who allowed me to interview them to understand how men think. I'm also extremely grateful for those men and/or wives who were willing to talk about the negative impact of pornography in their lives, as well as for the individuals who arranged those interviews. In particular, I would like to thank Barb Steffens, formerly of the National Coalition staff, and her husband Steve, for their insights and for arranging the home meeting in Cincinnati. Thanks also to Nancy and David French for arranging another important meeting, and for hosting me on another research trip.

A core group of wonderful individuals and organizations were of immense help in providing specific, detailed information as I researched the unfamiliar issues of pornography and outreach to those trapped in the sex industry. First and foremost, I must acknowledge Jerry Kirk and the leaders and staff of the National Coalition for the Protection of Children and Families, as well as Steve Watters at Focus on the Family. I'm also very grateful to the men and women of Citizens for Community Values, especially Eli McKenzie in Atlanta and Carolyn McKenzie in Memphis, as well as to Gene McConnell, founder of Authentic Relationships International, and Jim and Chris Sharp of Abba House in Atlanta. Special thanks to Victoria Teague, founder of Victoria's Friends, for getting me started.

Special thanks also to Sarah Parker for her willing research assistance at just the right time!

BOOK DEVELOPMENT

It helps having friends who are professional screenwriters and moviemakers when you get stuck as to plot development, editing, or just about anything else. As usual, I couldn't have written this book without the support, friendship and expert professional help of Lisa and Eric Rice. My—and my husband's—love and gratitude go deeper than we can express.

My sincere gratitude also goes to the many other friends who provided plot ideas or read the book for editing and feedback, including Calvin Edwards, Dave Gilmore, Nancy French, Jane Joiner, Jennifer Wheeler, Deb Goldstone, and Jenny Shea. Special thanks to Joe Proctor, the uncle of my helpful friends David and

Margaret Treadwell, for his primer on satellites, his insight into covert operations, and his devious plot ideas. Thanks also to Roy Leffew and Blaine Anaya for their insight and help on technical questions, and to Susan Rodenberg and Vernadette Broyles for help on battered women's issues.

PRAYER

The words I put on paper would be empty without the anointing of the Holy Spirit. Every moment that I am writing, I am so aware of my need of inspiration, guidance, and wisdom from the Lord. Perhaps the most important people to acknowledge with my deepest gratitude, other than my immediate family, are those dedicated individuals who have spent more than a year receiving emailed prayer requests and interceding for the book. I cannot express how much I have relied on your prayers and encouragement. My heartfelt thanks to: Elisha Barnett, Scott and Tammy Beck, Elizabeth Beinhocker, Steve Blum, Barb Bowlby, Vernadette Broyles, Kathia Campos, Martha Carter, Liliana Colgate, Christa Crawford, Gerry Crete, Alison Darrell, Mike Deagle, Betty Dunkum, Nancy French, Natt Gantt, Bob Gay, Deb and Michael Goldstone, Judy Hitson, Anne Hotchkiss, Jane Joiner, Kristen Lambert, Kathryn Lindstrom, Terri McCracken, Ruth Okediji, Sarah Parker, Linda Preston, Lisa and Eric Rice, Susan Rodenberg, Roger Scarlett, D.J. Snell, Andy Stross, Margaret Treadwell, Katherine Waitman, and Kyleen Wissell. Special thanks to Deb, Katherine, Liliana, and Lisa for their Wednesday morning prayers.

AND FINALLY...

Thanks to the team at We Care America, especially Dave Donaldson and Mike Owen, for modeling unconditional love to those in need, and for supporting my book-writing schedule. Much love and special thanks also go to my agent Calvin Edwards, and to the amazing team at Multnomah, especially Don Jacobson and Rod Morris. Your friendship means so much to me and Jeff.

To Jeff's parents, Bill and Roberta Feldhahn, how can I thank you enough for your constant willingness to drop everything and drive twelve hours from Michigan to Atlanta, just to help out so I can meet one deadline or another. You are so special to me.

To my parents, Dick and Judy Reidinger, and my brother Rick and his family—thanks for your constant love, advice, and encouragement even from the other side of the globe. A special hug to my mom, who is a terrific editor and always tries to help my words convey the love of Christ.

To Morgen and baby Luke, thank you for teaching me how to love more than I ever thought possible, and for loving your mommy even when she was distracted and in front of the computer for too long. I love you, precious little ones.

To my dear heart, my best friend, Jeff. Thank you for your honesty, your compassion, your constant help with everything from plot to edits, your prayers and your strength. Thank you for looking out for me better than I could look out for myself, for challenging me in the many times I needed it, and for your undying love. I could not have imagined how stalwart and rich your love would be, passing all my expectations or understanding.

Finally, my love and gratitude to our Heavenly Father, who relentlessly pursues all of us with an undying love. If you, the reader, do not yet know Him, I urge you to set aside some time and come to Him with all your questions, all your cares, all your skepticism, with an open heart. He is waiting for you with outstretched arms.

www.shaunti.com

Dear Reader,

Thank you for joining me on this journey. I would love to hear your feedback.

Please visit me on-line and share your comments. You can find sample chapters at my website, as well as other resources that you might find useful in investigating some issues raised in this book. You can also sign up to be on my e-mail prayer team. Go to:

www.shaunti.com

Or feel free to write me via e-mail or post:

ShauntiNet@aol.com

SHAUNTI FELDHAHN
c/o Multnomah Fiction
12265 Oracle Boulevard, Suite 200
Colorado Springs, CO 80921

I love hearing from my readers and, as always, I covet your prayers.

Sincerely,

YOUR ONE-STOP HANDBOOK ON SEXUAL PURITY

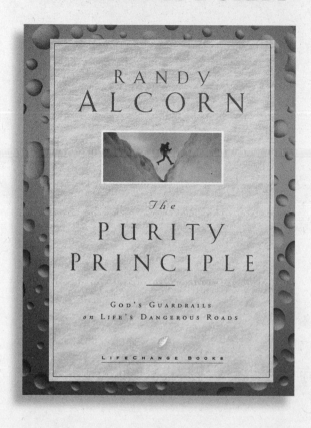

For thirty years, Randy Alcorn has been encouraging people—young and old—to pursue the rewards of sexual purity. Too often we settle for a compromised Christianity that's just a baptized version of the world's sad existence, rather than the abundant life God calls us to. This book deals with

- raising children to embrace sexual purity,

- providing an example of purity in the home,

- protecting purity in dating (at any age),

- and maintaining purity in marriage.

Biblical, practical, and concise, *The Purity Principle* is a one-stop handbook for individuals, families, and churches.

ISBN 1-59052-195-1

LUST TELLS YOU LIES.
THE TRUTH SETS YOU FREE.

I wrote this book for both men and women. Why? Because lust isn't a male problem. It's a human problem. Lust ruins our relationships, robs us of spiritual passion, and leaves us feeling hollow...

But the truth is that you and I don't have to stay on that treadmill of guilt and shame. God calls us to a high standard—not even a hint of sexual impurity. And He gives us everything we need to make it a reality.

If you're ready for a practical, grace-centered plan for defeating lust and celebrating purity, I hope you'll join me on a most promising journey.

—Joshua Harris

ISBN 1-59052-147-1